THE PLAYER'S DIARIES

THE PLAGUE DIARIES

Keeper of Tales Trilogy:
Book Three

RONLYN DOMINGUE

WASHINGTON
SQUARE PRESS

ATRIA

NEW YORK   LONDON   TORONTO   SYDNEY   NEW DELHI

WASHINGTON SQUARE PRESS

ATRIA

An Imprint of Simon & Schuster, Inc.
1230 Avenue of the Americas
New York, NY 10020

First Washington Square Press/Atria Paperback edition November 2018

WASHINGTON SQUARE PRESS / **ATRIA** PAPERBACK and colophon are trademarks of Simon & Schuster, Inc.

For information about special discounts for bulk purchases, please contact Simon & Schuster Special Sales at 1-866-506-1949 or business@simonandschuster.com.

The Simon & Schuster Speakers Bureau can bring authors to your live event. For more information, or to book an event, contact the Simon & Schuster Speakers Bureau at 1-866-248-3049 or visit our website at www.simonspeakers.com.

Manufactured in the United States of America

10 9 8 7 6 5 4 3 2 1

Library of Congress Cataloging-in-Publication Data
Names: Domingue, Ronlyn, author.
Title: The plague diaries / Ronlyn Domingue.
Description: First Atria Books hardcover edition. | New York : Atria Books,
    2017. | Series: The keeper of tales trilogy ; 3
Identifiers: LCCN 2016049056 (print) | LCCN 2016057440 (ebook) |
    ISBN 9781476774282 (hardcover) | ISBN 9781476774305 (e-book)
Subjects: | BISAC: FICTION / Fantasy / General. | FICTION / Fairy Tales, Folk
    Tales, Legends & Mythology. | FICTION / General. | GSAFD: Fantasy fiction.
Classification: LCC PS3604.O457 P58 2017 (print) | LCC PS3604.O457 (ebook) |
    DDC 813/.6—dc23
LC record available at https://lccn.loc.gov/2016049056

ISBN 978-1-4767-7428-2
ISBN 978-1-4767-7429-9 (pbk)
ISBN 978-1-4767-7430-5 (ebook)

THE PLAGUE DIARIES

THE CONTINENT

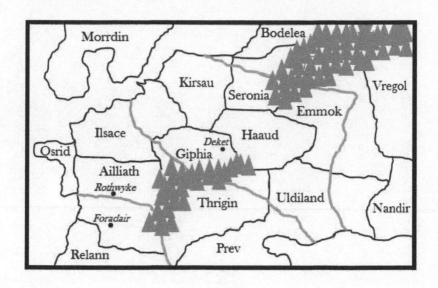

Prologue

FATE IS A LINE FREE WILL TWISTS INTO A SPIRAL. A PATH FRACtured into forks that lead to the same place. A snake that bites its own tail. The beginning knows its end.

This is the paradox: Free will slips among the twists of fate. Crosses the valley, scales the mountain, enters the cave. Finds a new way through fixed space. The end remembers where it began.

When I was a child, I knew—believed—none of this.

On a summer morning, weeks before I turned eighteen, a pigeon, a dove, and a sparrow summoned me to visit an estranged friend. I went to her cottage in the woods west of town. There, Old Woman revealed the symbol carved in stone at her hearth. She knew I'd once dreamed of this symbol but had long concealed its presence in her home from me. Then, she said it was known "the man Fewmany" was buying land where other stones lay, but not the reason why. She spoke of the missing arcane manuscript entrusted to my late mother, who was meant to decipher the text but didn't. Old Woman told me, "You are here to shift a balance, one with the potential to deepen our darkness or bear forth a hidden light."

Both were my fate, the darkness and the light, and the one I chose, a matter of free will.

I thought I had a choice to accept neither. I wanted no part of a prophecy, although my blood and bones knew it to be true. Foolish, because I'd read enough myth, lore, and fairy tales to know when one receives a call—hold a candle to a sleeping monster lover, search the world for a lost daughter, take a basket to Grandmother's house, spin straw into gold—one must heed it. That is fate. How one responds, that is free will.

So, descendants and survivors, here told is what happened to me, once as innocent as the girls in the tales I loved, and how it came to pass that I released the Plague of Silences.

- Part I -

ON THE SECOND OF JULY, I AWOKE BEFORE THE CLOCK'S SUM-
mons. By first rays, I was dressed and breakfasted, the satchel on my
shoulder, turning the lock of the row house's front door.

Across the street, a lamplighter extinguished the night's flames. At
the third corner on my route, seated inside the newsbox was the news-
speaker, his eyes pinned to a timepiece in one hand, the morning report
in the other. Several shopkeeps appeared on their thresholds as I waited
for my favorite market vendor. He had cherries, sharply sweet. I bought a
pint and poured it into a basket in my satchel, next to the boiled egg and
a heel of bread I'd packed for my midday meal.

By the time I reached the ward's edge, the nearby stable lot gate was
open and three carts were on the street. For twelve years, I'd walked
in their direction or sat next to Father on his two-horse cart, going to
school or to my apprenticeship in the translations office. But that day, I
was headed toward the grand homes north of town, to my first job.

I passed through four more wards, moving quickly through the one
which made me nervous, well-known for the unfortunate frequency of
burglaries, violent attacks, and indecent assaults. The narrow streets, de-
crepit walk-ups, and glaring residents did not refute the ward's reputation.

Once I crossed the town's official border, the road continued. I
approached the main entrance to The Manses, where several of the
kingdom's prominent families resided and my father once, perhaps still,
aspired to move. A man with a ruffed collar stood under a covered arch-
way, flanked on both sides by high wrought iron fences. He asked my
name, which I gave. When he checked a list, he said I was now included
among Fewmany's staff and could come and go as I wish. After I passed
him, I looked at the fine houses set back on expansive lawns. The only
hints of wildness were the sky itself and a flight of swallows streaking
blue through the ether.

The road forked. To the right I followed it, drawing closer to the great
house. I'd seen it before, once, when Fewmany invited me to his library
and offered the archivist position. At the manor's gate, I gave my name

again. As the guard glanced at his list, I tugged at my lace cuffs and brushed the front of my three flounced skirt. He studied my silver hair and tawny skin and stared into my mismatched eyes the colors of night and day.

"You'd be mistaken for no one but yourself, would you, Miss?" he said.

Sadly, I would not, I thought.

With each step along the curved path, my hands shook a little more until surely I looked as if I were having a fit.

At the drive's apex, I stared up at the manor's thick columns and the long windows grouped in sets of two. When I reached the double doors, I rang the bell, clasped my hands behind me, and stood straight as a blade.

The door opened.

"Good morning, Miss Riven," a man said. He bowed. "We weren't formally introduced when you came for the initial meeting. I am Naughton."

"Good morning," I said.

As he closed the door, I looked into the marble-floored hall. Impressive as before, a talon-footed round table stood on an elaborate tapestry rug decorated with animals. Within the recesses between the twelve closed doors were statues.

"Follow me," he said. Naughton led me to the grand staircase with its green marble steps and dark wooden railings. On the landing, near a long cushioned bench, I paused at the leaded windows to peer at the courtyard below and, beyond that, a stretch of green before a grove of trees.

"An arresting view," Naughton said.

I glanced at him. His forehead shone under his thinning brown hair, and his eyes, also brown, glinted with patience. He wore a black coat and trousers, a light gray vest with blue piping, and a flawless white cravat.

"Yes, quite," I said.

He escorted me up the west stair to the closest door on our right. As he searched for the key on his ring, I studied the bowed figures carved into the wood, most charred black. Fewmany told me he'd salvaged this door from a library lost to fire. The other eleven doors on that floor appeared to be identical to those on the first.

Once inside the library, Naughton invited me to hang my satchel on the ornate coatrack. Then he gave my instructions.

If I required assistance or refreshments, I was to pull the cord near the door to summon him. I could stroll the grounds and gardens and enter any room I found unlocked to view the magnate's art collection, but must make sure to close the doors when I exited. If I found a dog roaming the second floor, I should ring to have him taken away. As etiquette required, I shouldn't go below stairs, and neither was I to speak to the staff nor they to me. I was to use the water closet on the first floor, to the right and below the east stair's rise.

Naughton indicated a letter had been left for me on the table. With a nod and the promise of tea, he exited the library.

The letter was from Fewmany, a welcome in his absence. He said he was pleased to have my assistance to organize and catalog his collection and invited me to acquaint myself with the "nooks and crannies herein."

On that same table, large enough to seat forty people or twenty giants, I found three books, a map of sorts, and a box. The reference texts were on bookbinding and book collecting. The library's map noted where general categories were kept—history, natural science, et cetera—and where I'd find what interested me—myths, folklore, fairy tales, and the like. The last item was a delightful surprise, a box of stationery printed with the following letterhead:

FEWMANY ATHENAEUM
Miss Secret Riven, Archivist

I began my exploration. To the right of the entrance, near the coatrack, stood a supply cabinet with doors and drawers where pens, ink, bookstands, blotters, paper, wax sticks, pins, and scissors were kept. On top were a bouquet of red and white roses and two wooden book cradles.

At the enormous table were four chairs, cushioned in velvet, with high backs.

Not far beyond the table, centered in the space, was a fireplace, the stone chimney rising to the roof. The simple wooden mantel, curved at the edges, invited my touch. A movable screen, resembling chain mail, hung on a track inside the hearth.

The library itself seemed to span the entire length of the second floor, with a gallery accessible by six spiral staircases tight as a snail's shell. Along the east and west walls—and surrounding gallery—were rows and rows of bookshelves with leaded glass doors above and cabinets below. Throughout were brass sconces with cut crystal shades, held high by lifelike, masculine, disembodied arms, oil lit; I saw no evidence of candles.

Thick purple drapes framed the windows. The view west looked out to distant neighbors, the carriage house, and stables; the view north to the courtyard, the green, and the trees. Strangely, the south wall had no windows, instead more shelves and cabinets.

The books—so many books, hardly any space for more on the shelves or in the cabinets, which were stuffed with manuscripts and boxes of ephemera.

By the end of the day, my anxiety about the tremendous task before me, among other lurking concerns, gave way to pure giddiness.

How could it not? I was in a paradise.

That night, when Father and I sat down to dinner, the glamour had not faded. I was in rare spirits, glad to tell him what I'd seen and to show him the epic I'd borrowed, leather bound, gold gilt.

All was well; our conversation, amiable. He reminded me he would leave at the week's end to settle a land deal in Thrigin. Father was to have no lengthy carriage ride that trip, as every time before. He'd arranged to have passage on the new steamwheeler, which connected to a station outside of town. For weeks, he'd been agog reading about how they were built, how much weight they carried, and how fast they traveled.

"Iron can do what muscles cannot!" he said.

As the sole Geo-Archeo Historian at Fewmany Incorporated, Father didn't need to know any of that for his work, but his personal curiosity was indulged. What mattered were the maps he'd been studying, finished track lines and proposed ones, which veined across Ailliath and the kingdoms around it. To satisfy Fewmany's ambitions, Father would have to negotiate for the use of vast acres near and far.

However, there were acquisitions Father could never arrange for him.

After our dinner, Father brought out a cake Elinor, our daymaid, had baked to honor my first day. As he nudged a slice toward me, his hand brushed against the ceramic ochre bowl at the table's center.

Memory cracks with the slightest pressure.

There I was in the same place, but elsewhere in time.

Eleven years old again. Balanced across the edge of the ochre bowl filled with pears, the scissors gleamed, their violent whisper still in my ears. A foot of my black hair was gone, one inch of it cut by my father each night he punished me for telling a lie I had not told. Nearby, an exquisite illustrated book lay open to a page with a fox chasing a hen. And then, to Fewmany, who sat at our table, Father presented my drawing of the symbol.

Father, my mother, and Fewmany waited for me to tell where I'd seen it.

"In a dream," I said—and in that moment, I told the absolute truth.

As they looked at me, I wanted to grab those scissors and stab each of them through the heart. After they watched my hair grow back to its full length before their eyes, my parents glanced away, but Fewmany didn't. He and I matched stares, his amused, mine defiant. In spite of myself, I felt repelled by and drawn to him. Even then, I sensed a mystery connected us.[1]

That night's incident was never mentioned again. Father didn't explain why the symbol held such import or why the inquisition had occurred. Whatever I was presumed to know was significant enough for Fewmany to visit our house—under the ruse he was there to deliver documents Father had left at the office—to question me himself.

I hoped, of course, all had been forgotten, and if not that, buried. Because if either Father or Fewmany asked me again, I would have grappled with whether to lie.

I could no longer claim to have seen the symbol in a dream. I knew the location of one carved in stone less than an hour's walk outside of our town's borders, in the woods.

AFTER AN EXCHANGE OF LETTERS, MY SCHOOLMATES CHARlotte and Muriel and I agreed on an afternoon to spend together. We hadn't seen each other since our graduation in June. Charlotte was soon to be off for an extended visit with an aunt. Muriel had a holiday trip planned with her mother before entering a music conservatory in Osrid.

That summer day, on the gold-toned tile plaza in front of Fewmany Incorporated, the tallest building in town, I waited for them.

From the newsbox nearby came reports of local interest—a brutal robbery, a street repair in a certain ward—and an advertisement for Tell-a-Bells. *Don't let another to-do slip your mind. Get the self-communication aid everyone's talking about—and to—the one and only Tell-a-Bell. Keep that to-do list at the tip of your tongue! Make your bell toll today and never forget a thing. Visit* Time Matters *for the newest model, now with Whisper-Gear Horologics.*

A rumble disturbed the ground under my feet. Although I heard no sound, I thought it was the steamwheeler coming or going with freight. The tracks weren't far from the town's southeast edge and the river.

A two-horse cart approached. Tassels festooned the drays' harnesses. I returned the waves of the passengers.

"We're consumed with nostalgia," Charlotte said as she stepped down, her skirt lifted to reveal strapped walking shoes with buckles.

Muriel adjusted the tortoiseshell comb in her flaxen hair. "Old Wheel. What do you say?"

Their eager smiles prompted me to nod as my stomach knotted. The oldest ward in Rothwyke had been one of my favorite places. There I had enjoyed an occasional outing with my few friends, and my father and the caregiver I called Auntie took me there as a child to watch puppeteers and hear storytellers.

When I was five, Auntie fell asleep in her seat one afternoon, and the red squirrel appeared, urging me to follow him, which I did—into an alley, through a grate, along an underground tunnel, and out into the woods. Again and again, Cyril led me to the trees, to the quiet, to Old Woman. Those visits had been a source of joy and comfort once, but there came a turn, then a break, and I wished not to be reminded of how, and where, that all began.

"Goosequill's or The Dowager's Parlor first?" Charlotte asked.

The former it was, our favorite bookshop. Charlotte bought one of the new penny serials, noting they are "weak on intellect, strong on emotion," and Muriel, a "brooding novel" a friend recommended. Because I had access to the great library, I chose nothing.

Next, to the antiquarian shop, where the old shopkeep humored us although we rarely bought anything. That day, he allowed Charlotte to feign a languish on a grotesquely carved couch with one gnawed leg and Muriel to handle a miniature porcelain tea set. In a glass case where he locked away small treasures, I spotted an old coin, minted with a stag's head. He sold it to me for less than the cost of a clothbound book.

Hungry at last, we went to a teahouse for pastries and conversation. They prompted me to speak of my work as an archivist, as well as to describe the manor of, as Muriel stated accurately, "the magnate who owns half the kingdom." So I did, attentive to details, which seemed to satisfy their curiosity.

"But you haven't given up hope you'll be going to high academy, have you?" Muriel asked.

"I'm still on Nallar's wait list," I said.

"Are you certain that's what you want?" Charlotte asked. "If you go, I fear you'll suffer the same brutishness you did in school, or worse, and there will be no one to look after you. Besides, even if you completed your studies, how difficult it will be to find employment, biases being what they are. Not to mention, you need not. Your father can keep you well in comfort until you marry."

Her words didn't anger me. She was right, of course. I'd endured nasty harassment from several boys and cold treatment by the teachers who thought no girl should take the advanced courses I did. Those were meant for boys who would attend high academy, presumed a waste on me. Although always encouraging and ready to come to my defense, Charlotte never understood my ambition. It was peculiar, but I was peculiar—in appearance and character—and never believed what was inevitable for most women, regardless of station, was so for me.

"Charlotte!" Muriel said.

"I worry about her. I'm merely being practical," Charlotte said.

"Should I not go to the conservatory for similar reasons?" Muriel asked.

"Your choice is less provocative. It's not an academic institution," Charlotte said.

I looked at my friends, smart, genteel, pretty. "Muriel, she means well. But the pursuit of knowledge is in my blood, which is why I accepted the archivist position," I said, and said no more.

"Well, then, on the subject of high academies, I saw Michael Lyle after a play last week. He's set to leave for his in September," Charlotte said.

I sipped on my empty cup as they cut teasing glances at me. Never once had I confessed my infatuation, but the mention of his name ignited my cheeks.

"He has a prime intelligence," I said.

"His mind isn't the only prime quality," Charlotte said. We sputtered with giggles. "How could Nikolas interrupt you as he did? At last, you were talking to him! Details, please."

Her straightforwardness discomfited me, but I had no reason to withhold what happened at our graduation party. "You and Muriel were off dancing with the others, and I was sitting alone, with Michael nearby. He asked me a question and we started an innocuous conversation about cats—disappointing, I know, yes, *cats*—and then Nikolas appeared and asked me to follow him. He told me his father said he must attend a meeting about some dispute, which required them to depart the next morning. Nikolas thought he'd have the summer here before he left for his goodwill visits, but no. Once the dispute was settled, he went straight on to the first kingdom on his itinerary."

"The longsheets and newsboxes mentioned his departure. I had no idea it was so abrupt," Muriel said.

"Have you received word?" Charlotte asked.

"A few letters. He's well, and not yet travel weary. You know his sense of humor. Among his more memorable quips, he said he's 'on a diplomatic mission with a vague promise of adventure and constant threat of cholera.'"

We finished another pot of tea, then said our good-byes, knowing it would be some time before we saw one another again. The farewell was proper, clasped hands and tears held. Charlotte offered a seat on her cart—her driver was waiting—but I chose to walk home. Their company had cheered me, but the sadness at their leaving, and Nikolas's absence, weighed heavy once I reached my room.

I sat on my bed and, on my night table, placed the ancient coin next to the carved wooden stag Nikolas had given me years before. His eighteenth birthday was in three days. I planned to send the coin although it would reach him too late for the occasion. He'd appreciate the nostalgic reminder of the ancient stag who stepped from the trees the day I showed him the way to the woods, with Cyril the Squirrel as our escort. I still remembered when we returned to our schoolmates in Old Wheel, clapping at the end of a troupe's performance, and Nikolas splayed his hands above his blond head and bowed.

Why did I, should I, miss him so when I knew once we finished school, our ways would inevitably part? He'd have his duty as the prince of Ailliath, and I'd do as I planned—attend high academy, find some suitable employment, and live on my own.

The bruised ache in my chest flared as I thought of how he called me away from the party, led me to a vestibule, and said he was departing the next day. No warning at all, at his father's command. With no mind to propriety, Nikolas took me in his arms. We clung like heartbroken children until I pulled away and felt as if a piece of me had been torn out. My best friend since I was seven years old—here, then gone.

When would the raw feelings scar and the pain become a memory? I wondered.

AUGUST /35

DURING THOSE INITIAL WEEKS, I SENT LETTERS TO PRIVATE AND HIGH academy libraries requesting information on their organizing systems. What Fewmany wanted had been accomplished before, and I thought it best to consider the sum of functional options. As it was, most of his library was grouped in broad categories with little distinction among individual subjects. He might have remembered where each title among the thousands was placed, but I suspected even he had forgotten what he possessed.

As I walked among the shelves, annotating the map he'd provided, I observed Fewmany hadn't exaggerated his collection's diversity. Many of the volumes were what one might expect of a person of his station— the writings of famous men who put order to matters of the world and imagination. The definitive works by great historians, philosophers, and scholars.

Then there were the texts I couldn't account for then, specifically,

- Bestiaries and histories, popular in times past, which described with absolute conviction fanciful creatures and distant lands that either never existed or were greatly exaggerated, with two shelves dedicated to dracology alone;
- Volumes on lost civilizations, those verified by archeology and those speculated by legend, as well as books on obsolete religions, the beliefs, traditions, and rites no longer—or still rarely—practiced; and
- Esoterica and alchemy texts, most of which were manuscripts, and all distinguished themselves by the images within—drawings of recurring symbols, geometric shapes, vessels and hearths, beasts real and imagined, representations of the elements, and human forms.

As to the rest, I was unsure what appealed to him. Perhaps the rarity or reputation motived his acquisition if the topics didn't. There is, of course, prestige in ownership regardless of whether one has genuine interest in the thing owned. Although many books were clearly valuable, others seemed meant for reference rather than investment.

By now, I was content in my duties. Not only did my constitution suit me for the position, but also I was accustomed to spending vast hours alone. So often had I been left to myself—an only child with a mother who required my silence, hissing if I made a sound, as she bent over tattered books; a girl, then a young woman, with a father who traveled away for his work. In my last two years of secondary school, I became an apprentice at Fewmany Incorporated. I didn't mind the solitude in the apprentice's room, although I had Leo Gray's occasional patient company as he corrected my translation assignments.

At the manor, I rarely saw anyone but Naughton. He greeted me each day when he opened the front door. He was silent when he set a carafe of water on the table after I began to work and served morning and afternoon tea. Sometimes, I glimpsed another servant scurrying in the halls and near the lower-level stairs, which were below the west stair's rise. It was, after all, a proper manor, where servants were to be neither seen nor heard.

Not once was there a hint or mention of a spouse or children, brother or sister, cousin or elderly relative. My only contact with Fewmany was through letters, my questions promptly answered on his personal stationery—From the Desk of the Magnate—and waiting on the library's table when I returned in the mornings.

Then—an encounter.

I'd lost myself browsing the shelves again, but never had I lingered so late. I'd rung for Naughton to see me out, and I was halfway across the first-floor hall when the front door opened.

He was a shadow with a top hat against a rectangle of light.

I froze.

"Good evening, sir," I heard behind me. Naughton was suddenly at my side.

"Good evening, Naughton," Fewmany said. "And to you, Miss Riven."

"Thank you, sir," I said. My feet moved forward to match Naughton's pace as Fewmany approached.

With a pinch at the brim, Fewmany lowered his hat, and with his other hand, brushed his gray-streaked hair smooth against his head. Because of the sconces' dim light, what otherwise would have sharply glinted instead shone weakly—his amber eyes, the Tell-a-Bell at his ear, the ring on his right hand, the timepiece at his hip. As always, one of his coat pockets appeared stuffed full, its edge revealing a handkerchief. His coat, vest, and trousers were a dark gray wool, impeccably tailored. In contrast, the scarlet cravat at his neck almost seemed to throb.

"I trust your assessment of the collection continues to be engaging," he said.

"It does, sir," I said.

"And what of the inquiries made?"

"There are two replies outstanding. I've begun to compare the systems."

"Very well. We'll meet to confer when all is accounted. By the way, your messages regarding what you have borrowed are appreciated, but it will suffice to make a note and leave it on the supply cabinet."

"I will, and I apologize if the correspondence has been excessive."

"'Tis an indication of your honesty." The corners of his mouth twitched upward as his eyebrows lifted.

We bid cordial good-byes. The heels of his boots tapped against the floor, a whistled tune meeting the time of his step, as Naughton walked at my side then let me out.

I stood with my back to the door. In the distance, the castle's towers rose jagged into the pastel sky. Fewmany had neither said nor done a thing to provoke me, but my arteries pulsed as if he had. I'd been unprepared for the sight of him, not quite on my guard, although I had no reason of late, nor for years, to fear him. With squared shoulders, I walked into the twilight, crossed through the unsettling ward, and entered my house in the dark.

DIARY ENTRY 10 AUGUST /35

Dead, but the odor resurrects her.

The emanation was so keen, I pulled myself away from reading to investigate.

Father's bedroom door gaped wide as the billow threatened to choke me. What has he done? I thought as I held my breath and lifted the lamp. As expected, her wardrobe's bottom drawer was partially open. The dressing table still held the brush, mirror, comb, jewelry box, wedding ring, bottles. There was a dark blotch on the wood's surface. I remembered I'd heard him cry out, assumed he'd lost a button or noticed a raveling hem, but no—he'd spilled some of her precious essence, hadn't he?

He thinks I don't know he dabs a drop of perfume on one of her handkerchiefs and tucks it into his evening coat pocket. He doesn't perform this ritual every time he attends a performance, but it is why I rarely accompany him no matter how much I'd like to see the play or hear the orchestra.

Dead four years come October, but his room suggests she's away for a while, coming back.

His mawkishness is beyond tiresome.

Today, I received a letter from Nikolas. Obviously, mine to him are delayed because only now do I have his response to my decision to work in the library. I expected him to be quite heated, considering his antipathy for—that might be too strong—his long-held suspicions about Fewmany. I could tell Nikolas didn't like him the very first night I met them both at the castle, at the summer grand ball.[2] How long ago . . . twelve years! Since then, Nikolas has had encounters with him, however brief, and hears about the meetings Fewmany and his men have taken with the Council. His opinion has never softened.

Regardless, his reply was, well, polite. He congratulated me, stating I was sure to do a fine job while I was there, but expressed full confidence I'd be on my way to high academy. (Still waiting.) No word from Charlotte or Muriel yet.

Confound it! Knocked half a bottle of ink on my desk. Father and I, both clumsy tonight. Now, no reason really, the memory of the dinner after I was so sick with the fever, my hair sprouting silver, her words when she tipped the salt cellar, "Mind what is spilled, girl, and watch it doesn't spread."

Dead, but she is not gone.

BY THE MIDDLE OF AUGUST, I EXPLORED WHAT I COULD OF THE manor, outside and in.

The exterior was a testament to balance, symmetry, and proportion. On the front facade, every window was perfectly spaced and aligned. There were forty-eight on the lower story and sixteen on the second, all grouped in sets of two. I couldn't account for why the library's south windows were missing from the interior, but there they were on the exterior, covered with drapes like all the rest. Across the basement level, small windows caught the light like narrowed eyes.

Along the back facade, on the first floor, two glass doors opened to the courtyard and on the second floor, one huge central window allowed in northern light. As with the front, there were multiple windows, but also four doors. Two led into the west wing, for deliveries and servant comings and goings; the ones to the east wing remained a mystery.

The courtyard had gold-toned tiles—the same kind as the plaza in the front of Fewmany Incorporated—and a grid of planters filled with shrubs and flowers. Stepping off to the west, one approached the carriage house and stables, where four carriages and seven stallions had shelter. To the east of the courtyard were the formal gardens, fastidiously groomed, dazzling with color and texture. Among the flora were detailed sculptures of animals and stone pathways without the creep of weeds or moss. At the center, made of juniper, with walls too high for a giant to peer over, not a maze but a labyrinth.

Beyond the house and courtyard was an expanse of green, the sod cut to a plush cover. Three archer's targets at different distances, marred with holes, stood in the open, yards from a wooded area. I walked across the green and approached close enough to see what was beyond was a wild place. An urgency welled up in me—*go, enter*—but I resisted, determined not to be the girl I had been. Even if I'd heeded the impulse, I couldn't have entered. In time I'd see for myself that a locked gate and iron fence surrounded the acres of old trees.

As for the interior, the manor was a silent place with an irregular pulse. Elegant; in some ways simply, in others sensually. Fierce with beauty and light, and dark. Mysterious, where what was revealed only hinted at the maze of what was hidden.

The first- and second-floor halls had mirrored proportions, the same width and length, the same high vaulted ceilings. On either side of each main corridor, there were six doors, evenly spaced. Flawless white plaster covered the walls, crystal sconces lit the way, and art filled the space between the doorways, statues on the first floor and paintings on the second.

On the second floor, only the charred door near the west stair allowed entry into the library. The rest were locked. I suspected the last gave access to a hidden room; I'd counted my steps, and the library came forty paces short of the hall's distance. On the opposite side, I could enter only two rooms, one with glass display tables filled with brooches, bracelets, and rings and one with landscape paintings. The last door at the far end always smelled of an animal, dank and pungent.

As for the first floor, to the west, I found a ballroom two rooms wide, three locked doors, then a dining room. Across the hall was a chamber of mechanisms, another room filled with sculptures, and yet another, which seemed to be a split parlor, a wall separating the two sides.

But what of the wings, which flanked each side of the first floor?

At the time, they were a puzzle. From the second-story windows, which faced sunrise and sunset, I saw the long rooftops without a single chimney. An opaque glass pavilion connected each wing to the main house. In the first-floor rooms I could enter, there were windows with views of mosaic murals, ferns, and ivy, but I found no doors leading across. Not yet.

Curious as I was about what I couldn't see, there was enough to explore among what I was allowed.

My favorite, the one I visited most often, was the chamber of moving marvels. Hundreds of mechanisms were displayed on tables and stored in cabinets. Some of the contraptions had exposed gears, pins, springs, and wheels. I studied scientific machines—orreries, engines, magneto-electric shock devices—and many toys, including animals familiar and fantastic, carts that moved without horses, human figures waiting to be animated. Here, like in the other rooms, each item bore a descriptive tag, stating its approximate age, place of acquisition, and typically an anecdote.

One day after my midday meal, I played with a homunculus, which pounded a rock with a pickax, and the caged bird whose cheerful notes fluttered like its wings. I noticed two new acquisitions, or perhaps old ones moved from other locations. There was one of a woman who danced round and round on her tiptoes. The other was a boy who ran in circles chasing a dog, or with a shift in perspective, the dog chasing the boy.

As I was leaving the room, I saw Naughton approach the grand stair with a package in his arms. He stopped to look back when he heard the latch click.

"One of the most whimsical rooms," he said.

"A visit there always cheers me," I said.

"And him as well. He adores his automatons. With a little care and shelter, they do exactly as they were made to do. My favorite is the gilded bird," Naughton said.

"I like that one, too. There's a device I'm curious about, though. The tag is missing. It's a small metal box with concentric dials, and several metal arms pointing from the center."

"The Prognosticator, he calls it. Allegedly, it's a mechanical calendar of an ancient civilization. That's what his best minds told him. If one knows how to set it, the machine determines astronomical cycles."

"How fascinating. You've spent considerable time in there, I suppose. I didn't know the staff was allowed such entertainment," I said.

"We staff find beauty and joy where we can, do we not, Miss?" There was no harshness in his eyes, so very brown, but a gentle watching, like that of a deer. He turned to climb.

"Yes, indeed," I said behind him, smoothing the bristle in my tone.

I'd been put in my place. My service was different, but I was still among them.

THE MEETING WITH FEWMANY WAS SCHEDULED FOR NINE o'clock. I arrived at my table early, reviewed my notes, and made three nervous visits to the water closet. As I returned from the last trip, I heard a high-pitched yap. I turned around on the stairs' landing. The beast froze, then darted at me. A whistle pierced through the hall. "Mutt!" Naughton shouted. I'd never heard him raise his voice.

Unlike any I'd seen, the dog was no larger than a squirrel, with short fur, nubby legs, curved tail, pointed ears, and blunt muzzle. He leapt at my legs, barking as if alarmed.

When I scratched his head, he gazed at me imploringly. I withdrew the instant a twinge pierced through my forehead. He knew he could reach me. I could feel the pressure mounting, the force of his will and the haze of the image he wanted me to see.

"I no longer speak to your kind," I said aloud, my human speech unintelligible to him.

He barked again, frustrated, I could tell from his tone. His dumb noise filled me with relief. Throughout the years, I had learned to control the ability I'd had since I was a child, which was to communicate with creatures and plants.[3] By then, I wanted no part of that strangeness anymore, and I was determined to keep it at bay.

I returned to the library. Minutes later, I heard footsteps, then a firm *rap-rap, rap-rap* on the door. I stood next to my chair as Fewmany entered. He was shaved and shined, his coat pocket stuffed as always, top hat tucked under his arm, his red silk vest a flash of fire.

The dog whipped past his legs and dashed toward me. I scowled at Mutt but stretched my hand down in a friendly gesture. He licked my fingers.

Fewmany tilted his head. I noticed a rough scar under part of his jaw and chin. "Well, what-ho. He's savage to everyone save myself, Naughton, and a rare other. Now you, too."

I pulled my hand away, feeling exposed. "An anomaly, to be certain."

Fewmany snapped his fingers. Mutt followed him to the door. As Fewmany pulled the bell's cord, he nudged the dog into the hall and shut him out. The magnate placed his hat on the table. "Please sit down," he said. He reached his hand to the curved gearbox behind his right ear and switched off the Tell-a-Bell's mechanism. Now it couldn't ring and prompt him to recite his toll, a list of his day's tasks to do, which was surely quite long. That I had his full attention was reassuring, and discomforting. I stiffened in my chair and ignored the swirl in my belly as he settled on the seat to my right.

As we exchanged due pleasantries, Naughton served tea and placed two books at Fewmany's arm. With Fewmany's prompting, I explained what I'd learned from the library staff who had replied to my inquiries. He skimmed the subject category lists some had forwarded. To honor his request for a catalog, I suggested one comprising cards, which would, in time, be cross-referenced. Each item in his collection would be assigned a unique letter-number combination, which would be marked on the item and written on the card.

He looked at several blank samples I'd devised as I told him the book dealers' correspondence would be marked as well and filed by the item's title, or other identifier if one wasn't noted.

That he had few questions surprised me. In fact, he seemed quite taken with the thoroughness of my suggestions.

"A rational, orderly system you've recommended. I knew this challenge suited you. Well done," he said.

"Thank you, sir," I said. I hoped the blush wasn't too deep on my tawny cheeks.

"I'd like to study the category systems and review the card samples before I make a final decision. Would a response by next week's end suffice?" he asked.

"Of course."

He pushed the books Naughton delivered toward me and rested his right hand on top. The skin's texture suggested his age, as his face and form did not; he was at least as old as my father, likely older. The ring on his finger held my attention—a gold band engraved with interlocking knots and one pebble-sized red gem at the center.

"New acquisitions from my dealer, Quire," he said.

I'd found reams of correspondence from this Quire stored away. His letterhead identified him as William Remarque, but that wasn't how he signed his name, at least not to Fewmany. I thought it uncanny his surname, Remarque, was also a term for a small drawing in a book. As for his nickname, Quire, a term that referred to the folded leaves in a book, I assumed he'd chosen that himself as a nod to his profession.

I opened the first book to find several pages weren't cut, as if no one had ever looked at or read it.

"'Tisn't unusual to find a quarto untrimmed. Leave it as it is," Fewmany said. He reached for a pen, ink, and blotter as I turned the cover of the second text.

Loose at the title page was an annotation in Remarque's hand. He described the book as a chronicler's account of a man who claimed to be king of a vast region, who sent letters to the kings of many lands, but no one was certain he ever existed.

"The one you hold seems to me a testament for writing of one's own deeds rather than relying on historians," Fewmany said. "I wonder what will be written of yours truly."

I wasn't certain if he expected a reply, but I gave one. "I suppose that depends on who tells the tale."

"Astutely said," he replied. "Neither book has my mark. Nothing is to be stored without it. Observe."

I watched as he wrote on the first, middle, and last pages, near the margin at the spine. His mark, simply *fm*.

"Shelve them where you see fit," he said.

When he rose to leave, I stood on quivering legs as the tension bled to the floor.

"Again, well done," he said as he put on his hat. There was lightness in the tone of his parting words, "Good day, my keeper of tales."

"Good day, sir," I said. I waited until he left the library to smile at the gentle sobriquet, in spite of myself.

"CONFIRMATION ARRIVED I WILL NOT ATTEND NALLAR THIS AUtumn," I wrote in my diary, the twenty-fourth of August. "Unbelievable!

As hard as I worked at my studies, all I endured my last three years, the apprenticeship at Fewmany Incorporated. Father wasn't as disappointed as I thought he'd be. He said I can apply again and in the meantime, I have something purposeful to do. Yes, at least I have the library."

Still, my disappointment was blatant for days because Naughton, who typically said no more than good morning, Miss; your tea, Miss; and good evening, Miss, breached the bounds.

"I was informed you received distressing news of late. I am sorry, Miss," he said.

His empathy provoked a hitching cry in my throat. I assumed he knew of the note I'd left for Fewmany that I would remain as his archivist. "Thank you, Naughton."

That same week, I was on my way home, walking along a block of shops, when I saw someone pressed near the wall outside a haberdashery. He looked down as he shifted packages under his arm.

Michael Lyle. Suddenly, every thought and worry vanished. I wanted to thrust my hands through that wavy chestnut hair, trace the sublime angle of his nose . . .

Despite my liquefied knees and tied tongue, I managed to sally forth and unravel a coherent greeting. He smiled when he said hello. As he remarked on his summer and preparations to leave for high academy two days hence, I relished a pause to look into his moss-green eyes.

"Your plans?" he asked.

"I'll continue to serve as the archivist for a private library," I said. "Fewmany retained me in July."

"So then . . . ?" he asked. It was common knowledge who had been accepted and who was waiting among our classmates.

"No seat opened."

"Although I'm not surprised, I'm sorry to hear that."

"Not surprised?"

"I imagine it must be difficult to swim against the prevailing current in a skirt," he said.

"Shall we exchange costumes?" I asked.

He laughed with a hint of pink on his cheeks. After we shared our well wishes, I offered my hand—a socially acceptable but personally bold gesture—which he shook with a firm yet gentle grip. How I remained upright as every drop of blood rushed to my thighs, I have nary a clue. Woe—what was unrequited!

Then, I caught a glimpse of myself in a window. Light, how it reveals. That moment, my silver hair resembled the pelt of an aged animal. My eyes the colors of night and day shone like mismatched minerals. My skin was the color of a tea stain.

I stared at what Nature had wrought and realized it was high time to mask it.

The next day, I visited a ladies' parlor, spectacle shop, and jewelry merchant. My hair was black with dye, both eyes now brown behind tinted lenses, and my throat bright with a jade beaded necklace.

Although I never bothered much with fashion, I decided I must have something new for my wardrobe. What I'd worn had always been appropriate, timely yet inconspicuous. But I wanted—needed—a change.

After walking in and out of shops for hours, I settled on two split-busk corsets with a narrower waist than I'd worn previously, two skirts, three blouses, two dresses, and a new pair of side-lace boots.

Then, I noticed a whimsical sign of a tree decorated with a frock. There was a little shop wedged between two others, both among Few-many Incorporated's many enterprises. Curious, I entered through the narrow double doors. The space was barely wider than the outstretched arms of a tall man. Shelves and cabinets filled the left wall. A full-length mirror hung on a cabinet door. A long plank of wood angled into the room, held fast into the wall with hinges.

A tiny woman of mysterious age greeted me, Margana Bendar, the proprietress. I said I was in search of a new garment but with no particular type in mind. She opened cabinets to show finished examples of her work. I liked her attention to minute details.

I asked her fee, and Margana said that would depend on the design's complexity and materials chosen. I thought I might be able to have one lavish thing.

As Margana opened a book of fashion drawings for me to review, I stared at her beautiful pendant with a blue crystal at its center.

"It's a treasured family heirloom," she said.

A strange feeling came over me and my arms prickled. I asked no more.

I decided I wanted a cloak with sleeves for winter. Margana asked what colors I liked, then if she could surprise me with the design. She said it so kindly, as if it were a gift, that I accepted. She told me to return for a fitting in two weeks.

SEPTEMBER /35

ONE EARLY SEPTEMBER MORNING, I SKIMMED A LONGSHEET FA-
ther left on the dining table. A classified ad caught my eye. An apartment
for rent in a ward in walking distance to work, with its own water closet,
and at a price I could afford.

I posted a note of inquiry, scheduled a meeting, and went to look
at it. The ward was far more modest than Peregrine, where we'd lived
since I was four. Among the streets, there seemed to be fewer newsboxes
(less chattering noise), shops (the essential ones—dry goods, apothecary,
butcher, et cetera), stables (those of modest means, which included me
now, cannot afford a cart, horse, and livery fees), and performance halls
(although I seemed to have little time for such entertainments).

The building was a walk-up with an aging but clean facade, brass
railings, and two large pots filled with flowers. The attendant assured me
the tenants were respectable. The landlord tolerated no riffraff.

Once inside, the stairway was sturdy, the paint old but hardly cracking. The fifth-floor apartment was one large room filled with sunlight.
As I stood there, imagining myself in that place, I anticipated a pleasure I
hadn't known before, a sense of independence, a pride that I would, and
could, manage my own affairs. I signed an agreement standing at an old
cupboard next to the stove and promised to deliver a deposit by the end
of the week.

But first I had to tell my father.

The next day, I found him in his study with the curtains pulled open.
The morning sun brightened his table, covered with books, maps, and
documents.

Father didn't notice me in the doorway. He faced his treasured three-
hundred-year-old map on the wall, covered in thin veils marked with
battle sites, old roads, and other mysterious marks. He stood with his
arms folded, unshaved jaw set, the hair on his balding head tousled, his
ear absent the Tell-a-Bell. Nearby was the stool where I once sat. I felt
more tenderness than I expected then, remembering Father's pointing
finger. I learned the history of The Mapmaker's War well before it was
mentioned in my school lessons.

". . . Had the mapmaker's apprentice never crossed the river border,
none of this would have happened. Neither of us would be here, my pet . . ."

". . . Rothwyke wasn't Rothwyke then, but the site of the first battle, which later became Ailliath's seat . . ."

". . . The war waged for three years, surging through the lands north and east of Ailliath . . ."

And then there was his quest to prove a noble lineage, based solely on his father's apocryphal story of the land and title stripped from our family after this great war. No proof yet found.

Father startled, then shook his head as if to clear it. "You were a ghost for a moment."

A coil of black hair fell across my shoulder. There I was, like the dead crossing from another realm. I tempered my scowl. I'd intended no reminder of her.

"I have something to tell you. I've signed a lease on an apartment. I move in three weeks," I said.

"Why didn't you talk to me first?" he asked.

"To what purpose?" I asked.

"It seems reasonable you would. This is a significant decision."

"No more so than moving a kingdom away to attend Nallar."

"There you would have had supervised housing with a boarding mother and other young women for company."

"I'm not a child."

He sighed. "I'm stunned, to be honest. As it is, you live enough on your own, considering how often I'm away."

"Then what does it matter?"

"And Elinor is here several days a week, to look after things."

With no warning, my temper ignited. "I am not a thing."

"That wasn't my implication. Because of her, we live in cleanliness and order, errands done, meals prepared. How will you manage that on your own, working as you do?"

"I'll find a means."

"You've rarely had to do these tasks for yourself."

"I'm more capable than you think." My thoughts rushed to my hands wrapped around a broom handle, a brush dipped in a bucket, the edge of linen hung out to dry. I learned the chores of daily life at Old Woman's side. Father had no idea where I'd spent many hours of my childhood.

He rubbed his forehead. "In which ward is it?"

"Warrick. I'll have less distance to walk, and the block where I'll be is quite safe."

"Warrick."

"It's what I can afford on my own wages."

"I raise a girl to have a mind of her own, and this is the result." When he smiled, I knew he wouldn't forbid me. Whether he'd try to talk me out of it remained to be seen.

"I know how unseemly this will appear to most, but it's only slightly worse than my pursuing an education," I said.

Father gave a faint laugh. "Only slightly. I do wish you'd stay, though. A part of me was relieved you weren't leaving for high academy. Quiet as you are, our home would be quieter still without you. How very silent it will be with you elsewhere," he said.

"I'll be three wards away," I said.

"Distance is irrelevant when the presence is gone," he said. His eyes moistened. He stepped past me to enter the hall. "I'll make some tea."

My very heart felt sore. There was another reason I wished to go.

I wanted to be somewhere empty of memories.

ROTHWYKE DAILY MERCURY.

21 September /35. Page 3, Column 5

OLD WHEEL BETTERMENT—Last week, demolition commenced in our town's oldest ward. Behind Fewmany Incorporated, jagged piles of debris stand where the first buildings have been cleared away. The ward's grid of streets and squares will be replaced by what has been termed "a village unto itself," where residents will be able to work, shop, eat, drink, and live within a gated domain. Completion and leasing of individual properties, in what will heretofore be known as New Wheel, is expected within three years.

The Old Wheel Preservation Society, which attempted to negotiate protection of various historically significant structures, expressed disappointment in Fewmany Incorporated's actions. The conglomerate wholly owns the land and buildings of that ward. No restrictions exist to prevent this new development.

I'D FINISHED MY WORK FOR THE DAY BUT LOST MYSELF IN A book I intended to borrow. Evening fell without my notice. I packed the book in my satchel and slipped on my cloak. As I swept down the stairs, I heard footsteps and stopped before I collided with a man.

"Oh-ho, fire or foe makes you flee?" he asked.

Fewmany.

"I hurry because a portion of my walk home is uneasy in the dark."

"Have you not accepted the offer of a carriage to bring you here and take you home each day?"

"I wished not to impose." That, and I wasn't entirely certain he was sincere about all he offered when he first proposed my position. Indeed, he was.

"'Twas meant to spare you the muck and rabble of the streets. Wait in the hall," he said.

I stood near the grand staircase as he walked under the west stair. A bell pealed. He appeared moments later with a lit lamp hanging from his fingertips.

"The carriage is summoned." He gestured for me to walk forward as he remained at my side. "Has so long passed since I last saw my keeper of tales that the transmutation went unnoticed?"

"Sir?"

"Your appearance has changed."

I pushed up my spectacles and resisted the impulse to touch my hair. "Yes, sir."

"Well suited, with a cut of a scholarly jib," he said.

Although his tone hinted at nothing more than a kind observation, a flare of memory burned my ears. The night of the scissors and symbol, he had watched me transform before his eyes.

When he opened the front door, the lid of the horizon was already shut. We stood in silence until he finally spoke.

"Are you afraid of the dark?"

"That depends on where I am and what might be near," I said.

"Mmm, yes. How true," he said. Fewmany dangled the lamp. The light pooled on this boot, then the other.

"Are you afraid of me?" he asked.

His candor startled me as much as the question itself. I wanted to laugh, but a stronger impulse held it back. "Do I have cause to be?" I asked.

"'Twould be a pity if you did, as every accommodation has been made for your comfort."

"I appreciate each gesture, and I apologize if you've gleaned otherwise, sir."

"Still you don't speak my name, after all this time."

"You are my elder, and I've been taught to show my respect. Besides, to my recollection, I failed to ask, and you never indicated how I should address you."

"Fewmany will suffice." A change came over his face, one I could see even through the shadows. "Can you keep a confidence?" he asked.

"Yes."

I watched the light swing to and fro. I felt the weight of my hair and the satchel on my shoulder. The carriage rounded the corner of the manor. Part of me wished for the horses to hurry, to hold back what had become unbridled, but I did nothing to stop it. I wanted to know.

"It's a matter of bosom trust," he said.

"I understand."

He leaned forward and whispered, "I am known far and wide as Fewmany, but my given name is Lesmore Bellwether."

I couldn't read his eyes but he studied mine.

"When I struck out into the world, I tore away from my dirty roots. I wished to be free of it all. You understand the wish to have a name of your choosing, don't you?" he asked.

I did. I hadn't been called by my given name, Evensong, shortened to Eve, in many years. What I'd chosen for myself felt truer.

The horses clopped to a halt. The coachman opened the door. Fewmany illuminated my approach to the waiting escort.

"I shall keep it to myself," I said at last. I settled upon the taut leather seat, found a cashmere blanket at my side, and felt heated bricks near my feet.

"Have a pleasant eve, Miss Riven." He closed the door, pounded the side of the carriage, and shouted for the horses to ride.

What am I to make of him? I wondered as I peered out of the carriage window. As a child, I had been frightened of him. The night we first met, when I was six, I said not a word to him—I didn't yet speak—and he teased me in the cruel way adults do, "So, if I tried to eat you up, you wouldn't even scream?" When I was eleven, there was the incident with the scissors and symbol. Since then, Fewmany and I had had no such dramatic encounters, but I continued to hold my wary childhood impressions, as well as Father's actions, against him. My cautious feelings, entwined with curious ones, lingered.

For some time now, the magnate had done nothing to garner my distrust. In fact, Fewmany had been quite generous. Perhaps he didn't involve himself in the decisions regarding apprenticeships at his conglomerate, but I expected he did, for all of us whose fathers worked for him. Although I was the only girl.[4] As to my archivist position, he could have solicited far and wide and found someone experienced.[5] But he asked me, more confident than I was I could manage so immense an endeavor. I suppose I should have felt flattered by, rather than suspicious of, those opportunities. What I'd done to earn his favor, I was unsure. I resolved to continue to do my best and not harbor grievances.

As the carriage halted near the row house's steps, I had a sudden thought, born of all I knew of myths and tales: There is power inherent in a name. I decided he meant to put me at ease with something we have in common.

DIARY ENTRY 23 SEPTEMBER /35

My birthday, 18th. The weather isn't cold enough, but I wore the new cloak Margana made. It's a beautiful purple wool, which reminds me of one I had as a child, with appliqués of bird shapes along the back and sleeves. Father made reservations at The Trencher, which is more accommodating to my diet. He had roast quail and I a warm beetroot, fennel, and walnut salad. Almond custard for dessert.

The evening was pleasant enough, but I do wish Father would stop pretending he doesn't notice how besotted Mrs. Knolworth's sister is with him! He could have had his pick among several lonely widows and vivacious spinsters willing for a late start—dare I suggest, a discreet liaison—but he persists with his lovesick grief, which only seems to endear him more to them.

When we returned home, I opened a package from Nikolas. He sent a collection of fairy tales well-known in Ilsace, in that language. Pressed between the pages were flowers. In his letter, he said he gathered them at a roadside. "Because of this gesture, the coachmen secretly refer to me as The Dainty Prince. I am thoroughly emasculated."

I've not missed him so acutely of late. I keep my mind busy in the library and at night with books. But sometimes, as tonight, when I'm reminded of how he makes me laugh, or something brings him to mind, or my vigilance fails, I wish he were here, if only for the comfort of his presence.

Enough.

I'll send him a thank-you and tend to tardy replies. Oh—I must remember to send these with my new post address. I have my own cubby! Charlotte is now settled with her relatives and has made several acquaintances. She believes her aunt is determined to have her engaged by this time next year. For Charlotte's sake, may he be a man who appreciates her directness. Muriel seems happy at the conservatory. She says she practices for hours which pass like minutes.

I understand that feeling of immersion. Sometimes it happens as I work, even though to many it might seem tedious, so many books to catalog. But for me, there's always an element of surprise. Everything I touch receives a dallying perusal. My knowledge of the world increases one paragraph, one page, one illustration at a time.

Every evening, I spend in study, an endeavor which, although natural to me, has become almost insatiable. Anything I wish to learn, I can discover on the shelves. Well, then. Perhaps I'm not as angry about the rejection from Nallar as I thought I was.

OCTOBER /35

THE ANNIVERSARY OF MY BIRTH BLURRED INTO THE WEEKS PRE-
ceding the one of my mother's death.

Excited about my pending move, little did I think of the occasion until I had to decide what I'd leave behind.

I planned to take my furniture and clothes, most of my books, the let-
ters and odds and ends in my desk drawers, and a box of old drawings. But the faded blue chest, painted with little animals, and the nesting dolls—no. Those things my mother had kept from her childhood and given to me. She'd never expressed warm attachment to them. The chest had been in my room since I was a baby. The nesting dolls she passed down to me when I turned seven. According to her family's tradition, the firstborn girl received the old set and the mother purchased a new one for herself. My mother instead bought a vase to fill the gap on her shelves.[6]

I wasn't especially fond of the chest or dolls, but they remained in my possession, vestigial more than sentimental objects. Although I expected to have no children myself, I wondered, if I did, would I bother to pass them on, too, for the sake of tradition?

The blue chest sat in plain sight at the foot of my bed, but it had long disappeared from my notice. Not so the night before I left my room in my father's house.

I unlocked the chest. There, where I'd last stored it, was the illustrated folklore book written in my mother's native language, which I couldn't read. Slipped between those pages was the cipher she had drawn, four years earlier. Flushed with anger, my hand scraped against a knot on the chest's bottom as I made room for the nesting dolls, the stack of twelve to be precise. The thirteenth, the solid one which fit in the center, was already inside, along with the bag of gold ingots and the handwritten clue, which read "A map is to space as an alphabet is to sound." Those items, too, she'd left for me within the chest, four years earlier, before she died. The dolls, ingots, clue, and cipher reminded me of what I hadn't found, what remained hidden or lost.

The arcane manuscript.[7]

With a *thup* of the lid, I shut away the objects and the memories with them.

The morning of the move, Father insisted that he help even though I hired two bull-armed men for the task. As we waited for them to arrive, I looked at my new home.

The plaster was patched. One of the curtain bars was broken. The floors showed evidence where a wall once stood and a wide groove as if someone paced many wee hours. The long room served as parlor, bedroom, and kitchen. Next to the stove, meant for cooking and heat, was a large cupboard with a drop leaf. A door led to a tiny water closet with no basin, but there was an ancient privy and a hip tub with a modern spigot. Luckily, the building's placement on the corner—where there was no newsbox—allowed for much light through the windows.

The men placed my desk, carved chair, mirror, bed, night table, wardrobe, and bookshelf where I wanted them. Father carried my belongings up the four flights of stairs, defiant that his age winded him. As they stacked my boxes, I thought of what was to be delivered on my next half day—the new dishes and kettle, the secondhand reading chair, and the small table and bench. I contemplated what prints I wanted to hang on the rails.

Anxious to unpack, I opened a box of linens. I noticed Father peering out of the windows, his body a gray shadow against the streaming light. He huffed quietly and turned then, his fingers pinched at the ring on his left hand. I didn't ask, and he didn't say, what he'd been thinking as he stood alone. I reached into my box again, determined to ignore the unwelcomed presence he'd released in my space.

I wasn't successful. How happy I'd been, and how quickly that turned into a raw irritation.

Father only made matters worse when he offered, yet again, to find some way to extricate me from the lease and assist with rents in a more "suitable" ward, since I insisted on living on my own.

That was the issue—the appearance of my station, the reflection on him. Father wasn't conventional about other matters, namely my education or prospects. He had always encouraged my intellectual curiosity, although I wondered if he would have done so if my brothers had lived. I knew he expected me to finish high academy before I married, which is why he made no concerted effort to arrange introductions or pressure me as such.

What Father loathed were poverty and the marginal hints of it, which he had evaded by his wits and good luck. Born in Foradair, one of Ailliath's oldest towns and the kingdom's former seat, Father lived in a cramped walk-up with his parents, who worked as a chimney sweep and a laundry maid. There had been siblings, but all had died before he was born or while he was too young to remember them.

Like other boys of his station, he should have followed in his father's footsteps, broom in hand. However, in primary school, Bren Riven gained attention for his charm and intelligence. Kind strangers took an interest in him. Scholarships paid his way to fine schools; his genial disposition made him many friends, including those with influence and power. Proud in their own way, although they never said so, his parents—this I would learn after the plague—often remarked, "Who do you think you are?" and "So, you're too good for us now?" He meant no insult by his striving, but he suffered their derision and that of the neighbors. Still, after he graduated with honors from a high academy in history and geography, he returned to Foradair to work for a land speculator. His parents rarely visited his modest house; he rarely returned to the ward, that reminded him of what he wanted to escape. Once his fortune took a great turn, thanks to another native son, Fewmany—strange, that coincidence—Father couldn't bear anything that reminded him of his origins.

Although there were wards in Rothwyke far more desperate than Warrick, the mere sight of it roused a dormant anger with which he couldn't make peace.

Before he left my apartment, he urged me to allow him to send Elinor once a week. I refused. I could tend to myself, and Elinor, old enough to be my grandmother, need not have more to do and more stairs to climb. Our good-bye was on pleasant terms, at least. He kissed me on the forehead, something he hadn't done since—I couldn't remember when.

A FULL MOON WAS SET TO RISE THE SEVENTEENTH OF OCTOBER.

I'd rung for the carriage and was on my way downstairs when I stopped on the landing to adjust my full satchel. When I looked up through the windows toward the west, the twilight shimmered lavender and rose.

An impulse surged through me. I asked Naughton to unlock the doors to the courtyard and told him to have the coachman wait.

I walked out among the planters, looked into the sky, then cast my eyes to the trees beyond. Suddenly, my feet stepped ahead of my will, through the courtyard, across the green, and toward the grove. A high fence spanned as far as I could see, made of iron bars set close together, too narrow for deer to pass.

At the arched gate, decorated with a tangle of metal ivy, I set down my satchel. I tried the latch, but it was locked. My fingers clutched the cold bars as I peered between the gaps. The trees rushed me with their knowledge gathered from roots and branches: the grove was wide and deep; once it had been connected to the woods in the west.

Their message prompted my memory. When I was a child, my father—and the crow who visited our courtyard—told me that trees covered much of the land, but many were cut to build Rothwyke and the castle. Still more, I realized, to make way for the manors.

No sound reached my ears, but a vibration rumbled through my soles like a summons. For a moment, I lapsed, listened beyond listening, standing in that threshold space with the light and breeze and bird calls when I heard,

"Fresh air thins blood that's long been sitting."

I turned to see Fewmany behind me. A colossal key dangled from his finger.

"Would you care to join me for a stroll?"

Curiosity, as much as the promise of a wooded walk, prompted my acceptance. I stood aside as he turned the lock, stepped ahead of him, and heard the creaking hinges go silent at my back. I followed his lead at a fork in the path as we spoke of my progress with the catalog.

Then he changed the subject.

"This grove was once part of the nearby woods. Much of the land was cleared long ago, but this was left behind," he said. "Some weeks have passed since I entered the gate for a moment of quiet or a hunt."

I remembered the animal heads mounted on his office wall at Fewmany Incorporated. Most of the beasts didn't roam Ailliath or any close region. "How many acres do you claim?"

"All told and accounted for, millions. But here, enough for a long walk or vigorous chase."

"What do you chase?"

"Deer, sometimes boar, or whatever is obtained to roam until it meets a sharp demise."

"Have you always hunted?"

"Once to survive, now for sport, but the satisfactions are the same—cooked meat eaten, raw aggression fed."

Such is his bluntness, I thought as I stepped from the path to look closer among the undergrowth dotted with red, gold, and orange leaves.

A blur twirled at my nose, joined by another, then another. I leaned back as the bees spiraled around my head. When they darted toward Fewmany, he stood stiff, his eyes wild, as they zigzagged near his nose and mouth.

"Go away! Vindictive pests!" His arms swiped through the air.

"Be still, and they'll leave. They're scouts from the hive reading our faces," I said. Scouts, I thought, this late, in this chill. How odd.

As quickly as they came, the bees flew away. Fewmany exhaled with a contempt-filled huff.

I crept farther into the trees, brushed my toe across the ground, and lifted my spectacles to study a cluster of mushrooms. Impulsively my fingers pulled one from the litter. I sniffed the cap and bit into it.

"What-ho, what if it's poisonous?!" he said.

I reached down for two more. I offered one to him as I ate the other. He took it from me with caution.

"It's not poison." I ate a third as he stared at me, then at his mushroom. "If I'm mistaken, I'll be dead soon, at least by this time to-morrow."

Fewmany nibbled the top, which gave me a subtle twinge of satisfaction. His face revealed he liked the taste, and he ate all but the stem.

"How did you know it was safe to eat?" he asked.

"I learned it."

"Is there a book specific enough that you trusted you could take such a risk?"

"No. I was taught."

"By whom?" He narrowed his eyes.

My stomach lurched. I revealed something I hadn't intended to—the truth of it connected to matters I didn't want to think about—and I knew I must be guarded with my answers.

"A grandmother," I said.

"Mmm-hmm. A grandmother who lived in the woods?"

"Yes. I was young at the time. I remember the lessons well, though," I said.

"Was this your father's mother or mother's mother?"

"The latter," I lied.

"Your mother—peace be to the dead—was from a land far from here. Vregol."

"Yes."

"How old were you then?" he asked.

He detected something was amiss. That unspoken connection I'd felt with him before drew suddenly taut.

"I'm uncertain, but I remember I was small and didn't yet speak."

My answer held a conflation of truth and lies.

"Yet you recall with precision a fungus that wouldn't cause severe illness or death. You must have eaten many of them to retain the memory," he said.

"Until I could fill on no more. Surprising what one remembers with such clarity," I said. "So, as a child yourself, you knew the woods as a hunter . . ."

"Yes, yes. Hunter, scavenger, predator, prey. Such was a life on the margins where the woods met the pasture."

"Who taught you?"

When he pivoted on his heel and began to walk again, I knew we'd abandoned the prior topic.

"When I was a stealthy lad," he said, "a distant neighbor, a kindly woodsman, found me inspecting a dead rabbit with fresh wounds. The man said a hawk had dropped its kill. Strange I'd come upon it when I did. The man taught me to skin, gut, and roast it, then with no rude mention of my hungry look, showed me how to use a snare. This served me well until my body and appetite grew. The woodsman taught me to use a bow and arrow and gave me the use of his hound. In exchange, I was to share my kills. By then, my mother was reduced to bones and hair, so my sister—peace be to the dead, both—was the one who welcomed the fresh meat, shaving slivers of liver to eat raw while she stewed a thigh and fed the collie the heart."

"Why didn't your family eat the sheep?" I asked.

"My father didn't own them. He was a shepherd. We received a lamb in spring, a ram in autumn, and on occasion a basket of wool. The man who owned the land and everything on it was fair according to custom, and not unduly unkind. My father despised him, but I admired his horse and fine clothes and the ring on his finger. Once, I stood aside as they spoke and I realized that 'tis always better to own the sheep. There's far less monotony and uncertainty involved. A fierceness rose up within me I didn't know I possessed, a deeply buried monster with teeth and claws and fetid breath."

I glanced at his profile. A scowl tightened his face. The air itself seemed to weigh upon me. I wondered if he said such blatant things to other people.

Fewmany looked into the distance. "Ah, but what would you know of these matters? A fortunate child you were—yes?—given the boons of attention and necessities. You have been spared a certain striving."

His cloaked tone of envy bristled me. I heard myself blurt, "How confident you seem in your assumptions."

Fewmany gave a curious smile. "Why, she has small fangs after all."

"You misread me."

"Do I?"

"Appearances are deceiving at times."

He halted his steps and met my eyes as best he could through my spectacles and the fading light. "We shall have to see one of these days, won't we?"

Then he lifted his chin and peered behind my back. I turned my head. A fox sat on the path, her ears alert, her body aware.

"A fine stole it would make," Fewmany said.

The fox stared at me, trying to force her thoughts into mine. I stamped my foot and she ran into the bosk. As I followed Fewmany to the gate, I realized how many hidden eyes peered out.

Indeed, I could ignore them, but those who looked did not stop watching me.

Their witness, if I were to call it so, began the day of my birth, when—according to my father—a pigeon, a dove, and a sparrow flew widdershins in the room moments after I first breathed. When I was three years old, my mother took me to see her mother in a faraway village within a vast forest. There, I first experienced the profound beauty of Nature—from a single pale yellow mushroom to great stands of evergreens. There, I followed a swarm of bees into a hollow trunk where, to my amazement, one bee told me a story of a terrified girl tied to a tree, a wounded man, and his silver wolf. There, in that same tree, a queen bee stung me three times on the forehead.

Soon after, although I didn't speak—I was mute, in a way—I found I could communicate with creatures and plants, and they with me.

I was six when Cyril the Squirrel first led me to the woods, then seven when he showed me the way to Old Woman's cottage. For months, I hid as I watched her and listened to her tell myths and tales to the animals. One of the myths about men in blue coats moved me so intensely that I gasped, and she discovered me in the shade. That very moment, the knot in my belly which had been tied to my tongue loosened, breaking my seven-year silence.

Old Woman taught me to sow, forage, weed, and harvest. At her side, I learned to sew, stoke, wash, cook, and clean. She was the first I trusted with my secret—that I could speak to and hear plants, animals, birds, and insects. She gave me love and told me of my fate—and I tried, how I tried, to abandon both.[8]

ALTHOUGH I WASN'T YET BORED OF THE OPEN ROOMS, I'D DEVELoped a habit of checking all the knobs as I walked through the halls. Did no one enter those closed chambers? I wondered. If they were opened for cleaning, did the servants ever forget to lock them? Where were Fewmany's private quarters? Where were the rooms for guests?

One afternoon in late October, I tended my work, close to the fire Naughton had built, and felt a heavy throb in my forehead. I knew Mutt was at the door even though he didn't make a sound. I willed him away. He was strong, persistent. Then he started to whine and scratch. I should have rung Naughton to fetch him. Instead, I opened the door. Mutt grabbed my skirt in his teeth and tugged at the hem. The dog wanted me to follow him.

His nails clicked as he walked to the far end of the hall. My blood quickened when the dank smell filled my nostrils. He clawed against the door. Hatch marks marred the lower panel. Mutt wanted to get inside.

I glanced toward the stairs. No sound, no movement. So—I twisted the knob and gave the door a push.

Mutt rushed into the gap, I slipped behind him, and I closed the door behind me. Instinctively my hands reached to the left. Like in every other room, I found a table with a lamp and vesta on top. Wick lit, flame high, lamp raised, I peered into the darkness.

The chamber was filled with wolves.

Paintings and tapestries and mounted heads on the walls; decorated vessels and bronze castings set on tables; a ligatured skeleton; a case of teeth. Dozens, stuffed and posed, their preserved lips snarled, their bloodless paws on breathless prey.

I crept toward the east wall. Behind the dense drapes, the sun's brightness filtered to a weak glow. Between the windows hung paintings of the beasts in the midst of hunts.

Within a cabinet with glass doors was a carved chair, massive as a throne, and hung across its back was a coat.

Mutt stood at my side as I opened the doors and looked closely. The instant I touched it, I knew I should leave it alone, but my fingers brushed against the silver-gray fur and traced along a sleeve, which ended with a paw, the small bones intact. The hood lay forward, as if a hidden head drooped in sleep. I pinched a lock of hair, lifted the hood, and saw ears, eyes, a snout, and teeth.

My breath seized.

I arranged the coat as I had found it, shut the doors, and looked down at the dog.

He was silent, in voice and thought.

I extinguished the lamp, clutched the spent match in my hand—careful to put things as they were—and opened a crack in the door. Mutt darted around my ankles. I closed the door, quietly, quickly. As I stepped away, I turned to see Mutt with his leg lifted, wetting the chamber's entry.

I rang for Naughton. As I waited for him to take the dog away, I looked into Mutt's eyes.

Speak, I said without saying, allowing what I didn't want.

His answer was only an image.

A lamb, alone.

NOVEMBER /35

THAT NOVEMBER, I VISITED WITH LEO GRAY, HEAD OF THE TRANS-lations office at Fewmany Incorporated. He had written my letters of recommendation when I applied to high academies the prior year, and he agreed to do so again.

The walk to Old Wheel was miserable in the cold. I realized how quickly I'd become accustomed to the comfort of the carriage which took me to and from the manor each day.

As I neared the plaza, I heard the sound of falling rubble. I walked along a side street and found the passage blocked with ropes and a No Trespassing sign. Several buildings had been demolished. Steam puffed from the mouths of men and horses, who loaded and pulled the debris. The sight of the ruins made my heart ache.

New Wheel would be built upon ghosts.

When I approached Fewmany Incorporated's portico, I paused to watch King Aeldrich step down from the royal carriage, shake hands with a man who worked on the twelfth floor with my father, and enter the building under escort.

By the time I crossed the lobby, the group was headed up the pulley lift. At the giant carved desk, the attendant gave his rote greeting: "Welcome to Fewmany Incorporated, inspired by innovation, anchored in tradition. How may I help you?" I waited for my pass and skimmed the names of the enterprises carved into stone behind him. Four more had been added since I last counted. The conglomerate held—to name a few—haberdasheries, teahouses, taverns, apothecaries, dry-goods shops, longsheets, coal, jewel, and metal mines, quarries, timber land, arable land, banks, textile mills, armories, several steamwheeler lines—machines and tracks—and various other inventions, including the Tell-a-Bell.

At the translations office door, the familiar garlic and bay rum smell greeted me. Wesley jumped back when he let me in. Cuthbert and

Rowland, who rarely acknowledged my presence, leaned forward in their chairs.

"Ye gods, she walks again!" Rowland said.

"Forgive him, but the resemblance is striking," Leo said as he rose from his chair.

My hand drifted to my hair, black as it had been when I was a child. Last they'd seen me, it had been silver. From my hair, my skin, even my shape, I was the image of my mother, who had once worked as a translator for Fewmany Incorporated.

As Leo went to grab his coat, the men returned to their work. The office hadn't changed, although a luminotype of Leo's pretty wife now replaced the miniature portrait which had once been on his desk.

I meant only to collect my letters, but Leo suggested an escape to a teahouse.

He hardly sipped his drink as I told him about the library—it was wonderful to be in the company of someone who appreciated books as well—but wasn't surprised that I'd taken my own apartment. Father had mentioned it to him in conversation.

Leo said they'd been as busy as ever and had no apprentice that year. On personal matters, Wesley was courting (regardless of his harelip, he was well mannered and hardworking), Cuthbert's eyesight was failing (he was very old), and Rowland was as curmudgeonly as ever (oddly reassuring). Leo looked well, although I noticed a strain in his face. His wife and son were in good health and content.

He gave me nine envelopes with Fewmany Incorporated's seal on the flaps.

"I know you didn't apply to your mother's alma mater before, but consider it. I took the liberty of writing a letter. With your marks, class ranking, and translation skills, you'd be an excellent candidate for Altwort," Leo said.

"How thoughtful," I said.

"As a legacy, you're sure to find more favor among the committee."

"I imagine so. Thank you," I said. I had no intention to apply, though. Why would I want to contend with her shadow?

The sympathetic cast to his eyes said what he didn't. *Poor girl, missing her mother.*

We parted ways with a light handshake and my promise to keep him informed of my whereabouts.

❦

A FEW DAYS AFTER THE VISIT WITH LEO, MY DIARY CONFIRMS, I was compelled to think of her again.

One morning, I entered the library to find two manuscripts left on the supply cabinet, an indication they were meant to be shelved. Each had ribbons lolling out from the pages. That made me curious, so I opened both side by side where they were marked. The one on the left I could translate but not fully comprehend, as it seemed to be written in riddles. Among the pages, some elaborately rendered and colored, were drawings of beasts and humans—one creature strangely conjoined from a man and a woman—as well as sketches of laboratories, vials, tubes, and vessels, and all sorts of symbols. The breath thinned in my lungs as I skimmed the manuscript, suddenly anxious I'd see the symbol which had once interested Father and Fewmany.

I looked at the manuscript on my right. No symbols, no illustrations, only blank spaces where that should have been. The translation was in my native language, in my mother's handwriting, on the grid-marked paper she had specially printed.

I compared the manuscripts side by side. They were meant to be read in tandem. One page mirrored the meaning of the other. Fewmany had inserted his own thoughts along the margins of her translation. Apparently, he was trying to repeat the experiments.

No surprise he, too, sought to turn lead into gold.

I walked up to the gallery, past the medical and anatomy texts, past the erotica collection—included there presumably for their technical purpose, most written in foreign languages, most with detailed drawings from which I discerned much and quickly—to the cabinets which held the esoteric manuscripts.

A few shiny spots marred the immaculate wood floor. As I bent down, they scurried away. The nemesis—silverfish! One cabinet had the telltale signs of a feast, dust on a shelf and manuscript edges jagged from their chewing. For a creature which likes dampness, they were in the wrong place, and their presence alarmed me.

I left a note with Naughton for Fewmany to decide what must be done.

Through the following days, my concentration waxed and waned. The sight of her handwriting shouldn't have unnerved me. That wasn't the first time I'd encountered it among his collection.

I'd known for years she'd been a translator for Fewmany Incorporated, Fewmany's favorite, Leo once told me. Not until the magnate offered the archivist position to me did I learn she'd been a translator for his library as well.

When I was a small child, before we went on the trip to visit my grandmother, I saw collectors and couriers deliver tattered treasures to my mother, which she arranged in musty stacks on her tables. After our return from Vregol, there was no more of that. During the next ten years, I didn't see who brought the confidential documents from Fewmany Incorporated, although I realized at some point it had to be Father. As for the books and manuscripts which came one by one, I knew she was bound by agreement to translate for only one patron, but I didn't know who among the many collectors retained her exclusively. I had no context at the time to make the link to Fewmany himself.

Then, the summer before I turned thirteen, the arcane manuscript arrived.

A messenger presented it with the directive that she attempt to translate it, as all others who tried had failed. My mother forbade me to tell Father it was in her possession. I didn't ask why. I knew not to cross her. In retrospect, I know she meant to guard herself, as well as Father, against her disloyalty to the magnate. She violated her agreement with Fewmany because she couldn't resist the challenge.

But there is more, isn't there?

I couldn't forget the way my body pealed when she read the one word she could immediately discern on one of the pages, a name, the sound, *Ee-fah.*

Or how my muttering mother fell into silence, pacing, nightmares. The night she paced the parlor and repeated over and over, *I've been robbed!*

The fever that struck me and brought on twelve days and nights of dreams, terrible and beautiful, and my ability to speak a language I'd never heard before.[9]

How my mother took the arcane manuscript from its hiding place when I insisted the language I suddenly spoke—as she did, too, with her freakish gift—was the one in which the manuscript was written, but I couldn't read it.

The return from a twilight walk in the woods to find Father in the dark, who told me, "Your mother is dead. An accident. I believe she choked."

How she left for me a cipher for the lost? missing? hidden? arcane manuscript, as if she thought—as if she knew—she wouldn't live to complete the task.

DIARY ENTRY 25 NOVEMBER /35

Most days, I leave early and return late, and I've had few opportunities to encounter my neighbors. This afternoon when I returned from meeting Father for a performance (no perfume for matinees!), I met the last of them.

On the first floor are three elderly sisters, the Misses Acutt—one tall, one round, and one short—and their gray long-haired dandy of a cat, Sir Pouncelot (that is not a joke), who wears an embroidered collar. They are obliged to a solitary nephew, whose wife cannot wait until they're dead.

On the second, two women some ten years older than myself; Miss Jane Sheepshank and Miss Dora Thursdale, both secretaries, at Fewmany Incorporated and an accounting office, respectively.

The third, Mr. and Mrs. Woodman, rough faced, as if they once labored in the sun, always with a ready hello. On her off-day mornings, she bakes cinnamon buns and shares them. He works in a printing shop, and she works as a daymaid.

Then fourth, a family. I've met only Mr. Elgin, who has the most enormous hands I've ever seen—he's a mason—and have heard the voices of a woman and at least two children below me.

Everyone seems to keep to his or her own affairs, but is pleasant enough. They know I work as an archivist and have stopped giving me looks when they see me step on or off the carriage. One of the Misses Acutt recently needled me with questions of a biographical nature, and my answers only seemed to exacerbate matters. "So you have chosen to live this way, with your father's full knowledge. How liberal. And alone—even more peculiar than Miss Sheepshank and Miss Thursdale, not even sisters," she said.

In moments like that, I wish I had a cutting mouth! But I kept quiet, as one does to keep the peace.

It is strange for me, this proximity. I hardly remember the house where we lived when I was very small, only the corner of the room where I played as she worked, and I saw others when we went to market or for her walk. Possibly other times, but I have no memory. At our row house, only one wall was shared, and it was either thick or the neighbors were silent as owls, because I don't recall hearing voices or noises on the other side.

Here, that is not the case.

As tonight. It isn't the first instance I've heard Mr. Elgin shouting and slamming some object around. There was no other sound for some time, but when I went into the water closet to wash for bed, I detected a whimper.

A child is below. She hides; she listens; she waits. Her plaintive suppressed wail needles straight into my belly. My nerves are raw now, my senses too sharp.

DECEMBER /35

Dear Miss Riven,

How is it that you and I have never discussed our common interest? Books, of course, and related scribblings.

Would you be so indulgent as to join me for a convivial dinner, here at the manor, so we might confer on matters near and dear to our hearts?

You are invited at seven o' the clock, 15 December. Please inform Naughton of your reply.

Sincerely,
fm

Post script. A carriage will be sent for your comfort.

FOR MORE THAN AN HOUR, I FRETTED OVER MY ATTIRE AND managed to pin up my hair in time for the carriage's arrival. At the manor's door, Naughton greeted me with a tone more reserved than usual as he took my cloak. I heard music and looked around until I saw from where it came. On the grand staircase's landing was the quartet Fewmany had told me was on his staff.

Mutt scampered from a room and leapt at my knees. I gave him a pat on the head. A moment later, Fewmany stepped out, closed the door, and locked it.

"Good evening and welcome, Miss Riven," he said. He gave a deep bow. After he rose, Mutt licked the ground near his feet. What looked like crumbs dusted the floor and the fabric at Fewmany's coat's edge. Always, the mystery of what he kept in that pocket, but I made no inquiry.

"Thank you, Fewmany," I said with a curtsy.

His smile was relaxed. He clutched his lapels. A crimson vest blazed against his black pin-striped coat. "Join me in the library. Cook has an eye on the roast."

I must have given some indication of distress, because he gave me a quizzical look and asked, "Is there something of concern?"

My pause allowed for an assessment: I had consumed neither meat nor fowl since I was nine years old and declared to my parents I wished not to eat what I believed to have thoughts and feelings of their own. My diet had been a matter of habit, unevaluated until that moment. The girl I was once was no longer. I wondered how I might respond to the taste of flesh again.

"No, not at all," I said.

"Very good. Naughton, take him, please." Fewmany picked up the dog and handed the animal to Naughton, who walked off without a word. "Come," Fewmany said to me.

As we climbed the stairs, I nodded toward the musicians. The cello player returned the gesture, the only one who could without disturbing his instrument.

In the library, all of the chandeliers and sconces were lit, casting shadows which were inviting rather than ominous. Fewmany stepped toward a rolling table which held decanters and glasses of various sizes. He offered a refreshment, which I refused twice. He smiled as if amused and filled a glass of wine for himself. When he turned, I realized his Tell-a-Bell wasn't attached to his ear. I didn't know what to make of this, other than he wanted no interruptions.

"Mr. Gray sends his regards. I saw him this week. He mentioned some letters he'd written on your behalf," he said.

A jolt of surprise spiked through my gut. "I'm applying to high academies for next autumn's term. You know I've always aspired to further my studies."

"I admire your ambition and wish you well, though I'd be disappointed to see you go. Your work here has been superb, and there is much left to do," he said, then took a sip of his drink. "You could have asked me for a reference."

"I wished not to trouble you. All due notice will be given if I'm admitted," I said. I dared not add that as much as my desire to leave Rothwyke and start anew remained with me, the intensity wasn't quite as strong as it had been.

Fewmany peered at me with cool scrutiny, then waved his hand over his shoulder. "To the tomes!"

We walked among the shelves. He selected several works he found especially beautiful or interesting, setting aside his drink to point out a favorite illustration or oddity. I would have guessed he'd be pompous in showing off his collection, but he was almost boyish. He took delight in the details, including the caricatures and complaints written by long-dead scribes.

By the time we were called downstairs, our conversation had moved to what was within books and manuscripts—ideas, observations, and stories.

Although upon the offer of my position Fewmany said I could have his staff prepare my midday meals, I hadn't accepted the invitation. I resolved to change that as I enjoyed a delectable dinner. Chestnut soup, poached salmon, roast beef with a hint of blood to which my stomach gave some nauseating protest, and spinach.

Naughton appeared with a bottle. "Miss, may I?" he asked.

"No, thank you."

He filled a glass for my host. "Are you certain?" Fewmany asked me. "Falling on a full stomach, the cordial can't rise to the head."

My hands kneaded under the table. The liquid was a lovely golden brown, and the glass was rather small. "Well, then, yes please."

Fewmany raised his drink, and I did in return. The first taste was syrupy, nutty, with a hint of a sting. I liked it.

Then Naughton served dessert in bowls filled with red glimmering pods. I raised my spoon, anticipating an unknown sweetness, and took a bite.

Fewmany leaned back in his chair. "You've borrowed several books within a certain area of interest, that of myth and lore."

"I doubt any library would have a finer collection." Another spoonful crossed my lips. The tart jellied globes gave way to an ossicular crunch. Pomegranates, I thought, although I'd never had the fruit.

"So, tell me, Miss Riven, what accounts for your regard of these fanciful tales?"

"I'm not certain, other than I like them."

"An evasive reply, and spare of the intellectual vigor for which you are renowned. 'Tisn't reason enough to hold you in such thrall so long out of the nursery. Sit, and think, and give us an answer." His finger circled his glass's rim. The song of true crystal rang out.

A drop of the cordial fused with the heat in my belly. I was angry, no; offended, no; kindled, yes. No one had ever asked a question of me in that way, certainly not on a subject for which I had such zeal.

I paused to think, listening to the music drift into the room. What I said wasn't at all what I might have expected myself to say.

"At first glance, the myths and tales seem different. Sometimes, the names, places, and things mentioned are particular to a clan or a kingdom, a certain group of people, you see. But underneath, the tales are all the same. Stories of how the world was created and how it will be destroyed. Wise beasts and divine children and magical weapons. Heroes with weaknesses and villains with wit and guile. Transformative potions and impossible sacrifices," I said.

I waited for a response, but he kept quiet, rubbing the inside of his left arm as if it hurt.

"There's something deeper still. The stories open into a secret realm that's hidden by the ordinary one of our five senses. These are places where there is justice, truth, and innocence and goodness. And they are, too, places of strife and betrayal and rage and evil. They reveal our wish to explain and understand what is ineffable. To make sense of longing and pain. The stories are a quest for meaning."

Fewmany braced his elbows on the table. "So 'tis not as simple as you like them and read them for pleasure alone."

"Not any longer. My father entertained me with them when I was a child, and that was the purpose when I could read on my own. At some point, I knew there was more to them than an amusement, or distraction." As I paused to take another draught, I realized, then said: "They're a form of memory."

"Memory?"

"Of what is essential in Nature, human and animal, above and below." My arms prickled with gooseflesh, and a shudder whipped up my spine.

"Is that immutable?"

"Well, the tales themselves lead me to believe so."

"Do you believe so?" he asked.

"Yes, but I also believe we can choose the qualities upon which we act." Invigorated, I turned the question to him. "And you?"

"The truth of every man is revealed in the whole of his actions, not only the parts. '*Malum quidem nullum esse sine aliquo bono.*'"

"There is, to be sure, no evil without something good," I translated.

He waved for Naughton to fill his glass again. I declined, but reluctantly, and had another bite of dessert.

"Now then, as to what you described before, that the old stories are a quest for meaning," he said. "'Tis an eloquent opinion, dare I say, and at the risk of seeming condescending, which I don't intend, a mature one as well. I concede I'm not as widely read here, but I'm of a different mind on the message."

"What's that?"

"When I was a gullible boy, my illiterate mother—peace be to the dead—pulled the covers to my neck and told me of the ills and beasties that waited to befall. There was warning in the whimsies: Beware ogres and crones; beware the calling crow, wily fox, and black beetle spinning widdershins on its back. If a careless lad dared to stray too far from home or wag an impudent tongue, a dragon lurked to eat him alive, gobble him whole. My mother, she tossed salt, whistled in the dark, and covered the mirror when the veil between worlds thinned. My ignorant father—dead, I know him to be—told of the ruin brought on by crying of phantom wolves and sparing the rod. He declared things to be, so they were, as his father, and father's father, and all who came before. My father, he wielded repetition like a whip and used it like a sword. So, small lad that I was, I cut my teeth on fallacy and convention until I could chew my way out. The stories served the means of manipulation."

"That is a literal interpretation, but you have a point," I said.

Fewmany crossed his arms at his chest and brushed his hand against the scar under his jaw and chin. "Of course. Seek not to displease the powers that be, whether gods, kings, or fathers, the ones who create and destroy"—his voice became sardonic—"because there will be lightning bolts and hideous devourings and beatings and banishments. But if you obey, laud them well, you shall receive a bounty of boons. In the darkest days, wish for impossible rescues by virtuous mortals and benevolent forces. Believe that if you are truly good, that if you suffer enough, even needlessly, you will be delivered through wondrous intercession, and if you are bad, willful and prying, dear child, you deserve what comes."

"Not always. Sometimes one is delivered by her own cunning. And you've made an inadvertent suggestion."

"Of what?"

"The presence of hope."

He scoffed. "Hope, my keeper of tales, is an impotent thing, useless without action. 'Tis light without heat. 'Tis illusion without form. Unlike its brother, Despair, which thrives in its own prostration. This is the domain of superstition and rote, both effective determinants of people's behavior. Convince them of what they're told, and one can anticipate how they will react. Weapons are a brute's option. Capture the mind, and the body will follow."

"I haven't much pondered ideas as that yet," I said.

"Ponder, then. Even in your brief, what, eighteen, nineteen years?"

"I am eighteen."

"Old enough to observe the basic conditions of mankind." Fewmany sighed. "Men are simple, little more than animals but for the abilities to laugh and speak. They want for creature comforts of the flesh, and all else are mere trimmings. There must be enough to keep them safe, then sated. Not too much, not too little. Too much and they become complacent and entitled; too little and they become malcontent and demanding. The divide must be kept in balance, you see. All great men have understood this, and that is what, in part, has made them great."

I let the question loose. "Like you, Fewmany?"

"So 'tis, Miss Riven, so 'tis. I couldn't read a word until I was fifteen, but I was a scholar in the ways of the world. I simply chose to use what I'd observed rather than what I was taught."

I had no response other than to smile with appreciation. Such a conversation I'd never had before.

Fewmany took a bite of his dessert.

A rush of fear coiled with delight. I bit my lip to suppress a smile.

"Will you convey what has amused you?" he asked.

"In light of our conversation—we've eaten the fruit of the underworld," I said.

"Well, indeed, we have. And there is no mother in search of you." He grinned as if his belly were full, which it was.

JANUARY /36

Dear Secret,

I'm writing to you inches from a blazing hearth. Otherwise, the ink would be frozen solid and my fingers too stiff to hold a pen. Oh yes, it is cold in this valley among mountains. I've been swathed in lynx, sable, and bear (sorry to bring those images to mind), but that does little to keep my blood warm. That sort of comfort requires boisterous activity, intoxicating drinks, and flesh-melting proximity to fire. To think I've complained of the dusting we have during our winters.

I shouldn't be so misleading that I'm miserable. The land here in Bodelea is beautiful in its own stark way. The sky takes on a vibrant blue against the snow-capped peaks. You'd be awestruck by the trees, massive evergreens compared to the ones you've seen. I've learned to ski, which is almost as thrilling as a ride on a fast horse and perhaps as dangerous. Two afternoons ago, I almost failed to pivot in time to avoid a fir tree that uprooted into my way. Ha!

If I were to write about the banquets and meetings I've taken, I'd only repeat what I've told you in previous letters. Again, talk of trade, alliances, rumors of discord, threats of war, and inevitably, gossip. The intrigue of court, ever the same game with ever-changing players.

What has been different is one of my delegated companions. This king has two daughters, the elder promised, the younger not. Jorra, fifteen, has joined several excursions. I'd met her before. She attended my sister's wedding three summers ago. Every wedding is an opportunity to arrange for another, isn't it? She's beautiful and spirited with a bright laugh and probably a disappointment to her mother because she doesn't hold her tongue well.

I've enjoyed the goodwill visits thus far, although I have so little time to myself. Except for those moments one expects privacy and the hour before I go to bed, I'm with someone, talking, listening. I could demand more time alone, but I know what is expected of me.

Now I'm homesick. I'm thinking of my chair in my room. Now my

favorite tower where the guards let me play in peace when I was small.
And the woods where Cyril led our escape and it seemed there was no one
else in the world but the two of us. I miss that, Secret, the quiet, the respite.
I miss you. By the way, how are our squirrel friend and Old Woman?
You've not mentioned them.

I know your letters are delayed because I'm traveling, but do write. They
catch up to me. Describe what it's like to live alone so I may vicariously
experience what I'll never know. Tell me what you're studying from that
grand library. Assure me all is well, most of all.

To bed—I must be at my royal best tomorrow.

Affectionately,
Nikolas

BEFORE FEWMANY DEPARTED FOR A TRIP, HE OFFERED TICKETS
to a musical performance he'd be unable to attend. I accepted, although I
considered not going. First, my evening clothes had a snug fit, likely from
my indulgence in rich foods and my lack of exercise. Second, I had no
escort—when had I ever?—and Father was away. But I chose to go alone,
aware it would be somewhat scandalous.

The new performance hall replaced the premier one in Old Wheel,
which by then no longer stood. Once inside, I checked my coat and
slipped away to stand near a decorative urn filled with dried flowers.
From there, I studied the lobby, more opulent than the former one—
painted vaulted ceilings, polished brass everywhere, black marble floors,
red velvet tufted benches, a banister of dark wood, and not a single
candle in sight.

Then I turned my attention to the preliminary show under way.
Everyone strutted in their gowns and tailcoats. They gathered in talk-
ative clusters, organized by status and sex. Many people I recognized
because I'd been introduced to them throughout the years—twelfth-
floor men who worked with Father as well as other associates from
within and outside of Fewmany Incorporated; of course, their wives;
at times their children, some of whom were schoolmates. Among the
others were visitors from across the kingdom—men of land and title,
some of whom were on the King's Council; as well as their wives, or
women who were not.

The chimes rang out for us to take our seats. Conversations ended. Fingertips reached behind ears to silence the Tell-a-Bells. I hurried toward the stairs. With demure nods, I acknowledged those who stared at me quizzically. I didn't wish to provide, and neither was there time for, introductions.

An usher showed me to the private box with a superb view. I managed not to turn around as speculative whispers wondered who was taking Fewmany's seats. The box had a door with a lock. Heavy curtains framed the balcony's opening. Between two upholstered chairs I found a table, two sets of theater binoculars, a decanter of wine, and two crystal goblets.

There the drink sat without restriction. I poured the goblet one-fourth full and took three sips. The deep red thickened my tongue with the taste of smoke and cherries. On the rare occasion Father had offered a sip to me when I was younger, I had no desire for more. The flavor seemed bitter, nothing like the depth and richness I savored here. As I filled the goblet, my body tingled. I hadn't drunk enough for the wine to have such an effect, I knew. The response was delight, the discovery of a pleasure I didn't know I could feel. I stared into the goblet between sips, attentive to the warmth in my mouth and on my skin.

Eventually, I lifted my eyes. No expense had been spared in the performance hall. Luxurious green curtains, trimmed in gold, framed the stage. Opposite the stage, above the floor, were three balconies of tiered seats, gold gilded. Two levels of seats, box and balcony, flanked both sides of the hall.

Then, in the box directly across, I recognized King Aeldrich and Queen Ianthe. They leaned into one another with intimacy. A young woman approached and kissed the Queen's cheeks. Queen Ianthe held the woman's face, and I realized she was the eldest child, Princess Doria, better known as Pretty, whose return for a visit had been announced in the longsheets and through the newsboxes. Pretty sat between her mother and a man who wore a gold emblem at his neck. Her husband, a prince from Morrdin. When she touched his arm, he laid his hand on top of hers.

I swallowed a lonely feeling with a swig of wine, then drowned it with another. Their affection made me yearn for what I believed would always elude me. I could change my hair and cover my eyes, I could try to keep my inherent strangeness hidden, but I would still never be like other people. No matter where I sat, the adjacent chair would remain empty.

The performance included three singers—a woman whose voice reminded me of meadows, a man who evoked deep water, and a dark-haired boy who called down the stars. Their voices dazzled me. My imagination failed to conjure what it would be like to have a gift that made people smile, nod, and weep.

And weep the audience did, but unlike any instance I'd witnessed before. At first, there were only sniffles, as if the most sentimental among us had been touched. Then, with each song, more of the audience were overcome. Those who couldn't contain themselves sobbed with such intensity, they rushed out of the hall or collapsed in their seats. I held my breath against the emotions which swelled in me, both desolate and ecstatic. Why was this performance so stirring?

Then I heard it. Another voice. A child's—but not the boy's—which hid among the others, the harmony so perfect it was almost intangible. I leaned out to look for a fourth performer but saw no evidence. A trick of the acoustics, I wondered.

In the final solo, the boy stood at the edge of the stage. He sang without a flaw, but another otherworldly pureness touched our ears. Within moments, his voice and the other one mingled with the audience's wails. Those who remained silent sat transfixed. The cry that surged within me met a stronger force to suffocate it. No matter the box's privacy, no matter the outpouring around me, I refused what welled up. A grief for something unnamed and long lost.

At the end, the boy collapsed in tears. The woman took the child in her arms, and the man placed a paternal hand on the woman's shoulder. They bowed to effusive applause.

When the lights rose, I stayed in my place to scan the seats and stage below. The drone of leaving settled into silence. For the briefest instant, I thought I heard a sharp chirp and saw a small face peek through the closed curtains. My skin burned as my blood chilled.

Oh, I wanted no reminder of a bizarre occurrence from the previous summer involving a light-haired child only I appeared to be able to see. A peculiar, peeping little orphan named Harmyn who spoke of things that couldn't be known. Descendants and survivors, that name is familiar to you, and there will be more to say in due time.

As everyone left, I finished the last sips of wine, grateful for the soft drowsiness and blunted thoughts. The usher who discovered me suppressed a smile when he placed the almost empty bottle on a tray. He was close to my age, comely, a scar on his temple, his hands hidden in white gloves.

"Do you finish what's left?" I asked as I stood with a sway.

"That's not allowed, Miss," he said.

"Yes, but do you?" I asked, goading him.

He raised his eyebrow and smiled so conspiratorially, I wanted to abandon all good sense and kiss him, although I'd never kissed anyone.

"If ever there's a drop left in this box or the King's, Miss," he replied.

"It tasted of smoke and cherries," I said.

He tilted the bottle to read the label. "And rain. Among his favorites, this one."

We wished each other good evening. I walked home. I took the main routes. It was so late, I watched a news-speaker lock his box and place the evening's reports in a nearby bin. He tipped his hat as he crossed my path.

FEBRUARY /36

FEWMANY'S MELODIC WHISTLE ANNOUNCED HIS APPROACH AND his *rap-rap, rap-rap* prepared me for his entry. I stood next to my seat, the fire searing my back.

He laid his top hat on the cabinet next to a narcissus bouquet. Sleek sable cuffs and a collar trimmed his black coat. Pinned on the chest was a red rose crafted in enamel. He set a package wrapped in linen on the table's edge near me. "Unbound printed text, hand-colored copper etchings in gruesome anatomical detail. We are nightmares under the skin."

"Did you place your mark?" I asked.

"Ah, no," he said, reaching for my pen and ink. I unwrapped the book and counted to find the center page.

"I've been needled with inquiries regarding the solitary woman who sat in my balcony some weeks hence," he said as he wrote his initials on the first page.

"I wished to be inconspicuous," I said, but did not add I found it entertaining to be a mystery.

"Speculation was easily squelched once I revealed you to be my archivist and my right-hand man's daughter. What a curiosity you are, watchful as an owl, fleeting as a mouse, solitary as a cat."

"Such qualities serve me well," I said.

"But there were two tickets," he said.

"I know." Fewmany's silence begged for, if not required, an explanation. "Circumstances are such that my friends are away studying or traveling abroad."

"A paucity of those with whom to consort," he said.

"My father would have been pleased to accompany me, but he's been traveling, as you know."

"A paternal chaperone at your age seems, dare I say, unfashionable."

I pressed my spectacles against my face with a splayed hand. I willed the color to bleed out from my cheeks. When I looked at him, I could tell he was trying not to grin. "Yes, sir."

"A good, virtuous lass," he said. Fewmany finished his task and left the text where it was. "Next week, several guests will be coming for dinner. Two visiting lecturers and actors with a traveling play who are in Rothwyke through the month. Please, do join us."

"I'm grateful for the invitation, but I recall I have plans those evenings," I said. The refusal was impulse as much as instinct, which had little to do with Fewmany. Ever since I was a child, I'd hid when I could, even from my closest friends. The thought of a dinner at the manor among strangers, oh dread!

Before he could reply, his Tell-a-Bell released its *tinktinktinktinktink* into his ear.

"I'll have Naughton give you the exact date and time, should there be a cancellation. You are most welcome. Good day," he said, then began to list his toll of to-dos as he left the library.

I VACILLATED FOR DAYS WHETHER TO GO. FEARING IF I WENT, I'D fail at the etiquette, I searched the library for an appropriate book. Finding none, I purchased the latest edition of *Mrs. Swope's Primer for Proper Ladies*. I skimmed the whole and memorized the chapter on dinner parties. Once again, my curiosity proved stronger than my trepidation, so I attended.

Once there, I discovered little of what I read applied. We did gather for introductions and beverages served by a footman, but instead of the parlor, this occurred in a first-floor room which was always locked, filled with paintings and sculptures. With ease, Fewmany moved among his guests, and from their expressions and laughter, clearly they found him charming. From the way two women looked at him, I believe they thought him alluring, even handsome.

When Naughton called us for the meal, the ladies were not paired with escorts to dinner, there seemed to be no attention to rank or status in the seating, and even though Mrs. Swope instructed that no lady should take wine at dinner—lest it lead to sullied cheeks and reputation—the ladies did. Fewmany gave me a teasing look when I accepted a glass during the meal. I dared not say in front of everyone I'd recently acquired a taste for it.

I would not have spoken much, if at all, if Fewmany hadn't stated I was his "keeper of tales" and a scholar of myth and folklore. During most of the dinner, I listened to him and the other guests. I hoped Admiral Linville would give a more invigorated lecture than his dinner conversation indicated, or the audience might want to find themselves drowned at sea. His wife seemed inured of his pontifications as she nodded and took frequent drams from her wineglass. Professor Perch, a theologist, spoke on reincarnation, the belief one lives, dies, and is reborn again and again. As I'd never heard of this, I intended to search the library for a book to learn more. The four visiting actors were comical, especially Miss Sawyer and Mr. Billings, seated to my left and right, who told of their adventures.

During the main course—venison, of which I could eat only morsels—Miss Sawyer asked about my studies. As a child, she had adored fairy tales, and the enticement of make-believe was what led her to the theater.

"What we were told in the familiar ones are tame compared to their sources," I said.

"What do you mean?" she asked.

"The stories were changed. The tales borrow from older, far more primal roots. It was parlor entertainment at the court of Ilsace, and others, to create new tales. Also, there have been scholars of a sort who've recorded the lore told at firesides and in remote villages, only to sanitize what was spoken," I said.

"In what way?" Mr. Billings asked.

"In the old lore, far worse than fairy tales, there's unspeakable violence and cruelty. If a slipper doesn't fit, toes and heels are cut off. Children aren't abandoned because there's no food; they become the food. The wicked stepmothers in the tales we know—they are instead true mothers without compassion or remorse. And awakening kisses and bed-chamber visits, well, all is not so innocent," I said.

I glanced up to see the guests' eyes on me, from Mrs. Linville's offended squint to Fewmany's wide amusement.

Mr. Billings flourished his napkin, left his chair, and draped an imaginary garment across Miss Sawyer's shoulders. "Stand, Little Red Cape, you must fetch your basket to take to Grandmother's house."

She clasped her hands under her chin and batted her lashes. "Oh, but isn't it dangerous for a girl to go alone through the dark woods?"

"Let us find out," he said, smiling to expose his teeth.

Then and there, the two gave a hilarious bawdy improvisation of a tale everyone knew well. I tried not to blush as I imagined Mr. Billings at my neck instead of Miss Sawyer's when he declared "all the better to eat you with."

They bowed as we clapped at the end. The actors took their seats. Spirits remained light through the remainder of the evening. When I returned to my little apartment, I didn't mind the cold. I was warmed by something I hadn't enjoyed in months—laughter.

MARCH /36

Yourself and a guest, if you wish,
are cordially invited to attend
the Masquerade Ball to take place at the manor of
Fewmany on the evening of 1 May.
❦ Guests must be masked before they arrive and
remain so until they depart from the event.
❦ Carriages will be offered at the end of the
evening for those who require them.
❦ All due confidentiality regarding this
invitation and whatever occurs
that evening is obligated.
The honor of a reply is requested.

I accepted. Only a magnificent costume would do, so I went to see Margana the seamstress. She asked how much I wished to spend. Her eyebrows raised when I told her the amount, which I assured her I could pay. Again, Margana asked to create a design of my behalf. Again, I agreed.

The silver I'd saved from my wages would have paid her in full, but I knew I had another means to cover her fee.

The day I planned to go to Father's for a visit—and to get what I needed—I received the last response from the high academies to which I'd applied. So, I had news to share along with my errand.

Over tea, I told Father, "I've heard from the academies. Six rejections, two waiting lists, Erritas and Goram."

I expected him to be terribly disappointed, as he'd been the previous year.

"I'm sorry, Secret. How do you feel about it?"

My stomach twinged at his tone, inquisitive more than sympathetic. Father, although he had always been attentive in his own way, was rarely so direct. Neither was I, but I gave a frank reply. "I'm conflicted. I want to attend high academy, a prestigious one, and Erritas would be excellent, if I'm admitted. But I do enjoy my work and have evenings to read whatever I wish, and my experience as an archivist has as much worth as a conferred degree."

"Then there's nothing to do but wait to see if either opens a seat," he said.

I agreed, then excused myself to go upstairs to find a book—that's what I claimed—I'd put in storage.

I guessed, rightly, that the old faded blue chest with the painted animals was still where I'd left it. No dust coated the floor or baseboards. Elinor continued to clean it as a room even though Father had begun to encroach with his boxes of documents, books, and ephemera. Several were stacked in the far corner opposite the windows.

When I knelt next to the chest, I paused. The memory of how the gold came into my mother's possession rushed back.

She received the ingots as payment to attempt an arcane manuscript's translation. The messenger had assured her the compensation was to try, implying more was to come if she succeeded. Nearly a year after my mother's death, the same messenger appeared to ask about the manuscript. I had no idea where it was, or, at the time, where the ingots were. The messenger said there was no concern about the gold, but certainly for the manuscript.[10]

Eventually I searched for the text. The box in which it had been delivered was stored in the third floor's garret, but the text itself was gone. The gold ingots, the clue, and the cipher were all I had in my possession.

The chest's lock broke when I turned the key. I cursed under my breath. I shoved the nesting dolls aside, slipped the cipher into the folklore book, and reached for the ingots. I rationalized the gold I'd use for my costume was compensation for the trouble my mother had caused me. She died and left me responsible for something of which I wanted no part. If, or when, I found the manuscript, I told myself, I would return it to its rightful owner, and if the ingots came into question, I'd address the problem then.

I'd dropped the gold into my pocket and was reaching for the folklore book when Father's hand grabbed it first. As he lifted it, the spine opened, the pages spread, and the cipher fell to the ground. His grasp was faster than mine. He held the book in one hand, the cipher in the other. I blanched as he tucked the latter in the book's corner, balanced the spine in his palm, and turned the pages.

"I remember this!" he said. "Now, what was the name of the town? Far from your mother's village. Regardless, I found it in a small bookshop. Three attempts to identify a language we both spoke, and the clerk managed to convey it was printed in their native one. Local folklore. The rarest of finds."

I'd studied the illustrations when I was a child, but she never read any of the stories to me. She never shared Father's appreciation for wonder and whimsy.

He whisked the cipher away before he handed the book to me. My pulse sped to full gallop. "What's this?" he asked.

Father's eyes glanced at it before I snatched it from his hand. "Some old thing I made at one of those summer activities I attended. You remember. I took botany once, and woodblock printing, among others."

"You did enjoy those classes," he said.

Sweat dampened my palms. How I wanted to hide the cipher—and stem the rush of memory of those summers, those school-day afternoons, Cyril appearing to no one else's witness to lead me to the woods, to Old Woman. Father never suspected; neither of my parents ever knew.

"You're pale. Are you feeling sick?" he asked.

I wedged the cipher between the book's pages. "I'm fine. I have what I came for."

"Have you been eating well enough? Do I need to send Elinor to help at last? Or have you simply been staying up too late reading?"

"You know how I adore my books," I said.

I'm not sure he believed me, but he didn't pry any more. By fortune, he asked nothing about the cipher.

I stayed through dinner and allowed him to escort me home. When he lingered to chat with the Misses Acutt, I went up to my apartment alone. After I changed into my nightclothes, I stared at the cipher—two concentric circles mounted at the center of a square of paper.[11]

Outside of the larger circle were twenty-three small drawings, among them a flower, a boat, a wheel. Along the perimeter of that circle were the letters of my native language's alphabet, three missing. Through a triangular window in the smaller circle, I read the letters of an unknown alphabet—or code—used in the arcane manuscript.

As I turned the circles, I pondered the meaning of the only clue my mother seemed to give me: "A map is to space as an alphabet is to sound." Two years after she died, I found the cipher. Even then, I was baffled that she'd had the forethought to create it, as if she knew she wouldn't live to translate the text. I told no one but Nikolas about the cipher and my realization. Neither of us could say aloud what it meant if an accident had not ended her life.

Resentment seeped into my blood like a quick poison. I shoved the folklore book and the cipher to the bottom of my wardrobe, wondering why I couldn't bring myself to burn the cipher and be done.

BY EARLY SPRING, FEWMANY AND I HAD ATTAINED A COMFORTable rapport. That is, my trepidation about him dissipated, and his occasional visits to the library—to deliver an acquisition, return something he'd finished reading—ceased to agitate my nerves. Our conversations were brief, kept to inquiries about the catalog and usual pleasantries, but now and then, we would talk of books we'd found interesting.

When he invited me to a dinner with him and his book dealer, my impulse to decline reared itself but wasn't indulged. I had enjoyed the prior evenings in his, and his guests', company. As well, I was curious to meet William "Quire" Remarque. His correspondence with Fewmany provided information about new acquisitions as well as critiques of eateries in several kingdoms, detailed weather reports, and intrigue within their book-collecting circle.

Fewmany gave due warning that Remarque would "make a memorable impression." Fewmany did not overstate.

Naughton led me to the chamber of moving marvels when I arrived. As Fewmany made the introduction, I studied his guest. Remarque had a hirsute nimbus of silvery-brown curls and fleecy sidechops, truly piercing blue eyes, and a red speckled nose. He wore a black tailcoat and matching trousers, brocaded vest of orange chevrons, and gray-striped cravat. His boots were scarred, not scuffed. His Ilsacean accent failed to soften his blaring voice. I thought he might be somewhat deaf, but no. At dinner, we were not once asked to repeat ourselves. He appeared to be an insatiable gossip—the things he told Fewmany, in front of me—and a connoisseur of fine spirits.

Dinner was rousing. How Remarque managed to swallow and talk simultaneously was a biological phenomenon. His animation elicited stifled smiles among the footmen, and even Naughton barely suppressed a laugh at an extraordinarily lewd joke. Proper young lady that I was supposed be, I almost burst from trying to contain my appalled but genuine amusement.

Remarque entertained my inquiries about his work, and he asked of mine. We three discussed whether the penny serials sullied the appetites of an ever-growing reading public and foretold of the demise of books as we knew them.

Then at dessert, Remarque held his fourth? fifth? glass of wine against his stained lips and stared at me. "Doesn't she so remind you of her mother?"

My jaw locked in mid-chew. A needle of betrayal burrowed under my skin. Fewmany had mentioned no such connection before.

"At times, yes," Fewmany said. He set his jeweled eyes on me.

"A resemblance to be sure, that black hair and swarthy skin. See here, remove your spectacles. Do you have those same eerie violet eyes?" Remarque asked.

"Quire, some restraint," Fewmany said, raising his hand toward me in a halting gesture.

"Oh, that *was* rude, my apologies," Remarque said. "That aside, an unwonted beauty, aren't you. A strong mind, a thorough one. Quiet but not meek. No, you do not cede space among men, I can tell. Like her." He winked.

I took several sips of water to open my throat. "I had no awareness of your acquaintance."

"We entered Altwort the same year. My belated sympathies for her loss. Devastating to scholars and collectors who knew her work. And to her loving daughter and husband. An accident, I heard. She choked, did she?"

My tongue lay dead. I could only nod.

"I must ask. Do you have her gift?"

"Sir?" I asked.

"The knowledge of every language ever spoken."

For a moment, my sight dimmed, my body felt small, and my ears filled with her muttering, burbling, the stream of words in countless languages breaching her lips, while she worked, while she cooked, while she sat alone. My mother had been born with the ability to speak the languages of the entire known and ancient worlds.[12] If that weren't incomprehensible enough, she could also read and write them, a skill which for ordinary people required a teacher to learn. As a child, she'd been punished for this. As an adult, she used it to her advantage to make her own way as a translator.

"No. I'm schooled in classical ones, fluent in four modern, literate in three others, but that's all," I said.

"Miss Riven apprenticed in our translations office with distinction," Fewmany said.

"Well, then, you know the fellows! Cuthbert and Leo Gray and Pungent Rowland—oh, have I told you this story before, Fewmany?" Remarque began.

My eyes shut as I exhaled with relief. When I looked up, Fewmany glanced at me, with concern, with curiosity, I couldn't quite tell. I didn't care. He'd spared me whether he knew it or not. I declined the offer of a cordial and conversation in the library, stating I had the beginnings of a headache. Fewmany rang for the carriage as Remarque gave me an effusive farewell, clasping my hand in both of his with Ilsacean forwardness.

APRIL /36

MY DIARY FOR THE APRIL DINNER INCLUDED THE FOLLOWING: "Beautiful night, so clear and pleasant, dinner served near the formal garden. Ten guests. Most interesting, Professor Hawkes, archeologist who excavated a *tell* (city built on the ruins of another, possibly several!) in Nandir. Fewmany unlocked a room on the second floor—trophies. The sight of it unsettled me. His dragon's head joke—?"

I must have been tired to write so little, affected to remember so much.

That night, when we entered the room, one door away from the chamber filled with wolves, the space was bright as day from the lit sconces and chandeliers. Exclamations and gasps put me on guard as I followed the group inside, Fewmany at the rear.

The animals fascinated and sickened me. Heads and entire bodies of beasts and birds from all over the world, some almost as exotic as any in a bestiary. I observed details I could never discern from a description, illustration, or luminotype. When Fewmany announced we could touch them, I found myself next to a great stag. My hands swept across his shoulder to an old wound. How much I wanted him alive, to hear him tell what caused that gnarled scar. I hid to wipe my eyes, furious I couldn't be like everyone else who gaped and touched with simple awe, furious at myself for a lapse into my old ways.

I walked among the trophies with my head down, avoiding the faces as Fewmany answered questions about how he acquired them, some he'd hunted himself.

A guest noticed an empty mounting plaque on the wall and asked what was missing.

"The head of a dragon," Fewmany said.

The room filled with laughter, some amused, most nervous. Fewmany flashed a good-natured smile, but there was a stillness in his eyes. He noticed my gaze and held it steady for the beat of a breath. When he blinked, the light there was diffuse.

I remembered he'd made a similar remark the first time I was called to his private office at Fewmany Incorporated and I commented on the mounted menagerie on his wall.[13]

"Absent that, Mr. Goossens, an elephant's. You'll notice I haven't one yet," Fewmany said.

Then, before the Plague of Silences, the dragon menace was the stuff of longsheet and newsbox reports. Everyone knew of the random destruction it leveled on distant villages but none close enough to verify, it seemed. No one discussed—not publicly or among unfamiliar company—whether they believed or disbelieved the dragon existed. Regardless, for generations, the firstborn princes in many kingdoms were sent to quest and to take a scale from its body as proof of a confrontation.

At the castle, I had seen the display of red scales gathered by princes who became kings of Ailliath—from Wyl,* the first to quest, not long before The Mapmaker's War, to Aeldrich, who still held the throne.

A few years later, on the wedding day of his sister Ursula, nicknamed Charming, Nikolas discussed the quest with me, only that once. We stood on a tower as we looked out at Rothwyke and beyond. He was aware of the inherent symbolism of the act, staring evil in the eye. He also questioned the purpose of the quest—and the dragon's very existence.[14]

As Nikolas and I talked that afternoon, I thought of the stories Father told me and the myths I'd heard from Old Woman. Dragons as monsters, destructive and voracious; dragons as beings, wise and strong, old as time.

The night of Fewmany's dinner, I thought about the archaic echo in our modern era. The blur between fact and fiction, which, as it turns out, can be both at once.

DIARY ENTRY 27 APRIL /36

As of yesterday, I'm on a two-week holiday required by Fewmany. There has been no mention of the ball, but I assume there's a preparation taking place now, then a tidying up afterward.

I went for a last costume fitting. Breathtaking! Feathers cover the mask, which sits on my head by means of a little cap, and there is a tiny beak, which covers the top of my nose. The sleeves and the train of my dress are designed to resemble wings and a forked tail. The toes of my slippers have little claws. The way I feel wearing it, I could almost take flight!

---

* Wyl, pronounced *will*.

When I returned home, I saw a child whom I'd only glimpsed before but heard her name shouted often. Julia, who lives on the fourth floor, was seated on the landing. Sir Pounce slept on a blanket close by.

A greeting would have sufficed, but I introduced myself properly and asked her name and her age. She's eight, almost nine. Her brother Lucas, whom she "detests," is five. I remarked on the doll she held, whose name is Flowsy ("like flower," she said). She appeared to like me because she offered Flowsy's hand to shake and asked if I had a brother. I told her I didn't (too complicated to explain the stillborn ones to her) but I had a very dear friend who was as close to a brother as I might wish.

Julia asked his name. When I told her, she exclaimed, "That's the same name as the prince!" and her eyes widened, then squinted after I said he was one and the same.

"You're lying. Only a fine lady would know the prince, and you are not." She pressed her lips together as if she should say no more.

I've been truthful with my answers when asked about my circumstances and work, but apparently there are opinions calling me into question. I was somewhat insulted and amused by what Julia said and wondered what she'd overheard. Regardless, I told her, "I tell the truth. We attended school together and became very good friends."

Her mother called her, hidden behind the door. Julia stood to leave and peered up at me. "Could we be friends, too?"

How strange then, my eyes stung with the threat of tears. "Of course."

"Oh! You are my friend whose name is Secret. I mean, Miss Riven."

"You may address me secretly," I whispered.

A sweet smile, she has. I fear it's a rare one.

WEEKLY POST.

28 April /36. Page 2, Column 1

WALL PLANNED—In days of old, walls surrounded villages and towns. Walls defined boundaries and protected those inside. Enemies who appeared risked arrows through the heart, weights upon their heads, and boiling liquids on their flesh. When this barbarism waned, walls fell into disfavor and disrepair.

Yet continuous concern regarding the threat of foreign armies and the dragon menace prompted a lengthy negotiation to construct a new wall around our fair Rothwyke. An agreement was signed on Tuesday between Ailliath and Fewmany Incorporated.

As proposed, the new wall will incorporate much of the west green and a portion of the east meadowland, to accommodate future wards. Some designated areas of the wall's walkway will be open for pedestrians.

The main gate will be to the east, with smaller gates in the south and north. No gate is planned to the west, as the woods past the green create a natural barrier. When completed, the stone wall will be 20 feet thick and 50 feet high, and towers may exceed 80 feet.

In His Majesty's proclamation, King Aeldrich declared the protection of our kingdom and its people is of utmost importance. A representative of Fewmany Incorporated remarked the wall is for the greater good.

MAY /36

HALF AN HOUR PAST SUNDOWN, A CARRIAGE WHISKED ME through lamplit streets. Along the curved drive at Fewmany's manor, torches illuminated the way. A tent surrounded the house's front entrance. When the coachmen stopped the horses, the door flung open to a dark passage.

An ungloved hand reached out in the gloam. I took its offer. The young man smiled. I tried to thwart my audacious stare, but his loose trousers, naked chest, and comely face allured me. Once my feet reached the ground, I turned my eyes to the left. There stood a young woman, beautiful as the young man, who wore a silk frock with no sleeves and a low neck. The sight of their skin was shocking.

"Shall I lead you within?" he asked, my hand still clutched in his.

I almost returned to the carriage and the familiar press of night in my own room. But I didn't, allowing the man to walk me through the tunnel made of evergreen boughs. My footsteps didn't fall on marble but on flower petals so thick the walk was cushioned. A fragrance I had never smelled before surrounded me, a heavy but pleasant scent which made me think of blood and sap. I could see a bright light ahead and hear pounding music. Before I could study him, the young man released me.

The hall with its round table and familiar rug had disappeared. Vines covered the walls and most of the doors. Tree trunks reached from floor to ceiling. Boughs of greenery made an impenetrable canopy. Crystal and metal lamps hung above and the lush green carpets below belied the initial illusion. A brown rabbit darted from a grouping of ferns.

Behind my mask, I watched the other guests. They, too, had taken efforts to adorn themselves beyond recognition. Some were so wildly attired I couldn't tell whether they were men or women, although I determined that was the intent. Most, however, had chosen formal wear exaggerated in design and textiles.

A balding man with a bear muzzle mask wore a brilliant pink long-tailed velvet coat. He spoke with a woman whose bosom burgeoned far past bodily limits, giving shape to the two iridescent beetles that sat upon the striped orange and yellow mushroom that was her skirt. Her hair piled into a tidy nest on her head, out of which peeked a stuffed red squirrel, and the mask across her face was woven into the coiffed strands.

The music reached a crescendo then collapsed into silence. A squeal pierced through the applause. A woman burst from the northeast corner, chased by a laughing man whose cape dragged the floor. From the opposite corner, near the servants' stair, twelve people carrying trays heaped with food stepped into the hall. They walked gingerly, their bodies below the waist like sheep, with white fleece legs and hoofed feet, which forced them to step on hidden tiptoes. On their heads were hats with sheeps' ears. The men's torsos were bare, and the women's breasts were covered by triangles of fleece held in place by strings.

I followed behind them into the ballroom. The breeze through the open windows couldn't dissipate the weighty scent I'd encountered in the tunnel. To my right, in the distance, musicians stood on a dais. Below me, braided blue mats padded the floor. Ahead, several tables were heaped with every possible delicacy—meats, cheeses, fish, dried and preserved fruits, breads, pastries, custards. Crystal decanters held the gem hues of liquors and wines. Guests formed a line to the tables, each taking a platter and a goblet to fill.

Everyone spilled into the hall and sat among the trees as if at a picnic. I retreated to the darkest shadow I could find, sipped my punch, and ate until I couldn't swallow another bite.

In my hidden place, I listened to the music and observed the guests.

They ate and drank and talked and laughed. Among several, their hands and lips lost a sense of boundary. Rabbits and doves rustled below and above.

A rabbit hopped nearby, followed by another, then another. Soon a colony surrounded me, their noses sniffing at my skirt and nudging my hands. Suddenly, they scattered. In the space where one had stood, I saw black boots polished to a reflective shine.

"Oh-ho, what a furtive creature you are, my keeper of tales."

I looked up. My heart spiked into my throat.

He wore the wolf coat from the chamber, the glass eyes replaced by his amber own. A gold cravat shimmered at his neck as true as the metal itself. His vest was a red deeper than pomegranates, as were the matching gloves. His trousers were a silvery gray much like the fur which covered the rest of him.

I scrambled to my feet. "How did you recognize me?"

"I didn't. I rightly guessed your habits. Lone birdie in the bush," Fewmany said. *"Natura non facit saltum."*

Nature makes no leap.

"Come. There is nothing to fear. Join me in the ballroom," Fewmany said.

The scent I'd detected since my arrival urged itself further into my lungs. The music—mournful, sensual sounds pierced by sharp cymbal pings and dull drum thumps—became louder as I neared the dais. The performers wore robes and bright hats and played instruments I'd seen in books but had never heard before. Within the room, people danced to the strange rhythms. I noticed I'd fallen behind and quickened my pace to follow him.

With his back to me, he said, "Long ago, this was a night of release and renewal. Simply because it is forgotten doesn't mean the power is lost. We may still partake of the ecstasy of the old gods."

I felt a tremble spiral from my feet to my shoulders.

When he turned, he held out a stemmed glass the size of a bird's egg, full of a ruby liquid.

"Not so simple as wine, this is a rare libation I serve only on this night. Drink it, and no circumstances will befall that you haven't wished upon yourself."

Ecstasy of the old gods. A vivifying ritual. Yes. Blood and sap.

I took a deep breath as I reached for it. The first sip stung with heat, the second with sweetness, the third with a longing for more. I drank the vessel dry.

He took the glass. I detected a whirring warmth and turned to see a crowd forming. Fewmany gave a pleased smile. "Go. Find what you seek."

I felt heavy and open as deep water and wandered back into the hall, a sense beyond sight searching among the revelers.

Then I saw a man standing alone. I approached him. He wore a helmet with curved ram horns and a plate that covered his forehead and eyes. His garments were those of a hunter—boots, thick trousers, leather jerkin, and loose linen shirt.

Without a word, the hunter took the offer of my hand and led me behind him. On his back was a bow and empty quiver. We entered the ballroom, where people danced to the unfamiliar tones and melodies, unconcerned with proper steps, moving with natural rhythm. His hand brushed my waist. My hips began to sway. My fingers held the curve of his jaw and its astonishing firmness and heat. He was near my age.

Only once, alone, as a child at the castle's grand ball, had I ever danced. What was happening now seemed like a dreamwish fulfilled.

He struggled to find my eyes behind my mask's tinted glass. "What's your name?"

I laughed. "My name is Secret."

"From where do you come?"

"From below the sun and under the moon."

Slowly, with a grin, he circled me, stood at my back, and placed his hands on my hips. How long I, we, danced, I don't know because the music continued with no pause.

Minutes? hours? later, he whispered, "Will you join me for a walk?"

"Yes."

He led me through the ballroom, the treed hall, and into the northeast corner, where the doors were always locked.

Suspended among the vines, I saw a sign which read OPEN. The hunter pushed the door to a crack wide enough to enter.

Around his shoulder, as my eyes adjusted to the light of hundreds of candles, I discerned the distant movement of human forms, in their own skins and pelts. There were sounds I had never heard before, yet intelligible to some part of me because the heat of my blood pooled heavier in my thighs. On the floor steps away, a man and a woman animated an image I'd seen between the covers of a book.

I pulled him out to the courtyard. In the distance, two bonfires burned on the green. Although I couldn't see it, I knew the gate was open, and the wooded land called to those who went near. The pull was almost impossible to refuse, but I did, whisking past couples who hid among the planters.

I led him to the garden's juniper labyrinth. No farther than a step or two, we were entwined at the arms and on the cool ground. In the light of the moon and stars, he reared up on his knees, shrugged out of the bow and quiver, and placed his hands against his helmet. I pressed my slippered foot into his chest and shook my head. Rules for the evening aside, I didn't want to see him clearly—no—because under that mask, he could be anyone I wanted, anyone I dreamed of, and he was Michael, my chestnut-haired, green-eyed consort.

The hunter crawled toward me, pressed his hips against my right leg, and leaned the rest of his weight into his straightened arms. Then he kissed me, smooth as the ruby libation I, and likely he, had drunk. The ground rushed to catch me as he pushed me downward. Our lips parted. I touched his neck and shoulder, blood and muscle. Alive.

He swept my hand from his shoulder and guided it downward. What had weighted against my hip pressed into my palm. My mind contemplated the contours, lingering, until he groaned. I realized what I'd heard in the unlocked room.

My lack of fear frightened me, unable to discern will from drive. The hunter knocked away his helmet, brought his lips to my neck, and clutched my breast. He was urgent but not rough. I sensed no cruelty in him, only the ordinary debauchery of a decent man.

As the hooks came loose from the back of my bodice and the row of buttons from his trousers, I kissed him in search of the threshold. The night was cool. The shock of heat from his fingertips on my shoulder made me gasp. He froze when I touched him, unclothed, his tongue mute. Then he moved again, his hand under my skirt, over my knee, to the gap in the drawers where my thighs were bare, higher still at the part of my legs.

I held him in a gripping rhythm.

"Let go," he said.

I didn't, but I paused while his touch swept against my unchaste skin until a current ripped into every eddy in my flesh.

Then, before our bodies decided what to do next, he lifted away from me to his feet.

"Put on your mask. You know the rules," a man said. He was hidden outside the labyrinth entrance, but his arm held out the horned mask within the space.

I began to hook my bodice as the hunter fumbled with his buttons, then slipped the helmet back on his head. I hadn't seen him clearly when it was off, so occupied had I been. If I were to see him again, I wouldn't have recognized him. The illusion of who was behind the mask I could easily retain.

"Go back to the house," the man said.

The hunter grabbed the quiver and bow. With a shadowed glance that seemed wistful, he disappeared.

"Are you hurt?" the man outside the labyrinth asked.

"No," I said, walking into the open.

The man wore a dark coat and trousers and an unadorned mask across his eyes. His thinning hair fluttered in a gust of wind.

"Naughton! What are you doing here?"

"This isn't my first spring ball," he said. "Come along so that I may hail you a carriage."

"You had no right to interfere," I said, furious. The longing of the third sip had thickened within me and was slow to thin. I hadn't had my fill.

"All guests are meant to stay masked."

"What harm is there if not? You had no right *at all*."

He looked down at the ground for a moment. When he raised his eyes again, there was a hint of remorse. "No, I didn't."

The admission was as unexpected as it was sincere. It left me speechless. I suspected he'd been watching me all night, and I didn't know why. Nor did I ask. Part of me wanted to march back into the house to see what I was missing, but my mood was spoiled.

"I should at least bid good night to the host."

"This isn't that sort of party, Miss," he said.

I followed him without a word. Naughton opened a carriage door. Before I climbed in, I reached to remove my mask.

He grabbed, then released my wrist. "Leave it on until you're behind your own door."

As the horses pulled me away, I looked through the rear window. The moon was high, the sky twinkling. Smoke drifted above the manor from the hungry fires.

The raw trace of the hunter was still on my lips.

May /36

Dear Secret,

*Clutch your smelling salts. Prepare yourself for the great shock—Haaud
and Giphia are at war. The kingdoms, once again, at each other's throats!
I was on my way to the former when a messenger intercepted my envoys
with the news. Given the strained relationship between Ailliath and
Haaud, one I hoped to understand better for myself, my advisers decided it
best to postpone the visit. I attempted to convince them otherwise. No time
for a social call, they said, although I've not once perceived this twelve-,
now eleven-, kingdom journey as a holiday. They've been present for a
majority of my meetings. None has given an indication I've committed a
single calamitous gaff of diplomacy. If I've done well, they've made little
mention of that either.*

*I might return home by next summer because of this itinerary change.
Now I'm in Emmok visiting my sister. I'm an uncle again. Charming had
a son three months ago, a hale little fellow named Iwen. Pretty's daughters
are now seven and five, but I didn't first meet them as infants. What a
creature, a baby. Watching eyes and grasping hands. Did you know they
have a scent? I asked the nurse why. She had no explanation and seems
suspicious of me because I often ask to hold him.*

*I couldn't help but become pensive as he slept in my arms this morning.
As I write this, Deket is surrounded by arrow, sword, and cannon, but the
real siege is the threat of starvation. There are small ones like Iwen, and my
nieces, behind that town wall. Innocents, everywhere, young and old. I've not
turned a blind eye during my travels. The degrading poverty in Rothwyke's
southeast wards is in almost every town in our kingdom and the ones
beyond. In some of the remote villages, I've seen people so wan it hardly
seems possible they can rise from bed much less work a field. Then to a
manor or palace I go, as if to a magical realm where all is gold and fat geese.*

*I remembered that morning I took you to the fields, and as we rode out,
you told me of the orphan child you'd seen. I quoted my mother, "Fate has
its favorites." This thing fate, it's so arbitrary, I thought again today, and
then how cruel the complacency with which we regard it, stations low to
high. As if we are powerless against it. Is war a product of fate? Or for that
matter, love?*

No one speaks of such things at court.

I didn't intend to write such a serious missive, but you're not here to talk with me. So then.

Well, there's the option to abdicate should my constitution prove fatally flawed. Think now. Iwen could take the throne, or another future nephew, if I have no son to embarrass first. There are cousins on my father's side as well. Where would a philosophical prince go for his exile? Would you come away to see me?

Your account of the dinner with the admiral, theologist, and actors entertained me. I'm very glad you went and found pleasure in the company. I've noticed your letters are less frequent. You've mentioned before you wish not to be redundant because one day is rarely different from the next, but I don't mind. It's the closest I get to hearing your voice.

> *Affectionately,*
> *Nikolas*

Coincidence is not a synchronization of random events so much as it is a magnet drawing the moments together. So, although I wanted to dismiss what happened when I stored Nikolas's letter among the rest, a part of me knew I could not.

I opened my desk drawer, tilted the front, and was about to place his letter at the end of the stack when I heard an object roll forward.

I'd forgotten I had the cogwheel, but I remembered who gave it to me. The orphan child Nikolas mentioned—that was Harmyn, the strange little waif who wore mismatched clothes and yellow spectacles and who chirped and peeped as he walked. The one I thought had sung, unnoticed, at the performance three months prior.

The first time I met Harmyn, he gave me a flower. The second time, the cogwheel he'd found. The third, he told me the middle of Rothwyke was in the wrong place and led me straight to the grate in Old Wheel, over the tunnel that led to the woods.[15]

As I held the cogwheel, bronze with a missing tooth, I heard music as if from a music box, but the sound was too loud and too layered to have come from a neighbor's machine. As I tried to discern the source, my joints started to ache. A cold sweat trickled from my pores as the rupture broke through.

My throbbing feet stood in my apartment, but then the room seemed to vanish. I listened to a twinkling melody; underneath it, the smooth turn of gears; above it, the voices of children singing along.

Suddenly, my chest heaved with the blunt force of grief. The image took form—huge wheels turning, the music coming from them. I refused to endure it, threw the cogwheel out of the window, and leapt onto my bed.

I grabbed the carved wooden stag, stilling my breath until all I could feel was the whisper of air at the top of my lungs. Almost a year had passed since I'd had a mental rupture or a dream like this—the inexplicable sounds and images that came without warning and with the visceral presence of memory.

JUNE /36

THAT JUNE, CHARLOTTE REPORTED "ESCALATED WOOING" from a Mr. Frigget. He was ten years older, well established in his father's textile company, and a widower with a two-year-old daughter. She conveyed a fondness for him, although she wasn't ready to dismiss the attention of "the titillating—and titled—Lord Tyson-Banks." Her blatant inquiry of my prospects was as surprising as it was laughable.

I had never confided in her, or anyone, my doubt I would ever marry. No beauty did I consider myself, or beguiling. I couldn't fathom marrying for the convention of it, which I suppose most did out of necessity. There was little reason to fear I would end up like the Misses Acutt; between my own wages and eventually my inheritance, I would be secure.

Of course, I wanted to know the depths of love, and what I'd read in the better poetry, the occasional novel, and numerous myths and tales. What must it be like to feel cherished and to feel that way for another? I wondered.

Desire—that was no requirement for love. That had a will of its own, as I well knew, and although I might have regretted my actions later, I did wish my encounter with the hunter (oh, Michael—the primal lust) wasn't consummated only in my imagination. The knowledge I'd acquired from the library's erotic texts—useless, impotent!

But I could write of none of this. Not of my expectations, or of the stir awakened in me, not only carnal but also sensual, certainly not of the ball itself.

In truth, writing to my friends had been difficult for several months. Of course I told how I'd spent my days, of the books I'd borrowed, the dinners I'd attended with interesting guests, even what was displayed in some of the rooms. Still, there was much I hadn't said to Charlotte or Muriel, or Nikolas, who was closest to me. My letters were suitable for the eyes of strangers, with appropriate conveyance of affection, absent intimacies of detail and feeling. I withheld because I was becoming someone I didn't expect to be, uncertain she was someone they would care to know.

One indication—I removed myself from Erritas's and Goram's waiting lists. Either, or both, might have had a seat for me by the summer's end, but what had once been so important to me seemed less compelling. If knowledge was my true quest, I pursued it without limit in Fewmany's library. If escape was what I desired, I had done so without leaving Rothwyke, simply by choosing to live on my own.

Father accepted my decision without protest, which I found somewhat perplexing as he'd always expected me to attend high academy. He assured me the fund he set aside for my education would remain until I needed it and suggested I could apply my independent studies later, possibly skip a year or two ahead. When I told Fewmany, he was pleased to know I'd stay, but I sensed he wasn't surprised. However, my friends and Leo, all informed by letter and who replied within weeks, were taken aback; Leo, also disappointed; Nikolas, concerned. How unlike you, each one conveyed in some similar phrase or another.

And it was, for the girl I had been.

For the young woman I thought I was becoming, that wasn't so. She had fallen under a spell of beautiful things, delectable foods, astounding books, and fascinating people. How easily I could live that way, forever, she thought. As if the enchantment would last.

JULY /36

ON MY FIRST ANNIVERSARY AS THE KEEPER OF TALES, I STOOD AT one of the west windows. A flight of blue swallows twirled over the flat green land. I recalled I'd seen them on that day a year before. How much had changed within my own life, I thought, while the cycles outside remained the same.

Not long after Naughton served morning tea and placed an arrangement of lilacs and white roses on the cabinet, Fewmany *rap-rap, rap-rapped* and entered with Mutt at his heels. The dog ignored me to race up a spiral stair to the gallery.

Near my place at the table, Fewmany stood with his hands behind his back. "'Tis a year today that you have tended my athenaeum," he said.

That he remembered seemed sentimental, and unexpected. "It is," I said.

"You've earned a measure of my trust. I wish to bestow a boon," he said. I heard the *clink* before I saw the keys. In his left hand, one made of brass. In his right, a ring of them, seven of all sizes.

"Choose," he said.

"What do they open?"

"First decide, then I will tell you."

I glanced up at him. My fingers hovered over his palms. That instant, before a second thought, I reached to take both. My lips stifled a laugh as he cried out in surprise.

His eyes narrowed with a hint of mirth.

"You didn't say, 'Choose one,'" I said.

"'Twas implied."

"But not stated."

"Wily you are today, Miss Riven."

"What will they open?" I asked, the metal warming to my touch.

"The single one, the main doors to the house. The set, the door to the east wing and some hidden within."

"Where *is* the door to the wing?"

"First-floor chamber to the parlor's left, behind drapes that don't cover a window."

"To which I now have a key?"

"Yes. You must remember to lock what you open. Always. The keys are to remain here, stored in the cabinet. You may, of course, carry the key to the manor."

"I am glad for the privilege," I said.

Fewmany smoothed his hands past his lapels to the bulging coat pocket. "You're welcome, although I'm stung by your trick. Mutt! Come!" he said.

The dog gave me an appraising look as he passed, as if he knew something I did not.

The following afternoon, I entered the east wing for the first time.

Behind floor-length drapes, a door led into a tomb-black hall, not into the glassed pavilion between the main house and wing. Inside the hall to my left, as expected, was a small table with a vesta and lamp, which I lit. With apprehension, I walked ahead with the key ring in my pocket and, as was my habit, turned the knob of every door on both sides of the corridor. None gave entry. The hall forced me to turn a corner, left, where there were more locked doors, then left again. I realized the hall was U-shaped. In the dark warm silence, I continued onward.

At last, a knob circled at my touch, but the thrill gave way to panic. What if someone on the staff had failed to lock the door? Surely they were bound by the same rules I was. To have someone meet trouble for this—including me, now that I had a ring—was a matter I wished to prevent. My hands trembled as I tried my keys, hoping one fit. The sixth turned the lock. Relieved, I entered the room.

As my light shone upon the jars, revealing their hideous contents, I winced but didn't turn away. Closer I went with the lamp high to stare upon a two-headed piglet, a skinless arm twisted with vessels and muscle, a head with a monstrous brow, a perfect coiled snake, a tortured heart. Shelf after shelf were specimens, some as beautiful as the others were grotesque, all labeled with descriptive tags. I paused to stare at a fetus, the cord looped at his neck, thought of my two brothers, born blue before me, and shivered.

Aware I'd spent too much time away from my duties, I hurried off, locking the doors behind me, and returned to my table. I tried my best to concentrate, but my thoughts strayed to wonder what else was hidden behind those many doors.

"If you would, please, Miss," Naughton said as he set down my afternoon cup of tea, "ensure the doors latch when you leave the open chambers or lock the ones to which you have access."

"I'm quite certain I do."

"I only wish to impress a reminder." He paused with the pot near his chest, which prompted me to look at him. "Ever so many locks here, and so few keys. We servants keep an extra one to our entrance hidden under the boot scraper. One never knows when one will be locked out."

THE NIGHT OF THE TWELFTH OF JULY, I JOINED REMARQUE AND Fewmany for dinner, prepared to be entertained and hopeful Remarque would have no surprises.

After we ate, Naughton was dismissed, and we went to the library. Fewmany showed Remarque his new waywiser—an object I'd never seen before, but I knew what it was. Perhaps I'd noticed a drawing in a cartography book. How odd Fewmany left it there, when it seemed like an instrument he'd keep in his mechanism chamber.

As Remarque pushed the squeaky contraption around the library, Fewmany revealed what Remarque delivered. "Limited first edition of the newest translation of the kingdom's chronicles—from the era of The Mapmaker's War."

I brushed my fingers across the front board, a good leather, tooled with a detailed eye.

"I confess," Fewmany said, "ancient history rarely holds me in thrall. So often the language is stilted, spoiling the facts it means to convey, a putrid sauce over a fine meat. This edition is quite good, lively even—at least the chapters I perused."

"Such as?" The spine made that wonderful cracking sound when I opened it.

"An example? The account of how the people selected Prince Wyl's feat has a marked sardonic tone. Before that time, as you surely know, the people chose hunts or feats of strength, but this was the first quest to find the dragon and its treasure. The chronicler must have been of a rare minority mind, then, to insinuate the prince went to search for a figment."

"Unless the translator's interpretation of the text, rather than the text itself, reveals whose opinion it is."

"Trained as you are to mind these subtleties," he said.

"Meaning is malleable," I said as I studied the paper's texture.

"But fact is fact."

"As long as there's proof."

"Which has its own mutability." His eyebrow lifted with a goading tilt, and he smirked with good humor. Had I parried back, we would have bantered. He was in a sparring mood, one I'd come to anticipate and enjoy since the dinners I'd had among his guests and with him alone.

"The one you're holding is for my collection," he said. "The one on the table is for your father. The exhaustive annotations and closing analysis might well render him apoplectic with glee."

"You've been subjected to one of his half-delirious speeches."

"'Tis good for a man's blood to have something to pursue. Regardless, this volume shall, with luck, help him in his efforts."

I detected a restraint in him. I assumed he wished not to show an open affection for my father, which touched me. When he looked up, his expression was earnest, instead hinting of practical matters.

"Blood. Pursuit. What's this?" Remarque asked, handing the waywiser to Fewmany.

"My father believes he has an ancestral link to a noble family who had power before The Mapmaker's War. He's in a perpetual search to prove it," I said.

"Luck be with him. A thousand years since then, much has been lost to fire and purgings, assuming good records were kept at all," Remarque said.

Remarque walked away to help himself to another drink. As I set aside the book, I remembered the lecture I attended with Father when I was in my sixth school year. What bored me had invigorated him. The visiting scholar spoke on the topic of subtle inconsistencies found in the old handwritten chronicles.

Suddenly, the waywiser's noise grew faint. My eyelids drooped. As my body demanded sleep, my memory swirled among three moments.

At the lecture, sketching circles with dark intersections, which became not links but gaps.

The shiny pair of scissors that cut my hair and the drawing of a symbol from a dream.

The arcane manuscript's brown-red script and the name, *Ee-fah*, which pealed like a bell in my blood.

"Take this seat," I heard Fewmany say.

His hand gripped my shoulder—the touch protective, but touch nonetheless—and guided me to the nearest chair. A glass of water appeared. I stared at the ring on his hand, the gem round and red as a drop of blood.

"You were swaying as if you were about to faint," Fewmany said.

Remarque sloshed three glasses on the table. "Perhaps I should drink what I served you."

"No, please pass it here," I said as I reached for the sherry.

"You look flushed," Fewmany said.

"Fewmany, I'm all right. Thank you," I said, glancing up at him, the rough scar under his jaw and chin visible. I took a sip and shut my eyes.

Why those memories, why in that moment? My body ached the way it had during the rupture when I held the bronze cogwheel. I suppressed a groan of dread another might be coming.

"Hair of the dog, Miss Riven," Remarque said with his glass raised. "I'm told you're not going to high academy."

"I declined. I like my position here, and at night, I can study whatever I wish. I can always apply again."

He scratched furiously at his sidechops and some remote location obscured by the table. "Of course. It's not as if you'd have to endure a trial as your mother did."

"Quire—" Fewmany said with a tone of warning.

Not again, I thought. I should have said *No, sir* or something else to thwart what came next, because he must have taken some cue from my silence when Remarque told me,

"Her admittance was quite nearly denied. She had no formal schooling, word spread on that, and nevertheless a prodigy of languages, but the trouble was she was a woman. She took a written test to prove her skills, but those in charge didn't believe a woman could possess—my pun intended there—such talent. Being men of knowledge as opposed to superstition, they assumed she hid something, rather than that she was a witch. So, the head professors held a meeting, and she was forced to bare herself to prove she wasn't a man."

"How did you learn this?" I asked.

"A professor, or two, or three, told someone who told another. Boys will be boys, even after the fur has grown in." He chuckled.

"What a boor you are," Fewmany said.

I reached for my drink again, missed the grip, and splashed it on the table. I remembered again what she said at dinner only days before she died, "Mind what is spilled, girl, and watch it doesn't spread."

"I'm sorry," I said. "How clumsy I am this evening."

Fewmany found a cloth on the beverage cart and draped it over the puddle.

"Some respect for the dead, Quire," Fewmany said.

"I meant no offense. Oh, Miss Riven, have I upset you? My apologies! Bygones, yes? In the end, she eclipsed everyone, students and professors, and made an excellent reputation for herself. In my case, I failed most of my courses that first year and didn't return. I am more adept with books and manuscripts as objects rather than subjects."

For me, the night ended soon after. Remarque bid me a warm farewell. Fewmany rang for a carriage and waited with me. He asked if Remarque had disturbed me terribly—no, not terribly—and said Remarque's frankness suffered from a lack of couth but shouldn't be construed as malicious.

Fewmany was quite tender with me. Of course he assumed Remarque's anecdote had saddened me more than it did. In truth, what Remarque said helped to explain the hardness in her—that invisible wall no one but Father ever seemed to scale.

DIARY ENTRY 13 JULY /36

As I enjoyed Mrs. Woodman's cinnamon buns for a late treat, I heard it again. The last few evenings, downstairs, shouting and slamming—twice, the door, and pounding footsteps—then whimpering. That is Julia because after these episodes, Lucas yells as if he's playing a rough game alone. What Mrs. Elgin did after Mr. Elgin grew quiet or left, I could only imagine. She neither quieted the boy nor comforted the girl.

So I huddled on my bed, the carved stag clutched between my hands, as I thought, one doesn't know what misery hides behind a door or pleasant expression.

A terrible dread has seized upon me. All I want to do is lie down and slip into the breathless black, where I feel safe, calm, disappeared.

Later: the most vivid dream.

A haze of light crossed my closed eyes. I thought it was dawn. With lids half-closed, I tried to stand, but my body wouldn't comply.

Trees whispered with the night wind. An owl cried from a high branch. A swirling buzz circled my ears, and spots whirled around me. Bees, away from their hive. This frightened me because they shouldn't be out in the middle of the night. Something had disturbed them.

The woods crackled. A large animal approached. I trembled but couldn't move. Under my fear, I hoped if I had to die, the beast was quick to kill.

"You are far from home," a man said.

He moved into the moon's light to reveal himself, crouched like a bear. His hair and beard were white. A red cap topped his crown. He reached his arm toward me.

"Drink," he said.

I accepted the bladder. Water, cold and fresh.

"I know who you are, but why don't you tell me your name," he said.

I couldn't choose among the ones that came to mind and so I remained silent.

"Do you know who I am?" he asked.

I nodded. I did, although I had never met him. Nikolas had mentioned him to me several times when we were children.

Old Man took my hands in his strong palms. His skin shifted, unmoored by age. He held me with tenderness and patience, with love. My bones and muscles relaxed; my breath came full and steady.

Then he released me without warning. He flicked the tip of my nose, hard.

A hot expansive pressure filled the center of my body. I shook with the violence which streamed into my limbs. I went blind for a moment, intoxicated by what consumed me. He trapped my wrists together.

"Yes, feel it. Feel what has been neglected and starving. Feed it on its loss. Feed it on its need. And when it's full, tell me, where does the rage go, child?" he asked. His thumbs scratched across the insides of my wrists. "Here?" He grabbed me round the neck. "Or here?" One hand suspended close to my chest and the other pressed against my forehead. "Or here, where the poison eats from the inside out?"

With force, I knocked his arms away. I hoped he was hurt.

He laughed, dark and knowing. "Yes. The rage could go there. The strike felt good, didn't it? Good enough to want more."

I glared at him as I nodded.

Old Man took my left hand. "What you feel is power. It can be hate and become love. Rage to become compassion. Know this: Peace leads to greater peace. Violence leads to greater violence. If you fall in the water, the whole river knows it from your ripple, no matter how small the splash."

I stared at his hand. I remained inert, caught between the urge to pull away and the wish for him to hold on. My eyelids were leaden with the need for sleep.

"The time is coming to bring the pieces together," Old Man said.

I awoke with a startle and stared at the ceiling until my heart stopped pounding. When I turned over, I saw a feather tucked under the carved stag on my night table. I know I neither found that feather nor put it there.

AUGUST /36

SO—THIS IS HOW IT WAS FOUND.

Up in the gallery to store a book, I passed the esoterica shelves and noticed the floor was covered in silverfish, in greater numbers than I'd seen months prior in the same place.

I opened the doors to the shelves and cabinets. Several insects scurried from a lower-corner cabinet. On my hands and knees, I pulled out the manuscripts, looking for chewed edges and crumbs. Little evidence showed they'd feasted there. As I returned the manuscripts to their places, wondering where the silverfish lived, I paused to glance at one text from the middle of the stack.

Minuscule handwriting, strange alphabet, thin paper, single pages stacked.

The arcane manuscript.

Shaking, I took it to my table to study. I couldn't discern a single mark except for Fewmany's neat *fm* on the usual pages. Aside from a few nibbled notches, the manuscript was in fine condition, as it had been when my mother received it.

Cold dread trickled down the back of my neck.

I'd found the manuscript at last.

That Fewmany had it in his library—how was that possible?

I stayed so late, Naughton came in to see if he'd been mistaken whether Fewmany and I had a dinner scheduled. No, we didn't, but I told him to send up Fewmany because I had something to discuss.

An hour later, Fewmany came in whistling. His good mood didn't sour when I mentioned the silverfish.

Then I showed him the manuscript. "I found it when I tried to locate them. I've never seen writing like this. How did you acquire it?" I asked.

He turned the pages. "Oh, this. Your father gave it to me."

I pressed my toes into my shoes so hard, I thought I'd break my joints. "When?"

"Four, five years ago. Bren said he found it among your mother's effects—peace be to the dead—and assumed it belonged to me. I said it did not. His attempt to identify an owner was unsuccessful," Fewmany said.

"He didn't think it was hers?"

"No. He assumed it had long been in her possession, unclaimed, and gave it to me knowing I'd appreciate the curiosity."

"What did you think of it?"

Fewmany tidied the stack and pushed the manuscript away. "Unusual. Such a delicate paper. The writing meticulous. There are few corrections on the pages, as I recall, and the writing compared to nothing I've seen either."

"And you stored it away with no other inquiry?"

"Of course not. I sent a copied page to several high academies and a few pages to Quire. He and imminent scholars agreed with my belief it's written in a code."

"A code."

"Quire said the manuscript is worthless," Fewmany said.

In a glance, I searched his eyes, his face, his bearing for a hint that he withheld a detail or he lied. I detected neither. He had told me the truth as he knew it.

"'Tis late. Would you like to join me for dinner?" he asked.

"No, thank you. Cook provided an ample lunch today. I'll return the manuscript to its place and be off."

"You may borrow it."

I had every intention to decline but said, "Perhaps I'll show it to my father to see what he remembers."

Fewmany observed me for a moment, his lips slightly parted as if he weren't sure of his next words. "Very well, then, my keeper of tales."

That evening, I studied the manuscript by lamplight. My palms ached when I touched it, as if my body understood something my mind couldn't.

Still, I was torn. I didn't want the responsibility for it, but there it was—found. Although I'd imagined I would return it to the rightful owner and fantasized about burning it, I could do neither.

The manuscript belonged to Fewmany now. I didn't want to know what penalty I might face for losing or destroying what was his.

As well, the very thought of trying to break the cipher nauseated me. A mystery I didn't want to solve.

Two evenings later, the seventeenth of August, I took the manuscript when I dined with Father. I planned to make light of the issue, not to provoke him into a fit of melancholy.

He said he had cooked for us. Elinor was away for the evening with her daughter Bess, visiting from the village of Clyton. As I stirred the warming pot, I asked him to glance at what I'd left on the table. "I borrowed it from Fewmany. He said you gave it to him."

Father studied the pages. "Yes, I did. Not long after your mother died."

"Was it hers?"

"I didn't think it was. She wasn't one to keep many possessions. I checked the log she kept and found an entry, but it listed no owner's name. She had no other patrons then. I thought the manuscript was Fewmany's. But the manuscript didn't have his mark, which I knew was always there because your mother mentioned how appalling she found it."

"There are far more ostentatious ones than his. Regardless, did he claim it belonged to him?"

"No. I gave it to him, then, as a gift."

"But where did you find it? I was the one who stored away her reference books and records," I said.

"It was on her table that day," he said.

"I don't remember seeing it."

"I cleared some of what was there. There were documents for Fewmany Incorporated to return, one book of his, and that manuscript."

A hot rush flooded me. She had meant for *me* to find the manuscript, not Father. If I'd returned from school when I usually did—instead of taking that walk in the woods with Nikolas—what would I have seen?

What Father said he found? My mother on the floor near her work-tables, an empty bowl and a piece of bread, the furniture out of place as if violently moved. And the manuscript . . .

I laid the plates of stew at our places, the old ochre bowl between us.

"Why do you have the manuscript now?" Father asked.

I faced him, the memory of a time before trying to escape from where I kept it buried—the scissors, the symbol—then smoothed away a tendril of hair. "I found it in the library. When Fewmany told me of its history, I was curious to ask what you knew."

"It's a mysterious thing. I'm surprised he kept it. He told me it's val-ueless," he said.

"He likes his oddities. It should belong to someone who can appreci-ate it," I said.

Father touched my hand when I reached for the salt cellar.

"She would have been proud of you, my scholarly pet," he said.

I forced a smile, for his sake.

After dinner was done, I placed the arcane manuscript in my satchel and prepared to leave. Father saw me to the door. He opened his palm to reveal a treasure he bought from a peddler, a carved wooden bird with a forked tail, flakes of blue paint peeling from its back.

"When I saw it, I thought of you, when you were a little girl, outside in the courtyard with your flowers and visiting birds," he said.

I was taken aback by the wetness in his eyes. Suspicious, too. I wondered what he meant by the gift but said nothing except thank you.

I lay awake through much of the night trying to order my thoughts.

The facts. The manuscript arrived. My mother was paid to attempt its translation. She asked for more time when the courier returned for it. She made a cipher and left in the folklore book. She died.

The assumptions. She meant for me to find the manuscript on her table. The manuscript was written in code. Whatever the text contained, she thought it important enough to create a cipher. As for her death, she choked, as Father said, or she didn't choke, or die by accident.

The truth. She hated me. I hated her. And no matter what she left behind or what Old Woman said about the manuscript or what I was meant to do, I wanted no part of any of it.

The next morning, I returned the manuscript. It could remain in Fewmany's library forever, out of sight, out of mind, out of my hands.

SEPTEMBER /36

MY DIARY CONTAINED THREE SPARSE ENTRIES THAT SEPTEMBER. On the ninth, "Charlotte is engaged. She wrote, 'I'm too young to be a stepmother, evil or otherwise, but if I were to wait too much longer, I'd rot despite my purity! How exhilarating we may now hold hands and share a chaste kiss.' Yes, what Nature urges and Nurture controls. No word from Muriel, but I've failed to keep up correspondence, too."

On the thirteenth, "Phantasmagoria! We guests entered a black tent in the ballroom. All went so dark, could hardly discern the outline of those nearby. Around us, a smoky mist, drifting voices, eerie music. Specters and beasts emerged and disappeared. Gasps and screams from the audience at what we saw—and what brushed against us, cloth, hands, breath! Two ladies fainted and one man required a splash of water. Stayed behind with Fewmany to learn how the tricks were done. Images painted on glass, lanterns, thin metal sheets (thunder!), mannequins, ropes and pulleys. How easily we are deceived."

On the twenty-third, "19th birthday. Father traveling, sent package—three jars of honey which taste of three different flowers. From Nikolas, a book of 'hilariously sentimental poetry,' his favorite ones marked with ribbons. I think he's in Uldiland now, soon to Prev."

Then, near the end of the month, I received this note:

Dear Miss Riven,

I invite you to a hunt the morning of 5 October. You should arrive at the grove's gate at dawn attired for the occasion. Be prepared for the blood.

Sincerely,
fm

Post script. You are at liberty to decline.

THE GIRL I HAD BEEN NEVER WOULD HAVE CONSIDERED, MUCH less accepted, the invitation. The young woman I was then appreciated the unknown. What might be discovered in a conversation, behind a closed door, at the least.

Well before dawn, the alarm of my clock woke me. I dressed in my oldest shoes and clothing. Instead of pinning my hair, I let one black braid hang at my back. In my satchel, I packed a clean skirt and blouse.

I ate a small breakfast to curb my hunger, slipped into my purple cloak, and walked to the manor, surprising the guards at the main entrance and manor gate who expected no visitors so early.

Fewmany's figure was a dark shape in the ascending light. He stood at the open gate. He wore a jerkin over a loose shirt, knee-length breeches, and high boots. A pouch hung at his hip from a belt. His hair flared wildly about his head. There was a bow in his hand and a leather strap across his chest. A full quiver of arrows was on his back. On his right hand was a fingerless glove and on his left arm a sheath of leather. He allowed me through the gate and locked it behind us.

A blur whipped around my head, then his. He scowled, frozen. The unmistakable buzz of a bee lingered at my ear. I frowned. We stood together until the nuisance was gone.

"Remove your spectacles if you can see well enough without them," he said.

I placed them in my satchel.

"Set aside your cloak. Your skirt is too long. Running will be difficult. Will you allow it to be altered?"

I nodded. When he knelt in front of me and drew a short knife, I startled.

He looked up at me, his amber eyes clear.

"I won't cut you. Be still," he said.

A wide ribbon pulled away. The skirt draped to my kneecaps. I felt exposed to the elements, to his presence, but the anxiety was accompanied by a rush, as if something had been freed.

"Put on this belt. You'll have a role in the morning's events," he said.

The belt had a sheath, and within the sheath was a knife. I slipped it out to look. It was as long as my forearm, the handle made of bone, cool and smooth, the blade sharp with an edge of light. The weight of it on my body seemed to force my feet closer to the earth.

He instructed me to follow him closely. The wind was in our favor, he said, but we must take care to be as quiet as possible. He would rely on gestures rather than words, so I must pay attention.

"Are you afraid?" he asked.

"Yes."

"Good. What will happen will be all the more potent."

"What's that?"

"And spoil the surprise? This you must experience, not be told, my keeper of tales," he said.

We walked along a path. He stepped off, mindful of the leaves and twigs, and crept among the trees. I watched him move as if he'd changed skins, as if his fine suits covered an entirely different creature. I inched forward with my innate caution and ability to hide.

When he paused, I paused. When he stared at his feet, I tried to see what he did. As he scanned ahead, I peered around his side for a glimpse of what he hoped to find. I realized then I didn't know what he planned to track. I knew hunts could involve dogs and falcons, and weapons blunt and sharp, and that some seasons were better than others for one animal or another. Between us, there were a bow, several arrows, and two knives. I wasn't so fast or strong, and I didn't know what physical demands would be made of me.

I had the fleeting thought I might be in danger.

Yet as the mysterious pursuit continued, I detected a change in my senses. This wasn't the open connection I once had to everything that surrounded me, birdsong a note in my own. Quiet Little Secret by herself but not alone in the woods, long ago. No, this was defined by boundary. I noticed the press of my foot on the soil. I listened for the distance between my ears and the source of the chirp, rustle, and whisper. I perceived the space around me as definite. It was then my heart beat with anticipation rather than caution. I was after something.

He slowed his pace, raised his hand, and stopped. I couldn't see what he must have seen. He turned to face me, holding a finger in front of his lips. With grace, he sidestepped until he was aligned with a large oak and moved straight ahead. As I repeated his steps, more deliberate than he in my restraint, I scanned the area. The undergrowth rustled, but I didn't see what disturbed the branches.

We slipped behind another tree, then another. He held up his right hand, higher, twisting his palm to the fletched arrows in the quiver, as he bent upon his knee. I could see over his shoulder. A deer chewed the leaves near its nose. The doe stood in perfect profile.

Suddenly, she raised its head and flicked her tail. He didn't move. The deer remained still. After a few moments, she began to eat again.

As he raised the bow, I held my breath, my blood thick and forceful under my skin. He drew back the bowstring.

Stay, I said without saying.

She turned her neck. Her eyes met mine with recognition, shifted their focus away, and glazed with panic.

There was a quick whoosh, then a wet slap.

The deer kicked its back heels into the air and ran to its right between the trees.

He stood but didn't run. He searched the ground.

"Look for the blood trail. You will find spots. Walk slowly. When you find one, stop and look for the next. Follow how they connect," he said.

He found the first drops. The trail continued sharply to our left. He rushed ahead.

I sprinted behind him, surprised at his speed and my own. The sudden exertion transmuted air into flames in my lungs. We continued farther on, how far, I don't know.

Then I saw the fence, and against the fence, the deer. On the other side, the land was pasture and lit with early sun. Nothing was beyond the grass—no houses, no fences, no trees. I turned my eyes back to the animal.

The deer lay on its right side fighting to breathe. The arrow jutted from the space near its left shoulder. Small bubbles foamed at its mouth and burst to stain its fur.

He nudged me with his bow.

"Pay attention to your pounding heart."

He knelt next to the deer. He placed his hand near the wound, rubbed the blood between his fingers. He straddled the deer and heaved it inches away from the bars.

"Draw your knife and come here," he said.

I looked into his eyes. He didn't blink, and because he didn't blink, I was able to hold myself there. He stood his full height. I took the knife out and held it near my chest.

A thought rose with the action. One deep plunge in the right spot and there he'd lie, too. I shuddered because there was pleasure in the horror. A fleeting primal thrill.

"Listen. I will hold its head. You will draw the blade with one long deep stroke across its throat. Begin with the edge closest to the hilt, slide across smoothly, and all the way through. The hide is thick. You'll have to exert pressure."

He bent his knees, anchored into his legs, and grasped the deer by the jaws. It gave a weak struggle.

I knelt on the ground. The deer's eyes searched for mine. I ignored the excruciating throb in my forehead. I stared at a point on its neck, raised the knife, and did as I was told. In that brief instant, I felt as I never had before. Invincible.

Blood poured from the wound onto my naked knee. I dropped the knife and touched the wet thick smear. I smelled the animal dank and a hint of metal. My vision blurred as if a veil had fallen over my face. My upturned fingers were red. I didn't recognize my hands, or the curve of my breasts, or the black twist of hair that crossed my collarbone.[16]

When my focus returned, I walked toward the trees. There were eyes on me, the animals in full view—fox, boar, crow.

A single firm stroke swept against the back of my head.

"Well done," he said.

I turned to see him with a rag held out in offer. I wiped my knee, my hands. The dampness disappeared, but the stains lingered. With a lurch, I ran ahead and heaved a puddle on the ground.

"I did, too, the first time. The shock. The excitement," he said.

With my back to him, I leaned into a tree. A sensual breeze rushed around my bare legs. As the rough bark pushed through my clothes to my skin, I contemplated the force that emerged from nowhere within me.

"What was the surprise?" he asked as if he'd sensed what I was thinking.

I faced him. "The surge of power."

"How did it feel?"

"I've no measure or comparison."

"Nevertheless."

"As if anything imaginable were possible."

"You ventured far and deep," he said.

Blood smeared his clothing. With a spin on his heel, he turned south. He strode like a man in his youthful prime. I quickened my steps to catch up to him.

"Why did you invite me?" I asked.

"To see the true size of your fangs. My, how big they are," he said.

"Come along. I'll have Cook prepare a breakfast while we tidy up. Guess what you'll have for tomorrow's midday meal."

SOON AFTER I BATHED AWAY THE GRIME OF THE CHASE, I FELT DIFFUSE, AS if I'd been unmoored from my body. For days, the feeling continued. I'd lose my sense of time and place, finding ink pooled under my pen or blanking on a response to a market vendor. Sometimes, I'd lapse into that morning again—the raise of his hand, the pound of the chase, the tension of the cut before I finished the deer's life. The severing moment was open as a threshold, and while the deer crossed through, I remained here but aware of what hadn't closed.

I realized Naughton found reasons to come into the library more often. He left items to be shelved one at a time instead of in a stack, checked whether the drapes were closed to spare the collection the ruin of light, asked if I wanted a fresh pot of tea or the fire stoked. As he never did before, he lingered in his service, movements slow, brown eyes watchful, until I was sometimes irritated enough to say, "That is all, Naughton."

"Yes, Miss," he'd say with a bow.

The frequency with which I saw Fewmany remained the same, but a nuance softened our interaction. We seemed to know something of the other that hadn't been known before, although it couldn't be easily named or described. I felt close to him, and I think he had a fondness, even respect, for me that he didn't before.

This he revealed in the simplest way. He'd come in to recommend a book he'd finished, and in the midst of our conversation, he called me Secret. I surely reacted with surprise because his posture straightened.

"'Twas impetuous to address you that way. I hope I caused no offense," he said.

"None taken. Certain formalities seem dispensable of late."

"Indeed, we are more familiar than we once were," he said, his tone matter-of-fact, his expression relaxed.

"That is so." In my pause, I noticed the handkerchief in his bulging pocket matched the burgundy cravat at his neck. "If I may, then, ask a question about something I've long wondered."

"No harm in asking, is there?" he said.

"What do you keep in your pocket?"

He pressed his palm against it. "Bread crusts, which remind me of home, and two copper coins, which remind me of how I got away."

I nodded, needing no explanation. Years before, when I was an apprentice, we'd had a private meeting, and he told a story of his childhood when he found a bag of coins and bought enough bread to gorge himself. He wouldn't let himself forget the poor boy he once had been.[17]

Several days later, I received a letter stating he'd departed to address "some matters of urgency" and would return in January.

My own routine didn't change—days in the library; nights tending housework and reading, sometimes going to a performance or lecture— but I felt more lonely than I had in many months. I'd come to enjoy the company of Fewmany's guests, as well as his own.

Although I no longer lived with my father and didn't visit him as often as I could have, his concurrent absence—he, too, was traveling— left me unsettled. Everyone for whom I cared was gone.

One night, as I lay in my bed and heard Julia's faint whimper below, a deep sadness came upon me.

I slipped into the trough of it, swept away from my snug bed and cozy apartment, and found myself once again a small child. Once again, wondering where Father was, peering at my mother's back from a corner of the room through wooden bars, her silencing hiss when I made the slightest noise.

Her little fungus.

JANUARY /37

I HEARD A SMALL BARK, THEN A VICIOUS SNEEZE, AND THE *RAP-rap, rap-rap*. A warm greeting was on my tongue's tip as the door opened—this was the first I'd seen him in weeks—but all I managed was a bewildered smile.

On Fewmany's head was a tasseled nightcap, the fringe level with where his Tell-a-Bell should have been. His silk robe was embroidered at every hem. His slippers, instead of leather, appeared to be felted wool. His red eyes and nose explained why he wore bedclothes but not why he would allow himself to be seen in such a state. He placed a book on the table's edge.

"Good morning," he said.

"Good morning. What's the matter?" I asked.

"'Tis but a coryza proving impervious to the apothecary's store." He whipped a handkerchief from a robe pocket, and finding it sodden, dug in a different one for another. "With apologies," he said, then turned to blow his nose. "Three days in this condition, and the tedium from the quiet and the bed is near to putting me out of my mind. I can't read another word. I have nothing to amuse me," he said.

I laughed to myself. He was like a cross child, too restless to lie still.

"If you wish to sit, you can keep me company as I work," I said.

"I wouldn't want to be a bother," he said, stepping toward the cabinet. He traced his finger along the amaryllis, which had bloomed.

"Nonsense."

He pulled a high-backed chair to face the fire, called Mutt to his lap, and honked piteously several times.

He was silent so long, I thought he had drifted into a nap. But then, "What have you found of interest, of late?"

I told him of three books I'd read and liked.

"And what of the wing rooms?" he asked.

The wing rooms—ovens in the summer, ice caves in the winter, airless as tombs, endlessly fascinating. "I had only started to look through the one with pottery last we spoke, and it's now among my favorites. The mask room, however. I can appreciate the beauty but not the disturbing dreams they cause."

"If your explorations are complete, a new set is yours for the asking," he said.

"I would like that," I said.

"You have proven yourself faithful, Secret. I've no doubt of your fealty for that which belongs to me, and for me as well."

"That is true."

Fewmany peered around the chair. "I wish to share something which you haven't seen. Does this interest you?"

"Of course," I said.

Fewmany sent Mutt to the floor and walked past the fireplace. I followed him the length of the library to the back wall of shelves and cabinets. He set five books aside, then moved both hands forward. A heavy clunk suggested the turn of a lock and then a groan, the pivot of a hinge. Above a cabinet, six shelves moved forward like a door.

There was a hidden room, as I suspected.

"Come. Bring a lamp," he said as he entered the dark.

When I stepped past the cabinet, sunlight spread into the chamber. He had opened some of the drapes on the south wall. Mutt leapt in and began his inspection.

Tall cabinets with long, thin drawers rose up from the floor opposite the secret entrance. Across from that was another set of shelves with objects on display. On the walls were framed drawings—all of them maps. A table near the west-facing windows reached nearly the length of the room. Upon this were more maps, weighted at the edges with metal instruments and various objects. The map borders were decorated in color with foliage, puffed cheeks of the four winds, and fantastical beasts.

I lifted a copper globe, which fit perfectly in my hand. I could read the engraved names of distant lands. Where a shore met the sea, there was the phrase *HC SVNT DRACONES. Here be dragons.* I replaced the small globe where I found it.

"Within this chamber is the whole of the known world," Fewmany said. "As noted by the cartographers, to be certain."

I looked at a framed map. Triangles twirled from the center outward, cutting the land and adjacent waters into fragments.

"Curiosities, they are. Maps are alike in that what isn't charted has as much significance as what is," he said. "What you see there is an old map of Emmok. The main roads and the rivers, the intersections where towns and villages once thrived. Yet one does not see what might have never been drawn."

Fewmany pointed to a triangle colored blue and brown. Gold bled from the foothills, he claimed, and into the river. He knew this because an obscure geological text written sometime after the map was drawn told him so. At that time, the kingdom's name was different, but the land's prominent features were not. Fewmany hadn't intended to discover this fact, but he did, by accident. The mine was dead by then, scoured clean by water and pickax. He owned a tract where it flowed once. Rich arable land, covered in barley crops.

"Why did you want the land?" I asked.

"Because of what it yields—which I require of every acre I own. But in this case, and few others, as well as what it might. I'm in search of something yet to be found. An elusive acquisition. Tell me, if you could have anything at all, what would it be?"

"I have simple needs and wants."

"You are human and entitled to dream."

"Anything?"

"Mmm-hmm," he said.

I glanced at the instrument at the end of the table. It was round, mirrored, with one hole on its edge the diameter of a small plum. A heliotrope. I leaned over to inspect it and lurched back when I caught a glimpse of a face, realizing after a blink it was my own.

Fewmany sniffed and blew as I pondered. In my life, I'd imagined many impossible things. To be beautiful and charming, to have brothers born alive, to never be afraid, to leave Rothwyke and never return, and more I couldn't quite name. Most were a child's wishes, unattainable.

What I answered was unlikely to happen but truthful. "I would wish to have a library such as yours."

"Why?" he asked.

"There's pleasure in knowledge but more so in understanding, and that requires years of study in a suitable environment."

"How passionless."

"Then I will keep my answer and recall an open window with a slant of afternoon sun, and the brown smell of a tanned skin under my fingertips, and the smoked cherry taste of a good wine."

"Better," he said.

I walked to a cabinet filled with objects. Balanced against it was the waywiser Fewmany had acquired the previous summer. I took the

handle and rolled the wheel against the floor. The squeak was muted—he must have oiled it—but the noise irritated me still. As I put the instrument back in place, my shoulders seized with a torturous ache, which streaked into my hips, rooting me in pain through my soles.

A rupture was upon me.

I could do nothing but hold myself rigid as the waywiser before me disintegrated like a rotted cloth and another formed within my inner sight. It was worn, much used. Withered, ink-stained fingers wrapped around its handle,

held out in the offer of a gift. Affection and sadness flooded my heart as a name tried to whisper through.

As the rupture's violence reverberated in my bones, I opened the cabinet doors.

"What is the thing you seek but cannot find?" I asked. My hands reached toward the instruments as if they had a will of their own.

"A treasure as old as myth. Many have tried and failed. Many have died in its pursuit."

I twirled a compass in my palm. "Am I supposed to guess the riddle, or will you speak plainly?"

"The hoard."

The needle drew blood, and I felt the thick pull of sleep.

He took the compass away and offered a clean handkerchief. I pressed it against the wound. "Stories of it have descended through the ages. You know this and know it well," Fewmany said.

"It's also thought to be under careful guard," I said.

He laughed. "Oh-ho—a fire-breathing beastie, so we've been told. The infamous menace, bringer of ruin. Strange, isn't it, the havoc it wreaks, destroying villages across the world, and princes for ages have quested to face its fury, yet not one—not one—has bothered to slay it once and for all and claim its apocryphal prize."

"Perhaps there's nothing to find. No dragon, no hoard, no truth in it at all," I said.

"If it didn't exist, why would its legend endure?" he asked.

"Wishful thinking, like turning lead into gold."

He smirked, then sneezed into his arm. "I prefer to assume some recondite knowledge has been ostensibly lost, or instead misplaced, through the ages. Calamity or war, or the death of certain men and kingdoms."

"Possibly, the raiding and burning of libraries." I brought my hand to my mouth to suck away the blood. I thought of the empty plaque in the locked room of dead animals, waiting for a dragon's head. "Or a metaphor, the meaning of the story more important than the facts."

"The rational makes sense, but the irrational is far more interesting." Fewmany brushed his fingertips across one of the maps. "That said, there are plausible theories about this hoard. A warrior's hidden booty, a dead king's grave, the jeweled veins of a dark cave, the treasure of a lost civilization. But presuming a dragon were involved, what do the old tales tell us?"

Knowing him as I did, his words seemed guarded. A shiver streaked through my spine as an image came unbidden—the scissors and the symbol—and I looked into his bloodshot eyes. His brow arched playfully.

"That depends. In some traditions, the dragon is benevolent or at least harmless. We're familiar with the dragon as a creature who steals what it likes, keeps account of what it's taken, and exacts revenge if it's robbed. I'd advise caution if you proceed," I said.

Fewmany wandered around the center table and picked up the copper globe I'd held earlier. "Strange mysteries abound. A wise man allows for what cannot be explained." He placed the globe on its stand and turned to close the drapes.

I followed Mutt out and heard the lock slip as Fewmany shut the room. He left the library then, complaining he felt quite poorly.

For a long while, I stood next to the fire, giving no mind to the rupture or the memory of the scissors and symbol, warmer for the confidence he shared with me, the kind one would only share with an intimate friend.

ROTHWYKE DAILY MERCURY.

2 February /37. Page 4, Column 1

UNEXPLAINED MANIA—What caused the paroxysms among the adults in the ward of Warrick two days past? After four o'clock, people exhibited behavior unbefitting public display. Firsthand accounts told of men and women in the streets and shops with tears streaming down their faces, many trying in vain to hide what had come over them. Some erupted into fits of rage, howling into the air, pounding the walls with their fists, and whipping their carthorses until the beasts bled. Others became paralyzed in silence, immobile as sculptures where they stood.

No children were reported to sicken, but youngsters who were at the intersection of Turpery and Vine gave an account of what preceded the dramatic outbursts.

According to five children, a brown rabbit was seen darting across the cobblestones until it stopped near a drainage grate and began to scream as if in excruciating pain. As it screamed, a boy, described as urchinly with light hair and spectacles and approximately eight years of age, approached the animal and cradled it.

Several adults confirm seeing the rabbit, but none claim to have seen the child. The five youngsters insist the lone boy walked away with the rabbit singing a melody "in a high voice like a bird." In the ensuing moments, the adults around them lost their composure or seemed to "fall asleep with their eyes open" where they stood. No adult has come forth claiming to hear the child's song.

The paroxysms afflicted the victims for approximately one hour. Through the evening, the ill effects were exhaustion, nausea, tingling of the extremities, and inability to concentrate.

Learned speculation suggests a miasma brought about the unpleasant events, though there are those who blame that day's full moon and sorcery.

WEEKLY POST.

2 February /37. Page 2, Column 1

DANGEROUS GROUND—Rothwyke Services is investigating the sudden appearance of a crevice one block south of the New Wheel development. Several workers report feeling subtle tremors in the past weeks, which they presumed were related to construction. The crack is, at present, five yards in length and reaches to a depth of two feet. Mr. Beardsley, lead officer at Rothwyke Services, dispelled rumors that the weight and rumble of steamwheelers have caused this geological instability.

MARCH /37

Inviting your and, if desired, a guest's attendance
at the Masquerade Ball.
Revelries to ensue at the manor of Fewmany
on the evening of 1 May.
❦ Guests must be masked before they arrive and
remain so until they depart from the event.
❦ Carriages will be offered at the end of the
evening for those who require them.
❦ All due confidentiality regarding this
invitation and whatever occurs
that evening is obligated.
The honor of a reply is requested.

The invitation was left on the table, the writing on the envelope in Fewmany's hand. I placed my cordial reply on the supply cabinet, awaiting Naughton's delivery.

For months, I'd pinched and saved in anticipation. I wouldn't take another ingot to pay for my costume, but I would spend lavishly. When I visited Margana, I told her I wanted something to fill those who saw me with awe.

"I will do my best to oblige," she said.

THOSE FIRST DAYS OF THE MONTH, I ENJOYED A CHEERFUL, EX-pectant mood. Fewmany invited me to a dinner with a large group of guests. Although Remarque was among them, I accepted.

On the twelfth of March, I was seated next to a scientist and a lit-erature professor, both in Rothwyke to give lectures. The former was a woman, Dr. Bechgert, her Kirsauan accent distinct. She spoke of her theory that disease was caused by organisms, spread by contact with any fluid which harbored them. A controversial assertion, she said, which caused her great derision among her colleagues.

The latter was an older man, with very kind eyes, who taught at a high academy where I'd been rejected twice. I made no mention of the slight. While Remarque talked loudly at the other end of the table, Pro-fessor Karkes and I slipped into an exclusive conversation. When he re-vealed Fewmany told him of my interest in myths, a subject he included in his courses, we spoke for some time before he said he particularly liked creation myths and told of his favorites.

Perhaps I meant to impress him, perhaps my enthusiasm got the bet-ter of me, but I abandoned my dessert to tell him one I'd heard but never found in a book.

It was the first myth in the cycle Old Woman taught me and recited to the infant animals born near her cottage, which began, "Do you re-member, small one, before you opened your eyes, The Great Sleep, which came before All That Is?" The myth told of the red dragon who came into being to witness the creation of the world.

When I finished, I sensed Fewmany's attention. I looked at him across the table, his finger on the lip of his glass, a satisfied grin on his face. I understood then, Professor Karkes was a gift Fewmany was pleased to bestow.

I smiled back at him as Professor Karkes patted his pockets. "I must jot a note," he said, finding a paper scrap and a pencil nib. "Tell me, Miss Riven, from whom did you hear it?"

"A woman I knew once," I said, suddenly cautious.

"I've never heard a myth quite like that. Do you know where she learned it? Was she from Ailliath or elsewhere?"

"I don't know," I lied, almost in a whisper. "I was quite young when I knew her. Her stories stayed with me."

"Understandably," Professor Karkes said.

For a time, Dr. Bechgert, the professor, and I spoke of the war between Haaud and Giphia. At last, the town of Deket was back in Giphia's control, but there was cause to worry Haaud was preparing for a greater fight, next with Kirsau.

Our entertainment that evening was a performance by one of the guests, a violinist, and Fewmany's staff musicians. When the hour became late and the guests bid their thank-yous and good-byes, Fewmany asked me to join him and Remarque in the library. He promised not to keep me but a few moments.

Because of that assurance, I agreed, although I'd avoided Remarque all evening out of fear he'd say something to rile my nerves. Up the stairs I went with Fewmany, discussing Dr. Bechgert's theory.

When we entered, Remarque was bent over the table, lamps lit.

"Expert among experts, what do you say?" Fewmany asked.

"My opinion hasn't changed," Remarque said as he pushed the arcane manuscript toward the table's center. "Paper doesn't endure like parchment, and given the condition, it cannot be that old. Virtually no foxing. It should have a more pronounced smell. And it's so thin—only the finest artisan could craft a material so delicate that's still durable. I've seen enough alphabets and syllabaries to know what is legitimate, and although it was written in a system, I don't think it's a language."

"Other linguists concluded the same," Fewmany said.

"And no provenance! You know how that irks me, Fewmany. If you plan to dispense of it, I will not broker it. I have a reputation to uphold," Remarque said.

"Your integrity is at no risk," Fewmany said. He picked up the manuscript and offered it to me. "'Tis yours, by right."

I stepped back.

"Hers?" Remarque asked.

"I'll explain the circumstances later. Secret, take it."

The brush of our hands, or the touch of the paper, sent a shock through my arm.

My manners, I remembered. "Thank you. This is unexpected, unnecessary."

"How did your mother obtain it?" Remarque asked.

"I don't know," I lied.

"When did she get it?" Remarque asked.

"I'm not certain," I lied again.

"Did she speculate of its origin, because if anyone could attest to—"

"Mr. Remarque, my mother, as you well know, was a terse woman. Why this manuscript was in her possession, I have no idea. What she thought of it, or what she might have known or speculated about its content, I cannot say," I said. Suddenly, I wanted nothing more than to be huddled under my quilts, sipping stale air until my thoughts went black.

To Remarque's protest, I wished them a good night and thanked Fewmany again for his gesture.

I rang for the carriage, walked downstairs, unlocked the door, and waited for Naughton to bring my cloak.

Moments later, Fewmany whisked into the hall as Naughton appeared from behind the stairs with my cloak on his arm.

Fewmany peered down at me. "As usual, I apologize for him, and if I caused you any distress or embarrassment, I am sorry."

"Neither of you meant harm," I said.

"Their absence is a wound thinly scabbed, no matter the time passed," he said.

I thwarted a laugh. To him, to anyone, I would have appeared to restrain a swell of grief. He had misread me completely. "Yes, of course," I said.

Naughton stood at the door. His presence wasn't that of a servant, detached, almost unseeing, but of someone observing.

"Shall I wait with you?" Fewmany asked.

"I will, sir," Naughton said as he held my cloak open.

"I'll be all right on my own, thank you." I slipped into the garment. "The carriage will be here soon enough."

The men looked at each other, then at me. They were hesitant to honor my wish, but they did. I stood outside with my back to the door, the manuscript pressed against my chest, and stared at the castle's outline. A scuffling noise turned my attention.

A fox approached the steps with a skulk of them behind her. All at once, they raised their heads in a cry, running in circles until the carriage frightened them away.

WHEN I HEARD THE KNOCK, I WAS STOKING THE STOVE'S COALS to heat the kettle and take the chill from the room. Rarely did anyone come to my door; Father if he came to take me out for the evening, one of the Misses Acutt in search of Sir Pouncelot, or Julia to say hello.

The visitor wasn't a neighbor. A man stood opposite me, his blond hair catching the light from the sconce near my doorway.

"My apologies. I must have the wrong address," he said.

"Nikolas. Come in," I said.

"Why, Miss Riven, what dark hair you have—again."

With the ease as if he'd done so before, he leaned in and kissed my cheek. I glanced behind him. His guard stood at the top of the stairs. Once Nikolas stepped inside, I closed the door. He looked exactly as he did the last time I saw him.

"Surprised you, have I?" he asked.

"You weren't expected back for months. Suddenly, here you are," I said.

I invited him to sit as I checked the kettle. On the hook by the door, he hung his coat over my cloak and walked to the windows. He peered into the falling darkness, then around my room. He stepped toward my night table, touched the carved stag, and smiled without comment.

This was only the third time he'd been in my private space—the first time after the fever, the second after my mother's death—and his presence felt more intimate now than it had then.

"A cozy little home you have," he said.

"Thank you. How was your return trip?" I asked.

While I prepared cheese sandwiches and tea, he stood at the cupboard and began to tell of his journey. He took the plate to the table when I served our cups. As we sat across from each other, Nikolas alive and well and glad to be home, I could make no sense of the conflict within me— the relief and the reluctance of seeing him after almost two years.

"Enough of that. And you?" he asked.

I told him what I'd written in my last letter, which I'd sent days before. Nothing unusual.

"I have to ask, because you haven't mentioned them. How is Old Woman? And Cyril? Is he impossibly still among us?"

For an instant, I thought to lie and soon regretted that I didn't. "I don't know."

"What do you mean you don't know?"

"Precisely that. I haven't been to the woods in some time."

"Since when?"

"The summer you left."

That impassive expression of his smoothed every line in his face. He was thinking, and as it had always been, I couldn't tell what, other than he was and deeply.

"Your eyes—the colors are lost behind the glass. Your hair—the silver hints at the roots, but the rest is covered black. Your heart—forgive me, but where did it go?"

I was shocked, then angry. "I merely said I don't know because I haven't gone, and you rush to undue judgments."

"Are they? I could hardly wait to surprise you, and your reaction was at best cordial. In letters I received, yes, you said you missed me sometimes, but I rarely felt any depth to it in the past months. And you don't seem at all concerned you have no idea what's become of Old Woman or Cyril, I know for whom you once had great affection, and I thought for me as well."

He knew nothing about my last visit to Old Woman. I had no desire to tell him then, or ever.

"I'm sorry to disappoint you," I said.

"What's happened to you?" he asked.

"What do you mean?"

"You're not the Secret I left."

"This you can say after a few words of conversation."

"You forget we knew each other beyond words, before you ever spoke one."

"I'm not that girl any longer," I said.

"Who are you, then?" he asked.

"A keeper of tales."

"Is that a title, or a pet name?"

"Pardon?"

"Nothing. That's *what*, not *who* anyway." He shook his head, pushed away from the table, and walked toward the door. "I'm sorry I came unannounced and certainly disappointed I harbored expectations of a happy reunion." He snatched his coat. "Perhaps we can see each other again under more convenient circumstances. That is, if you have time between now and when I leave for the quest." He fumbled with the key until the lock turned free.

The door closed with a harsh *thunk*.

A sob lodged in my chest.

It weighed heavy when Julia stopped me on the stairs the next morning to say she'd seen from her window "the handsomest carriage in the world with *four* horses" and her mother said the man she watched step out was the prince himself.

"Was it him? Your friend, Nikolas?" she asked.

"Yes, it was he," I said, although I wasn't so certain after our argument.

The pressure of tears returned when I agreed to meet him at a teahouse a week later. We'd never been so uncomfortable with each other. I tried to blame my behavior on a harrowing day—how tired I was after work—but he didn't believe me and said so. He tried to figure out what had caused the distance; I tried to keep it. As I watched him walk away, angry and hurt, I wondered if what was happening was how a friendship ended—once parallel paths, violently forked—each going toward whatever fate or possibility beckoned.

Still, the cry remained caught even after Father informed me he'd received an invitation to Nikolas's departure banquet, addressed to us both. Of course he was on the guest list; Father had risen to be an important man, thanks to Fewmany. My inclusion, under the circumstances, seemed to be a formality.

APRIL /37

ON THE TWENTY-THIRD OF APRIL, FEWMANY AND I HAD DINNER alone. After the meal, he suggested a walk through the grove, as the weather was so fine. Whistling what sounded like a folk song, with odd discordant notes, he poured two glasses of wine, handed one to me, and pulled a ring of keys from his pocket.

I hadn't been to the grove since the hunt. Had I asked for a key or his escort, the request would have been granted, but I'd kept away on purpose. The memory of what happened was still numinous. I felt expectant as he walked beside me across the green and unlocked the gate. A waxing moon shone down through a star-spattered sky. The breeze carried a warm, wet scent. I thought of the evening soon to come. A feast, the flesh. I hid an anticipatory smile behind a sip of wine.

He led us into the trees. We strolled for a long while, our conversation as easy as ever. A fox darted in the distance, yipping to others who answered.

"Do you recall the conversation we had in the map room some months ago?" he asked.

"I do."

"Is your answer the same, that if you could have anything, it would be a library like mine?"

"Yes."

"What if I were to give it to you?"

"What? Why?"

He halted his steps. The moon pierced through a gap in the branches, casting a glow in his eyes, against his Tell-a-Bell, within the red gem on his ring.

"If you allow me to obtain what I desire, I will give you my entire collection." He did not blink. "That, and your favorite objects from the rooms, a beautiful manor in which to hold them, and a guarantee to maintain the luxuries to which you've been accustomed here, until the end of your days."

My breath caught. My hands shook. My bottom lip fell, but I couldn't speak. Had he just . . . ?

Fewmany smiled softly. "Ah, no, Secret, what I propose is not of that sort, though I'm flattered."

I stood there, somewhat embarrassed by the assumption and—dare I admit it?—somehow disappointed. He waited for my response.

Finally, I asked, "What you desire, what makes you think I can help?"

He balanced his glass near a tree, laid his coat on the ground, and rolled his left sleeve to the elbow.

"Because I know you know where one of these is carved in stone," he said.

Burned into the underside of his arm—the symbol.

His palm closed when my fingertips brushed across his skin to the relief. He flinched as if my touch hurt him, but he didn't pull away. What I felt was not anger or betrayal, although both would come in time, nor did I feel manipulated and seduced, although I had been. In that moment, I felt trusted, not only because I knew he was about to reveal a secret but also because he was so suddenly, nakedly, vulnerable.

When I met his eyes, he drew back and covered himself.

"Who did that to you?" I asked.

"I did. Here's a tale of wonder for you," he said as he slipped into his coat and took up his glass. "When I was but a frog-voiced lad, I spent many a night exposed to the dreadful dark, but safe from the stinging strap. Once I ran farther than I'd ever run. I slept in the cradle of a tree. Morning brought hunger's gnaw—no strangers were we—but also light to see that I was lost. For a moment, I was also free. I spied a cottage from my nestie-bed and thought to sneak about for food. I found a comb of honey on the table and bread golden brown in the hearth.

"Hello, mousie, an old woman said to me. I jumped out of my skin and missed it in the landing. I meant to run, but I knelt before her and blubbered shamefully. Boohoo. Boohoo. Pitied me, she did, then fed me solid as a rock. I slept in her bed and filled my belly at the sun's summit and at its return to rest. I slept again that night on a pallet at her feet. Safer in darkness or light I'd never felt.

"I knew I couldn't stay, but I didn't wish to go. She knew, the old woman, she knew. Before she sent me away, she took me to her fire. 'Look at this stone,' she said, 'and see where the triangle points. Follow this symbol wherever you find it, child, for it will lead you to the riches you desire.' Then she had me exchange my worn shirt for a clean tunic and told me to watch for rabbits, who would guide the way.

"So I set off in the point's direction until I found myself in a village far from my own. A man seized me and tied me up like a pig. My father had put a bounty on me, a sum paid in my sister's rough hand in marriage. I returned to my toil, to what seemed like my loathsome fate, furious I'd been forced to stop my search. But then I found the jewels and coins the old woman had sewn into the tunic's hem and buried them in a secret place. With those, after a cutting clash with my father, I escaped." He rubbed the red gem in his ring.

"To where?"

"The unknown at first, back into the woods. I followed rabbits, which led me in circles until one left me at a vacant hut with a cold hearth and the symbol in the stone. I knew then there were others who knew of a treasure, for what else explained the old woman's words and what she gave me? In time, I made my fortune, and here I am. But I have never found what I truly wanted."

"The hoard," I said.

"'Tis but a name for what is hidden and yet to be claimed."

"What does that symbol have to do with the treasure you assume exists?"

"That, your father and I hypothesized together. As best I could, I described to Bren where I had seen the two identical stones, many miles apart. I sent men to scour the land, find them again, map the locations, and bring the stones to me. I believed they were an ancient guide to those who knew how to follow them."

"Has he always known what you sought?"

"Since I realized his particular talents would be useful and his fealty assured. 'Twas Bren who observed the symbols' proximity to a trading route and mines as well as battle sites from The Mapmaker's War and—in the way a true scholar apprehends what cannot be readily seen—recommended a careful survey of certain lands. Then—huzzah!—another was found, then another—some laid not far from an abandoned port or exhausted mine—enough to floor a few square feet of a small chamber."

If he knew how close one such old woman was, he didn't reveal it. Rothwyke was built on the land where The Mapmaker's War's first battle took place. There was no mine or abandoned port, but it was near an old trade route. Was it missed because there was no reason to look, based on their assumptions?

"If anyone can help you find what you suspect is lost, that person is my father. You know his tenacity well," I said.

"The best of qualities have their limits and their complements." His eyes met mine with a glimmer I couldn't read. Was it affection or certainty that reflected back? "We've come to know one another, my keeper of tales. Confide in me. You've met an old woman who keeps a stone."

"What makes you think so?" I asked, wanting to tease out how he could be sure.

"A sense beyond common ones. You were convincing in your denial as a girl, so guarded, as I would have been had someone asked of what I'd seen. We knew to keep quiet, didn't we? Through the years, my belief endured doubts but couldn't be shaken."

"Why not?"

"You are not an ordinary young woman, and this you have evinced time and again. 'Tis not only your intelligence and determination, but also your willingness to go beyond the limits of, let us say, convention. Then there is the mystery of your hair, such dramatic changes when you were younger, the growth, the silvering, as if you are endowed with a quality that defies the laws of Nature. I believe this to be so, because I have observed animals behave most strangely around you, as now, daring to come near, as if they have a special knowledge about you." He stamped his foot. The trees and shrubs rustled. Hoofs and paws scrambled. "I suspect you have powers, so to speak, latent ones, something I sensed, too, about your mother."

A sharp twinge ripped at my navel. I remained silent.

"Regardless, and aside from that," he said, "anyone can stumble on the stones, or like my men, be told where to search. However, I believe only the rarest persons are given hints to what greater things await."

His words, so veiled, but hiding nothing.

"How do you know I didn't merely stumble?" I asked.

He smirked with good humor. "Your own body betrays you. That was a draught for courage if I've ever seen one, and I've seen many."

I had taken a heavy mouthful of my wine, feeling the heat rise through my face.

"I'm not angry, Secret. You have no reason to be afraid," he said.

"So, what if I have?"

"Do you recall what I offered you this evening?"

"Yes."

"What I ask is that you do what my men and I cannot. Go to the places where the old women live. They will tell you how to follow the stones and how to reach the treasure. I will cover every expense for your travel and provide any means you require to obtain the information. All I have promised is yours—if you lead me there."

All he promised is mine, I thought. A library, a manor, the luxury. Study and solitude.

"Well then?" he asked.

"What makes you think one would reveal to me what wouldn't be revealed to you?"

Fewmany dipped his finger in his wine and traced it along the glass's edge. A singing chime rose high. "Now the mundane world meets the magical one. You are the adept here. What do the old tales forecast will happen to an innocent girl with a dead mother?"

I smiled because what he said was witty and smart, and I adored this side of him, the banter, how I felt in those moments a worthy match.

"What is said to happen to shrewd men with great fortunes?" I asked.

"'Twouldn't that depend on who tells the tale? After all, '*malum quidem nullum esse sine aliquo bono.*'"

"There is, to be sure, no evil without something good."

We grinned at each other. Mine ebbed when an owl hooted, and I knew in my bones the call was meant as a message.

On the walk back to the manor, I declined the offer of another glass of wine, as it was nearly midnight. He rang for the carriage and waited with me until it arrived.

The coachman remained seated as Fewmany opened the door. He offered his hand to help me inside. My palm fell into his firm warm clutch. A jolt surged through my arm.

There is a force between us, I thought as I settled on the cushion.

"You understand what we've discussed is with utmost confidence," he said.

"Of course."

"We'll talk again next month," he said.

I'd forgotten for the moment my holiday had begun so the manor could be prepared for the ball. "Perhaps I will see you before then."

"Oh-ho, yes," he said with a conspiratorial grin.

The door shut. As the carriage pulled away, we waved good-bye.

DIARY ENTRY 24 APRIL /37

Margana did one last fitting on my costume but refused to let me stand in a mirror to see until the final touches are complete. I also brought an old gown for new trimmings. Nikolas's banquet is in six weeks. No matter the stale blood between us, I won't fail to see him off.

I do feel strange today, as if I've been through a shock, which I suppose I have. What Fewmany asked of me! To at last know the reason they questioned me that night. Of course they didn't explain why when I was a child.

What great trust he has bestowed—to tell me, to include me.

The symbol joins us, has always joined us.

Whatever skepticism I hold about an actual dragon's hoard, there is surely some core truth of a treasure, since it so often has appeared in myths and tales. Father's theories might address the mystery—a warrior's plunder, a lost mine. A reasonable explanation.

But what if Fewmany is wrong that the symbols lead the way? What if this is an esoteric matter, like the symbols in his alchemy texts, figurative rather than literal?

Still, what if he's correct? How is it possible no one has achieved what he aspires to do? There is a first for everything, isn't there? Imagine if I can aid this. No greater find has ever been discovered.

Later: nightmare.

A man stood before me but didn't reveal his face. From his throat to his groin was a gnarled scar, desperately knit. The wound destroyed his navel. I knew his name but couldn't speak it. He was my husband and my father—but not both at once. I reached out to him and wept with grief for the agony he endured and for a grief that was my own. I loved him and he suffered with pain I couldn't imagine, pain for which I knew I was responsible. I touched my hands, my lips, wet with blood.

This man—I dreamed of him before, during the fever. A warrior with a gold breastplate, the father of a child dancing at a ritual fire. The child's mother, dancing, too, costumed as the Red Dragon.

This man—no, please, let this be imagination, madness—I'm remembering the visit to my grandmother's, the day of the picnic, the first day I heard beyond hearing and saw beyond seeing.

I followed the bees into the hollow tree, and one told me of the terrified girl running through the woods, three men chasing her, tying her to the tree, and the man who tried to help her, horribly wounded the length of his body, and his wolf digging him up from the dead.

Now I'm thinking of the queen bee's three stings on my forehead as my mother tried to claw me from the dark hollow . . .

I don't want to, but I feel now as I did after the fever.

The ancient language I awoke speaking. The dreams and ruptures I've suffered since I was a child. That arcane manuscript now hidden in my wardrobe. There is a link among them.

At the center of it all is the symbol, isn't it?

I ROUSED TO A TAPPING, THEN REALIZED IT WAS A KNOCK. MY eyes ached and my head felt stuffed with gray. I wanted to lie quietly and let whoever was there go away, but another round shook my door. As I slipped on a robe, I noticed my diary was open on my desk.

There in the hall was Naughton holding a package.

"I'm sorry, Miss. Did I wake you?" he asked.

"Yes, but I should have been up by now. I never sleep so late." The scent of cinnamon buns wafted up the stairs, what Mrs. Woodman made at the end of every week. This confused me as much as Naughton's presence.

He handed the package to me. "I decided to deliver it instead of sending a courier."

I thanked him and expected him to leave. He did not.

"He's been in ebullient spirits these past few days but no reason has been divulged. The staff is inquisitorial why that might be," Naughton said.

I was surprised he'd be so forward, but then I realized he'd never come to my apartment for any reason. For a moment, I was amused. "Are there rumors?" I asked.

"There is speculation of an agreement of sorts."

"Nothing of the kind they perhaps imagine, I assure you."

He smiled with apparent relief, but his eyes were troubled.

"What is it, Naughton?"

"There have been others."

"I don't understand."

"Others who've captured his interest, on whom he has pinned a hope. When they have failed him—as they have, although I cannot attest to how—their falls from favor have been hard."

"You have no idea what's been spoken between us," I said. A flare of jealousy scorched through me. Others?

"I don't need to know, Miss. This dance I've watched before, even when I didn't see his partner. You would do well to take your leave and never return." His brown eyes carried a look of warning.

"I will not. Cannot."

"You need make no decision at the moment, but do take some time to think. Good day," he said, bowing slightly.

I shut the door, laid the package on the table, and stared at my desk. I remembered the dream I'd had the night before—but no, it had *not* been. Mrs. Woodman baked on her off day. After the terrible dream, I'd slept through an entire day and the next night.

An anxious thrum rose in my blood. I read the note folded under the package's ribbon.

Worth the wait, my keeper of tales.

fm

Wrapped in the paper was a book. The first and last pages didn't bear his mark. It seemed immaculate, a quarto still uncut, thin paper protecting the brilliantly colored illustrations—a frog wearing a crown, a girl with impossibly long hair, a fox chasing a hen . . .

I'd seen the book before.

Not in the library, but in my father's house. It was the same book Fewmany brought the night he questioned me about the symbol, the pages laid open on the table near the bowl and scissors. At first, I laughed as if this were an old joke between us—oh, he kept that old thing all these years, what a misunderstanding that was—but there was a hitch. The laugh verged on a cry.

Even at the age of eleven, I knew the book had been meant as a bribe, withheld because I did not, and could not, tell him what he wanted to hear. Now it was a reward. Then, if I had told him the location of a symbol, my guidance would have been a simple answer to a simple question. Now I wasn't unwitting. I knew what he wanted and why, and he believed I could do what he couldn't, as a girl wandering the woods, at the mercy of crones, alone and motherless.

My eyes shut.

Mother.

What had she known as she stood silent the night they questioned me? What did she know as she created the cipher, before she died?

When I looked down, two wispy antennae emerged from the top of the book's spine. The silverfish crept across the table. As it crawled over the edge, I watched dozens of them stream from my wardrobe to the floor. They skittered as I approached, disappearing into cracks along the walls.

There was no escape for me.

A yielding calm quieted my pulse as I opened the wardrobe to get the cipher and arcane manuscript. Logic wouldn't bridge what had just occurred any more than it would explain what was to come in the hours, weeks, and months ahead.

I pushed everything away on my desk and stared at the cipher. On a sheet of paper, in three columns, I named each drawing—flower, boat, etc. Then I listed the letters from the large circle and copied the strange alphabet revealed behind the small one. I realized each drawing was meant to correspond to a letter in my language.

What was the connection?

I remembered the one-sentence clue my mother left behind: "A map is to space as an alphabet is to sound." I recited this again and again, attentive not to the meanings of the words but the sounds of them. I held the image of a map in my mind—and what came forth was the word, the *sound* of it—in the ancient language I spoke when I roused from the fever.

There was something familiar to this connection between image and word. I pondered how I communicated with creatures and plants. What came first was an image, connected to thoughts and feelings, and then a translation into language.

I studied the drawings and named the wholes and parts aloud in the

ancient language. Flower. Petal. Stem. Leaf. Pistil. Stamen. I tested com-
binations of letters and sounds with the first sentence of the manuscript.
I aligned a letter in my native alphabet to a drawing. A sound within the
foreign word matched the letter. BOAT matched with *B*, LEAF with *E*,
JUG with *G*. The window in the smaller circle revealed symbols in the
ancient language.

I understood how the cipher worked. The sound of a letter in my
alphabet mirrored the sound from the other.

Suddenly, the manuscript's first line came clear: THIS WILL BE THE
MAP OF YOUR HEART, OLD WOMAN.

I skimmed the first page, the mention of learning shapes—circle, triangle, square—a question posed, AOIFE, WHO TAUGHT YOU TO DRAW A
MAP? That name—*Ee-fah*—pealed through my veins. Further, I read . . .
Aoife hid and played in the woods. She had no interest in what entertained most girls. She drew the hidden realms of bees and ants.

SEE, YOU BECAME A MAPMAKER.

She was an apprentice. Her elderly adept, Heydar, gave her a waywiser. Prince Wyl built a tower to ease her work. She traveled through
the kingdom, charting. At the bank of a river, men emerged from the
forest.

YOU STUDIED THE FIVE MEN IN YOUR DESCENT. BLUE COATS,
WHITE BELTS, FLAXEN LEGGINGS, TANNED SHOES.

My body shook with the force of a seizure. A noise made me look
up. There on my windowsill sat a crow with a narrow bald stripe across
his chest. I'd seen the scarred bird before, years ago, as I spoke to that
strange little peeping child, Harmyn . . .[18]

A crack split me from groin to crown. All the ruptures and dreams I
wanted to forget streamed into the gap.

I remember stumbling down the stairs, then falling on the building's
doorstep. Passersby stared. "Soused—this time of day!" someone said.

Above, hawks and crows circled; between, pigeons and doves cooed;
and below, a mouse and a cat scampered at my feet. A dog put his head
in my lap.

Follow me, he said without saying.

My right foot dragged behind my left. People glanced as if I were
afflicted and gave me space to clear them. I recognized a shop here and
there, then could make no sense of the sights. I was lost.

The dog led me through wards. Buildings in disrepair, drains spilling into the streets, alleys full of refuse. A newsbox report—mining village in Seronia—dragon menace—laid waste—charred bodies. Tell-a-Bells chimed and the people's tolls rang out in response. I tripped on a buckled sidewalk and saw a figure crouched in a doorway dressed in worn clothes. The child looked up, with a cracked yellow spectacle lens. Suddenly, I called out a name, a question, a memory.

"Harmyn?"

A cluster of garrulous women walked by, and after their languid passing, the area was vacant. I looked left and right but saw only people and horses.

More voices, then, some clear, some not. "You lost, girl?" "She looks good enough to eat, and I'm hungry." Animals around me, my guards, my guides.

At the town's edge, the dog prodded me forward. In the distance, ahead of the trees, was the stone wall, nowhere near complete.

At the woods' margin, through the young leaves, a stag emerged, the scars on his shoulder raised. The dog nuzzled me, then ran. The stag led me through the trees to a huge rounded rock, a marker for this particular place and a guide that pointed to another, which I sensed I'd seen before.

Feel for the groove. Trace its line off the rock, past the trees, and into the glade, the stag said.

I approached a cottage with blue shutters. I called out but there was no answer. Inside, the hearth had warm ash, but no fire, no embers. I sat in the shadows next to a cauldron, the impression of the symbol under my fingers.

I felt abandoned, then furious.

I ran. The woods tore at me as I plunged deeper than I'd ever been. I ran from what stalked, then chased me, even as I slept, ever since I was a child.

Exhausted, I sat on a dead log. I stared at my hands, which felt gloved by another skin.

"So, you've returned," he said.

I looked toward the voice and saw a solid shadow. Part of me filled with the instinct to flee, the other with the peace of surrender.

"You cannot be alone now. Whom do you wish to help you?" he asked.

I searched myself for a name. So many names, near and far, past and present. Faces shifted like mist in my mind's eye.

"Nikolas," I said.

The owl above my head screeched. Old Man carried me to a giant hollowing tree. He nested me within, the space softened with his large cloak. The warm wild smell was a comfort, as well as the familiar touch of whiskers and small paws. Cyril's.

I stirred at the sound of hoofbeats and footsteps. I heard the voices of two men, which first panicked, then soothed me. One gave instructions to the other one.

When my body was moved, I was too weak to fight or assist. "Secret," a man said. "I'm here." Then consciousness spiraled away.

I AWOKE THRASHING IN A STRANGE BED.

Hands pressed into my arm. "Do you understand me?" Elinor asked, her eyes heavy with concern.

"Of course I understand you." I glanced around. "This is the spare room. Why am I here?"

"You've been ill, talking nonsense, breaking into rigors every few hours."

Oh no, I thought as fragments came back to me. She put a cup of water in my hands and went out to find my father.

He had the same worried look on his face as he did when I awoke from the fever almost five years before. I had no doubt there was a link between the two.

"That was the worst case of acute dyspepsia I've ever seen," Father said lightly.

"What do you mean?"

"Prince Nikolas brought you here after your dinner. You were quite sick, but it was later evident the vomiting and sweating weren't because of a bad meal."

"What's the date?"

"The third."

I sighed. I'd lost several days and missed the ball.

"I took the liberty to inform Fewmany. He said you are on holiday through next week but not to rush your recovery."

"That's all?"

"He mentioned your understanding." Father smiled, but it was restrained. "We'll talk of it later. For now, I expect you to stay here until you're well. Elinor and I have worked out an arrangement. Oh, and the prince should be here to see about you this evening, as he has these nights past." He seemed to resist the temptation to say more.

I nodded. I was exhausted, in no position to argue, although I wanted to be in my own home alone to make sense of things. After a bath, I lay in bed thinking, as Elinor checked on me throughout the day. She served Father and me dinner in the room. Soon after we'd eaten, Nikolas arrived.

As he walked up the stairs, I heard him refuse Elinor's offer of tea. He knocked on the half-open door before he entered, then sat in the chair nearby without a word. The look in his eyes was wounded and worried.

"I'm sorry," I said.

"For what?" he asked in a clipped tone.

"For being so cold since your return and forgetting I have no truer friend than you."

"That sounded sincere."

"It was."

He sighed.

"I remember nothing after I was inside the tree. How did you find me? What happened?" I asked.

"An owl came into my room and dropped strands of silver-tipped black hair on my bed. It flew at my door, and there was no question you were in trouble. I had my horse saddled and left without a guard—you know what a breach that is—and the owl led me to the woods. Old Man said you called for me. There you were in that tree, with Cyril, barely conscious. Old Man told me nothing and left me alone as you became sicker. I didn't know what else to do but take you home to your father. I managed to get you on the horse even though you fought me as if you feared for your life and I couldn't understand a word you said.

"So, I told your father we met for a late dinner which hadn't agreed with you. I think he thought you were drunk, because he brought in a bucket and a glass of willow powder. He tried to look stern, but I believe I saw him hide a grin," Nikolas said.

"At last his good girl had a lapse," I said, thinking Father might not be so amused if he knew what limits of propriety I'd violated since I left his house.

"After you finally fell asleep, I returned home. I stayed awake through the night wondering what happened but certain you hadn't gone mad. The owl, Old Man. No, something uncanny was afoot."

The time is coming to bring the pieces together, I remembered from the dream months before.

"Just now, when my carriage stopped at your door, a fox bolted into the alley. A murder of crows sits on your rooftop, and beetles are crawling over the front steps. They're here for you, aren't they? Do you know why?"

I looked into his eyes. I stifled a cry of recognition. He was still the blond boy with the gold cup I met long ago, the same boy I led into the woods who believed me when I said I could speak to creatures and plants, whom I trusted and adored above all others.

"I don't know why. Not yet. I don't want to speak too loudly. Come closer," I said. He pulled the chair next to the bed. "What I'm going to tell you is what I know now, which is a part of a much greater story."

"Very well, then," he said.

I tried my best to think clearly, to connect one thing to the next.

"Do you remember when I told you about the cipher my mother made and the arcane manuscript she didn't translate, the one that went missing?"

He nodded.

"I found the manuscript at last"—I didn't tell him the details then; this was complicated enough—"and several days ago, I broke the cipher and read the first pages."

"Yes . . ."

"And do you remember when I was horribly sick with that fever and my hair began to turn silver? I'd just turned fourteen."

He rubbed the scar on his right hand, as he had that day he came to see I wasn't dead, that same wound healing, scabbed. "I do."

"I told you then I had strange dreams, but I didn't describe them. There were three I still remember clearly. One was of a ritual dance at a fire, with a child dressed in white and someone dressed as a red dragon. In another, I was shackled and a man tried to rape me and somehow I escaped. And the last—I dreamed of a spiral stair and a cave filled with treasure."

"Go on," he said.

"What I didn't tell you was I awakened able to speak a language I didn't know. For days, I could think, but not speak, in our native one. Of course my mother knew the strange tongue, but she didn't explain why I suddenly spoke it," I said.

"When I couldn't understand what you were saying when I found you—"

"Almost certainly I was speaking it." I took a deep breath. "But before all that—before I found the cipher or had the fever—when we were eleven, I drew a symbol for you I'd seen in a dream. You didn't recognize it, but something rippled between us, some perception for which we had no words," I said.

"It was made of shapes—a triangle, square, and circle, with an opening in the middle," he said.

I nodded. "I've had other dreams before that and since, all vivid and potent. And I've had what I call ruptures, which happen when I'm awake. The ruptures are physically painful, aching and tearing through my body, and images always come with them. Those and the dreams—there's no other way to describe them other than . . . memories that aren't mine."

There, I said it. I named what I couldn't before.

Nikolas remained quiet.

"I don't know what the manuscript is yet—a history or a biography—and it's written in the language from the fever. Strangely, the person who wrote it used the pronoun 'you' throughout, not 'I' or 'she,' as if she were addressing herself. The subject appears to be a woman named Aoife, who was a mapmaker, and a friend of Wyl."

He nudged back in his chair. "Wyl?"

"One of Ailliath's early kings. There's mention in those first pages of a prince named Raef," I said.

"Ancient history, then. Raef was Wyl's younger brother.[19] Who is this Aoife?"

"I don't know other than what I've read thus far. She was from a noble family. Her father and Wyl helped her to become a mapmaker's apprentice."

"I've never heard or read her name. She would have been alive around the time of the war," Nikolas said.

"The *Mapmaker's* War," I said.

We both shivered and rubbed our arms.

"What I said about the memories that aren't mine . . ." I said.

"Yes?"

"When I've had those moments, it's as if my very being is filled with thoughts and feelings and sights and sounds I can't attribute to my own experiences or imagination. The moments are—visceral—as if something has been unleashed from deep within.

"I'm not insane, and I'm not lying, Nikolas. I've remembered three moments that appear in the manuscript. A few months ago, I had a rupture when I handled a waywiser—that's a mapmaking instrument—remembering an old man's hand. The day of Charming's wedding, when we went to the tower, I had a rupture then, too, there was a man with green eyes—the manuscript describes Wyl as having green eyes. And then after the summer grand ball many years ago, I had a dream of men in blue coats, and Aoife describes them on the last page I read."

"Those were your first words to me. 'I dream of blue men,'" Nikolas said.

I shut my eyes to sudden tears. Yes. He remembered. The bed shifted. When I looked up, he was leaning against the mattress.

"What about the symbol?" he asked.

"It's real. There's one in Old Woman's cottage at the hearth. I expect to read of it in the manuscript. At this point, I don't think the mention of Aoife learning shapes—circle, triangle, square—is mere coincidence."

"So, the confusion when I found you?"

"Too much converged at once. I was lost in whatever returned," I said. "It's more complicated, still."

"Well?"

At that moment, I decided not to mention what Fewmany had asked of me. There was too much to explain, too much I hadn't sorted out for myself.

However, Nikolas needed to know what Old Woman told me the last time I saw her.

"Not long after you left for the goodwill visits, I saw Old Woman. She revealed things to me I didn't want to know. She said she's from a people called the Guardians and that she's an elder who volunteered to live alone in the woods. These elders are supposed to help those who need safety," I paused, thinking of Fewmany and the woman who'd given him refuge, "but they're also meant to watch for children who were foretold in their legends. She said we—you and I—are among them. We're here to 'shift a balance,' but she didn't say how or for what reason. She even mentioned the arcane manuscript. She knew it was important and that my mother was meant to translate it."

"But then the manuscript and the cipher were left for you," he said.

"I don't know why." I shuddered again when I remembered what else Old Woman told me. "She also spoke of a legend about a woman who was exiled and escaped a war."

Nikolas held the scar on his hand as if it hurt. "Anyone else who heard this would think you've lost your mind. But I don't. I'm not surprised."

I waited.

"Remember the night we met?" he asked.

"Of course. When I first saw you, I thought your eyes were the color of myth"—I watched Nikolas smile, as if touched—"and you invited me to play and took me to hide in the meeting chamber."

"Before then. I saw you, so small, so silent, there under the shadow of those adults, Fewmany and your parents, and I walked up and said to them you kept a secret."

"Yes. That's when I knew my name, beyond what I was given."

"You never told me that. Well, what I said then—I didn't understand why I said it, only that I must." He paused. "Among my many attributes, it appears I am prescient."

I laughed. I wanted to touch him, but a familiar hesitancy rose up. This wasn't the first time I'd felt like a beaten dog who fears the tenderness she wants because the moment could cruelly turn. As I tried to force my reach for him, he wrapped his hand on top of mine. I leaned to rest my cheek on his shoulder.

"Whatever is to come, I will not fail you," he said. I nodded. Where the queen bee had stung me, he kissed my brow as if he'd sealed a promise.

WHEN I RETURNED TO MY APARTMENT, THE EIGHTH OF MAY, nothing looked disturbed. Placed on my table was a note from Margana, who had tried to deliver my costume and banquet gown and had returned them to her shop for safekeeping. The windows were closed. The stove's ashes hadn't been cleaned. The cipher and the manuscript were where I left them.

Those two items, and my diary, I stuffed into my satchel, intending to store them in the safest place I knew.

I walked through the northwest wards and along the edge of town. In the distance, I saw the wall's low rise and avoided the construction as I crossed the green and stepped into the woods.

Cyril the Squirrel, once red, now gray, too old to be alive, was there waiting. He led me to a friend I hadn't seen in so long, the great tree with the spiraling trunk—Reach. He greeted me with a low drone, which hummed in my feet. As it had always been, his voice was too deep for me to understand, but I sensed what he conveyed.

I've missed you, too, I said without saying.

I continued on, finding the path which led to the glade, and crossed through to the garden beds, filled with vegetables. I could hear the random noises and smell hints of the sheep, goats, and hens kept near the cottage. When I looked toward the door, Old Woman stepped out, tying a blue kerchief over her white hair.

"Secret," she said as she took me in her arms.

"I'm sorry," I said, holding back tears.

"All is forgiven. If you're here now, something has happened. Come in," she said.

We sat at her table. I looked toward the hearth. The symbol carved in stone was clearly visible.

"From where do you come—the true home you left?" I asked in the ancient language of the fever and the manuscript, which by then I suspected was spoken by the Guardians.

"First, how did the tongue come to you?" Old Woman asked, speaking it back to me.

"The fever years ago, and the manuscript is written in it." I took the arcane manuscript from my satchel. "It's the one my mother was asked to translate. I broke the cipher she left. I can read it now."

"So, there *was* an early written form of our language, as we were told in our legends. You have it there. Incredible. To your question, well, I wasn't specific when you were a child. You knew I came from a village outside of Ailliath, and what my life was like there, but I didn't divulge fully. Do you remember the myths I told you?"

I nodded.

"Then you'll recall Egnis the Red Dragon found a child in a river. She roused the infant back to life with her fiery breath, and with Ingot the Gold Dwarf and Incant the White Wisp, raised the child they called Azul. When the Orphan came of age, determined to join their humankind, Azul made friends and built villages throughout the known world where people could live in cooperation and peace. They declared themselves the Guardians, who vowed to protect the Red Dragon and all she surveyed.

"I am a descendant, born and raised in one of the few surviving settlements. One of the few, because many generations before, the people split in their opinions about the way they lived. There were those who believed our settlements should be insular, everyone keeping only among themselves. The rest believed others should be welcome to live among them or that the Guardians should go out to share their ways. In time, it was said, the outsiders who were allowed in brought trouble and those who left the settlements were drawn into the troubled world.

"Then, slowly, between that and many wars, the settlements disappeared, and the ones that endured became islands among themselves.

"In spite of this, some traditions remained. Since the founding of the first settlements, Guardian elders were asked to go within themselves and see if they were called to serve beyond our hidden borders. They were needed to give safety and comfort to those who were lost and searching, and later to watch for the children to come, the ones foretold.

"And here we are," Old Woman said. "I'm sure you want to know what is about to happen, but I can't tell you. I'm here to give you guidance and haven. Everything is known, but not revealed to one and all."

"Possibly, the manuscript will help," I said. I told her I'd read the first few pages, then repeated everything I'd told Nikolas about the manuscript, the language that came with the fever, the dreams and ruptures. "There's one other thing I must tell you. What you said about Fewmany—that he was buying land and taking any symbols he found, but no one knew why?"

She nodded.

"He wants the hoard. The dragon's treasure."

"Why does he think the symbol has a connection to it?" she asked.

"It doesn't?"

"What did he tell you?"

I repeated the story he told me about the old woman who found him in the woods, how he'd tried to follow the symbols and was caught before he could trace where they led.

Old Woman rested her forehead in her hands. "She meant to guide him to a settlement, not to riches like gold. Oh, we take that risk so rarely. She sensed something about him, about how dire matters were for him."

I felt a shadow of fate turn its heel on the boy Lesmore Bellwether, but my compassion didn't eclipse my anger at the man he became. "What about the symbol?"

"It connects to the realm, where there is a treasure, but the way is indirect," Old Woman said.

"So, the treasure mentioned in the myths—it's real."

"Both in the literal and figurative senses, yes."

"And does a dragon guard it?"

"Gold has value only to humans."

"That's not an answer to my question. Is it protected?"

"My people are protecting *her*, not the treasure. There are Guardians who remain alert to signs of trouble. They can't live in the realm, but they can cross into it, and if the boundary is breached, they respond. We believe if there was any attempt to injure or kill her, the consequences would be catastrophic. As the myths tell us, 'All would dry in endless light or all would rot in endless dark,'" she said.

"It's a myth. A fragment of truth shrouded in a story."

Old Woman looked at me for a long moment. "Well, you may soon be called to find out what that truth is."

AS SCHEDULED, I RETURNED TO THE LIBRARY ON THE ELEVENTH of May. When I entered the manor, there were no signs of the ball, and the usual doors were locked when I checked them.

On the table was a letter from Fewmany, who was away on a trip and hoped I was feeling well and asked to see me for dinner one week hence. I wrote a short reply to accept the invitation and belatedly thank him for the storybook.

Naughton served morning tea with his typical formality.

"I haven't discussed this with him yet, but I'm going away soon," I said as he poured a cup near my hand.

"Taken my heed?"

"I will say your advisement is duly noted."

"Very good, Miss," he said.

In the days which followed, Old Woman promised to give me shelter if I chose to go into hiding. Father, who poured forth the historical minutiae of the "endeavor" with which he'd been involved, was curious to learn how my help would advance, as he put it, "the acquisition." Nikolas, who by then knew what was asked of me, wished I could remove myself from any involvement but understood I couldn't do so without danger.

"You must trust me to figure this out. I must engage with him, but with guile," I said.

"That isn't in your nature," Nikolas said.

"You'd be surprised what's in my nature," I replied.

Understand this, descendants and survivors: My outward calm was a veneer. Even though the task was inevitable, I couldn't bring myself to read another word of the arcane manuscript out of fear of what would be revealed. I knew to refuse Fewmany's request would have imperiled me and possibly my father, considering the knowledge we both possessed. Regardless of my protective feelings, I contained a growing anger toward Father for what he'd done to allow, even encourage, Fewmany's interest in me.

And what of that interest? How confused I was, questioning whether Fewmany's regard for me had been genuine or a ruse, and in light of that, wondering if my once dark instincts about him had been enchanted away.

The evening we met for dinner, Fewmany's spirits soared high. I was careful to give no impression anything was different between us. We didn't discuss our business until we were alone, in the map room, as I requested.

With glasses of wine in hand, we stood over a large map on which he'd plotted each location where a symbol had been taken, those where it was likely stones were placed, and others that were still speculative. I remembered seeing maps in Father's study similarly dotted, but I had no idea what was marked. The reach extended through more than twenty kingdoms, heavily in those closest to Ailliath. I saw Geo-Archeo Historian Bren Riven's influence then; the concentration was to the north and east where The Mapmaker's War had spread more than a thousand years before.

Fewmany said he'd provide several maps to remote locations, places not yet explored but where he was certain stones had been placed. If I found an old woman, but she wouldn't divulge information, I was to travel onward.

He planned to send me out with a group of trusted men, for protection and to attend my accommodations, but that I protested. I believed it would be better for me to go alone. There might be less notice if I traveled as a young woman going to visit my grandmother—the story I planned to use—than a woman on a journey with men, to whom she had no relation. On this point, he was reluctant, which I sensed was not a matter of trust but insurance. I had value. My loss might cost him his prize.

It was agreed I'd receive an allowance for travel and write if I needed more. He expected I'd keep him apprised of my whereabouts but be cautious to conceal my purpose. When he asked how soon I could depart, I determined within three weeks, which would allow me to move from my apartment and tend my preparations. At that moment, Fewmany gave me leave. I need not worry about the library until I came home again.

He extinguished the lamp. I took our glasses, drinking the last drop from mine. We walked out through the hidden door, which he locked, and crossed the library.

All I have to do is give him what he wants, and this is mine, I thought. If I find it. When.

But I understood the task I agreed to do for him was part of a greater call I could no longer avoid. I felt no peace in this, only the dread of a reckoning.

I set the glasses on the table and brushed my hand along the surface. That I would be leaving struck me with a piercing sadness.

"That seat is yours when you return. The manor will be empty without you, Secret," he said.

I nodded. He pulled the bell, opened the door, and walked downstairs with me. Mutt greeted us in the hall. I scratched his head. He licked my fingers and said, *You will not be alone. It is known who you are.*

At the door, I reached into my pocket for the key, but Fewmany had already unlocked it with his. Reluctantly I held out mine. "I won't need this," I said.

He took it from my hand. "With thanks."

"I expect to see you at the banquet, so let us delay our farewell," I said.

"Good night, then, my keeper of tales, my seeker of treasure," he said. He closed the door behind me with a bow.

Moments later, the carriage arrived with Naughton standing on the tailboard. He had never done something like this. He helped me to my seat and held the door's handle for a long moment.

"Thank you, Naughton," I said.

"In your service, Miss. He said you will be away for some time. Be watchful while greater forces guard and guide you."

"I didn't know you were superstitious," I said.

"I'm not." He took the cravat from his neck and gave it to me, then shut me inside.

When the carriage entered town, I held the cloth toward the street's lamplight. The silk was a certain shade of blue.

DIARY ENTRY 23 MAY /37

As of today, my post service cubby is closed. Personal belongings (diary, some books, old drawings, some clothing, shoes, the carved stag, the ingots, my own silver) are stored with Old Woman. A few other things I've moved to Father's, but the rest I'm giving away. Jane Sheepshank and Dora Thursdale were glad to have the table, bench, and dishes. Mrs. Woodman took the wardrobe. The Misses Acutt delighted in the prints on my wall and invited me to help hang them, which required rearranging several paintings and embroidered pieces. Mrs. Elgin wants the bed for the children.

This afternoon, I gave Julia four illustrated books and the carved blue bird. She was so overcome, she threw her arms around me and kissed my cheek. I'd never held a child before. I will miss her when I'm away.

Although I'd prefer to stay with Old Woman until I leave, it's better I spend the days before my departure at Father's. Nights, to be precise. It is strange to sleep in the spare room, which was always closed off, waiting for no one.

My days I spend walking in the woods with Cyril. I have become soft and my sensitivities are blunted. I will require all my strengths for what's ahead.

And I broke my spectacles. On purpose. I must also see clearly again.

JUNE /37

THE EVENING OF NIKOLAS'S DEPARTURE BANQUET, THE SIXTH OF June, Father and I stood at the front door waiting for the carriage. I thought of the moments before the summer grand ball long ago, how I watched my mother preen him and how happy I thought others might assume us to be.

Father grinned. "I'd almost forgotten the true colors of your eyes. I find myself focusing from one to the other like a stranger."

"You look handsome," I said. "But for the ring, you appear to be an eligible swain."

He hid his left hand behind his right. A whiff of perfume irritated my nose. A clatter and clop slowed on the street outside.

"The carriage is here," he said.

At the castle, in the Great Hall, we made our way into the crowd. Father stopped to greet acquaintances every few steps. I waved to former classmates I recognized, then bolted from him when I saw two friendly faces.

"Charlotte! Muriel!" I called above the murmuring clusters. They approached with smiles, both dressed in stylish gowns.

"The silver is gone," Charlotte said.

"Has it grown black again?" Muriel asked.

"Hidden, is all. I didn't know you were attending," I said.

"The conservatory allowed me leave for the occasion," Muriel said.

"I decided to return home a bit sooner to attend wedding preparations. You'll receive your invitation any day now," Charlotte said.

I knew I'd be far away then, but I decided not to say so. They would get letters explaining I was sent away on a matter for the library. "How wonderful, Charlotte. I hope you're very happy."

A fanfare of gleaming horns announced the ceremony's start. A voice called us to find our seats and reminded those with Tell-a-Bells to switch them to silence. My friends and I parted. Father waved at me from the front row below the dais. Several yards away, Fewmany shook hands with a man who must have been a king. Something had been opened or sealed between them; I could tell by the pleased expression on Fewmany's face.

I paused. Two years prior, I sat across from him in his office, the blind menagerie behind me, fear viscous in my blood, curiosity thicker. I had no material power like noblemen and magnates, but an intangible one he sensed, he stalked, he seized.

What might he own with the wealth a treasure as great as a dragon's hoard could bring?

As I stood there, my eyes fixed on him until he looked at me and smiled, I couldn't deny my affection. Impossibly, I considered that man a friend, and I hated him for it.

Once the audience was seated, there was a procession of dignitaries and attendants, dressed and coiffed almost as finely as they would be for a coronation. Nikolas's sisters, Pretty and Charming, along with their children and husbands, placed themselves in front of cushioned chairs. The King and the Queen wore bejeweled crowns and purple velvet robes. Their faces alit with pride when they saw the last man walk across the dais.

Nikolas turned to the cheering crowd. He wore dark green fall front breeches tucked into high black boots. An old leather jerkin covered his torso. Around his waist was a thick belt held closed by a copper buckle. From his shoulders draped a purple robe edged in golden silk. The sapphire clasp at his throat glinted with a stray catch of light. The crown disappeared into the gold of his hair but made comical spikes at the top of his head.

How strange it was to see him then as the prince I had never known.

He searched the faces below and didn't cease until he met my eyes. Nikolas bowed his head ever so gently, an almost unnoticeable gesture, which made those near me turn to look nonetheless. I nodded back, feeling as I had the first time I met him, warm and light.

The ceremony continued with speeches and a ritual involving wine. King Aeldrich at last stood.

To the right of the dais, a man sat poised with a pen and ink. A bound book lay open before him. He was the official chronicler that evening. As was our kingdom's tradition, that night was the first time the king would tell the people of his own quest taken many years before.

To a hushed crowd, King Aeldrich told his tale:

For almost a year, I traveled across many kingdoms which spread beyond our own. Some of the clues my father gave me were helpful, while others proved to steer me from course. One day, I came upon a great hill, where I rested. I heard a thunderous rumbling in the valley far beyond. For a moment, I thought a storm was coming. But I saw a puff of smoke rise slowly, slowly, from a line of trees.

I knew I was close. I took my horse to the valley and left him some distance from where I believed the dragon was. I approached with only my sword to protect me.

I wove my way among the trees. The rumbling grew louder. I knew it was the beast stomping his way to his cave. Carefully, I passed through the brush and peered at him. Such a creature I had never seen! It loomed above me like the towers on this castle. I watched him for a moment to study his movement. It was slow but powerfully strong.

Suddenly, he lifted his head. His nostrils flared. It had caught my scent. Slowly, he turned around, these tiny eyes scanning the brush oh so carefully.

Then I had an idea. I could climb a tree, and as it tried to get me, I could slice across his chest and my scale would fall. I scampered to the closest tree. With sword in hand, I managed to climb several yards from the ground.

"Dragon!" I called. "Here I am, you odious beast!" It viciously tore among the limbs trying to impale me with a claw, finally wounding my leg in the attempt. I held to the tree with my left arm and swung with my right. I nicked the beast twice, and that made it even angrier.

Then, to my horror, the beast grabbed me in its huge claws.

My sword fell to the ground. I watched the beast's eyes glaze over. He was ready for the morsel I'd provide for him. But then—I remembered the dagger on my side. As the dragon drew me closer to its mouth, I pulled the dagger from its sheath. I cut the dragon's chin, and he roared. I looked straight ahead and saw nothing but a great wall of red. Clutching my dagger, I drew it across the beast's chest. Two half scales fell to the ground, and then one whole one. Hoping I could survive the fall, I sliced across the flesh that gripped me. The dragon dropped me.

I fell hard on my side and was winded. With the only strength I had left, I reached out for the scale and stood on shaky legs and ran as fast as I could to the woods. A blistering heat blew across my back, and I knew he'd gotten me with his flame. I dropped to the ground and rolled under the shrubbery.

The dragon stomped along behind me. I scrambled across the ground on my belly like a serpent, going deeper into the thicket. Thorns tore my skin, but I ignored the sting. Finally, I inched my way to the end of the brush and started running. I had survived the clutches of the dragon to return home in triumph.

As the audience applauded, he called his son to him. Two attendants carried forward a table and whisked away a decorated cloth. The king presented Nikolas with gifts. A satchel of gold. A hunting dagger. A sword intended for battle and designed for beauty. Outside in the stables, well fed and rested, was his favorite horse.

"May Fate and your wits keep you safe," the King said. "The pride of your ancestors and the future of the kingdom will ride at your side. Return to us soon with a red scale and a good story."

The King shook his son's hand and clapped his back.

"My people, I present to you my brave, honorable son, Prince Nikolas, ready to embark. All hail!"

The crowd rose to its feet. Hail! Hail! Hail!

As guests dispersed to find their seats at the banquet tables, Fewmany maneuvered away from vies for his attention and walked toward me. How little he had changed since the night I met him in that same hall—his hair still lightly oiled, the Tell-a-Bell and timepiece gleaming, his boots brightly shined. There I was in his shadow, no longer the child he frightened with the words *So, if I tried to eat you up, you wouldn't even scream?* My fear of him had shape-shifted. It was now founded, and in check.

"Good evening, Miss Riven," he said. "'Tis a momentous day in the kingdom, the prince leaving for his quest."

"Good evening, sir. Indeed it is," I said, playing along.

"What-ho, where are your spectacles?"

"Broken. How bright everything is."

He stepped within intimate distance. "All preparations made?"

"I received the allowance, quite generous, thank you, and the maps."

"What are your thoughts as you prepare to go?"

"How unusual it will be to walk in the bustle of the world," I said.

"'Tis a brutal one you enter. Mind your purse and your instincts," he said.

A shockingly tall man interrupted us. Fewmany made introductions, then attempted to hurry the conversation, urging the lord with a parcel of land to sell to make an appointment with his secretary.

Nikolas suddenly appeared at my side.

"Good evening, Fewmany. How honored we are to have you as our guest," Nikolas said.

"Good evening, Your Highness." He bowed. "Please accept my sincere gratitude for the invitation and wishes for a safe, triumphant return."

"Thank you. I do hope I'm so fortunate. I apologize for any interruption, but may I have a moment with you, Miss Riven?" Nikolas asked.

"I believe we were about to part ways, weren't we, Miss Riven?" Fewmany said.

They addressed me but kept their eyes on each other. And then—the tug. Fewmany drew me toward him without a touch. He'd sensed something he couldn't identify. I pressed my toes through my slippers.

"Yes, we were, sir," I said.

"Assure me you won't leave for the evening without a farewell," Fewmany said.

"I mind my manners," I said.

"Your Highness, Miss Riven . . ." Fewmany stepped away with a bow.

"How proper we are," Nikolas said.

"What is it, my liege?" I asked.

Nikolas leaned toward my ear as his mother approached with an exquisitely dressed, impeccably poised, very beautiful young woman next to her. "Meet me on the tower after midnight," he said.

Before I could ask which one or why, he slipped away to Queen Ianthe's open arms. She kissed his cheek and linked her elbow in his. The young woman clasped her hands in front of her, eyes bright and lashes fluttering.

I joined the merriment. Charlotte and Muriel waved me toward a group of former classmates, among them Michael Lyle. To my surprise and relief, my infatuation had vanished. He remained perilously handsome, but I felt no urge to trace my hands over every inch of him.[20] We had a pleasant if pedantic conversation and parted ways to enjoy a happy evening.

When a hidden clock struck twelve, Nikolas thanked his guests and took his leave so that he could rest before his journey at dawn.

Before I searched for the tower, I told Father I would meet him at the hall's entrance when he was ready to leave. Then I wished a good night to my friends, who seemed prepared to see the festivities to their close. Finally, I looked for Fewmany.

He was in conversation with two of his twelfth-floor men and two Council members. My approach didn't distract them, but my direct address—"My pardon, good sirs. Might I have a word with you, Fewmany?"—brought bewildered looks.

Fewmany walked with me to a quiet corner.

I stared at his coat pocket, the bulging shape covered with the handkerchief, as always, as long as I'd known him, from our first encounter to this parting. I glanced over the rough scar at his jaw, his smooth-shaven cheek, to meet his amber gaze.

"I'll be leaving soon. It will be some months before I see you again," I said.

"Travel safely and swiftly, and bring back word of the boon," he said.

"I'll do my best."

"You have my full faith, Secret. Farewell."

"Farewell." I clutched his left arm over the symbol's brand. His hand pressed mine until I released.

With no time to wallow in thought, I exited the hall, stood in the courtyard, and saw a mouse running in circles. I followed it to the gatehouse. A guard stepped aside from the stairwell to let me pass. I found Nikolas leaning against a space in the battlement. When I called his name, he gestured for me to approach.

Standing next to him, I looked out to Rothwyke. In the streets, people were celebrating his departure with music and dancing. To the south, I could see the outline of Fewmany Incorporated. To the west, where the waning moon traveled, the woods were too dark to see.

"My father gave me a map," Nikolas said. "It's a long journey, but the terrain isn't too harsh. The roads are well marked, with several villages to find supplies."

That moment, I remembered a rupture that cracked through before he'd left for the goodwill visits. There was a door with a bobbin and latch, and a man entered a room. The map he was about to see was a lie, and the last one the mapmaker ever drew. I suspected Aoife's manuscript would reveal the image's meaning, but all I could tell Nikolas then was,

"The map is false. It's connected to Aoife and the war somehow. She knew the truth."

"What do you think that is?" he asked.

"The dragon isn't part of the known world." I thought to myself, Neither is the hoard.

"Not on a map."

"No."

"Then how am I supposed to find it?"

"Something Cyril wanted me to tell you makes sense now. Follow squirrels. Stall when they stall. Hide when they hide. I'll add, if you find a cottage and see the symbol carved in stone at the hearth, you'll be safe there."

Nikolas stared into the distance. "We stood in this same place three years ago when I questioned whether the dragon was real and if the quest mattered anymore. I was afraid then, as I am now, but the need for the truth is stronger than the fear."

"I understand," I said.

"Which is why you won't refuse what Fewmany asked of you."

"That's my quest. You have the dragon. I have the hoard. If any old tale is true, they're in the same place."

He curled his arm around my back and drew me toward him. My cheek pressed against his chest. I held him tightly, one ear turned toward the stairs, the other to his heart. Unlike the last time we were separated, I wasn't going to pull away too soon, and from his grip, I could tell he wasn't either.

"So then—why don't you come with me?" he asked.

His tone was light, but I didn't think he was kidding. "Because I'm meant to travel alone, unnoticed, and I suspect you're going to attract attention along your way."

"Perhaps we'll cross paths," he said.

"Possibly."

I slipped back then. "I should go. You need your rest." Hesitantly, I raised on tiptoes to peck his cheek good-bye, but somehow he moved or I did, and although it was only for an instant, brief and chaste, there was a kiss.

"I suppose that makes this a proper farewell," he said with a bashful grin, so unlike him.

Despite the blush in my cheeks, I laughed. He reached for my hand, clasping it gently, and I began to ease away.

"Be careful," he said.

"And you."

"Secret, I—"

I waited through his pause. "Yes?"

"I'll miss you," he said.

"I'll miss you, too," I said.

He released me and waved good-bye. As I went back to the hall to find Father, fighting a rush of complicated tears, I wondered whether Nikolas had meant to say something else.

DIARY ENTRY 7 JUNE /37

As I write this, a bee hovers between my eyes. A messenger, she says, who will tell the others I'm on my way. In my satchel, I've packed bread and cheese, a change of clothing and my cloak, the allowance, and the manuscript. Old Woman waits outside to see me take my first steps on the journey. Once I begin, I cannot turn back.

- Part II -

Part II

FROM THE START OF MY JOURNEY, ANIMALS WILD AND TAME served as my escorts. The first nights, they guided me to cottages where hearths bore the symbol. Not one old woman showed herself, although I found, each time, a pot with a warm meal to eat, a basin of water to bathe, a gown for sleeping, and candles by which to read.

I walked several miles a day, but these cottages weren't as close together as they appeared. They were, in fact, many miles apart, distances I couldn't travel so fast on foot. Aoife's manuscript revealed the mystery. Before she embarked on her own quest, she had been given an incantation to ask the elements to show her the way. Subtle forces directed Aoife's steps, and animals led her to what she called "links"—hollow trees—which connected what she described as "gaps," thin places where time and space looped and compressed.

I needed no incantation. Since I was a little girl, creatures escorted me along hidden paths and into hollow trees. As a child, I didn't realize I'd traveled to remote places when animals led me into the hollows, which, in retrospect, happened often. Now an adult, I wondered what was to come of my bond with them and the quest they guided.

As the new moon rose in secret, seven days after I left Rothwyke, I slept through that night and into the start of the next. When I awoke, I found my black hair had fallen out, pressed into the pillow like a nest. My fingers clutched my scalp and slipped through new silver strands, which reached to my waist.

That very evening, I began to travel only under the cover of darkness.

My escorts remained nearby, leading me on, but familiar comforts were no longer arranged. Rarely did I cross the threshold of an old woman's cottage or abandoned hut. Shelter was as likely to be an empty space within a tree or under a dead log. Many nights, I huddled on my cloak, my satchel as a pillow. For the first time in my life, I experienced hunger. I couldn't always forage enough to eat. When I became weak from only water and enough fruit, mushrooms, or greens to stave the pangs, I had no choice but to enter a village or town to buy food.

When I encountered other people along the way, most acknowledged me with a nod or a wave, but with suspicion, because what kind of unaccompanied woman walks alone in the dark? The more wary strangers stopped me. Each kept one eye on mine, the colors of night and day, and the other on the satchel I carried.

What is your name? they asked.

It is Secret, I replied with a steady voice.

They expected no name as that. Their pauses of silence gave me the chance to continue along, unless a quick one asked,

From where have you come?

I answered—through the woods, across the valley, over the hills.

Where are you going? some asked.

My grandmother's house, I said, which was a ruse, as well as the truth.

The menacing strangers sometimes spoke, but beyond words, I sensed their intent to do harm. At those moments, an animal—boar, fox, bear, lynx—emerged with grunts or growls. The strangers looked at the creature, and me, and backed away in fright.

Yet I wasn't afraid. Often uncomfortable, sometimes miserable, but the physical conditions forced me into my body with an ascetic pureness that transformed into an ecstasy when my needs were sated. How surprised I was by this surrender and the wholly new silence it offered. My mind was so quiet. Empty. No thought remained for long because as soon as one surfaced, one of my senses pushed it away. I'd feel a breeze rush on my damp neck, hear the song of an unknown bird, smell the essence of a sleeping forest. I welcomed the respite from myself.

I WALKED THROUGH THE SUMMER AND INTO AUTUMN. THE DAWN of my twentieth birthday was rose and gold, the trees flaming red, orange, and yellow, a tang of frost on the wind. As I settled down to sleep under the roots of a tree, a fox curled against my stomach to keep me warm. When I awoke again, I walked in the light of a full moon.

Days later, I found the first clue that Nikolas was somewhere near. In an unattended cottage, I discovered a round rock in the center of the bed. Under its weight were a blue feather and three long silver filaments of hair. Then I saw three gold strands one-fourth the others' length. He'd left a message in the language of our childhood.

I didn't question the mystery of our parallel journeys beginning to converge. Having read Aoife's manuscript several times by then, I recognized this was inevitable, a pattern repeated from a thousand years before. As for the gifts, I took delight in leaving treasures and looking for others in return—feathers, pebbles, a fallen nest, a snake's skin.

Four months after I left Ailliath, although I'd become slight from miles of walking, a visceral heaviness slowed my steps. I knew, without the aid of a map, I'd crossed a border into the land where my mother was born.

It was then the silver wolf allowed glimpses of her lithe beauty as she slipped among the trees. She was neither figment nor ghost, but an echo of memory, of another wolf from another time.

In the manuscript, Aoife told the tale of her husband, Leit,* the warrior who suffered a sword cut from his throat to his groin as he stood powerless to save a little girl tied to a tree. His wolf, with the aid of bees, sought to heal him. Leit's flesh sealed, but the deeper wound never fully closed.

And the tree . . . I was certain it was the one outside my grandmother's village where I'd hidden as a child, where a bee told me of the girl, the wound, and the wolf, where the queen bee had stung me.

THAT LATE OCTOBER AS THE MOON WANED, A BADGER LED ME TO a cottage where an old woman, her irises eclipsed by milky whiteness, invited me to come inside.

"Welcome, waited one," she said in the Guardians' language.

Near the fire at her hearth was a shallow tub filled with steaming water. On the table, a full meal. On the bed, a clean dress and nightshirt and layers of quilts and furs.

"What you seek is near. For now, eat, drink, sleep," she said. She put on a blue wool cape and closed the door behind her.

After I bathed and ate, I climbed into bed and slumbered as the sun warmed the heavy drapes.

I awoke with a weight at my side. My eyes flew open. The cottage was dark. I'd slept into the following night.

"Well, then," a man's voice said.

He was a shadow against the fire's glow.

"What are you doing in my bed?" he asked.

I sat up in shock, a stumbling apology at my lips, my body a pyre of fear.

"Secret." He took my hand.

My fingertips brushed the ridge of a scar under his thumb. His head was edged in gold.

---

* Leit, pronounced *lite*.

"Nikolas," I said. "Is this a dream?"

"I'll tell you when I wake up," he said.

In a daze, I watched him roll a blanket on the floor. I lay down again and heard a loud sigh, the tumble of a log, and the sputter of embers.

When morning came, I was alone. I leapt up and ran outside. Under a tree, only yards away, a man stood with his back to me, his hands sweeping through his wet blond hair, his shirt tight on his damp skin.

He turned when he heard the crush of fallen leaves and caught me as I coiled my arms around his neck.

"So it was no dream," I said as he let me down.

"Not unless you're still asleep," Nikolas said. He scratched his beard, roughly cut. "Miss Riven, you are indisposed. Attire yourself properly while I make breakfast. The quest awaits."

That first morning together, we packed what we had and set out on foot. The wolf padded steps ahead.

Nikolas told me that during the first week of his journey, he didn't take Cyril's instructions to follow squirrels. Curious to see where his father's map led, he followed the roads from one place to the next. He realized soon enough that he was being trailed by a guard and otherwise watched.

Because the kingdoms that sent their princes to quest announced the departures, it was known far and wide Nikolas had begun his. Some of the attention he garnered didn't surprise him. He'd been told by other princes he'd receive invitations to make all sorts of merry with games of chance, intoxications, alluring women, and feasts. He anticipated the beggars and robbers along the way, and was equally grateful he could express kindness or turn a blade with convincing threat.

Yet if danger seemed to press too closely, he noticed alert eyes on him. Several times, a man, once a woman, interrupted the exchanges. Without his request or welcome, these people distracted the others. Often, they suggested a crossroads to take, a landmark to notice, or a place to avoid.

"Did they wear a certain shade of blue?" I asked.

His face was still.

"Any article of clothing, or a collar or a cuff? Or a band on the wrist, even a prominent jewel?"

"Some of them did. One fellow pulled on the brim of his hat such that I thought he was afflicted."

"They are the Guardians," I said. "Like Old Woman and Old Man, but they watch the roads."

"How do you know?"

"I read the manuscript," I said. "Before I speak of that, tell me why you stopped following the map."

"Because twice along the way, someone tried to sell me a dragon's scale. I don't know what they were, really, dark red and tough as horns, but I knew then my journey was meant for something other than a noble task. So, I sold my horse, kept an eye out for a squirrel, and escaped the guard," he said with a bitter tone. "Well, then—what of the manuscript?"

I asked if he wanted me to tell him or if he'd prefer I translate aloud when we rested. He wished for both, so as we walked, I told him what I learned.

"What we were taught about The Mapmaker's War is, at best, incomplete. The apprentice blamed for provoking the war—the one who was never named in our history books—was not a man, as assumed, but a woman. She wasn't merely an apprentice but Ailliath's mapmaker, and she wasn't executed by sword, as we were told, but instead exiled. Her name was Aoife," I said.

Aoife was the daughter of one of the king's most trusted advisers. Because of the influence of her friend, Prince Wyl, and her father's lack of objection, she trained with an adept mapmaker and learned the trade.

What we were taught in school was this: The unnamed apprentice found a hidden clan across the river that separated Ailliath from another land. The people there were considered wealthy, protective of their stores, and richly armed. When Ailliath's advisers learned of this, they feared invasion but took no action. Several months later, the apprentice returned to the clan and warned the people of a possible attack. It was recorded that the clan took up weapons against the kingdom's sentinels on the river border. Thus, the war began, and the apprentice was executed as a traitor.

Yet, in her manuscript, Aoife stated she was sent to map Ailliath's river border, and she decided to see what was on the other side. When her boat approached the shore, five men in blue coats stepped out from the cover of the woods. One led her to the hidden settlement within the trees. Two crewmen followed behind her, and they, too, saw—or rather felt—what she did. A sense of peace they'd never known.

"The blue men from your dreams," Nikolas said.

I nodded and continued.

Aoife didn't hide the fact that she crossed the river, but she also didn't reveal all she'd seen. Prince Raef, Wyl's younger brother, questioned her crew in secret. The cook described the village and told of a child he met, who spoke of a dragon and its hoard, which her people protected.

When Wyl was sent on a quest to find this dragon, Aoife departed on her own to see for herself. Months later, they found each other in a faraway land. Soon after, in this distant realm, they saw a great treasure in a cave—but no dragon.

On the journey home, Aoife became pregnant. When they returned, they learned Raef had visited the clan's settlement, saw the people's riches, and deemed them a threat to Ailliath. Wyl revealed his scale—which Aoife knew he found on a mountaintop—and said he'd seen a hoard that included many weapons. Meetings were held to determine what the kingdom should do. Aoife's father and her brother, Ciaran,* both in the king's service, believed there was cause for alarm. However, the King chose not to act; that is, not to invade.

By then, Wyl had severed a betrothal to a princess, compensated her father with land, and married Aoife. Soon after, she bore twins, a girl and a boy.

Without anyone else's knowledge, Aoife returned to the settlement out of fear that the King and his advisers would change their minds. Aoife believed the people meant no harm and posed no danger.

Soon after, the King died. Wyl took the throne. On Wyl's orders, armed men from Ailliath crossed the river—and the war began. Aoife was imprisoned and forced to draw a map to the hoard at Raef's demand. When she finished, she was exiled as a traitor. The two guards sent out with her were instructed to kill her, but one of the men let her go free.

"What happened to her?" Nikolas asked.

I told him she wandered for months in search of another Guardian settlement. She'd been told such places existed across the known world. The abiding peace she'd felt in the settlement she first encountered was what she sought in another. Finally, she found one, and the people accepted her although she had come from Ailliath, the kingdom that started the war. Aoife described how kind and patient the Guardians were toward her, how they lived cooperatively and peacefully, with affection and compassion. However, she struggled with profound guilt.

---

* Ciaran, pronounced *keer-ahn*.

Aoife blamed herself for what happened. She believed she caused the war. Had she not crossed the river, perhaps none of the events would have happened. Although the people who'd lost warriors forgave her for what responsibility she had, she couldn't forgive herself.

Several years later, she married Leit, one of the Guardians' greatest warriors. He had fought in the war and returned months after its end, bearing a horrible scar the length of his body. This wasn't a battle injury but a wound he received when he witnessed a little girl's violent death at the hands of three men. The men left Leit to die, buried alive, but his wolf companion saved him.

Leit believed a darkness, which had always been among people outside of their settlements, had become worse and would spread as the war had. No one, not even the Guardians themselves, was safe.

In time, Aoife and Leit had one daughter. They named her Wei.* She was one of the rare children the Guardians called Voices. Nearly all Voices were girls—few were boys with limited abilities—born with extraordinary gifts.

"As soon as they could talk, they could speak any language of the world," I said.

"Secret—like your mother?" Nikolas said.

"I'm almost certain she was one of them. She had violet eyes, like all female Voices. I don't know if she had the other abilities, being able to heal people with light and sound, or how much she knew of the past, present, and future. The Voices were blind, too, but somehow compensated beyond ordinary senses. My mother didn't focus her eyes like everyone else. It was as if she looked past people, instead of at them. And sometimes, she was clumsy, stumbling around in unfamiliar places or if furniture was moved in the house. I wonder now." With a clenched fist, I rubbed off a trace of unexpected wetness from my lashes. I heaved my satchel to the other shoulder. "So, about Wei . . ."

In the manuscript, Aoife described the difficulty of having a child like Wei and the training her daughter needed to use her gifts. Other Voices, including an ancient one named Sisay, served as Wei's teachers. Then, when Wei was seven years old, she was chosen for a special role. She agreed to spend the next seven years accompanying warriors who patrolled the trade routes, watching for threats.

---

* Wei, pronounced *why*.

Wei witnessed the strife of the world when she traveled with them. Other people's pain affected her deeply, and she wanted to give comfort. When she was an adult, Wei challenged the Guardians' traditions and provoked much disagreement. Although no one who found a Guardian settlement and wished to stay was denied a home, the people didn't openly welcome newcomers. Rarely did the Guardians leave to live among those outside their settlements.

Wei believed that the pain of the world would continue as long as others were not taught to live in peace within themselves, their own homes, and their villages. She believed so genuinely in their ways—to which Aoife had been drawn so strongly—that Wei suggested her people invite those from the outside to come to them or for Guardians to leave and live as examples in other places.

"What happened to Aoife?" Nikolas asked.

"That, I'll read aloud to you later," I said.

For a long while, we walked in silence. Each time I glanced at him, I could tell he was thinking.

"I'm Wyl's descendant. You—are you Aoife's? Does this mean we're distant cousins, many generations removed?" Nikolas asked.

"You're descended from Wyl and his second wife. Whether Aoife is my ancestor, I have only my dreams and ruptures as proof, which are all described in the manuscript. Whether we're distant cousins, possibly. Aoife's brother, Ciaran, raised her twins after the exile and never sired children of his own. My father has long believed he's descended from a noble family that fell out of favor. If that family was Ciaran's, then we are."

By midday, we were famished. Although Nikolas wasn't a hunter before, by necessity he'd learned to catch fish and trap small game. While he fished, I foraged for greens, nuts, and wild apples. As we ate, the wolf lay under a tree in full view.

"An intimidating escort," Nikolas said.

"More so than a squirrel."

"I assume she's leading us, rather than only you, at this point."

"Yes. But there's a place I must go before we continue with your quest," I said. "During The Mapmaker's War, there was a village that revealed the location of a Guardian settlement. The Guardian warriors kept the fighting away from their own people, but it was a horrible battle. When Wei was an adult, she moved her family and several others there in an attempt to reconcile the betrayal. I believe this is the same village where my mother was born, generations later, where the blood mixed and no one remembers its source."

THE NEXT FEW DAYS, WE WALKED AS SILENCE FLOWED INTO CONversation and back again. Nikolas spoke of his adventures during the goodwill visits. I told him of the beautiful things I'd seen at the manor and of the interesting people I'd met, but nothing about Fewmany himself.

One evening, I told Nikolas what happened when I was eleven, when I drew the symbol, my father cut my hair to force me to tell him where I'd seen it, and Fewmany questioned me as well. Although Nikolas had known nothing about the night of the scissors and symbol, he remembered how unusually guarded I'd been at the time, aware something had upset me. He was glad to at last know why, sorry for what I'd endured, and angry on my behalf.

When we stopped to rest, I translated from the manuscript so that he could hear Aoife's own words. We wondered what her story revealed that we'd understand in due time. We discussed our fascination with the Guardians' culture so different from our own, from the care they gave to their children to the openness allowed for affectionate, as well as amorous, expression.

At nightfall, the wolf led us to abandoned dens and crumbling shelters. Between Nikolas and me, we had his coat, my cloak, two blankets, and the wolf providing her warmth. Neither of us was comfortable, but we were safe.

The end of that week, the wolf led us to a cottage where someone had laid out clean clothing, hot food, and thick blankets. We fell asleep on pallets next to a fire.

In the middle of the night, I awoke with a busy mind and went to sit in a clearing under the stars and moon. During the months I'd been alone, my journey had seemed almost unreal, as if at any moment, I could decide to slip away from the path of fate. Disappear. Never return to Ailliath. Do as Aoife did—begin again, elsewhere. Once Nikolas joined me, I knew matters of consequence had come down to us. I had no idea what we'd be called to do, what peril we'd face, or what would become of us in the end.

A rustle made me jump. Nikolas stood behind me wrapped in a blanket. He sat down at my side and draped it around us.

"You're shivering," he said.

"I'm cold," I said, a half-truth.

"Why are you awake?" I asked.

"I never quite fell asleep. There's something I need to tell you."

"What is it?"

"The scar under my thumb. I never told you how I got it. I often thought I had a vivid dream, but that wouldn't explain the wound.[21] Now, well, I suppose there's much that can't be explained at all," he said.

"True," I said.

"When you were sick with the fever, I was sick, too, but not in the same way. I had excruciating aches deep in my bones for three days. Nothing eased it. All I could do was pace my room like an animal. Finally, in the middle of the night, I lay down exhausted.

"The next thing I knew, it was dawn, but I was in the woods. I didn't remember leaving my room. I'm not sure if it was *our* woods or somewhere else. I was half dressed in trousers and boots. Old Man was there. He led me to a group of boys my age sitting on the ground. Most of them looked as if they had come from other lands, based on their skin, hair, and eyes. Everyone was tense. Several older men came through the trees carrying drums. They wore blue tunics and had scars on their faces. One had a missing eye. The rhythm they pounded, I'd never heard anything like it or felt the way I did. So alert, aware of my heartbeat.

"A man near our age walked into the circle wearing a vest made of skins. He looked each of us in the eye as if to intimidate us. Then Old Man appeared again with a chalice. He told the young man to open his arms. Old Man put his fingers in the chalice and painted a red stripe from the man's shoulders to his palms and smeared it across his face and throat."

"Blood," I said. I clenched every muscle to stop quivering, but it only made it worse.

"Old Man told us to drink. We couldn't refuse. Some of the boys retched. I managed to keep it down. It tasted of metal and honey. The drumming became louder, more forceful. None of us could sit still anymore. Then Old Man gave the young one a hunting horn and pointed to the trees. He went off quick as a deer."

"What did you do?" I asked. I thought of my own hunt—the knife, the doe, the blood.

"Old Man said he was our prey. We could use no weapons, only our wits and bodies. The one who brought him down would be the victor. There would be a prize. The drumming stopped when Old Man held up his hands. A moment later, three horn blasts rose up in the distance. 'Get him,' Old Man said.

"I was never one for a hunt, but I was that morning. I felt more alive than I ever had. I wanted to catch him more than I ever wanted anything. But I wasn't alone. The others tripped, punched, and wrestled each other, trying to slow each other down. When I got caught, I fought back hard. I discovered a ruthlessness I didn't know I possessed, more physical strength and agility, too. As if I didn't know myself at all.

"I took a drink at a stream, sat still, and listened. The prey could have been anywhere. Even though I didn't hear anything, I knew where to go.

"I found him resting on a log. He saw me and started to run. I was exhausted and sore and bleeding and filled with rage. He was so close but out of reach. I surged toward him, grabbed his vest, and held on as he dragged me until we fell.

"That's when I lunged on top of him and the vest burst. Blood covered us as I subdued him. The feel and smell of it made me savage. I wanted to kill him. I could have. Only when he cried out in a human voice, in words, did my senses return. Somehow, I held him down long enough until he stopped fighting.

"Old Man approached us. I got up and placed my foot on the man's back. Old Man smiled as if he were pleased. I shook hands with the man when he stood next to me. He left, and soon after, I began to shake as if I were having a fit. 'Let it release,' Old Man said, although I wasn't sure what he meant. When I calmed down, I asked Old Man about the prize. He grabbed my wrist, and I felt a sharp pain under my thumb. The blood was mine then.

"He told me the scar would always remind me of what I'd done and what resided within. He said, 'At another hunt, you will be the hunted.' The next thing I remembered, I was in my room, clean, in different clothes, but the cut was raw."

I discovered my hands wrapped tight around Nikolas's arm. "What do you mean, another hunt?"

He stared into the sky. "My turn came a few weeks ago, before we found each other again. I wore the blood vest. I was the prey. I've never forgotten how I felt when I was the hunter—the savage instinct, the power I wanted over someone, something, else—and I won't forget what it was like to be the one pursued, terrified and humbled."

I didn't tell him then about my encounter with Old Man in my dream, the rage he provoked me to feel, or the hunt I had joined with Fewmany, by my own choice. "Why do you think you were called to do it?"

"I believe I was meant to learn from the extremes. Who am I between them?" He nudged me with his elbow. "Quick, look up. Falling stars."

When I finally slept again, I dreamed of initiation, fire, and blood.

AN ARCANE KNOWLEDGE AWAKENED IN MY BODY. A PART OF ME knew this place, this cold, this forest. I knew my grandmother's village wasn't far away.

We trudged through the day's chill. I stopped to forage for mushrooms. When I found a cluster of pale yellow ones, I told Nikolas about the first mushroom I'd ever seen, that same yellow type, on the carriage journey years ago, to this same place. I remarked on the kind coachman who acknowledged its beauty but warned me of its poison. I didn't mention my mother, who told me not to touch the dirty fungus.

At twilight, the wolf loped ahead toward a clearing where there was a bonfire. Someone called out from the shadows. We waved in acknowledgment. Two people swept their arms high to gesture us toward them. I didn't feel there was a threat—neither did the wolf—but I was reluctant to go to the strangers.

Nikolas, who always enjoyed a festive gathering, slowed his steps.

A cheerful cry rose up.

"They're welcoming us. Let's go," he said.

We and the group exchanged greetings in different languages. After several tries, a young woman and I discovered we could both speak Seronian with adequate proficiency. Nikolas and I sat down with bowls of fish stew and mugs of ale. Everyone seemed able to communicate with gestures, pantomimes, and facial expressions, conveying more than seemed possible.

I studied the group in the firelight. Memories of the long-ago visit to my grandmother returned in glimpses. I remembered the people with their black hair and swarthy skin, like mine; their bodies strong and solid, although I'd grown more slight. As I watched the men, I sighed at the sudden thought of my stillborn brothers, wondering if they would have been tall, broad, and dark.

Three of our companions brought a lute, hornpipe, and drum into the circle. As they began to play, the young woman, Vasi, poured out the contents of our mugs and filled them with something else. Wine, sweet and heavy. I took several quick sips to make the heat rise and quiet the pangs for what I'd had at the manor and the company with whom I shared it.

Nikolas looked at me with his eyebrows lifted.

"As you know, this isn't my first taste," I said.

"Certainly not," he said. He tapped his mug against mine.

As the music played and people danced, we ate pastries filled with dried fruit and drank more wine. Between the drink and the fire, I was warm and relaxed. I tried not to stare at the drummer, the lines of his face striking in the flames' light.

Suddenly, Vasi dropped at my side. "Nikolas—husband?"

I laughed. "No."

"Cousin? Brother?"

"Friend," I said.

Her eyes brightened. She rose up, stood in front of him, and beckoned him with her finger. He shoved his mug toward me and followed her to the dancers. Vasi positioned his hands without looking away from his eyes. There, she taught him one dance, then another, the sounds of laughter adding notes to the songs.

I'd had another mug to drink by the time a young man with straight black hair and light eyes held out his hand to me. I almost declined, an old reticence revealing itself, but at last accepted his kind offer. I had watched everyone enough to replicate the steps of something like a waltz, although that song was slower, the rhythm sensual, not too quick, not too slow.

Nikolas glanced toward me several times. Vasi's palms pressed against his chest. His left hand held her waist, his right, a bottle.

Someone pulled Vasi away for the next dance. My partner slipped from my fingertips, and there was Nikolas with his hand lifted, open. I took it and, with my other, grasped his shoulder.

A man spoke a loud comment in a teasing tone. The others laughed. Although I had no idea what was said, I blushed. After one last sip, Nikolas dropped the bottle at his feet. The weight of his touch pressed into my side.

His eyes were glazed but focused on mine.

"Do you know what I've liked most about this quest?" he asked.

"What?" I asked.

He raised his arm to allow me to spin. When I faced him again, he said, "Not being watched and followed almost every moment of the day. At home, nearly every word and movement monitored. Always, a guard a few steps away. During the goodwill visits, much of the same, knowing I was never free of scrutiny."

His hand slipped to my waist.

"But I had an escape when we were children. No adults following me in the woods. No one telling me what to do or how to behave. No one ready to plunge a sword or take one for me. You never showed the way to anyone else, did you?" he asked.

"No," I said. "Only you."

He spun me again, three times, his palm on my side once more.

"When we were little, did you enjoy being away from the world? Did you like being alone?" he asked.

"Very much, and I liked not being alone when I was with you," I said, smiling at the memory of the two of us content in each other's company.

"Here we are now, untold miles from Ailliath, adventuring as we did when we were children." He released my hand, tucked a lock of hair behind my ear, and traced his finger along the side of my face. "However, we aren't children anymore."

The wine's soft blur lifted. The waxing crescent moon beamed between us. My blood raced. My breath shallowed. The look in his eyes I'd seen before, but not from him.

A couple stumbled into us, their apologies lost in drunken giggles.

"Excuse me," Nikolas said as he walked off into the trees.

He was gone for so long, Vasi asked if I wanted to have a friend look for him.

"I think he might be ill," I said.

She gave a twisted little smile. "Sick, yes. When he comes back, tell him you're invited to stay. We're here through the night. Unless you have somewhere to go."

I neither heard nor saw the wolf, so I assumed she knew we were safe. I accepted Vasi's offer and walked among the group thanking them. Soon after everyone settled, Nikolas returned.

"We're here for the night. Are you feeling unwell?" I asked.

He nodded, then fell asleep as soon as he cocooned himself in his coat.

I lay awake, blaming the wine for what might have nearly happened, listening to the fire crackle and the nightcalls of hidden lovers.

THE NEXT MORNING, NIKOLAS SLEPT THROUGH THE GROUP'S DE-parture. When he awoke, he had a throbbing headache. I made a fire, heated water in the pot he carried, and found a bark to make him a tea. Eventually he muttered he'd had a "merry night" and didn't remember much and hoped he'd not been "churlish." I assured him he did nothing of which to be ashamed, although I wasn't sure if his memory was as cloudy as he claimed.

We started out after midday and hardly spoke, but I sensed his good spirits returning.

Late in the afternoon, we stopped to rest. A loud call rose in the forest. We looked around for the source. The blare came again, closer. Fallen leaves crackled. A stag showed himself. He raised his head as his bell silenced every other sound.

My hips and shoulders dropped with a forceful ache. The scent of evergreen suspended in the air. With different eyes, I saw another stag of a former time. Melting ice covered his rack like crystals. He watched her—Aoife—and his pause was an invitation to follow, to lead her to the place which would become her new home.

The silver wolf joined the stag. They bowed to each other, then to us. We returned the gesture and walked toward them. I touched their faces and felt a surge of strength. Nikolas reached, too, and they allowed him three soft strokes.

Come, they said.

We followed the animals to a dirt road. The stag stepped aside, grazing my shoulder with his nose, and let the wolf lead us to a village.

The summer I'd spent with my grandmother had been reduced to images. Ahmama's braided white hair with the black streak. Her nesting dolls in her aged hands. A house with no halls. The woods filled with unfathomable beauty. I didn't remember this path although I'd walked it many times.

The wolf darted away. Nikolas followed at my side.

Many cottages were in disrepair with sagging roofs, rotted shutters, and unkempt walks. I recalled a populated place, but perhaps it had been sparse then, too. A large dark-haired man leaned on his hoe in a plot of leeks. He gave us a cautious stare as he whistled a piercing series of six notes.

Ahead, a tall elderly woman stepped outside her door with a cloth in her hand. I approached with a wary smile. The woman narrowed her eyes but seemed more curious than worried.

With Nikolas behind me, I halted several steps from the woman's door. I nodded and smiled, and the woman did the same. The villager uttered a phrase I didn't comprehend.

Suddenly, I was furious I didn't know the language. The only words I remembered that belonged to them were *ahma* and *ahmama*, "mother" and "grandmother"; *ahpa* and *ahpapa*, "father" and "grandfather." Of all the languages I'd chosen to study, I never considered I might need to know this one. I asked in several languages whether the woman understood the words I spoke and finally in the ancient Guardian tongue which hid within me.

The old woman shook her head.

"Zavet," I said.

The woman squinted her slightly slanted eyes.

"Zavet. My *ahma*," I said, almost in tears. "Ahmama—" I didn't know my grandmother's name, the key to my connection there. How could I not know my own grandmother's name? Why hadn't my mother told me? Why hadn't I asked? If I had, and was told, why didn't I remember?

I gestured toward the cottages around us. "Ahmama? Ahmama?" A forgotten name sprung to my lips, spoken to me only once, that of my mother's dead brother. "Szevstan?" The woman's head tilted. "Zavet. My *ahma*." I pointed to myself as I said my given name, the one I was known by almost twenty years before. "Evensong. Eve."

The woman studied my face. "Zavet!" she whispered. "Eve . . ." Her eyes softened. She touched her hand to her chest. "Tasha."

"Nikolas," Nikolas said.

Tasha invited us into her cottage. She gave us cups of goat's milk and brown bread. As we started to eat, she held her hands up as if to say, Stay there, and wrapped herself in a cloak before she left us alone. Nikolas and I waited until she returned almost an hour later with Vasi at her side. I smiled in greeting as my heart sunk. She was not who I hoped to see.

"Tasha thought I might know how to talk to you," Vasi said in the language we spoke in common. She smiled at Nikolas as she sat down across from us and looked at me with kindness.

"Do you live here?" I asked.

"I came to visit cousins. Some you met last night," Vasi said.

"Where is my grandmother?" I asked.

Vasi glanced at Tasha, their expressions sorrowful. "Dead. Two years ago."

The grief shocked me as much as what else welled up. I remembered only fragments of my visit that summer, but deep within, I hadn't forgotten what I felt. Love for her, loved by her. My elbows hit the table. I rested my head in my hands. "My grandmother is dead," I said to Nikolas. He touched my back. I shrugged him away.

"What was her name?" I asked.

"Katya. Tasha wants to know why you're here and if your mother is well," Vasi said.

"I've come to ask how the people here remember her," I said. My mouth dropped open when I realized what they should have known. "She died six years ago. My father sent a letter. Did it not arrive?"

Vasi turned to Tasha. They spoke rapidly, with sharp inflections and a melodious lilt, some of the words familiar. The Guardians' language, as well as their blood, had mingled in this village. Tasha's expression was confused, then mournful.

"She's sad to hear of this. If the letter arrived, she doesn't know. Your grandmother didn't mention a death," Vasi said.

I wondered if my grandmother kept this news to herself and why she did. "Well, then," I said, "tell me what Tasha knows."

I interrupted with few questions as Vasi translated Tasha's words.

The people of the village knew Zavet was different soon after her birth. The strange violet eyes against her swarthy skin made her appear otherworldly, although they agreed she was beautiful. She spoke months before most children learned their first words, and those villagers who had traveled afar confirmed her babbling wasn't in their language alone. Slow to crawl and walk, she was a clumsy child, prone to bumping into anything in plain sight, yet—they noticed—she was graceful when she walked within the forest or through a crowd.

But the people feared Zavet. Almost incessantly, she muttered and burbled, sounds and sentences, sometimes if she were in conversation with invisibles. When she sang, the air shimmered and those who heard her voice wept with a conflicted joy. When she spoke to others, she spoke of things she couldn't possibly know, of private thoughts and hidden deeds, of the present and past, and, sometimes, of the future. When she noticed someone was injured or sick, she hummed as she touched them, and although it was said this gentle magic healed many, none asked for the cures.

Among the old ahmamas and ahpapas, there were stories of others like her, girls born long ago, many who died soon after they became women. A curse among a few of the families, some believed, but the worst for Katya's, a lineage that barely survived the loss of so many daughters.

The people knew of, and condoned, the punishments Zavet received. When she didn't quiet herself, when she spoke of things she shouldn't, when she had fits in which she screamed in pain and pounded her head against the ground, her parents locked her in a room, or beat her with a switch, or dropped vinegar on her tongue. Only Szevstan, her older half brother, stood in her defense, pleading with them to see the cruelty made her worse. He was the only one who believed she was a wonder, not a witch.

When Zavet was seven, she, like many others before her, disappeared. Katya sent her into fosterage with the hope her daughter could be cured or at least taught to control what strangeness possessed her. Each time she returned home, only to be sent away again, the peculiar child was quiet and contained but ever darker. She never spoke unless spoken to, and never of where she'd been. The spring she returned and learned Szevstan had died—a cut from a lathe that festered into gangrene—no one heard her talk, scream, sing, or cry.

During the next several years, the people of the village knew what became of her through rare letters she wrote to her mother, her father since dead. She was a student at a high academy, then a translator of books, then married. Only once more did they see her, when she arrived with a young daughter and stayed for a summer.

"Did my grandmother speak of that visit? Of my mother?" I asked.

Vasi shared my questions. Apprehension clouded Tasha's eyes. I couldn't understand what she said, but her tone was grave. Vasi took a long breath before she replied.

"She said your mother wanted to be left alone and had little to say to anyone. Katya spent much of her time with you, which gave her much joy. Tasha wants you to know that. But before you and your mother left, there was a terrible fight. So much shouting she and other neighbors heard. Later, Tasha asked what happened. Your grandmother was very upset, very ashamed, and told her, 'They tortured my daughter.'"

I remembered a story my mother told of her time in fosterage, being tied naked to a bed with a bag of salt in her mouth to draw out the evil. "What was done to her?" I asked.

"Tasha doesn't know. Your grandmother said little else except the acts happened in several different homes. I'm sorry to have shared so much sadness," Vasi said.

"Szevstan. He was good to her, truly?" I asked.

Vasi conveyed my question. Tasha smiled at last and answered with cheerfulness.

"There was a tender love between them. He carried her on his shoulders and took her into the forest for walks. She smiled and laughed with him, and he could calm her in a way no one else could. He was a kind young man, and a talented woodworker. He made beautiful little chests. Everyone liked him," Vasi said.

The faded blue chest she kept, I thought. Szevstan must have made it for her.

A brief conversation passed between the women. "Tasha offered a place for you tonight. Let me show you where I'm staying so that you can find me if you have more questions. I can point out where your grandmother's house still stands."

Nikolas and I followed Vasi down the village's main road. Once I had my bearings, we returned to Tasha's, where a group began to gather with food and drinks. They had come to welcome me, Katya's granddaughter, Vasi said. Regardless of the smile I showed them, I was numb inside and wanted nothing more than to be alone.

The night was freezing by the time the guests left and Vasi returned to her family. Tasha showed us to a room with a bed piled with quilts and where logs blazed in the hearth. I wondered if the generous fire was a sacrifice of her own warmth later in the winter. I reached for her hands in gratitude. She kissed my temple and left us.

"Take the bed. You look exhausted," Nikolas said.

"You take it. I doubt I'll sleep."

He paused as if he were about to argue but didn't. He helped me make a pallet on the floor. I sat with my back to the fire as he covered himself with a layer of quilts.

"I want to tell you what they said." So I did, what Tasha revealed about the child my mother had been, how her parents and people of the village treated her, and what happened between her and my grandmother at the end of the visit long ago.

He looked at me with sympathy. "I'm sorry, Secret. She suffered terribly, and it must hurt to know this now."

I nodded, because that was the easiest response to give.

In time, I drowsed and found myself

hidden in the corner of a cluttered room, peering under the legs of a chair at the feet of an ogress. She smacked her leathery lips and sniffed as if she detected a scent. There was a smell, a hideous feral stink, a reek worse than death because this belonged to something alive, lurking, lying in wait, and when her matted arm reached for me in the dark—

I gasped awake. The ogress. It had been years since she loped through my nightmares with that stench, familiar, elusive, terrifying.

I put on my cloak and went outside to breathe the frigid air. I walked to my grandmother's house and entered without a lamp or candle. I didn't want to see. I wanted to feel. In each room, my hands stretched out to find the edges of nothing. The furniture was gone. My thoughts filled in the blankness—a cupboard against that wall, a table in the center of this room, a mirror near that doorway. I crawled on the floor, my hands in the dust, searching for a button, a bead, a strand of hair, something that belonged to her. All there was, was dust.

In the silence, I searched myself for a memory of the argument between my mother and grandmother, but nothing came. Instead, I heard my mother's voice, months before she died, the nights she paced, repeating, *I've been robbed, I've been robbed, I've been robbed.*[22]

And she was. She was born as gifted as Wei, Aoife's daughter. What the Guardians treasured and nurtured in children like them, the rest of the world feared and suppressed.

There—a reason, an explanation, a key that unlocked what I'd long buried. My body began to shake as the truth surfaced, tearing through my guts to my heart and throat as I returned to Tasha's house and saw Nikolas fast asleep.

I sat near the bed and hovered my hand near his, but I couldn't make myself touch him. I wanted comfort but the very thought of reaching for it made me recoil with humiliation. When a wail rushed into my chest, I trapped it with a held breath.

Nikolas stirred. "What's wrong?"

"Nothing. Go back to sleep."

"You're sitting here on the floor." His hand fell on my shoulder. "You're cold as if you've been outside. What is it?"

I shook my head and fought to freeze the trembling in my hips. I knew if I started to cry, I wouldn't stop. When his palm cupped the back of my neck, I remained still, afraid of what would happen if I leaned toward or away from him.

"Tell me," he said, so gently that I did.

"She killed herself," I whispered.

"Who?"

"My mother."

"Why would you say this? How do you know?"

"Because I do. I've always known, but I could never admit it because a part of me wanted to believe it was an accident, even someone murdered her, but no, she planned it."

"But—why would she do that?" he asked.

"Something happened she couldn't live with any longer. Something she knew became too much. She had horrible nightmares before she— she died. I remember Father trying to console her, telling her she was home, she was safe. This was the same time I believe she read all of Aoife's manuscript. She had to know about the Voices by then. I think what she found out shattered her. What might have happened to her in another place, in another time? Who might she have been?"

Nikolas kept his hand on my neck. "I'm sorry. So sorry."

My teeth clenched against a sob, not from grief but rage, as I wondered who I might have been without a cold, distant, broken mother who hated my strangeness, too.

My memories clawed to the surface, but I didn't tell him any of this, not then.

That after seven mute years, I spoke words to her for the first time in my life, and she asked, "Why now?" "Aren't you pleased?" I asked, and she said, "I was accustomed to my silent child." She didn't inquire what happened, showed no sign of emotion—not confusion, surprise, joy, nothing—and returned to preparing our dinner.

When I revealed I could speak to creatures and plants, I chose a day her spirits were bright, a rare good mother day. The stories I told entertained her, but she turned on me, saying she once thought she could hear things, too, and suffered for this mistake. Her advice was to ignore the thoughts. Her final words about what I shared: "I don't believe you."

Days after the fever, when I awoke speaking the ancient language, she had no explanation for how that happened. I tried to tell her of the dreams and ruptures I'd had since I was a child, of things I couldn't possibly know, that I believed something uncanny was at hand. But she dismissed it all, without a word or gesture of kindness, sympathy, or understanding.

Sitting there on Tasha's floor, as those moments and so many other secret, silent ones knotted within me, I wished I'd never been born. Better if I hadn't, I said to myself, then jolted as a shock streaked through my navel.

Nikolas stroked the top of my head. "I don't know what to say."

"You don't have to say anything. I don't want to talk about it anyway," I said. I covered him to his chin, went to my pallet, and curled into a ball, shallowing my breath until I was beyond thought and feeling, disembodied.

THE NEXT MORNING, I PLACED A FEW COINS ON THE BED, AVOIDing a protest from Tasha for the gift. When we left the room, we found Tasha and Vasi preparing breakfast and two bundles of food. They kissed our cheeks as we thanked them. As we walked from the village, they and several others waved.

Once we were out of their sight, the silver wolf emerged, although I didn't require her guidance. A sense beyond sight and sound compelled me to step into the trees.

"We're close," I said.

"To what?" Nikolas asked.

"What you've traveled so far to find," I said.

"So soon?"

"That is relative, isn't it?"

Nikolas kept up with my rapid steps under the bare branches, across a wide glade, and into the trees again.

The wolf kept to my side as we approached the petrified tree. Around it, bees swirled. When I was a child, the hollow had been open on one side. Now the wood within its trunk was rotted full away. The dead tree stood as if on two legs, straddling realms.

I touched the edge of the tree's dark twisted scar. My palm was moist. When I drew it away, the ancient wound wept. I thought of the little girl tied to that tree, her life taken there in Leit's witness. I thought of myself, hiding in the dark from my clawing mother. There were terrified others, I was certain, with whom the tree had suffered.

My forehead pounded with the rhythm of my heart. "This is where the queen stung me," I said.

The bees' hum rose as we stepped into the hollow. As they streamed back and forth, in and out, we paused. We looked up to see wattles of new comb—a store of gold.

Quietly within, I focused on the object of the quest. I imagined a resplendent red dragon. It flew, breathing fire and light. Egnis, she who first saw All.

I touched Nikolas's chest. When he glanced at me, I gestured for him to follow.

THREE STEPS—AND WE ENTERED THE REALM.

Although the forest looked like an ordinary forest, we were in no ordinary place. The air crackled without a sound, ignited without a spark.

We soon came upon the foot of a mountain. I touched its side and peered along its rocky face. Above its summit, the sky spread wide and blue. Nikolas stepped along its base until he came to the opening of a cave.

Within were treasures heaped upon treasures. The hoard.

Objects for every human use lay in the heaping piles. Cauldrons, kettles, pots, cups, goblets, knives, spoons, bracelets, buckles, necklaces, rings, brooches, swords, shields, armor, daggers, spearheads, axes, saws, picks, shovels, wheels. Jewels and metals reflected shards of the sun.

The sun.

"Look. The spiral stair Aoife mentioned," Nikolas said.

At the top of the passageway, the lintel bore the circles of gold and silver and their amethyst union. I remembered the myths Old Woman had told, my fever dream of the image, and Aoife's description of the same sight.

Soft light at the entry invited approach.

We climbed the steps. Gems and crystals gleamed in the corridor, but the source and extent of the light defied explanation.

We emerged through a circle of blue sky. The air was cool and thin. As Aoife's tale described, there was an unlikely orchard of trees, in fruit and bloom. I plucked a fig the size of my thumb. The stem leaked white. I tasted the tender ripeness and remembered my old friend Fig Tree who grew in the courtyard of my childhood home.

I crept to the edge of the zenith. The world turned between my ears, its oceans and deserts and valleys and forests. All at once, there it was—I could see it—contained by the same sky and covering the same sphere.

I glanced over my shoulder to find Nikolas. I called his name and followed his answer. In the widest, deepest, softest nest I'd ever seen, Nikolas lay on his back.

"What bird built this?" he asked.

"One large enough to mistake you for a worm."

Hungry, we pulled fruit from the trees. Figs, pomegranates, apples, oranges, plums, cherries. When we were full, we returned to the cave. Outside the hollow of the mountain, we saw a human shape.

He was the color of gold from head to toe, from his triangular cap to his thick beard to his heavy little boots. His eyes sparkled bright. A scorched leather vest covered his chest. He twirled a pickax on his shoulder.

"I am called Ingot," he said.

The Gold Dwarf of the myths.[23]

Ingot shook our hands with his own—small, blunt, callused, scarred, and strong.

A shimmer drifted next to him. The vapor assumed a form, its garments loose, its hair flowing. She opened her mouth and released the song of birds and babble of brooks and rustle of leaves. Yet, within the matrix of sound, we understood words.

"I am called Incant," she said.

The White Wisp of the myths.

Incant gave us with light kisses.

"Where is the dragon?" Nikolas asked.

The dwarf laughed. "You'll get your proof, good prince. Now, come with us."

The dwarf and the woman-wisp led us back into the cave farther than Nikolas and I had explored. Ingot uncovered a wooden chest that reached his waist. He opened the lid. Three manuscripts lay stacked in a neat row, and there seemed to be more underneath. I recognized Aoife's handwriting.

"You have the missing one," he said.

"How could you—" Impossible, I thought.

"Messengers assured us it was safe with her. Isn't that so, my sister?" Ingot said.

"Yes, my brother," Incant replied.

I held my satchel. "Please, no. I want to keep it awhile longer."

"Other texts await your attention, upon the first's return," Ingot said with a smile.

The dwarf shut the chest. The woman-wisp led us from the cave to the forest's edge.

Nikolas and I followed them to a cottage decorated with tile mosaics. The panels of the door were carved with frolicking beasts. Inside, the furniture was crafted by adept hands and scaled for giants.

"This dwelling and its contents are gifts from Azul's children, as are the treasures you've seen," Ingot said.

On a round table, four crystal goblets circled a painted clay decanter. Fruit, cheese, and nuts filled a shallow bowl. Slices of meat covered a silver platter. Two gold plates, each flanked by a knife, fork, spoon, and napkin, were set before two high-backed chairs.

"Eat," Ingot said. Nikolas and I ate with ravenous delight.

"Drink," Incant said. We four sipped a maroon wine. "Listen," the dwarf and the woman-wisp said together.

Hear us.

A nexus of time and circumstance has come again.

Through many cycles, a pestilence has survived and strengthened at every turn. Its manifestations seek to divide and conquer, to use and deplete, and to ban- ish and ignore. It takes many forms and guises, but its essence is unchanged. It is a Lie.

You are called to usher in a release. The wait has been long for you, but the onus is not yours alone. Among you are helpers, many who do not yet know who they are. Among you is a child, whom the mystery of All That Is has provided to guide the way.

For the release to begin, three tasks must be completed within one moon month.

The first vial marked with the circle must be drunk by the child.

The second marked with the triangle must be left in a bowl in the sun.

The third marked with a square must be poured into flowing water.

At essence, what is within them contains its own cure.

Understand, none will be spared a role in what is to come, and some will die. This is inevitable. Know, too, that you can refuse this summons, as others have before you. This choice is yours to make, but its burden, as well as its consequences, are shared by all, past, present, future.

Whatever you choose, your world will never be the same again.

When I glanced at Nikolas, he shrugged at a loss for what to think or say next.

"We have comforts for your rest," Incant said.

She led us to a stream. On opposite ends of a bend, we bathed in warm waters and dressed in soft nightshirts and thick robes.

When we returned, the cottage was candlelit. Ingot stoked a tremen- dous fire. I settled on a cushion with my back to the hearth. Nikolas sat across from me. Incant served sweet hot milk in heavy mugs.

"The nights are cold here," the dwarf said.

"The sun has been swallowed. Sleep," the woman-wisp said.

The door closed. We looked at each other but didn't speak. After my hair was dry and the milk was gone, we went to the huge bed, Nikolas to the right, I to the left. I burrowed under quilts, sunk into the mattress, and fell into a deep dreamless sleep.

The next morning, we awoke, dressed, and breakfasted. We packed our belongings. The satchel which held Aoife's manuscript was heavier with the three vials I was given the night before.

Dawn muted the sky in pink and violet.

"We can't leave until I get the scale," he said.

We walked around the mountain and found a green valley.

Nikolas stood with his hands on his hips. "Show yourself, dragon!" He walked farther into the valley, scanning the cloudless sky.

Egnis, I whispered. *Come.*

A shadow cast upon the ground. As we looked up, the darkness took form and landed.

Red, so red, scarlet crimson ruby.

A lithe tail undulated around her body. Wings flared bold and ready, the vessels pulsing under pressure. She reached her neck down and released two plumes of smoke from her nostrils. She was myth and story, nightmare and reverie.

She was.

Nikolas squared his shoulders.

I crept forward and touched a loop of the dragon's tail.

Elegant, Egnis uncoiled. She thrust her upper body vertical. A plate of metal armor covered her chest. Her thick forelegs were bent at the joints, her fierce black claws almost touching. She blinked her ancient impossible eyes.

"You know why I stand before you," Nikolas said at last.

I felt Egnis smile.

The dragon rolled her spine, fluid as water, and slipped the armor over her neck and head. When she arose, she revealed the scars from old wounds. The long scales which spanned her chest were nicked and broken. She didn't stir until Nikolas met her eye. With a deft pinch, she ripped a scale from the side of her body. Blood trickled from her skin. She placed the transparent object into his palm and lowered her face to his. An intense silent communication flowed between them as he held the tip of her nose. As Nikolas stood taller, his bearing shifted from strong to powerful. He bowed to her, and she to him.

Slowly the dragon extended her left claw to me. She relaxed the muscular toes. In her palm was a single white flower with a yellow center. I stared at the blossom.

Your proof, Egnis said beyond words.

I accepted the gift and the message it carried. Behold: Beauty.

She unrolled her black forked tongue. At one tip was a jeweled brooch. The symbol itself—the configuration of the circle, triangle, square, and flame—was engraved in the gold, surrounded by gems. On the other tip was a gold coin embossed with the symbol strung on a leather cord.

His proof. The child's amulet, she said.

I hung the amulet around my neck and placed the flower and brooch in my satchel.

Egnis brushed my cheek with her chin and leveled one eye with mine. I stared into her pupil—the shape of the symbol's center—into a black void that held everything and nothing. Through the darkness in the light, I saw myself reflected in my entirety. All I was, all I had been, all I was to be; all I had known, all I was forced to forget. In that moment, I was infinite.

She rolled back on her legs, stretched to her full height, and lifted her head to the sky. Her mouth opened.

Violet flames curled from a column of fire. Her wings spread wide, beat once, and she was gone, lost in a swirl of clouds.

Nikolas held out the scale to me. I touched it and looked into his eyes, the color of myth deeper. His fingers locked with mine as we took one last look at the valley, the mountain, and the sky.

A bee guided us away. We crossed the realm's threshold and carried its mystery through to the other side.

OUR JOURNEY HOME WASN'T THE IDYLLIC ONE AOIFE AND WYL shared generations before. While their travels took them through miles of wild forest, the animals often guided us into villages and towns. Each time a creature led us into a hollow tree—there was always one not too far from the boundaries of a place—we found ourselves in a different kingdom or another region of the same one.

If I couldn't forage and Nikolas couldn't hunt enough for us to eat, we used what coins we had left to buy food. Unless the village was small, we could often walk among the people with little notice. In the large towns, we encountered the familiarities of home—shops and teahouses and businesses bearing the same names, goods, and interiors as ones from our land. This was evidence of Fewmany Incorporated's reach, well beyond Ailliath's borders.

During those weeks, I developed a new sensitivity. I received messages from the ground which I couldn't interpret, no images or words, only feelings, sometimes sensory, other times emotional. I called upon the creatures and plants to explain.

Here, once, there was a quick stream from a distant river, a toad said.

Where you stand was once a deep well into a sweet spring, an ancient yew said.

A wide road much traveled once passed here, an owl said.

This place mourns its barrenness, a grasshopper said.

Here, this place rages for its pillage, a bear said.

There is grief for the pain of those who once lived here, a crow said.

The earth itself remembers, I thought, then recalled what Old Woman told me after my beloved Fig Tree was cut down years before. She said the tree and I were witnesses for each other; we shared the other's story. I pondered then, could it be Nature held what we'd forgotten, what we didn't want to remember? If so, did our blood hold a tale primordial? A balance of chaos and order that humans discovered they could destroy?

Attuned to me as they were, the creatures and plants sensed my wonder, then revealed the horror. From hollow tree to hollow tree, untold distances among them, the animals led us to holes in the earth where adults and children emerged black as shadows, coated in soot. The creatures showed us to mills and factories where the smallest crawled among grinding machines and young and old stood at saws, looms, kilns, and forges, breathing gray noxious air.

They guided us to mountains with empty veins, valleys where nothing grew, forests leveled to stumps, rivers and lakes stagnant and foul. The life stripped away. Scorched, barren, laid bare.

They took us to villages reduced to smoke and ashes, towns with breached walls and fetid streets, fields covered in blood. Where there were people, the survivors went through the motions of living with the blank eyes of the dead. When I heard them speak, I recognized the clipped inflections of Kirsauan in some places, the burr of Giphian in others.

Look, the creatures and plants said. *Look at what your kind does to itself, and us.*

The creatures and plants gave no explanation why they took us to see those things, but I understood, in some way, they revealed proof of the pestilence.

As Nikolas and I made our way back home, we were ready for the journey to end, but neither looked forward to the return. I'd have to confront what I promised Fewmany and now, without a doubt, couldn't deliver to him. Nikolas had to contend with the farcical quest on which he was sent and what he discovered when he strayed from the path.

We also had a choice to make—whether to accept our call. Some nights, we discussed what had been tasked to us. How could we decide when we had no idea what would happen? Could we bear the responsibility if our decision led to ruin? Other nights, we hardly spoke at all. He held the scale, brooding in a way I'd never known him to do. I'd sit next to him with my satchel, aware of the manuscript, vials, brooch, and amulet within.

The closer we came to Ailliath, the more I felt a reversal in each step. A thousand years before, as war spread throughout the land, Aoife traveled through a winter of exile to find refuge with the Guardians, at last finding a peace she had never known.

We were returning to the very place that war began, a war based on misunderstandings and lies. I felt no peace, only dread tinged with hope, aware Nikolas and I carried a power to correct what we didn't understand.

ROTHWYKE DAILY MERCURY.

---

21 December /37. Page 2, Column 3

RIFT BLAMED FOR TOWN'S ILLS—Geologists have yet to explain the cause of the crevice widening in New Wheel, first noticed in February. There is speculation the instability is significant and responsible for mounting problems throughout our town.

Buildings in almost every south and central ward has mild to severe foundation damage. Some shopkeeps and residents state that cracks in exterior and interior walls appeared within a matter of days.

Forty-eight blocks to date have been barricaded to cart traffic due to holes and cracks in the cobblestones. Recent closures are listed on page four of this edition.

Concerns mount regarding the condition of the town's drainage system, which once reliably cleared after routine street cleanings and rainstorms. Based on reports from physical inspections, more than half of the underground pipes are compromised. Some sections are so decayed that water pools in those areas. Diversion pipes and ditches are being built to allow for excavation below the streets and replace what is damaged.

Mr. Beardsley, lead officer at Rothwyke Services, stated his men are repairing the most severe areas first. Engineers are studying where the failures might occur next, but doing so, he noted, proves difficult because the town's drain system map has a number of inaccuracies.

WEEKLY POST.

21 December /37. Page 1, Column 1

WALL BEHIND SCHEDULE—Unexpected difficulties have thwarted faster work on Rothwyke's wall yet again. Residents will remember the mortar used in the first weeks began to crumble after setting and required all work to be dismantled and rebuilt. Late this summer, torrential rains saturated the ground, rendering it too unstable to transport materials, in spite of the trackway. Now commerce colludes to slow progress. An unnamed source reports the cost to acquire and move the necessary stones is far more than estimated. Negotiations with the Council's defense committee are expected to resume.

"SOME WELCOME FOR ANYONE," NIKOLAS SAID WHEN WE NEARED Rothwyke and our fox escort ran off across the meadow.

Some welcome indeed. Deep ruts marred the east road. The standing stones, which held advertising placards, had sunk into the ground and leaned at precarious angles.

Two men stood guard at the entrance, where none had ever patrolled in recent memory. They gave us wary looks but left us alone.

As we walked through the wards, the newsbox clamor was familiar, but a faint raw odor stirred and we had to be careful of the streets, dangerous for us but worse for horses and carts.

We looked unkempt. Nikolas was unrecognizable with his beard and laborer's clothing. Some people were unkind, sneering at us. Go back to your side of town. Where are the street cleaners when you need them? Lazy riffraff.

Old Wheel was no more. The buildings that were supposed to be constructed in its place seemed far from complete. We ignored the warning signs and trespassed. We walked to the alley to see the grate where we once entered the tunnel to the woods. The cobblestones above it had collapsed. My soles ached as I felt a groan rise from the ground.

When we reached the green on the west border, we saw the piles of stones and soil, the workers' camp, and the wall's low rise.

"How is it possible so much hasn't been done?" he said.

At the woods' margin, we found a dense barrier of tangled bare branches and vines, which hadn't been there before. We crouched through an opening large enough for a deer. In the high reaches of the trees, crows perched.

We take turns at watch, a raspy voice said.

Cyril crept down a trunk to Nikolas's offered hand. The squirrel indulged a few scratches before he vanished into the trees.

"You still intend to stay with Old Woman?" Nikolas asked.

"I'm not ready to face my father, or Fewmany."

"That will make it difficult to see each other. You don't want to be seen in town, and I doubt you want a guard following me here."

"I mean to protect her, too."

"I'll do what I can to slip away, but it won't be often."

"Then in between, we'll write. I'll find some four-legged messengers."

He smiled. "Do wings count? Because wings are faster."

"Wings count." I paused. "We haven't made a decision."

"We were given no indication we have to rush. There's time," he said.

After all that had happened in the two months we traveled together, our parting felt abrupt. He held his arms open. Without a hesitant thought, I clutched him around the neck. We stood there for so long, my muscles ached, but I didn't want to let go.

He released me and wiped his fingers across his lashes. "With appreciation for your reliable escort, Miss Riven." He bowed dramatically. "Good day."

When I arrived at the cottage, Old Woman was tending her animals. The sheep, goats, and hens looked up. Cyril chattered, and she turned around. As soon as she was through the gate, she embraced me and led me inside. I placed Aoife's manuscript on a high shelf with Old Woman's handwritten texts full of plant lore and the old log I kept as a child when she taught me her knowledge. Old Woman insisted I rest as she prepared the ritual of care—a shallow tub of hot water, a full kettle, a pot of beans and savory herbs, the table set for dinner, an extra pillow placed on the bed.

From the chest where I'd stored my belongings, I pulled out a clean nightgown, a pair of slippers, and my carved stag, the last of which I set on the mantel.

Well into the evening, I told her of the journey, what I learned from Aoife's text, and the call we'd been given. I showed her the vials and what the dragon gave me—the brooch, the amulet, and the flower, which I'd pressed within the manuscript.

"What's happened here since I was gone?" I asked.

"Something I've never seen before," she said.

Not long after the first work began on the wall, she told me, there was an assault on the woods to expand the open space between it and the stones. At first, men armed with saws, axes, and scythes came at the bosk, bramble, and branches. Each night, the trees and plants grew back faster than was possible, and more men were sent to chop it away. Next, the men tried fire, but each time, the wind stalled and heavy rains doused the flames. The plants rallied and grew more impenetrable than they'd ever been. Then when the men came with sacks of salt to poison the ground, the animals and insects gathered in defense. The creatures chased, kicked, gored, and stung those who dared to approach the margin. Now, Old Woman said, wolves, bears, and boars prowled the area day and night while swarms of bees and hornets watched from the air.

I looked at Cyril. *The plants and creatures aren't doing this only to protect the woods from the wall, are they?*

No, he said. *There's a greater purpose, but we don't know why or what it could be.*

"Surely, there's a connection with what's been asked of you," Old Woman said.

"I think so," I said.

Soon, we retired for the night. When I settled next to Old Woman, I braced against the sudden memory of sleeping with my mother in the bed at my grandmother's house long ago. She'd kept a space between us, a breach I didn't cross. I listened as Old Woman fell asleep with soft snores, Cyril's little whiffles echoing her, and I wished for Nikolas's quiet. As I waited to drift off, I didn't expect how much I missed him.

NIKOLAS VISITED THE TWENTY-SEVENTH OF DECEMBER, LONG after dinner, fully shorn and well dressed. In all the years we had played and strolled in the woods, he had never been introduced to Old Woman.

"A pleasure to meet you at last," he said with a bow.

Old Woman curtsied. "For me as well, although I've watched you from a distance since you were a small boy." She kissed his forehead, then sat to mend a skirt.

He checked to make certain his horse was tethered and we set out for a walk.

"How did you get away?" I asked.

"My parents left two days ago for a trip. No one will be looking for me. I told the guard I needed a ride alone and bribed him with a bottle of brandy."

"It's that simple?"

"Depends on the guard."

When I asked what happened when he returned to the castle, Nikolas said his parents were happy to see him alive—and clearly surprised he'd come home so soon. When he showed them the dragon's scale, they congratulated him but asked nothing about his encounter and little about the journey itself.

As for the damage in Rothwyke, he said no one yet understood the cause of the holes and cracks in the streets and buildings. As for the wall, there had been problems for months. Nikolas said when he suggested to his father and several Council members that there should be a halt to the wall's construction to assess the delays, he was told, "Time is money. The longer the building takes, the more it will cost."

Unsatisfied with their responses, Nikolas made inquiries of his own. The residents were frank with complaints, the builders unwilling to say much, and those accountable had only pat answers, empty apologies, and eager assurances. He learned, too, several residents and workers had been injured—tripping into holes, debris falling on their heads—and there were at least nine attributable deaths.

"No one I've spoken with, with the power to do something, seems that concerned for people's safety. There's blood on multiple hands—Rothwyke officials, Council members, my father, Fewmany," he said.

The mention of his name made me flinch.

As we continued our walk, I told Nikolas about the attempt to cut, burn, and salt the woods' margin and how the plants and animals had joined in defense. We stopped when we came to Reach. Nikolas sat at the ancient tree's roots. I placed my hand on his twisted trunk and felt his low drone rise into my feet.

"Remember the places we saw on our way home, the ruined land and villages? I wonder now if we were shown that as a warning," I said.

"Ingot and Incant—" Nikolas paused, as if saying their names was an invocation. "They told us whatever we face is already here. So something has started. Still, we don't have any idea what will happen if we open the vials."

"The ground itself is opening up. How could it be worse?" I asked.

"Everything becomes abysmal?" he said.

I smirked at the pun.

"I know I sometimes make light of things, my obligations included, but I do take this seriously. I have the people of this kingdom to consider," he said.

"Not only Ailliath. Remember we were told, 'Whatever you choose, your world will never be the same again.'"

"Then it's an even greater responsibility."

"Now think about Aoife's manuscript. Leit told her about the darkness in the world, that after the war he feared its spread and even the Guardians wouldn't be spared its effect. Our ancestors instigated that war. You aren't Wyl, Nikolas, but his legacy is yours, as Aoife's is mine. The decisions they made affected more than themselves and Ailliath alone. Had they chosen differently, we wouldn't be standing on this land, or exist at all."

"We're supposed to do what they didn't."

"Yes, I think so."

"What's that?"

As I embraced Reach, I felt a groan rise from a deep core in the ground and flow into an unfathomable center in me. The groan spoke my name. A wisdom older than my body, older than the great tree, opened the hollows of my bones and filled the marrow. Until then, Reach's voice had always been too low for me to hear, but for the first time, I received a message he had to give.

"Tend what's within," I said.

"I don't understand," he said.

"Neither do I, but that's what came through Reach. A feeling more than a thought."

"Within what? Our own borders? You mentioned war. Well, there's no trouble here—yet—but we know there is beyond us. Giphia and Kirsau are battling Haaud and have been for months. Or did the message mean tend what's within Rothwyke? The streets, the buildings, the wall—either there will be compromises to fix things, or some disaster will force a decision."

"No, that's too literal, I think. Remember what else we were told: we're to 'usher in a release,'" I said.

"Or not," he said.

"Again, we're back to the vials' mystery and what could happen if they're opened." I sat on one of Reach's roots with my arms crossed over my knees. "And then there's Fewmany. He's connected to all of this, somehow. I have no choice but to contend with him."

"He asked you to find the hoard. That's it. All you have to do is tell him you couldn't find what he wanted. He won't know any differently."

"He might not, but I can't do that. Egnis gave me the brooch for him. His proof. Proof of the hoard? But that can't be the only reason. I must see something through. I have to—" I paused, stunned by the clarity with which the words came. "I'm meant to stop him."

"From doing what?" he asked.

"I don't know," I said.

"Secret—"

"I can't explain. I simply know this."

Nikolas exhaled a sharp breath. He looked up through a gap among Reach's limbs. "The moon isn't quite full."

I glanced skyward. "It's waning. The new one is several days away. We could wait another moon cycle, or two, or—"

"It's decided, isn't it? No need to wait for another one, assuming you find the child who must drink the first vial. How are we supposed to figure out who that is?"

"I already know," I said.

JANUARY /38

YEARS BEFORE, I'D ENCOUNTERED A CHILD WHO WAS INVISIBLE to adults. Literally invisible, perhaps not, because one can easily overlook what one doesn't want to see, but invisible enough that the orphan was trampled and ignored by passersby in the streets. The child lived with an aunt and uncle, or so I was told, and stumbled around Rothwyke chirping like a bird. Small, with light hair and yellow spectacles, Harmyn wore mismatched clothes, and because the orphan wore trousers, I assumed Harmyn was a boy.

As I traveled home from the quest, I believed I knew the child who was meant to take my mother's place. Harmyn's unsteady gait, peculiar revelations, and hidden eyes made me wonder if the orphan was a Voice. Although generations before, a rare boy was born a Voice, I expected what was to come required a child with great powers—a girl.

Before the new moon, I told Old Woman about Harmyn and asked for her help. I had neither the means nor experience to care for a child, especially one like Harmyn. For months, or longer, we'd need a place to stay until we knew what the vials unleashed.

On the evening of the new moon, the fifth of January, I called the animals to guide me. A rat escorted me from the woods to a walk-up in Elwip, an impoverished southeast ward, and scurried to a door on the musty third floor. I knocked. As I waited, I thought of my apartment in Warrick, the modest but tidy building, and my neighbors, whom I hoped were safe and well. When I knocked again and received no answer, I tried the knob, and it turned. Inside, the apartment was dark, cold, and cluttered.

I called Harmyn's name.

Scuffling noises came from another room. A child emerged.

"Do you remember me? My name is Secret. Several years ago, you gave me a flower, and an old bronze cogwheel you found in Old Wheel, and—"

"I remember. Why are you here?" Harmyn asked.

"I'm here to ask for your help, and in return, I will lead you somewhere safe," I said. I held the amulet out on my fingertips. "I believe this is meant to be yours."

Harmyn walked closer and touched the symbol. I slipped the cord over the waif's head. Her hands reached to clasp the gold circle.

"Wait here," she said as she left the room, then returned wearing a wool coat and a knitted cap and carrying a little bundle.

"Will your aunt and uncle look for you?" I asked.

"I've left for days and they never cared that I came back. They won't now," she said.

Once we stepped outside, a mare clopped her hooves to get my attention. I hadn't called for any animal's aid, but a volunteer arrived anyway. I helped Harmyn onto the saddle and climbed behind her. She seemed so small when she leaned against me, no more than eight or nine years old. "How old are you?" I asked.

"Twelve, last month," she said.

We didn't speak again as we rode through town and into the woods. When we entered Old Woman's cottage, my elderly friend greeted us. "You can see me?" Harmyn asked, shocked.

"You're taller than a rabbit and shorter than a ram, wearing a cap and coat," she said.

Harmyn smiled as she accepted a mug of cider and a seat at the table. "I need to see your eyes," I said. "Please."

Hesitantly Harmyn removed the yellow-tinted spectacles. Behind those lenses, her eyes had always appeared brown. Without them, her irises were a perfect shade of violet, circled with indigo.

My entire body ached, skin, muscle, bone, blood. A veil within me slipped, and there was a baby in a man's arms, her black hair softly tufted, her eyes . . . her eyes violet.

Sing for your ahpa, Wei, the man said, his voice straining to find the notes, the infant answering with the sweetest trill, the first song of a Voice.

Old Woman gasped. Harmyn turned toward the sound.

"I'm going to ask you a question in an unexpected way. I want you to answer if you can. When you look at me, from where on your body do you see?" I asked in the Guardians' language.

Harmyn touched her forehead, which was covered with scratches and scars.

"Have you always been able to understand any language you heard?" She nodded.

"Have you ever been able to know people's thoughts or feel their feelings as if they were your own? Did you ever help someone with the sound of your voice or touch of your hands?" I asked.

Harmyn trembled. "Who told you? I was wicked once, and I don't do that anymore."

"You were not wicked. If you had lived among people who accepted you, you would have been called a Voice. You would have been thought of as very special. My mother was like you. She was punished, horribly, for the things she could do."

Harmyn wiped away a tear. "They said I was lying. They said I was wicked and I had to be quiet, stop singing. I tried so hard, but sometimes, I can't help it. The words stream out and so does the poison that gets inside and makes me sick."

"What poison?" I asked.

"You won't believe me," she said.

"I will. No matter what you say."

"A poison that comes from other people. Sometimes I can hide and it doesn't find me. Sometimes, I can't, and when I can't, I get very sick," she said.

"I don't know what the poison is," I said, "but I was told there's a pestilence—like a grave disease—already among us. I don't know if the poison has anything to do with it, but I do know there are helpers, like Old Woman, and you, who might be able to make things better."

As well as I could, I explained what I learned in the realm and why I'd sought her. I reached for the vial. "The child who wears the amulet must drink this."

"What will happen to me?" she asked.

"I don't know, only that it must be done first," I said.

"Do I have to keep hiding my—gifts?"

"Never again."

"Do I have to go back to Aunt and Uncle?"

"Old Woman will keep you safe here."

The orphan nodded. I touched a lit match to the wick in the vial's wax seal. A tiny elliptical flame leapt as its heart burned violet.

Harmyn tasted the liquid, smiled, then finished the rest. Seconds later, her skin flushed. Her limbs palsied. Before Old Woman could reach her, she crawled into a corner. When we tried to touch her, she cried, shrieked, kicked, and punched. For hours, bruises and cuts appeared on her face and hands, and raw bloody marks circled her wrists. All of the wounds healed before our eyes. As if insane, she babbled in a deluge of languages. Memories of my muttering mother, lost in tongues, streamed back to me. This, I endured as long I could until I had to escape outside and let the cold numb me to the bone.

In the moments when Harmyn was quiet, we offered water and food, which was refused, as well as comfort, which was rejected.

The next afternoon, Harmyn finally settled. Old Woman led her out for a short walk. When they returned, Old Woman tucked the child in bed.

Through the rest of the day and night, we kept an uneasy vigil. We had no explanation for what had happened. Harmyn slept without a stir, her breathing so slow and shallow, it seemed she was near death.

Not long after dawn, Harmyn rose from the bed with her arms outstretched, as if feeling her way through the dark. "Everything is a blur. I can't see anymore! Take me outside!"

Old Woman draped her in a blanket and led her through the door. I watched as Harmyn smacked her forehead with both palms. Old Woman whispered to her, and the child began to wail.

As I started to panic, afraid of what was happening to Harmyn now, I thought of what Aoife taught her gifted daughter. "Breathe," I said. "Stand still and feel your feet on the ground. Press them down. Breathe."

Harmyn did, then peered from left to right. The sky was a flat plane of muted blue. The ground was a dull brown where the snow had melted away. A lone pine stood out green behind a copse of bare trees. On a high branch, a black crow with a bald chest cawed.

Suddenly, she touched my face and hands. "You *seem* as solid as you feel." Harmyn did the same to Old Woman. "And you." The child stepped toward the distant trees. "It is so beautiful. Is this what you see? I've known light and shadow and shapes and thinness, as if everything were made of ghosts. But look at this!" She turned to face us. For the first time, she looked me straight in the eyes. "I have to match what I see with what I feel."

The rest of the day, we witnessed her discovery—touching everything—furniture, linens, pots, tools, Cyril, the sheep, goats, and hens, water trickling in the stream, rocks on the bank, dead leaves, dry bark, the bones of a rabbit.

Whatever pain the vial's liquid had inflicted, there was a gift, too. Harmyn could at last behold the world through her own eyes.

DIARY ENTRY 10 JANUARY /38

Poured the second vial's contents into a bowl and left it in the glade. It's a foul dark liquid which reflects the sun. Fragments of rainbows appear when I look at it from certain angles.

Later: the liquid is gone.

DIARY ENTRY 13 JANUARY /38

Is this because of the vial? We can't leave her alone or something
ends up spilled, torn from its roots, or ruined. She threw my carved
stag into the fire and laughed as she held me off with the iron! I
wanted to slap her. No food is pleasing, no pillow soft enough,
no kindness accepted. Such as, I offered to buy her new clothes
because all she has is what she brought with her, and wouldn't
she like some clothes that look like what other children wear (she
dresses, well, like an orphan—from another century!) and she went
rabid, screaming I can't make her wear anything she doesn't want.
Old Woman calmed her with a promise to sew tunics and trousers
from old dresses.

While that's infuriating enough, Harmyn unleashed one of the
Voices' gifts on us—knowledge of the past. All day, I hear barbs. I
know what your father did to you. Snip, snip! I know what you did
at the ball. Oh, oh! I know what happened to your brothers. Gasp,
gasp! I know lots of things you want no one to know, my little
fungus. Once she hissed at me and told me to go in the corner.
Turned my blood hot, then cold.

She does this to Old Woman, too. I try to remember what I
learned from Aoife—pause, breathe, be kind—but sometimes it's
impossible! I've lashed out several times, which meant Old Woman
had to calm me and Harmyn. Old Woman doesn't raise her hand
or voice, but I can tell the restraint she shows is sometimes almost
beyond her limits.

If this is how she acted with the aunt and uncle, they must have
lived every single day at their wits' end. What was I thinking when I
brought that child here? Oh no—what was I thinking when I agreed
to heed the call? Or when I agreed to see where the symbols led?
Yes, move backward, where did it all begin?!

When I know Old Woman is watching her, I run off into the
woods. Better than losing my temper.

WITHIN A FEW DAYS, HARMYN'S UNPREDICTABLE FRENZIES GAVE
way to silent obstinacy.

I could hardly stand to look at her.

One night after Harmyn was asleep, Old Woman told me to meet her outside near the vegetable garden. She confronted me about my disappearances and how cold I'd been toward the child. She listened without interruption as I told her I couldn't take it anymore. I was sorry I'd taken Harmyn there—I despised her—and wished I'd never found her much less given her the vial.

"What I'm about to ask of you is something you will find painful because you so rarely received it," Old Woman said. "Harmyn needs your attention. To be ignored is a torment for every child, and for some, it is torture. Whatever was between you and your mother, I could sense it. You never had to tell me. You appeared at my door clean and well fed, but that didn't mask your loneliness."

I took a step aside. She grabbed my arm.

"You will listen, but you don't have to speak. My assumptions are, you spent untold hours alone, even when you were in her presence. You learned to hide when you were sad or frightened, because you weren't likely to be comforted when you were. You wanted affection and kindness, but you received indifference instead."

A knot seized within my navel and wrenched the root of my tongue. My sight blurred.

"I am sorry, Secret," she said. "You were a precious, gifted child and you suffered. I did my best to give you what I believed you needed, but I could never make up for the lack. Still, I know you love and trust me, otherwise you wouldn't have returned here. And no matter the behavior you see now, Harmyn trusts you and wouldn't have followed you, or taken the vial, if not. For you to disappear as you do, and refuse to look at or speak to this child, is an act of abandonment.

"You do hate Harmyn, but not for the reasons you think. Another part of you loves this child, even though the feeling leaves you confused. I'm here for you both to give the patience and understanding I can. I'm having a difficult time, too, because none of the children I've known was as troubled as Harmyn, or as exceptional. I'm grateful we have Aoife's manuscript. It's the only guide we have to help this Voice." Old Woman looked at me as if she had something else to say but kept quiet.

I knew what she held back. *As no one helped your mother.*

Old Woman released my arm. I turned to the comfort of the woods, as I always did, this time dizzy with rage.

❧

DURING THOSE FIRST WEEKS OF JANUARY, NIKOLAS AND I EX-
changed letters on slips of paper, delivered back and forth by birds. He
told me what occupied his days, and I apprised him of Harmyn's condition.

Harmyn remained silent and sullen, but in the evenings, when I
read aloud from Aoife's manuscript, she was completely attentive. She
listened to the story and to Old Woman and me when we talked to her
about being respectful with her gifts, such as not intruding on people's
thoughts.

The night was late when Nikolas visited without notice, the nine-
teenth of January. When he stepped inside, Harmyn looked up but didn't
move from her pallet.

He knelt near her. "We haven't been formally introduced. My name
is Nikolas."

Harmyn's fixed scowl vanished. "You can see me."

"Oh, am I not supposed to? Is this a game? If so, you are the worst
hide-and-seek player I've ever met," he said.

"I'm Harmyn." She stared into his eyes. "You knew that. Secret has
written letters telling you how awful I am."

I opened my mouth to respond, but Old Woman cut me a stern look.
I held my tongue.

"You look quite ordinary for a monster," he said.

Harmyn pressed her lips together but failed to stop the grin. "What
should I call you, because you're the prince."

"My true friends call me Nikolas." He slipped a satchel from his
shoulder, reached inside, and held out a package. "Cookies, which of
course you won't share."

"Thank you, Nikolas," she said.

"You're welcome." He lifted the satchel to the table. "Pastries for
you all, and staples. With three people to feed, I thought you might need
more supplies. Secret, I brought books, too, as you requested."

"I, we, are most grateful," Old Woman said as she moved to store it
away. "Tea?"

"Don't bother. I came to speak to Secret."

As I gathered my scarf, mittens, and cloak, I watched Nikolas talk
with Harmyn, awed and jealous of his ease with her.

Once we were on our way to the stream, Nikolas said, "You told me she's twelve, but she seems much younger. From her appearance, I would have thought her a boy."

"I thought so, too, until I knew she was a Voice. Old Woman said to let her dress as she wishes, although I think that will make trouble for her she doesn't need. Regardless, we have bigger concerns with her than that."

"She's still being difficult?"

"Harmyn spoke more to you in those few minutes than she has in a week. No tantrums lately, only a quiet that seems sad, but also near to explode. None of the chirping she used to do, and she hasn't sung once, even though I know she can."

"More time, then," he said.

"I suppose. Why did you come to talk?" I asked.

"Several reasons. First, your father came to see me. He's afraid you're dead."

My chest tightened. "Understandably. He hasn't heard from me since June."

"He said he placed longsheet ads in several kingdoms, but received no legitimate responses, and then appealed to my father for aid—a favor, considering their dealings through Fewmany. My father said he'd look into the matter, but in all these months, no information has come. Your father hoped I'd be willing to help."

"What did you tell him?"

"I promised to have our messengers and envoys inquire about you at their stops. I'll keep my word to him, but I think you'll have to send a letter soon to assuage his fears, if you intend to keep hiding."

"I'm not ready to deal with him."

"Secret, he cried in front of me."

I shrugged.

"That's harsh."

"He betrayed me. He knew all along what Fewmany wanted. My father used me to gain his favor, to gain something for Fewmany as much as himself. If I was promised a library, Father was promised a prize, too," I said.

"Well, then, Fewmany. We were both at a meeting this week—ongoing contention about the wall—and he asked about you," Nikolas said.

"Did he?"

"He asked if I knew you were attending an assignment on his behalf. I said you told me at my banquet that it had to do with an acquisition for his library. Then he wanted to know if I'd heard from you because he'd received no word himself."

"What did you say?"

"That you had no reason to write me because you knew I'd be away on my quest, and that if your assignment was proprietary, perhaps your silence was an act of discretion."

"A shrewd reply."

"I have my moments. Clearly, he suspects something."

I stopped at the stream's edge, listening to the burble and flow. "He sensed a connection between us that night. He surely knew we were schoolmates but not that we were close friends. Aside from that, he might well be wondering if you saw what I sought for him and if I saw what you sought on your quest."

"On that topic," he said, "I've read the quest tales in the kingdom's chronicles. Every one, starting with Wyl and ending with my father. What Aoife wrote about Wyl's quest—that's not what appears in the official record.[24] There, it says Wyl fought the dragon and got a scale, but Aoife said he didn't. In all the tales, there's always a fight, and the scale is often taken by force. Sometimes there's a mention of the landscape, and the dragon is always red, but nothing is congruent with what I—we—saw."

"You don't think what's recorded is true."

"No. I'm convinced *none* of them saw her. Do you think my father would have told his own story the way he did if he had? That was a performance, make-believe, but exactly what people expected to hear. After seeing her, I am more than the man I was. Do you understand?" he asked.

I nodded.

"It's our tradition that the king publicly tells his tale before he sends his son on the quest. Why is that? Part of the ruse? The mystery? But I want to tell what I saw now."

"There are people who won't want to hear it, especially those who rely on the prevailing perception of the truth."

"These are likely the same people who believe we have to build this wall to protect us from an invading army—or the ever-elusive dragon menace. Absent a real threat, the assumption of one is enough."

"If you told now, you'd break a tradition, but more than that, you'd expose"—I paused—"a lie that's been told for centuries."

"And am I prepared for the consequences?" he asked.

"Yes," I said.

"If I say nothing, that's almost like lying. If I tell the truth—that she exists, there was no fight or force, we have no reason to fear a dragon menace—what would happen? Possibly, no one would believe me, or nothing at all would change. What should I do?" he asked.

"I don't know. Whatever you decide will have its own effects."

He sighed. "I came to talk but also for some quiet. If you'll indulge me," he said, turning one elbow outward.

I accepted the offer and the solace of a peaceful walk.

OLD WOMAN AND I WERE IN THE VEGETABLE GARDEN, TENDING what endured the winter, when Harmyn ran out in her nightshirt.

"Give me your hands," Harmyn said. We held out our palms and she grabbed them. "I had a dream I opened my right hand to the morning sun and my left to the evening moon and the light of both never faded. Feel this."

My blood and bones filled with currents, like water.

"Is that all you dreamed?" Old Woman asked, lightly brushing the hair from Harmyn's forehead.

"I walked through Rothwyke at night. The poison was there, but it wasn't invisible like it used to be. I could see it, very dark. It poured out of doors and windows and into the streets and the ground. It came after me, and I let it. I put my hands into it and there was light, then fire. I touched my chest, until the poison drained out of my feet, and then the fire melted me from the inside out, and I turned to gold."

Old Woman glanced at me with tears in her eyes. "How do you feel after this dream?"

"Very old, as gold is old, and very new, as every breath."

When Old Woman touched Harmyn's shoulder, the child started to cry.

"I'm sorry. I couldn't help how terrible I've been. I didn't want to be. Something happened after I drank what you gave me. I remembered many awful things, things that happened to me, and things that didn't. I've hurt so much these last weeks, my body, my heart, my head." Harmyn wiped her face on her sleeve. "No one has ever been so kind and good to me, Old Woman, and we fight, Secret, but I know you want to be good to me, too. I will try very hard to be better."

Harmyn wrapped her arms around Old Woman's waist. The look

in Old Woman's eyes was a challenge. Cautiously I laid my hand on Harmyn's back.

That night, under a waning moon, Cyril whiffled opposite Old Woman's soft snore as I tried to fall asleep. From her pallet near the fire, Harmyn whispered in the Guardians' language:

"There once was a couple who prayed for a child, year after year, until one day, their wish was left on the doorstep. The baby they thought they wanted, they didn't want at all and less so when it began to babble and sing in many tongues.

"They kept this baby hidden because they were ashamed of it. It talked and sang and chirped, but the couple didn't like that, so they covered Baby's tongue with bitter liquids and tied it into chairs and whipped it until it couldn't cry.

"When Baby learned to behave, they dared not send it to school for fear it wasn't fully tamed and left it alone while they went to work. Baby discovered the door was always closed but rarely locked, so Baby left to see what was outside. That is how Baby found out being quiet for so long had made it invisible, and being invisible meant being empty, so the poison had a place to fill."

I clasped my arms as the sudden urge to hold her came over me. "I'm sorry, Harmyn. No one should be treated that way. Terrible things like that happened to my mother, too."

"And worse, because she never got to know what I know."

"What's that?" I asked.

"We are all born made of gold."

DIARY ENTRY 31 JANUARY /38

The last task is done. Released in the stream. The vial had an amber liquid which smelled of honey and almonds. Now we wait.

4 FEBRUARY /38

CYRIL'S NERVOUS PAWS TAPPED ME AWAKE.

"The King and Queen are dead," Harmyn said.

"You must go to Nikolas," Old Woman said as she handed me a dress.

"But, if someone were to recognize me—"

"This isn't the time to worry about such a thing! Cover your hair. Here, put on Harmyn's spectacles," Old Woman said, moving with the speed of someone half her age.

Outside the cottage, a horse shivered under his sweat. I climbed up, and he galloped a direct route to the castle. I heard the first of the morning's newsbox reports. Again and again—The King and Queen are dead.

At the wooden gate of the castle's outer wall, a guard peered from a barred window.

"I'm here to see the prince. Tell him Miss Evensong is waiting."

He studied me, hidden under my worn purple cloak. "Haven't you heard what happened?"

"That's why I've come. I'm an old friend. I beg you, please, ask if he'll take my visit."

I heard him speak to someone behind the gate and watched another guard walk toward the castle. The remaining guard ignored me. Sometime later, the man returned, shouting to his fellow guard to allow me inside. I rode the horse up the drive and through the gatehouse, hitching him on a nearby post. A well-dressed servant, whose steady manner reminded me of Naughton, led me across the courtyard, past the keep, through a corridor, past another courtyard, and to a building newer by a century than most of the castle. We walked through a series of lavish rooms to a staircase. On the residence's second floor, he showed me to a door flanked by two guards. One with a cleft chin looked familiar.

I knocked, heard a shout of "Who is it?" and gave my name, Miss Evensong. A bobbin released the latch. The hinges groaned.

"How did you know to come?" he asked. He shut the door.

"Cyril woke me, and Harmyn said your parents were dead."

He slumped into a chair near the fireplace. "Why are you wearing those spectacles?"

"I didn't want to be recognized." I draped my cloak on a chair next to him.

His eyes were blank. I touched his shoulder. When he wrapped his arms around me, I swayed back, startled by the urgency.

"What happened?" I asked.

"He never became conscious again. Father stopped breathing, then Mother collapsed over his chest, and she died, too. The physician could find no cause," he said.

A shake started in my hands. I pulled away and moved a footstool to sit across from him. "Before that."

"Earlier in the day, I sat in a meeting about the wall with my father and Council members, as well as Fewmany and his men. I wasn't attentive. I kept staring at the crest in the chamber, at the red scales. That night, I went to my parents' parlor. I asked my father to tell his quest tale again, which he thought was unusual, but he indulged me. I noticed his recitation was practiced, as if he'd memorized it. Then he started to laugh."

"Laugh?" I said.

"'Is there something you want to tell me, son?' he said. 'I have a question,' I said. 'What color are its scales?' 'Red, of course,' he said. Then I handed him the one Egnis gave me. 'Where did you buy that one?' he asked me, amused. I told him, 'I didn't. I stood in front of that red dragon as she pulled it from her body. Go to the meeting room,' I said. 'See for yourself. There is only one like mine in the crest. The one Wyl brought back. Like those of a snake, the dragon's scales are transparent, like this one. Their color comes through the skin.'"

Nikolas leaned forward. "'You're teasing us,' my mother said. 'Oh, no,' I assured her, 'I am not.' He could tell I was serious and muttered something about how with more time and experience, I'd understand why this is done. I knew what he meant. For months, I've turned the meaning of the quest around in my head. Power in the illusion of threat, the control it allows, the sway of tradition. When I went to their room, I was thinking of the people in our kingdom, even those beyond, and of myself, and that's when I felt it fully—the betrayal. I wasn't told the truth as a boy and was expected to lie as a man. The dragon menace was a figment all along.

"That's when I told him, 'As fathers before, Father, you lied to me.' Mother tried to hush me, so I said to her—wondering if she remembered how many times she soothed me after I had nightmares about the dragon—'Did you watch me go, knowing the truth of the quest?' The moment she said she did, he slumped in his chair. Then all was in an uproar, guards dragging him to his bed, one running off to find the physician.

"They were both dead within hours."

"I'm sorry, Nikolas."

He stared at me. "The third task."

"Done, four nights ago. Tonight is the new moon, the start of the month."

"We were told some would die. Coincidence or consequence?" he asked.

"Coincidence," I said, trying to reassure him, although I had no idea what to think. "You can't blame yourself."

"I can't? I've never been as angry as I was when I spoke to them. Furious because I realized what the lie had cost the kingdom and what it cost me, all my life."

"What if the truth is as bad as the lie but must be told anyway?"

"Well, it appears the truth killed them," he said with a bitter chuckle.

A knock and the call of three names interrupted us. I stepped away to a window as Nikolas allowed them entry.

"Your Majesty—" one said.

For a moment, I could hear nothing else.

Nikolas was king now. The address declared him so.

The men told him of burial plans, asked how he wished to notify his sisters, and promised to draft an announcement to give to the people and send to kingdoms near and far. As they discussed details, I looked around the bed chamber, paneled in a warm-toned wood and trimmed in dark green. There were two wardrobes, a table with three chairs under one window, a large bed with one long chest at the foot, pegs near the door that held a coat, a satchel, and a hat, and shelves near that, which held books and various objects. A sword in its sheath hung above the lintel.

When Nikolas closed the door behind them, I could see from across the room he was trembling. I knew that feeling—how the tremors come and go after the initial shock of death and the numbness can't return soon enough. I took his arm and guided him toward his bed. He splayed out on his stomach. I sat on the edge. My hand hovered above his back. I didn't want to touch him, to feel that raw grief, but I forced my palm to fall between his shoulders. His sob struck me in the heart and spread its dark weight into my arms. I rubbed his back until he was quiet again.

He rolled to his side. "Don't leave. Please."

He piled pillows at his headboard, told me to sit against them, and before I realized what was happening, laid his head on my lap. I stared at the door, aware of how this would appear if anyone came in, but I didn't move. His parents were dead. Who would deny him solace now?

Then, without warning, Nikolas brought my hand to his lips and kissed my fingers. A bright pulse streaked through my body, its hum still there after he loosened his grip.

"Sleep, Nikolas," I whispered, and he did, even after I slipped away to read near the fire, until there were more knocks at the door and men in fine suits requiring his audience.

THE FOLLOWING DAY, KING AELDRICH AND QUEEN IANTHE WERE buried side by side in a vault under the castle. I wasn't there. I didn't hear Nikolas's address to the people, although I read his words in the next day's longsheet.

He was close to my thoughts; he and my mother, or rather, her burial as I stood hollow near Father, so many eyes on us, Nikolas's filled with sympathy, Fewmany's with pity.

I sent him notes twice a day, and I knew my excuse for not seeing him was selfish. I didn't want anyone to know I returned from my journey, lest Father or Fewmany find out. There was a reason I couldn't confess, though. Nikolas's grief exposed how little I'd felt when my mother died.

Old Woman warned that my actions hurt him more than I thought they did. Harmyn, who admitted she "glimpsed" what troubled me, wanted to help. I knew she needed to practice her gift. I didn't mind as she hummed near me, soothing as a cat's purr. The instant her hand gripped my arm, a black feeling rushed up from my belly. I refused to let her touch me again.

A week after the deaths, Nikolas arrived in the middle of the afternoon. Old Woman and Harmyn expressed their condolences, then left when Old Woman said they had some foraging to do.

The door closed.

"I know why you've kept away, but if anyone could understand what these few days have been like, wouldn't it be you?" he asked.

I looked at the floor.

"Don't you remember? I've lost both, not one. I don't have the luxury to hole away in my room or the woods. I've had not a daylight's moment of peace. Briefings on state matters the Council thinks I must have *now*. Already the curries for favor. A pact to review. Piles of reports and letters. One discussion about when to hold the coronation even though that's nothing but a matter of ceremony. Even questions about what I want for dinner," he said.

He threw his overcoat on the table and tore the cravat from his neck. "If that weren't enough, I know who had allegiance to my father, but not whose fealty is genuinely mine. Whom can I trust? Whom can I not? Who trusts me? Because—this is as unforeseen as much as it is obvious— there's a rumor they were assassinated, and another that I arranged for them to be poisoned. The court of Ailliath in chaos. But wait—the worst may soon come. What else will the vials unleash?"

When he swiped up the iron poker leaning against the hearth, I stepped back. He stabbed at the logs. "And I can't stop thinking of their stagnant blood and worms coming through the rot. I wonder if I'm going mad. Did you think such things when your mother died?"

I'd had those thoughts, but without any horror, only a sense that something was over. How could I admit to him I had never missed her? "Yes, I did."

Nikolas sat down and touched the stone carved with the symbol. "How did you make them stop?" he asked.

"I never figured that out. Eventually they ebbed away until they were gone."

"I miss them as if they were parts of my flesh ripped out. Tell me it will feel no worse than it does now."

"This will ease," I said.

He curled his head to his knees and began to cry. I was shaking then, remembering my own twisted grief, shocked but not sad, abandoned and released. I forced myself to put my arms around him. He hugged me back. In all the time he spent with me in the months after her death, never once did he hold me, but that was my limit, not his.

We were still sitting there when Harmyn and Old Woman returned with Cyril at their heels.

The child knelt at Nikolas's side and curled her hands around his arm. His body stiffened.

"Harmyn, you're to ask permission first. We discussed this. Let him go, or ask his consent," I said.

"I can help, but that means I have to see inside. May I?" she asked.

"The way Wei did?" he asked. I'd read the manuscript to him. He knew what Voices could do.

"Yes," she said.

He nodded.

Her lashes fluttered. As her breathing slowed, his became shallow and rapid. Old Woman stood near me to watch as Harmyn's face shifted through emotions light and dark, then froze in pain. Tears dripped over her cheeks as Nikolas pitched forward with a keen so raw, Old Woman let out a hitching cry and I fought the one rising in me.

"Listen. There was no other way. Don't blame yourself. I feel what you do, I can see it, it's chewed a hole in your side—yes, where *that* is," Harmyn said as he shook his head. "Egnis showed you the great man you are and the great king you could be. The sacrifice is unbearable"— Harmyn choked back a plaintive sob—"but it must be borne."

She began to hum an unfamiliar melody, but when Old Woman began to sing the words in the Guardians' language, my mind and body fused together a memory not my own. This was a song people sang in Aoife's settlement, an ancient hymn all the Guardians must have known.

When Harmyn lowered her arms, Nikolas faced her. Her cheeks were pale, her eyes too bright. She pressed her palm against his forehead, then pulled it away. "Better?" she asked.

"Better. Thank you," he said.

Harmyn winced as she stood.

"What's wrong, child?" Old Woman asked.

"That was hard. I want to take a nap," she said as she curled up on the bed.

Nikolas went to cover her, folding the blanket's edge at her chin. "She's already asleep," he said as he turned to us. "That was—that was—"

"Beyond words," I said.

DIARY ENTRY 27 FEBRUARY /38

Harmyn has been going to town in the middle of the night. This shouldn't concern me as much as it does, because she used to do this all the time. She said she needed to "practice" and to learn if the "poison" still hurt her as it once did. People still can't see her (yet?) but some can hear her. If she says hello or sings a little, they look around trying to find the voice. Glimpsing people's thoughts and memories is as simple as turning her attention to them, but if she touches them, her awareness is much stronger. She promises she didn't do that much. As for the poison, because we've taught her to breathe and keep her feet or hands on the ground, Harmyn discovered she can let it pass through like water, similar to what happened in her dream.

However, she's noticed something she didn't before.

Everyone is filled with "shadows," inside their bodies. Sometimes they seem to disappear, but they can come out again in an instant. The shadows are grayish and thin, or black and dense. Children have them, too, but theirs aren't as dark or thick. In the past weeks, she's noticed the shadows changing, getting darker, heavier, more of them.

These shadows make the poison, and the poison makes the shadows, she said. As poison, it moves and gets into other people. If the poison stays, it makes shadows, or makes the ones already there worse.

She said she understands now what happened after she drank the first vial. She had shadows that made her act hateful, and that poison entered me and that made my shadows angrier.

Old Woman wondered if the shadows are related to memory. Harmyn confirmed they are. Harmyn wouldn't tell what she'd seen in Nikolas, but when she sat with him, one of his shadows lightened ever so slightly. I asked why.

"Because he was willing to see it," she said.

DIARY ENTRY 5 MARCH /38

Through his notes, I can tell Nikolas has his sense of humor again. He still grieves, but he says it's not as acute. Rothwyke continues to crumble; the wall rises still slowly. He's admonished me for avoiding my father (Father has seen him again) and Fewmany, and he's right to do so, but I've needed time to think. How careful must I be with

Father, not knowing what he might divulge to Fewmany, and how careful must I be with Fewmany, knowing how magnificently I must deceive him.

I've asked him to search for a certain map Aoife mentioned, even though it might no longer exist.

ON THE FOURTEENTH OF MARCH, A HORSE CARRIED ME FROM the woods to town. Although a note would have prepared Father for my return, I decided to appear without warning. At the threshold of my childhood home, I knocked instead of using the key hidden near the steps.

"Hello, Father," I said when the door opened.

He crushed me into his chest. I submitted until I needed a full breath and pulled away. He touched my head. "You're silver again."

I walked into the parlor, which looked the same as always. On the table next to his favorite chair was a lit lamp and a cup. I draped my cloak over the settee.

I accepted his offer of tea. When he returned, I was sitting in the chair across from his.

"Where have you been?" he asked.

"On a long journey, on Fewmany's behalf," I said.

"That I know. I've been worried sick. I even appealed to the prince to find you. Not a single letter in all this time to tell me you were well."

"Rarely was I near a post service."

"That you were alone, far from civilized places—"

"I was quite fine on my own, I assure you."

He closed his eyes. They were damp when he opened them. "I'm so relieved you're home. I've missed you."

My mouth remained shut.

"Tell me about your journey," he said.

His Tell-a-Bell whirred into its *tinktinktinktinktink*. He batted at the side of his head, fumbling for the mechanism, and pulled the device off his ear.

"What you want to know is whether I found what I was sent to find," I said. "Per my agreement with Fewmany, I'll tell him, and only him, what I discovered. Whether he tells you is up to his discretion."

Father's expression shifted from shock to anger to assent. In this instance, I was almost a colleague and not quite his daughter. He smiled slightly. "You remind me of your mother now. She wouldn't speak of confidential matters that involved him."

Whatever I thought I might say then, about the night of the scissors and the symbol, how he used me to win Fewmany's favor, vanished. There was something else to say first.

"Let me tell you about your wife," I said. "Do you remember the manuscript you gave to Fewmany, the one you found on her table? Well, I've read it."

Father, so rarely at a loss for words, sat without a sound.

I explained how it had arrived by courier, that she forbid me to tell him about it, and that I suspected the language I spoke when I awoke from the fever was the same one in which the manuscript was written. Then I told him before she died, she made a cipher for it.

"I don't understand." He twisted the ring on his hand.

"She meant for me to find the manuscript and translate it."

"Why? You be direct with me, Secret," his voice firm, his tone fearful.

Now wasn't the time to explain the manuscript's relevance to Fewmany's pursuit of the hoard or the truth about how The Mapmaker's War began. Nor was this the moment to describe my journey to the realm and all that was unfolding. "Why? I'm not sure, entirely, but what I learned helped me to understand her," I said. "The manuscript tells of a people lost to history and the special children born among them they called Voices." I described their gifts and how they were treasured if they were born to those who understood them, reviled if born elsewhere. "Once, there were others like her, same eyes, same gifts."

"Others like her," he said with a smile. Then his face darkened. "As you know, your mother didn't speak of her past. She protected you from a great deal of ugliness. When we courted, she told me about the things she suffered. She always feared I'd have a change of heart about her, but I didn't. Each time she spoke of the past, it felt like a gift of trust as much as a warning. You wouldn't believe what was done to her. Evil things called good. Her body, her mind, violated."

He wiped his fingers across his eyes. "Once she divulged a horror, she never spoke of it again. Aside from her ability with languages, her other oddities seemed to vanish, but I knew she hid them instead. Zavet had uncanny moments that seemed a glimmer of her secret self, sometimes prescient dreams." He paused, his gaze on me reluctant, then looked away. "She'd remark about events of which she could have no possible knowledge. Sometimes, she seemed to have eyes in the back of her head."

"In a way, she did. She was blind," I said.

"Ridiculous."

"She was blind in the way we experience sight. She herself might not have realized it. That's why she moved slowly, why she was clumsy."

I stared at him as his eyes focused inward on his own thoughts.

"She learned she wasn't alone. Not the only one. That must have given her comfort. She died"—his voice cracked—"she died with the knowledge. *That* was why she was so peaceful those weeks before."

Dread gushed under my skin. The truth pushed against my throat, but I held it back. I couldn't tell him she killed herself. Not yet, not then. I couldn't bear to watch the grief ravage him as it had six and a half years before.

So all I did was nod. Yes, Father. What a good girl I was.

"Where are your things? I'll take them up to the room and find clean linens," he said.

"I'm not staying," I said. His expression fell with disappointment. "A friend is allowing me to stay with her."

"Miss Sheepshank and Miss Thursdale? The Misses Acutt?"

"Another friend. You don't know her."

"Why won't you come home?"

"This hasn't been my home in years."

He winced. "Is there something you wish to say to me?"

"Do not tell Fewmany I've returned. This is a test. Don't make me regret I've come to you first. I'll see him soon."

His mouth gaped as if he were about to reply, but he closed it.

"I'm going to the courtyard," I said.

He followed me into the kitchen. He turned at the dining table, the same ochre bowl at its center, to put the cups away in the basin. I didn't glance at her worktables as I stepped toward the back door and pulled the great bobbin and latch.

In the courtyard, I stood where my old friend Fig Tree had been. I thought of the hours I'd spent in her company, feeling content as I sat under her limbs. There was no flame, no fire, but the ground under my soles felt as if it had recently burned. I crouched to press my hands against the meager warmth, a gesture that echoed through the whole of my life.

DIARY ENTRY 20 MARCH /38

First day of spring. This morning as I went to fetch water, I sensed
something was wrong. I called to the plants and trees but received
no reply. I know they heard me because when I asked them to move,
they bowed and bent. But they cannot speak.

DIARY ENTRY 23 MARCH /38

Today, the plants can't hear. They don't respond to anything I say.
They give me messages, however. Images of stillness. The sky soft
with dawn's glow, the moon's cool light, animals enthralled by a
breeze. It is reassuring they aren't distressed, although I don't know
what afflicts them. Of course I suspect the vials.

DIARY ENTRY 27 MARCH /38

Yesterday, I realized they can't move. We can communicate again,
though, and they conveyed the wind causes pain, pushing against
their stiff limbs and stalks. Buds I expected to see open by now show
no signs of unfurling.

When I finally told Old Woman what I'd noticed, she said she'd
sensed an eerie lull in the woods but couldn't determine why.
Harmyn suggested we go into town to see what's happening there, so
we did, with me disguised. Everything is paralyzed there, too—trees
along the sidewalks, potted flowers, ivy clinging to walls. I didn't say
how worried I was, but I didn't have to. Harmyn felt it and held my
hand on the way home.

Then this evening, I went to Reach with hope the ancient tree
could tell me what's happening. I saw the margins of his leaves were
deformed, and I asked how he was. He heard me, and I received his
reply. In the dark between my eyes, a seed ruptured into a sapling,

which matured into a great tree, season to season, until its leaves withered and dropped and its bark shriveled.

He's dying.

Then the image of the dead tree changed. A crack formed in its trunk, widening and deepening, until there was a hollow through and through. On the other side of the hole was a tiny sapling, its young leaves open and green.

I thought of the petrified tree where I'd been stung and Nikolas and I crossed into the realm. A thin place it straddles, and I believe Reach knows he will one day do the same. As for the new sapling, I don't know what he meant.

I was already in tears by then, and was more overcome when he revealed his memories of me, of secrets I'd told him in words and tears. He also showed me other children, throughout ages, sitting at his roots, some happy, some sad, all of them seeking his comfort.

I asked how he sickened. Reach answered with visions of rain and underground flows and a great flood. I didn't understand immediately, but then I realized: The water wasn't the cause but the carrier. What I poured from the last vial contaminated the water, an element essential to life.

What have I done?

28 MARCH /38

As we readied for bed, we heard a horse approach the cottage. Harmyn peeked through the door and let Nikolas inside. He greeted us, scratched Cyril behind his ears, and set a satchel of food on the table. While Old Woman and I put it away, Nikolas presented a box filled with paper and coloring sticks to Harmyn. She told him she'd never had a plaything like that, adding, with shame, she'd never learned to write or draw.

"I'll teach you a technique you can master in minutes," he said, pulling a seat next to her. Soon enough, Harmyn found a comfortable grip and practiced as Nikolas held a sheet of paper steady.

Old Woman welcomed Nikolas to stay but declared it was well past

Harmyn's, and her, bedtime. After one more drawing, Nikolas told them good night, and we left for a walk.

"How did you manage to get away this time?" I asked.

"I told my trusty guard Hugh I was leaving, got on my horse, and rode away."

"What was the bribe?"

"No bribe. I realized I'm king now and I can change the rules if I wish," he said, throwing his arms out in a magnanimous gesture.

"You're joking."

"Next, I'll have someone tarred and feathered for my amusement."

"Have you chosen your victim?"

"The magnate himself, but half the Council might overthrow me if I did."

A protective feeling came over me for Fewmany, unwelcome but there nonetheless. "At his mention—did you find the map?" I asked.

"Maps. The original, and the copy. I was surprised either still existed. You won't believe how beautiful they are, or the others of hers in the archive. Wait until you see them."

"Others . . ." I said. "So, your map for the quest was different?"

"The one I used sent me south, then due east into Thrigin and Uldi-land. This map is more, how do I put this—adventurous. Crossing rivers and mountains. It's an irreplaceable artifact."

"The only one who would appreciate that better than I is he, and that's why it must be an ancient one."

I pulled an envelope from my skirt's pocket and gave it to Nikolas. "Please have that delivered to his manor. It states I'll see him soon."

As we walked, we filled in the details we couldn't fit into our letters. Our steps led us to Reach. I didn't want to tell Nikolas yet that the tree was dying. My heart felt bruised when Reach gave a deep sigh as Nikolas rested his hands on a huge limb.

"How long ago it seems, the first time you showed me the way here. He knows things about us no one else does, doesn't he?" Nikolas asked.

"Old Woman once told me, 'Sometimes, trees are the only things that stand still long enough to listen and remember.'"

Nikolas brushed his palms along the limb, walking toward me. "A silent witness."

"Who never forgets." I closed my eyes when I realized we were part of Reach's final memories.

When I opened them again, Nikolas was looking straight at me. He dropped one hand from the tree, placed it on the curve of my waist, and kissed me.

This wasn't like the one before the quest. This kiss was insistent and ardent. My lips parted and my fingers wrapped around his neck of their own volition. When his hands cradled my face, I drew away, breathless.

"Why?" I asked, my common sense flooding back.

"I wanted to. I think you did as well."

The kiss had lingered far too long to deny it. "But we're—We can't—This isn't—"

He took my hand—that was all—and the blood rushed swift in my veins, every shallow breath ablaze. I wanted the feeling to stop, and I didn't.

"I've loved you since we were children. You've been my best friend, always. That hasn't changed. But now. Secret, I'm in love with you."

I tugged my hand away. "This can't be."

"Why not?"

"Because you're my best friend and I'd prefer not to compromise it or, worse, lose it to some irreparable dalliance. Aside from that, even if I were from a family of land and title, I haven't the right blood," I said.

"The heart is blind to such distinctions. Right blood—that doesn't matter to me, and I know it doesn't to you. Every day, more now than ever, I'm crushingly aware of what's expected of me, what people want from me. With you, there's no pretense. I believe you love me for who I am rather than what. I've never doubted whether your esteem for me is genuine," he said.

I blinked to fight back confused tears. "Of course it's genuine. I feel the same. Regardless of my—idiosyncrasies—you have been the truest of companions."

When he searched my eyes, I knew I'd met him only part of the distance.

"You stand there as if you're being interrogated. Why is this so difficult?" he asked.

"I haven't thought of you, of us, in any other way."

"Never?" he asked.

"Not a single conscious thought," I said.

"And now?"

"Now I must because, although I wish I could, I can't deny I returned what I received."

"Why would you wish that?"

"I don't want to sacrifice what we share for the sake of curiosity."

"I might be curious where my emotions could lead, but curiosity isn't the impetus, I assure you," he said. "My impression is I haven't been rebuffed, yet for the purpose of clarity, you meant to kiss me back, and you wouldn't be opposed if it happened again."

I smiled, relieved by his humor. "Isn't one supposed to be engaged to take such liberties?"

"Too late. That makes me a cad and you a woman of questionable morals. An answer, please."

"Yes, and I would not."

He pecked me on the cheek. "Good night, Secret," he said, then walked off into the dark.

As I made my way back to the cottage, I could hardly tolerate the thrum in my body and the lightness in my head. Again and again, I returned to the moment he touched my waist and kissed me. By the time I settled in for bed, my head battled with my heart.

This is preposterous—and unseemly, I thought. What would come of such an entanglement, no doubt finite, could only lead to heartache. And he was no ordinary man. There was a limit to the latitude he had over his own life. He was a king, for whom the future was prescribed, including his choice of a wife, not that such a thing was even his intention in my regard.

I also thought of Aoife and Wyl and the ruin they brought. Had Wyl done his duty and married the princess betrothed to him—or if Aoife had refused him—either decision could have altered the events that led to the war, and where we were now. To risk a repeat of that past, in any variation, wasn't something I wanted to do.

In all the years I'd known Nikolas, I'd never hoped for anything more than his companionship. That alone had sustained me, my trust in it inviolable. Yet if I were truly honest, there had been moments, a gesture, word, or look, when a boundary blurred between us.

That night, he crossed it, and I joined him there.

Although every rational thought compelled me to, I knew I couldn't turn back.

DIARY ENTRY 29 MARCH /38

Well, then. The plants are fine today, all faculties as they were before. But the animals—now they can't speak.

I noticed this when I awoke. There was no birdsong. Harmyn was with me when I stepped outside and called out. A fox, sparrow, and beetle came forward. I asked them to turn in a circle, which they did, and when I asked them to call to their own kind, I could see how the fox and sparrow strained, but there was no sound. When Cyril returned from his forage, he had no voice either.

There's no denying a cycle has begun again. I'm worried, but not yet afraid.

Another cycle has made its turn, too. Old Woman has been telling the Myths of the Four to the newborn animals, as she's done every spring. It's a comfort to hear them. The stories enthrall Harmyn as much as they did me when I was little. She listens and asks questions, fascinated by the Great Sleep (What is it? Where is it?) and Egnis (Why was she so wise?) and Azul the Orphan (Who left Azul in the river? Was Azul a human? How did they become so brave?).

DIARY ENTRY 1 APRIL /38

Fourth day. No change in the animals.

I'll see Fewmany in three days. Harmyn warned me to be careful about what I plan to do. I didn't tell her, but she glimpsed me (with apologies) and him. She said he's never been so close, and he truly believes I can lead him to what he desires. Of course I can, I said, but I won't. She became very grave then. "He's vulnerable in a way he hasn't been in many, many years. This is your advantage, but it's also dangerous."

4 APRIL /38

ON MY WAY TO MEET FEWMANY FOR THE FIRST TIME SINCE MY return, I noticed how subdued the town was. Aside from the usual bustle and clatter, the creatures were as silent as the ones in the woods. The horse who volunteered to carry me made no sound at all, not even a whiffle. I heard no pigeon coo, dog bark, or rat squeak.

I'd left the cottage early so that I could ride the horse into Warrick past my old walk-up. The lights were dim behind drawn curtains, including my former apartment's. I wondered if the Elgins were having a peaceful night, if Mrs. Woodman had baked her cinnamon buns that morning, if Miss Sheepshank and Miss Thursdale had finished their weekly stack of periodicals, if Sir Pouncelot was trying to decide among the Misses Acutt's laps.

When I arrived at The Manses, the guards at the main gate and the manor's entrance greeted me, remarking how long I'd been away. When I reached the house, I hitched the horse and walked up to the front door. My hand slipped into my satchel, reaching for the key, which was no longer there. What the body remembers, I thought as I rang the bell.

"Good evening, Miss," Naughton said when he opened the door.

"Good evening," I said.

As I entered, I looked at him—hair thinner, eyes alert, his vest piped in blue. I grabbed his arm and dragged him into the ballroom.

"I know that blue and why you wear it," I said. "Why didn't you tell me? You're a spy, aren't you?"

He gave a slight smile. "A warrior, first and foremost. He had to hire me, of course, but I volunteered for this service many years ago, as he rose and our Elders determined he should be watched. He's long been considered a threat to the balance of All That Is."

I wanted to ask dozens of questions, about his life and his duty, but there was no time. I suspected there was little he would, or could, divulge.

"When you came here, I was informed who you were believed to be," he said. "I was told to protect you, but not to interfere with your dealings with him. I failed in my detachment at times, but my allegiances held firm, conflicting as they are. I've been told a great change is at hand. You and the King accepted a call. Do you know what's to come?"

"Not yet," I said.

He nodded, led us out, and shut the door. I looked ahead to see Mutt scrambling against the marble floor. When I reached down to scratch his muzzle, I felt how much he wanted to speak but couldn't. My ears instead filled with the sound of a grandiloquent aria, artfully whistled.

"What-ho! A sight for sore eyes. My keeper of tales," Fewmany said.

My hand reached out before I thought twice. As Fewmany clasped it in greeting, I couldn't deny—although the admission angered me—I had, in some way, missed him.

He held firm a moment longer than necessary, his gaze exploratory. "How different you seem, almost . . . radiant. Ah, the silver returned!" he said.

"There were few parlors along the way," I said.

He seemed unchanged—his amber eyes without an extra line, his hair with the same streaks of gray, the pocket of his coat stuffed, the Tell-a-Bell, timepiece, and ring shiny as ever—but the scar under his jaw and chin was swollen and red.

"What happened?" I asked, pointing.

"'Tis the result of a nightmare flailing, that's all. A bottle of your favorite wine awaits. Come."

Once inside the library, I sighed, unprepared for the way the smell and light and familiar objects made me feel. Content, secluded.

"There's still time to gather a costume," he said, whisking an envelope from the table and holding out the ball invitation to me.

As we settled in the high-backed chairs near the fire, he reached to the table between us to pour our drinks. "Quire visited two weeks hence. He asked of you and said he missed your, what was it, 'attentive and inquisitorial company.'"

I accepted the wine he offered and set it aside. "Do give him my regards."

"So long away without a word. Where have you been?" he asked.

From my satchel, I withdrew his gift. On my open hand, the jeweled brooch sparkled. He plucked it from my palm, bent toward the flames, and pressed his fingertip across the engraved symbol.

"Beautiful, isn't it," I said.

"Unequaled by any I've ever seen," he said.

"Nothing you've ever heard or read conveys the enormity or splendor of the place where I found it."

"Then tell me now," he said.

I heard an undertone in his response, a challenge for a good story but also for proof. I had to feed him, gorge him, whet his appetite for even more.

"Beyond our land, a blue sky consorts with a black mountain, and within the belly of this mountain is a cave filled with the light of the sky," I said, then described the treasure of a thousand kingdoms. I told of objects meant for war and for home, made with hands which knew the needs for beauty and function. So much gold, silver, copper, and tin; so many emeralds, rubies, sapphires, and diamonds. How was it possible for a hoard like this to exist, with still more hidden beyond the glowing mouth of the cave?

"What of the dragon?" Fewmany asked, his tone impartial, his eyes searching.

"What makes for good lore isn't necessarily the truth."

"No vicious beastie guarding its booty?"

"No. Unless it was away collecting another prize, as it's said to do."

"No guards of any kind?" he asked.

"None that I could see."

"An old woman led you there, to a treasure that vast."

"The old women know where it is, and no one tried to stop me." As I breathed calmly, he searched under my skin. "Few would have the courage to make a journey to find it, much less the endurance to reach it."

He cocked his head, the edge of his teeth visible.

"Remember what motivation I had to persevere. You do recall our agreement," I said. Finally, I sipped my wine. The dry smoky heat released a wave of pleasure.

"I do. But tell me, after seeing what you saw and taking what you did, why would you return to me and reveal what you have? Why not keep it for yourself?"

I anticipated his doubt in the tale's legitimacy, but not a doubt in me. My lashes dampened. I didn't speak until I forced back the tears, which gave him a moment longer to notice what I wished I hadn't felt.

"As I've told you before, I have simple needs and wants," I said. "Your offer was generous—and more than enough. I promised to do my best, and that's what I've done. You once asked for my gratitude, enthusiasm, and fealty, which I believe I've given in every manner in which I've served you. What else must I do to prove it?"

He leaned toward me. "'Twas not a question of your character," he said softly, perhaps too softly. "You, my bonny archivist, have proven yourself time and again. Surprised me as well, haven't you?"

My ears heard the hiss of silver, my tongue tasted the ruby of desire, and my skin felt the wet of blood. I pressed my forehead into my hand. Why are you doing this? I asked myself. Why didn't you stop when you had the chance? In that pause, I surrendered to fate's long reach. I was never the pawn Fewmany thought I was or I believed myself to be. He never had the power he thought he did. We were echoes through time, with Raef and Aoife's distant deeds unresolved. This old pattern would somehow, and soon, be altered.

"I've been honored to be in your service and by the trust you've placed in me, beyond my responsibilities as your archivist. There have been . . . experiences . . . these past years which have revealed me to myself in unexpected ways," I said.

"Such candor," he said.

"I want you to know of my appreciation."

"There's never been a question about it. But why do I feel as if you are about to drive a blade gently?"

"I don't intend to return to the library. My work is done. I think you'd agree."

"A fraction of the collection is cataloged. I'm not mistaken to say you found pleasure in your duties."

"Let's not pretend you chose me for that sole purpose."

His eyes searched me, searched me deep, but what he sought—my fear, my need, my innocence—I cloaked with my certainty.

I stared back. "Your instincts were right about me, after all. You hired me, then gained my trust as I gained yours. Now what you want is within reach, and what I want is within mine."

"I'm a man of my word, this you know to be true, and what I have promised, I shall deliver, once I claim the boon. There aren't yet heaps of chalices and blades in my possession, but you will be there to witness when I do."

I delved into my memory. The library's collection, my favorite objects from the rooms, and a manor to keep me in luxury all of my days were my rewards for his attainment.

"I will provide you with a map," I said.

"I asked specifically for your lead."

I hesitated for the briefest instant. "You didn't stipulate how I would lead you. That detail wasn't part of the *nudum pactum*."

Fewmany's brow rippled with tension, his expression confused. "Are you—are you *refusing* me?"

"Yes."

Disbelief numbed every feature of his face.

"I've violated nothing but your expectations, Fewmany."

He set down his glass with a slosh and went to stand near the fire. His back was to me as he gripped the mantel.

"That brooch is a token of what you seek. I risked my life and my limbs to obtain it. What more do you want from me?" I asked.

"What could I offer to change your mind?"

"Nothing. For you to honor my compensation when you return will suffice."

"So confident, are you, I will find it with this map."

"Yes."

Then he turned. He stood on the hearth stones, split by shadow and light. He appeared ageless, then ancient. When I blinked, I saw him as he was.

"Secret."

"Yes?"

"What do you think I would do if I discovered you deceived me?"

His voice chilled my blood, but I wasn't afraid. "Everything in your power to make certain I never touched a thing I loved again."

"How right your riddle." His mouth bowed in a cryptic smile. "How soon do you expect to produce this map?"

"Possibly by the time of the ball."

"Less than a month." He sat again, sipped his wine. He reached the brooch toward me like an offering.

I withdrew. "No, it's yours. I brought it as proof."

Fewmany pulled it to his chest. "Thank you," he said with surprise, even suspicion. "You have no desire to keep it?"

"That isn't what I value," I said. I looked to the gallery, the books in the closed cases. "I read in a text not so long ago, 'Gold spent is gone. A tale can be told again.'"

"How precious," Fewmany said as he pinned the brooch to his lapel. His now.

DIARY ENTRY 5 APRIL /38

The din this morning—chirp bellow grunt howl croak whir—
because the creatures can speak again, but they cannot hear. Cyril
crept toward me as I stood listening. When I picked him up, he stared
into my eyes. He confirmed what Reach told me. The sickness came
through the water.

Nothing is spared the need of water.

We will sicken as the plants and creatures have. They've been our
warning.

Old Woman and Harmyn know now. We had a talk. I asked
Harmyn what she'd seen in town of late. She said people's shadows
are becoming darker and there are more of them. (Mine are, too, she
told me.) She still has shadows, but they aren't the same for her. What
she drank from the vial forced them out, she doesn't have as many,
and they're light, like veils; she can see through them. Old Woman,
she said, has light shadows, and that hasn't changed at all. Why? I
asked. Because Old Woman was born among the Guardians; that
makes her different somehow.

So, at the moment, we assume the shadows will get worse, and the
sickness will affect them.

As for when the sickness will strike us, I don't know for certain,
but I think there are clues connected to cycles. I was told to release
the vials within a moon month. The first sign came on the first day
of spring. The illness has lasted for fixed periods. At worst, we might
become ill right after the animals, less than two weeks. At best, with
mercy, a few months. The start of summer.

Now I must tell Nikolas.

THE NEXT DAY, I CHOSE TO WALK TO THE CASTLE RATHER THAN
accept an escort from the horse grazing outside the cottage. I didn't go
alone, however. Through the woods and across the green, a fox ran ahead.
Once I reached Rothwyke's edge, a mastiff loped at my side.

As I passed through the wards, I watched how people treated the
animals—horses, mules, cats, dogs—all of them deaf, most of them confused and afraid. Some people tried to soothe them with kind voices and
caresses. Several ignored them with stern faces. Others screamed at or

struck them, furious that the creatures wouldn't listen, wouldn't behave, wouldn't be quiet. When I found an animal alone, I waited for a sign of welcome and gave it a reassuring touch, all I could give.

At the castle, a guard brought me to the Great Hall and told me to wait. Nikolas and I hadn't seen each other since the night we kissed. Under other circumstances, I might have been more nervous, expecting an awkwardness between us, but then, my worry was for greater matters.

Half an hour later, he arrived with a guard walking a few paces behind. Nikolas looked commanding in his dark blue coat and trousers and green damask vest. His smile suggested he was glad to see me, but it faded the closer he came.

"This isn't a social visit," he said.

"It's not."

He led us through the Great Hall to a crossroads among hallways. I recognized it immediately. I'd been there the night of Nikolas's fourteenth birthday. I'd slipped away from the scavenger hunt, crept through the gold-gilded corridor lined with oil lamps, and peeked into a private chamber where King Aeldrich sat alone. This was his son's office now.

One wall was still covered in weapons, the shelf with the gold sword still there. To the right of that was a large window, the casements open. Inside was a desk decorated with marquetry and an imposing carved chair behind it; near the fireplace, four upholstered high-backed chairs in a semicircle with a low table in front.

Nikolas leaned against the desk. "What's happened?"

I explained what I'd witnessed among the plants and animals. He'd noticed how quiet the stables were the week prior but hadn't given it much thought. I said they couldn't hear now, and within a few days, they wouldn't be able to move.

"The people will suffer, too. The Plague of Silences—" I paused. I had named it. "The Plague of Silences won't spare us."

Only then, although I'd read it several times, did I grasp the prophecy Aoife recorded in her manuscript. Sisay, the ancient Voice who trained Wei, had told Aoife: "In an era yet to be born, you will speak to a grandchild. With this child, and others whose time has come, beginning in the land of your exile, a great hush will force a reckoning between lies and truth. The future will depend on those who survive."

I sighed, unable to comprehend the whole of it.

"A plague unleashed to fight a pestilence," Nikolas said as he moved to the window. "Well, no wall can stand to that."

I walked over to him. Below us, an older woman stepped through a kitchen garden bordered by rosebushes dotted with early blooms. "We don't have much time to prepare," I said. "I think we'll be struck at the start of the summer. As to how long we'll be sick—weeks, possibly months. For plants and animals, there's a duration for each phase, but I don't know if that will hold true for us. I've received no word of a spread beyond Rothwyke, but I think it will only be a matter of time before that happens."

"The panic this could cause. I'll have to involve the Council." He stood with his arms folded, his features calm, his sight fixed in the distance. At that moment, I knew Nikolas's role in what was to be. Beyond the virtue of his birth, he possessed a quality of his essence. I'd seen it the first night we met as children, and in his words and deeds ever since. His gift was judgment, fair and clear.

I touched his arm. He turned to me. "You are a man who can find the balance between fact and intuition. You ally the mind with the heart and align evidence with conscience. Regardless of what's to come, I know you will lead as a king among men, not only as a king, because your aim is not power, but truth."

I watched his eyes temper, the color of myth set strong and ready as a blade. The might of words at the right moment.

"Is that what you think of me?"

"Believed, always, although I couldn't say so in words until now."

"May I prove myself worthy of that opinion." He glanced at the clock on the desk. "I'm due in a meeting."

On impulse, I smoothed the silk at his neck and flattened his coat's lapels. I blushed when he smiled, conscious of the intimacy conveyed. At least for a moment, we forgot the kingdom was in peril.

DIARY ENTRY 13 APRIL /38

Second day the animals can't move. Yesterday, I watched as the effects set in. The sheep, goats, and hens staggered and tumbled. Birds scuffled along the ground and twirled from the sky like dead leaves. Insects fell over and couldn't right themselves. Cyril dragged his back legs behind him. By the evening, the beasts were in hiding. They know what happens to those sick, lame, or injured. Their instincts serve to protect them.

Much of this morning, I worried they'd all die of thirst and hunger, but as I checked on Old Woman's animals and the ones I found hiding, I saw they're in a state like sleep. A temporary hibernation. All of them appear to dream sometimes, moving their paws, hooves, claws, and making noises. Their breathing and pulses are slower by a great degree. Birds usually vibrate in my hands, their little hearts beat so fast, but now the throbs remind me of a clock's *tick, tock, tick, tock.*

Harmyn was with me as I walked, and I let her pet them. Sometimes she hummed, which seemed to soothe them. They responded with little twitches and even slower breaths. She surprised me, though, when she said they have shadows, too. She couldn't see into them, as she had with Nikolas, but she could sense feelings from the shadows.

Fear and grief.

15 APRIL /38

IN THE WEEKS SINCE I'D SEEN HIM, FATHER AND I EXCHANGED letters—I'd reserved a post cubby—but I found excuses not to meet again. The last letter I received, he said he knew I'd visited Fewmany and that the search, as he called it, was over.

I agreed to meet at an eatery, a neutral place. We attended the usual pleasantries, and soon after we ordered our meals, he started with the questions. First, he inquired about the symbol, and I replied I still had no idea what it meant. As to where I found the stones, I said they were in places he'd identified, although that was a lie because I didn't use the maps Fewmany gave me. He wanted to know how I managed to find the location, to which I said little, and what the treasure looked like, to which I said no more or less than I told Fewmany.

When he asked why I resigned my position, I said I needed time to rest and plan what to do next. I assured him I had the means to remain on my own, but I refused to tell him where I was living.

"Where is my little pet? Where has she gone?" he asked.

"She grew up and went away."

"How far?"

"Far enough."

He looked wistful then. "Will you come in her place?"

"No," I said.

Then he scowled, his mouth hard. "Always hiding. Always withholding, weren't you?"

That he said it stung me more than the truth of it. I always had to, I thought. An old unease welled up within me, the same feeling I had when my mother's dark moods leached out, warning me to beware. Never once did she hit me, but the threat was always there. I could feel it. She inflicted the wounds of silence instead.

However, there were moments I failed to keep my guard with my parents. I failed, by choice, when I told my mother I could speak to creatures and plants. By outburst, when I expressed how devastated I was when they cut down Fig Tree. By accident, when I made the drawing of the symbol. Sometimes I failed when I had no control at all, as it was after the fever.

In those moments, I received no comfort or understanding, in words or gestures.

Of course I hid. Of course I withheld.

I had no intention to speak of these matters then, but what he said hurt me, and I wanted to hurt him back. "She didn't choke. She killed herself, you know."

He looked as if I'd punched him in the throat. "Why would you say such a horrible thing?"

"Because it's true."

"How could you know that?"

"Someone who expects to live doesn't make a cipher for a manuscript she was entrusted to translate."

When he started to twist his ring, I wanted to tear it off his finger once and for all.

He sat speechless, staring at his hands, and when he looked at me again, I couldn't read his face. It wasn't blank but too full. "She wouldn't have left me that way. You will never speak of this again, do you hear me?" he said with fury in his voice, one I hadn't heard since the twelve nights he cut my hair to force me to talk of the symbol I'd drawn.

All I could do was nod as he refused to admit the truth. He could hardly look at me when we parted ways, and said only, "I'll be away in Osrid, four weeks."

16 APRIL /38

ON THE EVENING I WENT TO COLLECT THE MAP FOR FEWMANY, Nikolas and I had dinner first, upon his suggestion. How comfortingly conventional this seemed, sitting down for a meal, and how unnervingly unfamiliar because we weren't quite the friends we'd once been.

When I arrived, I was taken to the courtyard where our graduation party had been held nearly three years before. Nikolas stood on the walkway speaking to a guard, the one with the cleft chin. He introduced me to Hugh and reminded us how we'd met. During the summer grand ball almost fourteen years earlier, Hugh found Nikolas and me in the meeting chamber's secret room, where Nikolas had led me for a game of hide-and-seek.

"A pleasure to meet you under less surreptitious circumstances, Hugh," I said.

"Yes, Miss," he said. His eyes cut from me to Nikolas. Hugh strained to thwart a smile.

Nikolas's face turned pink. He made a guiding gesture for me to walk ahead. In the center of the courtyard's lawn were a blanket, cushions, and trays of food. As we ate, we spoke of pressing matters, but not for long. For at least an hour, the conversation was a respite from what was behind us and what was ahead, the two of us talking as we had hundreds of times before. The only difference—we held hands as Nikolas sat with his back to the guard, shielding me from his view.

When we set out for the library, Hugh followed nearby and waited outside. The library was in the oldest part of the castle. I couldn't help but notice how much smaller it was than Fewmany's. New oil-lit chandeliers brightened the room. In the center was a map case, three desks with book cradles, and three cushioned chairs. Tall glass cases and open shelves lined the walls, accessible by ladders set on tracks. I shut my eyes as I breathed in the fragrance. How I missed that smell and the things that released it.

Nikolas opened a drawer in the map case. The rustle of parchment made my heart race. Knowing what I was about to see made it skip beats.

He laid two maps side by side, each about two feet square, one almost a mirror of the other.

As I touched the original, prickles stung the inside of my hand. Aoife's map to the hoard had been kept dry and in the dark.[25] The colors remained vibrant, almost as if freshly inked. There were no tears, but a dog-eared corner and a deep wrinkle along the right edge, a flaw in the skin. Aoife had taken great care to draw the rivers, mountains, and forests. Along the path she charted, she sketched towns in miniature and with dimension. Among the trees, beasts peered out—deer, boars, bears, foxes, wolves, one handsome stag, as well as a unicorn, griffon, and basilisk. In a desert, there was a line of camels, and in a sea, whales, narwhals, and seals.

Only one bird appeared, a blue swallow, its wings smeared to a blur, flying near the X drawn within a region to the north.

The X had no literal meaning. Geography was a limitation to which the realm was not subject. The realm could be entered from anywhere, given the right circumstances—a hollow tree which straddled one world and another, the escort of bees, the understanding to walk through. What Aoife had drawn was an approximation, a measure of time and distance, as the world was then.

A map shows time, in its own way, what space looked like in that point in time, I thought. What is written of an event—before, during, and after—is also a map of time, of perspective.

For a moment, I stared at my hands, the shape, my father's, the skin tone, my mother's. What map of lives are hidden in me? I wondered.

"Did you notice the dragon?" Nikolas asked. He pointed to a cluster of pink clouds. One drifted from the rest, its edges forming a tail, wings, long neck—ruby red.

"You said it was beautiful, but it's beyond that." I stepped aside to look at the copy drawn for Raef so he could search for the hoard.[26] That one was stained, creased, revealing it had been folded, with two roughly sewn patches. Much of the fine detail was missing, but the swallow and X appeared in the same place.

"Dare I ask, what will he think?" Nikolas asked.

"The copy is from the same era. If he suspects it's a modern forgery, he'll have it authenticated, but I'm not concerned about that. He's nearly as knowledgeable as the experts he retains," I said.

"I cannot believe I'm turning this over to him."

"What other option is there?" I said. I helped him roll the copy and slip it into a leather cylinder.

"What happens after you send him wandering and he returns without his prize, looking for you?"

"That won't happen."

"You don't know that."

"Somehow I do. I told you before, I'm meant to stop him. How, that hasn't come clear yet. Please, trust me."

"I have something to discuss with you." He braced his arms against the case. "I want you to address the Council about the plague."

I shook my head.

"You can describe what happened to the plants and creatures because you observed it yourself. You were the first to notice the affliction because of your gift. You know how it will spread because of what they revealed to you," he said.

"Yes, and I'm the one who released the vials, remember? Do you want me to reveal that, too?"

He didn't reply.

"What would happen to me before everyone sickens? Or after? What then? There will be a need to blame. If there's a person who can serve as the target, I'd be the one if anyone else knew what I did," I said.

"You're right. You can't disclose that," he said.

"But I can disclose how I know?"

"Yes. This knowledge gives us a chance to prepare. You observed the duration of the illness and the phases in a specific, not cursory, way. Like a natural scientist might, an astute one for certain. I know you said you don't know how long it'll affect everyone. But it will affect us, eventually. If you're right, within weeks, about nine by my count. I can't let this befall my people without trying to help them somehow."

Old memories of the child I'd been slipped from hidden places. A trail of ants. A creeping beetle. *So ugly. So stupid. That's witch talk! I don't believe you.* Fig Tree, green then gone. I fought back against the cry that knotted in my throat.

"What is it?" he asked.

"No matter what it looks like to you, I wish I didn't have this ability. To know things, to feel things from them. And it makes me like no one else, a freak of nature. For a while, when you were away for the goodwill visits, I made it stop. The absence was so wonderful. So normal. But it came back and I couldn't shut it away again."

"What if what you believe to be a curse is a boon? Think about it. If you couldn't do this, we wouldn't know what to expect. We couldn't plan."

"If I hadn't poured the vials, it wouldn't have happened at all."

"It's done. This is the result."

I stared at Aoife's maps. If her manuscript was a guide, what direction did it give me? What was I supposed to learn from her?

As if he sensed what lay unspoken deep within me, he said, "I doubt you have the option to hide anymore."

I burst into tears. When he tried to hug me, I stepped aside. Undeterred, he took my hands. "If you hadn't told me to follow squirrels, would I have wandered without aim?" he asked.

"Possibly."

"If you hadn't been there to take me through the hollow, would I have reached the realm?"

"I don't know."

"Well, I know," he said. "You were meant to be there all along."

"I wish it weren't so."

"But it is."

I brushed my damp nose against my shoulder, but he wouldn't release me.

"Consider my point of view. If I alone sat before the Council and told them a bizarre sickness had made lesser beings—"

"They're not lesser beings!"

"Love, I know."

His tender response stunned my tears away.

"Imagine if I tell the Council we'll get sick as they did, unable to speak, hear, or move for weeks, months, to come—with no legitimate authority, no man of science to substantiate what I say," he said.

"Except a witch?"

"You represent a realm of mystery whether you like it or not," he said.

"Whether others fear it or not," I said.

"I think even the greatest skeptics hope for the miracle of the unexplained."

"Many have suffered when they didn't." I thought of my mother, of Harmyn, untold others like them, perhaps like me, too.

"I could command you to speak, subject you to interrogation and worse, with nothing more than the stroke of a pen. I know what power I wield. Don't think for a moment I forget."

A rush of anger urged me to glance up. Expecting a threat in his eyes, instead, I saw a plea.

"I don't ask for my own credibility. I ask for the sake of Ailliath's people and for everything that depends on air, water, and light to survive."

In good conscience, I couldn't refuse him. "Very well. I will." Then because I wanted to, I clasped my arms around him and held tight.

DIARY ENTRY 19 APRIL /38

For the animals, the plague is over. But Cyril is still ailing. He called me to his basket this morning and said, "It was not only my role to guide you, Secret. It was my honor. Bury me near Reach, where I was born." I kissed his whiskered nose in promise.

Through the day, Old Woman cradled him in her arms in the shade. Harmyn sat with them, humming softly. I knew he was gone when I heard Old Woman cry out. I went to them only after I controlled my own tears.

When I went to Reach with a shovel, I received no greeting. His limbs swayed when I touched them, but the life was gone. I dug a hole facing east under the canopy. Old Woman brought Cyril's little body shrouded in a blue cloth. We buried him with dozens watching. The creatures had come to pay homage.

Once we went inside again, Old Woman lay down exhausted. Harmyn held her hand and hummed songs she seemed to know. Strange that Harmyn still won't sing, but nevertheless, the humming gives comfort.

I've sent a mouse to deliver a message to Nikolas about what happened.

Later: this arrived at midnight:

Dear S—Our intrepid Cyril, gone! How impossibly old he was, but his departure from us is no less heart-wrenching. Please convey my deepest sympathies to Old Woman. She has lost a treasured companion today. I'm thinking of her in her grief. And you. And myself. We all adored that magical squirrel. With love, N

26 APRIL /38

EIGHT WEEKS BEFORE THE SUMMER SOLSTICE, A QUORUM OF THE Council met. The advisers who lived too far from Rothwyke to travel in time would receive confidential letters about the proceedings.

When I entered the chamber with Nikolas, the men halted their conversations and stood as he walked toward the table's head. They straightened their shoulders and switched off their Tell-a-Bells. I felt them study me. Some seemed curious, as if I were an unexpected guest; others seemed dismissive, as if I were a servant.

"Good afternoon, gentlemen," I said.

Nikolas invited us to sit, nodding at me to take the one to his right marked RESERVED. The crest of dragon scales—Nikolas's own among them now—hung on the wall behind his chair. Nikolas welcomed the Council members and Rothwyke's mayor, Mr. Pearson. He introduced me as a lifelong friend who had attended the same secondary school he did. He added that my name might be familiar to those acquainted with my father, Bren Riven of Fewmany Incorporated. My presence would be explained soon.

During brief reports from the members, I looked around the chamber. A chronicler sat in a corner taking notes. At each place on the polished table was a teacup on a saucer, and along the table's length were several teapots. Portraits of the last four kings hung on the wall opposite the windows. Curtains woven with metallic threads covered the wall far across from the crest. I wondered if anyone crouched in the secret room behind them.

When I heard a change in Nikolas's voice, I looked at him.

He flattened his hands against the table and informed them of what was to come—a plague which would render every man, woman, and child unable to speak, hear, and move.

A few men suppressed their guffaws. The rest stared in disbelief.

"I realize that seems impossible, but this is no jape. I asked Miss Riven to speak because she is especially able to address the phenomenon. Their attention is yours," he said.

With an assured tone, I described what I observed among the plants and creatures in Rothwyke and in the woods. For the plants, the plague's three phases were of equal duration, each lasting three days, and for the creatures, seven. I assumed our people would be afflicted for weeks or months. Because the plants had entered the initial phase on the first day of spring, I predicted a cycle of Nature was involved. I believed the people of Rothwyke would sicken on the first day of summer. In time, the plague would spread beyond the borders of our town and kingdom.

"Miss Riven, how do you know this?" an old man with wiry side-chops asked.

"I have an unusual affinity with creatures and plants," I said.

Several men couldn't contain their laughter. Despite the humiliation singeing my cheeks, I continued. "Disbelieve me if you wish. I'd be incredulous, too, if I were in your place. However, those of you who live in Rothwyke, who have animals kept for service or as pets, you know their behavior was abnormal for three weeks. This happened, too, to the wild ones."

"We aren't potted plants and dumb beasts," another man said.

"No, which makes us far more vulnerable," I said.

"What's the cause of the ailment?" someone asked.

"I don't know, sir." To them, there was no way to explain what we'd been told in the realm.

"How is it borne?"

"Through water, I believe."

Several of them pushed away their teacups.

"How do you know that, Miss Riven?"

The man's tone was suspicious, accusatory, threatening. I took a slow breath to quell my anger. I remembered when my mother told my father I'd awakened from the fever speaking the ancient language. Father's response rushed back to me: "Once upon a time, we burned women like you at the stake." He smiled when he said it, but what made his humor dark was the belief that what cannot be explained is tainted with evil, done with malice.

I looked into the man's eyes with my strange ones the colors of night and day. He reared back in his seat. Because I couldn't tell the truth Reach and Cyril revealed to me, I said, "On that matter, I'd refer you to the research of Dr. Bechgert, from Kirsau. Listen, gentlemen, we have eight weeks to prepare. We can spend it concerned with the source and its transmission, but that will do nothing to stop the spread. We in Rothwyke will be the first, but we won't be the last. We can serve as an example to others, for better or worse."

"This is preposterous!"

"How are we to know this isn't a trick?"

"Or that the messenger bears no culpability?"

I blinked at the man who'd called out the last question. "If I meant harm, why would I reveal what's coming? I'll sicken like everyone else. If I don't, persecute me, then. For now, take me as a loyal subject with good intent."

The advisers rubbed their chins, crossed their arms, and tapped their fingers. Nikolas nodded at me with authority, but his eyes conveyed an affectionate pride.

"Which brings us to the other reason you're here today, good men of the Council and Mayor Pearson. We must plan for what's to happen," Nikolas said. "Miss Riven, you may stay, but I expect you understand our remarks are confidential."

At once, the men began to talk over one another. Nikolas made no attempt to quiet them, observing their demeanor with dispassion. Finally, in turn, they began to speak. They called to station sentinels in Rothwyke and throughout Ailliath. Of course, there weren't enough men in the king's service, so one man suggested a call for volunteers, another to require conscription of able-bodied men. Some advisers insisted there wasn't time enough to train them all, but several noted that didn't matter because anyone can figure out how to use a sword. Hiring mercenaries would be expensive, but those already-trained men could be rallied quickly. Many voiced their fear of what neighboring kingdoms would do once they learned of our vulnerability, especially as war spread around us—Ilsace now aiding Giphia to fight Haaud and protecting its border with Kirsau.

As they argued, I thought of Aoife, centuries before, listening as a few powerful men debated risks and anticipated threats that would affect so many. She wondered then about the power of words, how one could plan a strategy without them. "What kind of war could happen in the midst of silence?"[27] she wrote. Now I pondered the same in different circumstances.

I looked at Nikolas. Days earlier, we'd had a long discussion. He told me he'd consulted with various advisers, contemplated the history he'd studied, and considered what Aoife included in her manuscript—her and the Guardians' perspectives on war and peace, within one's self and the wider world. He wanted to challenge the way order had always been held. I agreed but was afraid the approach would fail. For so long, threat had been the means to obedience.

"Gentlemen," Nikolas said, "we have the option not to react as if violence is inevitable."

"Your Majesty, there's sure to be civil unrest—"

"—chaos—"

"—and if we are attacked from the outside—"

"—force will be necessary—"

"What lasting peace has that ever brought?" I asked before I could stop myself.

"What did she say?" one whispered to another.

"What lasting peace?"

The Council stared as if they expected me to say something else. So I did, because I would never get a chance like this again, and even though I knew, as it had been for Aoife, the men would not hear much less heed me.

"We choose the evil we do to each other, and because of that, we can choose the good," I said.

They scoffed and snickered, making no effort to hide their condescending grins. Nikolas gave me an imperceptible nod, conveying his accord.

"If only things were as simple as that fairy-tale notion," a man said at the table's far end. "Now then, to these grave matters, how are we supposed to defend ourselves, Your Majesty?"

"From what?" Nikolas asked. "Gentlemen, I'm not naïve enough to think there will be no aggression, but I believe that will come from within more so than without. I won't turn armed men among my own people. If they turn against each other, it's to their own detriment. What I propose is different, but that doesn't mean it will be ineffective."

With that, Nikolas ordered a census of every person living in Rothwyke first, then in every other town and village in the kingdom, as well as a tally of available food and supplies and how much would be needed if the plague lasted a year.

He announced a delegation of the town's people would convene in three weeks, to which Mayor Pearson had already agreed. Before then, in each ward, the residents were to meet as a group, state their ideas and concerns, and select two representatives, a man and a woman, of any age, of any occupation.

To the kingdoms which bordered Ailliath and several beyond,

Nikolas would send a letter about the plague, intending to prepare rather than frighten them about what would spread past our borders.

I could see the conflict on the men's faces. Many of the Council members disagreed with Nikolas's proposals. Most had known Nikolas since he was a boy, which might have made them feel fatherly toward him, but now he was a man, their king, a role that demanded loyalty and respect he hadn't had time to earn. If enough of them refused to cooperate or tried to usurp him, the plague would be only one of our worries.

"I speak for myself here, but perhaps for my fellow advisers when I say I have serious doubts this will work," a man said.

"—this requires more discussion—"

"—hear, hear!—"

"—indeed, what if this fails?"

"What if it doesn't?" Nikolas asked.

"What if we perish?" a liver-spotted man said.

"Then what have we truly lost?" Nikolas said.

Nikolas stood with his fists against the table. "Lord Milton, Lord Ashby, and Lord Sullyard, you are entrusted to organize your fellows. By the end of the day, I require a list of who you've chosen among you to take charge. Within three days, I require a written account of your initial plans. All heads are to report their findings directly to me. Mayor Pearson, we'll discuss arrangements for the town delegation. All of you, remember my intentions. I've been clear." He paused. His eyes shone with tears. "I ask you to honor my father by honoring me. There was peace during his reign, as I wish to have in mine.

"Gentlemen, gentlelady, our meeting is adjourned."

As the men rose from their seats, Nikolas asked me to stay. I answered what questions I could and tried to ignore the looks that pierced my way.

After everyone left, Nikolas held the door half-shut. Behind it, he reached out his hand formally for a shake, and I took it. "This is for a job well done," he said. Then he pulled me forward and kissed me. "That was because you're brave and brilliant and I love you."

1 MAY /38

ON THE NIGHT OF THE BALL, I DRESSED AT MARGANA'S SHOP. She'd kept the costume she made for me the year before. I'd paid for it and said she could it sell to someone else, but she refused to do so. After making the final touches, Margana stepped away with a look of awe.

"It's beautiful," I said, peering into the mirror.

"Yes, it is, but you give it life. You are exquisite," she said. "And your accessory makes you formidable."

I reached my hand to the silver wolf. Together, we'd crept from the woods to the shop so that I could get ready for the ball. The wolf indulged a quick stroke of one ear before I leashed her.

When I arrived at the manor's entrance, once again I accepted the offer of a man's hand. He was dark eyed and dark haired, from the curls on his head to down the length of his body. When he noticed the wolf, he tried to pull away, but I held my grip.

"She isn't the one to fear," I said.

I released his hand and drifted inside toward the heady music and scents. Throughout the main hall, lanterns cast light on plush scarlet carpets and velvet cushions on the floor. Silk veils, saffron and moss green, streamed together across the ceiling and draped down over the walls.

Compared to the costumes two years prior, several of the guests' disguises were far more revealing, with precarious bodices, gauzy codpieces, and skintight seams. What was alluring on some appeared comic on others. The guests sipped dark spirits and devoured their food. I felt the urge to have a drink, a taste, and knew I must not.

Find him, I said to the wolf, holding fast to her leash.

She escorted me through the hall. The gawking revelers cleared the way for us.

As I approached, I expected him to recognize me in that disconcerting way of his, as if he knew me by scent more than sight.

Fewmany laughed with two companions who were attached at the hip—the woman dressed as a man, the man dressed as a woman. The pair turned their faces. Their smiles receded as their jaws dropped.

His amber eyes flickered behind his muzzle mask. Fewmany tilted his head, then rose to his full height, his wolf coat fitting him like flesh.

"Ravishing!" the woman as man said.

"Divine!" the man as woman said.

They glanced at the wolf, then studied me, up and down.

A silver crown, tipped with crystal prisms, rested on my head. A simple white mask covered my eyes. My braided silver hair snaked over one breast. A shimmering beaded web, delicate as any orb weaver's, cast itself across the décolletage. Black as a void, the dress traced my curves. White flames flared across my belly, and the fiery tips licked all the way to my feet. On the long black cape, silver fernlike fronds splayed high from shoulder to shoulder. In the cape's cascade, a tapestry of silver birds and beasts danced against a darkness deep as night. Down the cape's sides to the end of its train, the border was jagged as thorns.

In one hand, I held the wolf's leash and in the other, the strap of a cylinder.

"Good evening," I said, nodding to him and the two guests. "I wish to thank the host for his invitation and solicit him for a word."

The glint in Fewmany's eyes shifted with mercurial speed, from astonishment to suspicion to recognition. The conjoined guests bowed a gracious good-bye as Fewmany stared down at me.

"My keeper of tales, 'tis a provocative transformation. I see you've brought a guest this time," he said, stretching his hand to the wolf.

Her quiet growl warned him to withdraw.

"To transform is the point, isn't it?" I asked.

I noticed an addition to his costume. Pinned into the fur at his chest was the jeweled brooch. Gratifying though it was to know he cherished it, seeing the symbol exposed conspicuously disconcerted me.

"I've come with a gift. I must give it to you in private," I said.

Fewmany smirked.

"No, this is something you truly desire. I'll wait for you in the library."

Before he could reply, I walked to the grand staircase. I ignored the sprawled couple who blocked my passage halfway up.

The library's door was locked when I tried to enter. Soon enough, I heard footsteps. He let me in and locked the door behind us. For a heartbeat, then two, I realized I had no means to escape. The wolf pressed against my leg.

In the dark, my hands found a lamp but no matches. I walked past him and took a vesta from the mantel.

He placed his mask on the table. "You never cease to intrigue me," he said.

"Which is one reason why we're friends," I said as I offered the lamp to him. When the light shone near his face, I winced. The red streak under his jaw and chin was no better, still swollen and now raw. A dark shadow loomed under his right eye as if he'd been punched.

"Your neck, and your eye," I said.

He took the lamp with gloved hands. "Nightmare flailings. Both will heal."

"Let's go to the map room," I said.

We walked the length of the library with the wolf between us. If Fewmany was frightened, he gave no hint. He opened the hidden room. *Go*, I said to the wolf, dropping the leash, and she stepped over the cabinet. I heard the humming murmuring crowd downstairs.

After I lit a second lamp, I took the map from the cylinder.

"Will you still not consent to let me follow you to find it again?" Fewmany asked, his tone suggesting an invitation, not a command.

"And spoil the surprise of what you'll discover? That you must experience yourself," I said, rephrasing what he'd said to me the day of the hunt. That he raised the issue again felt intrusive and ill timed. I excused this as some effect of the night's preoccupations. "Help me fix the corners."

We gathered heavy objects—the etched copper globe, an astrolabe—and placed them down. Fewmany swept his eyes across the chart. He curled one corner to feel the front and back, peered close at the inks, and studied the two sewn patches. "It looks ancient. You couldn't have drawn this."

"It's genuine. More than a thousand years old."

He shivered as his finger traced the X. "Explain."

"I didn't travel this route, but what you see marked is the destination. My father was right about the connection with The Mapmaker's War, not only because some symbols are near battle sites. From your library or his, I read some apocrypha about a map drawn for Prince Raef to find the hoard, not long after Wyl returned from his quest to seek the dragon. The map was well described, down to the swallow."

"How did you obtain this?"

"The royal library. I asked a favor of Prince—King—Nikolas—we were schoolmates, as you know—to conduct research on my father's behalf, for his particular quest. Tax documents, land records, et cetera. Had I not found this map, I would have drawn one for you, not quite as lovely, or as valuable."

"This is stolen."

"A bottle of ink spilled; I apologized profusely; the archivist went out for cloths; I folded the map, slipped it under my skirt. No one's looked at it in centuries. It won't be missed."

His incredulous squint vanished. He laughed. "What corrupting influence inspired this larceny?"

"I refrain from comment," I said.

The silver wolf let out a huff.

"However, the map lacks an important detail," I said. "When you arrive, you must look for a dead tree, a hollow through and through, large enough to stand inside. Near this tree is the cave entrance."

"Hidden in plain sight."

"So to speak. The chances of stumbling upon it are almost nil, and the journey to it requires fortitude."

Fewmany gripped the copper globe over the words *Here be dragons*. "If the kings of Ailliath have known where the hoard is, 'tis strange they haven't claimed it."

I puzzled over his remark. How strangely literal it was for him, as if he'd forgotten what drew us together and sent me out in the first place. "The symbol's mystery remains. The night you asked for my aid, you said you believe there are certain people who are led to great things. Perhaps not all princes are privy to its power."

"Not so for you, my keeper of tales, my lady of the beasts. Your power is no longer concealed, is it? Do all animals respond to you as this one does?" he asked.

"Yes."

"Our hunt. The deer. She saw me but did not flee. I always thought that unexplainable. So—she was under your command," he said.

"Yes." I could admit that, but not to the remorse for what I'd done.

He observed me, then dared to stare into the wolf's eyes. "Fascinating creatures, wolves. The way they hunt. Watch. Stalk. Chase. Bite. So different from the pathetic sheep, the way they cluster together, so effortless to cull the weak who lag behind, so easy for the collie to control." He took a deep, audible breath. "Well, then. My hackles are raised. 'Tis time for the libation. My guests demand release."

Each of us took a lamp. The wolf leapt over the cabinet. Fewmany locked the hidden room. As we stepped across the library, I allowed the sadness for what it was—that I'd never see it again, touch these books, discover their secrets. As he slipped the lupine mask over his head, I extinguished the lamps' flames. When the key set the door's lock, I stifled a cry.

Together we walked down the west stair and stopped on the landing. The wolf sat at my side, the leash slack in my hand.

Fewmany surveyed the guests who scurried below, quick and agitated. I sensed his pleasure in their thrall.

They're waiting, I thought.

The murmur quieted as pointed fingers and wide eyes turned toward us. Except for the music, the hall was almost silent. A torrent of warmth seared my limbs.

"Exhilarating, isn't it?" he said.

I glanced up at his dilated pupils fixed on mine. My thighs, belly, breasts, mouth burned. My gaze returned to the revelers.

"Oh-ho, yes, they see you. Fearsome and beautiful," he said.

"Your consort," I said.

"Were we to honor the old gods." He offered his arm to me.

I accepted, one hand stroking the fur down to his wrist.

"Come," he said softly, then again and again as he moved through the horde, parting the way into the ballroom.

The music pounded in my ears. The heavy erotic scent leached into my skin. With averted eyes, a sheep-legged man held a crystal decanter out to Fewmany. He poured the first small glass. I took the ruby libation. A drop flowed over my tongue.

The glass hovered close to my heart. My left hand dropped the leash and floated high, light as a trance. I grabbed the snout of his mask, lifted it from his head, and let it drop. With might, I clutched the fur around the brooch, dragged him toward me, and kissed him. His mouth softened in welcome then trapped my bottom lip against the edge of his teeth. When I felt him smile, I bit back, holding firm until the molten primal rush rising in me forced him to recede.

"Forgive me," I whispered, holding the red welt under his chin.

As I swept into the hall, the wolf at my side, I gave my glass to a young man whose tight costume allowed no mystery of his contours. He resembled the detailed statues within the manor's collection, but he was conscious, warm, alive.

He swallowed the drink in one gulp. "Join me for a dance," he said.

My hands slipped along the front of his body. How I wanted to, my blood lasciviously laced, but when I looked into his eyes, I knew whose I wished to see in his place. Desire was not enough. Nikolas was asleep, safe behind the castle's walls, where this longing could not yet touch him.

DIARY ENTRY 2 MAY /38

Nikolas delivered the public statement, repeated by the newsboxes. It's supposed to appear in the longsheets tomorrow. Soon, every longsheet and newsbox in Ailliath. Although several advisers urged him not to, he sent letters to the kingdoms on the continent. They'll have months, possibly years, to prepare, rather than weeks, if it comes to that, he said.

Harmyn and I talked with Old Woman about returning to her village. Harmyn doesn't think she'll sicken (something to do with her shadows), but if she did, we can't care for her alone. Once I sicken, she can't be expected to tend me even with Harmyn's aid. She wants to stay to help however she can. In the end, we convinced her, but she didn't tell us when she'll leave.

I'm afraid to be left alone with Harmyn, though. Sometimes, we still rile each other. When I watch Old Woman with her, and think about how Old Woman was with me as a child, and is still, I see the Guardians' ways in practice. Aoife wrote about their patience and kindness, a reflective rather than reactive way of treating others—my old friend does that. I'm learning, I'm trying, but I've never been responsible for another person. We won't lack for shelter or starve— we have the cottage; what we can't grow or forage, Nikolas will surely help—but to care for her. Can I do this? And eventually, I'll have to tell Father.

8 MAY /38

Dear S—I could have waited to talk to you rather than risk a debilitating cramp from writing another note with infinitesimal letters, but I couldn't get away tonight.

Delegates' mtg went well enough, better than I or certainly Mayor P & Council members expected. 82 delegates attended—representing, from census # received, 45,326 citizens, 1/4 children infant to age 17. You were right to suggest separating the groups for discussion. (How unaware I was in school the boys were so outspoken, the girls so silent, and didn't consider this continues long after.) When they arrived, they segregated themselves straightaway, women & men, by station. Random groups wouldn't have been helpful, not w/ emotions high as they were.

Morning session was congenial; 10 small groups total & they had similar lists of concerns. What about the availability & cost of food; how would they stay in their homes if they couldn't pay mortgages & rents; how would they be cared for if the last stage left them paralyzed; how would civil order be kept, etc. After the midday meal, when they discussed how to address the concerns, there were arguments within the groups but worse with cross-talk among the groups.

Mayor & advisers did as I asked; they didn't interfere—much. I knew most of them were annoyed, even angry. I should be demonstrating strength & leadership with clear edicts. As with all kings before me, declaring what's for their own good. Hrumph-hrumph-hrumph. But what's about to happen is unprecedented. How can they, or I, claim to know what's best for a family in Elwip, Warrick, Peregrine?

While I listened today, I thought of Aoife. Not until she found her new home with the Guardians did she start to unlearn the expectation of power & force. How she came to see the tenuous balance of caring for the whole with respect to the parts, & that in every moment, there is a choice—& not an absolute answer. These things, I must understand, too, if I am to lead, or guide, with compassion instead of might.

Many plans still to be made, but we have a sense of what must happen. Rationing, without a doubt. Most agreed we should have voluntary service through charity orgs & leagues; new ones possibly—there was agreement we'll need ward gardens to supplement our food supply. How we'll manage the third phase when we can't move, that will take more thought. I ordered the mayor to map the town into 12 areas and have each elect a person to serve on a committee with men from the Council. That's sure to be well received.

I know there wasn't a good reason for you to attend today, but I still wish you'd been there. Fawning adoration for my regal prowess would have been welcomed. That, & you would have felt, as I did, history taking a turn.

With love,
Nikolas

14 MAY /38

ALMOST A YEAR HAD PASSED SINCE I LAST SAW MY NEIGHBORS IN Warrick. I'd thought of them on occasion, but as the plague's threat became ever more imminent, I was concerned how they would fare, especially the Elgins' children and the Misses Acutt.

A greyhound steered Harmyn and me among the streets. Throughout our walk, Harmyn held the amulet at her neck and studied the people we passed.

"The shadows are thick. Everyone is afraid . . . so much anger, too . . . and some want to know who to blame," she said.

"She walks among them," I said.

"It's not so simple," Harmyn said, "and you know it."

The walk-up's facade looked the same, no cracks or crumbling, but the front door required force to open. The jamb appeared unlevel.

I knocked on the Misses Acutt's door. The tall one came first. "Why, Miss Riven! Lovely! Leave the door open for some air. Who have we here?"

"Miss Acutt, this is my friend, Harmyn."

"A pleasure to meet you," Harmyn said.

"Such a polite boy!" she said. Harmyn shook her head at me to leave the comment alone. "We must have cookies. Sister! We have visitors!"

Tall Miss Acutt hobbled to the cupboard as the bedroom door opened.

"Did you call me? Oh—look who's returned," Short Miss Acutt said.

After I introduced Harmyn, this time eliciting a comment on her "costume," I asked of the third sister. Tears rushed to their eyes.

"She left us this winter. Pneumonia. She did not long linger. How we and Sir miss her," Short Miss Acutt said.

"I'm terribly sorry. I know how dear she was to you," I said.

Tall Miss Acutt laid a plate of cookies on the table. "Yes, yes. Child, eat."

I nodded at Harmyn to accept the treat.

"How is your father?" Short Miss Acutt asked. "We've missed the little chats we'd have when he'd come by to see you. So dashing! If only one of us were twenty years younger—"

"Sister, thirty, at least—"

"Ah, bygones. The bloom has fully faded."

"He's well, and I'll be sure to tell him you inquired," I said.

"Now then. What of this plague? To think we'll suffer as poor Sir did. Sister was convinced several times he was dead. He didn't once move a muscle, not even when we carried him or tempted him with a morsel of fish," Tall Miss Acutt said.

A questioning meow piped up. Sir Pouncelot crept out, circled my ankles, and walked toward Harmyn. She bent to pet him.

In the hall, footsteps tapped on the stairs heading out. A face peeked in. "All's well, Misses?"

"Hello, Miss Thursdale," I said.

Dora stepped into the apartment. "What a surprise—and your hair, too. Your assignment is complete, then?"

"It is. How is Miss Sheepshank?" I asked.

"Jane has had a good turn. A recent promotion at Fewmany Incorporated, head secretary for the Office of Mining and Mineral Rights."

"And you?"

"I remain at Foxworth and Trent. Did Jane tell you, Misses, of the Woodmans?" Miss Thursdale asked.

"She brought us the good-bye note this morning," Tall Miss Acutt said. "They're not the only ones fleeing with all they can carry. I've heard people have been leaving ever since the King announced the plague, the well-to-do sending their families to distant lands, those like us going as far as we can."

"I've heard some towns closed their borders and sentinels are turning them back," Short Miss Acutt said.

"That seems dubious. Unless someone is stopped and asked, no one would know whether one is from Rothwyke," Miss Thursdale said.

The building's front door banged open. Lucas whisked up the stairs. Mrs. Elgin lagged behind with a basket in her arms. When she saw our group in the sisters' apartment, she nodded, prepared to go on, until Short Miss Acutt called to her.

"Good afternoon," I said to Mrs. Elgin.

"Miss Riven, good to see you're well," she said formally. "I can imagine what you're discussing."

We nodded.

"Strange, isn't it, how this happens not long after the prince returns. The King and Queen die mysteriously, then the animals fall ill. I heard a newsbox report that no prince has ever completed his quest as quickly as this one. Something's odd about that, don't you agree, and suddenly, there's a contagion in our midst," Mrs. Elgin said.

"Oh, but remember, strange things were happening soon after he departed. The ground problems in Old Wheel, the bodies—" Tall Miss Acutt said.

"Bodies?" I asked.

"My sister meant skeletons, old bones, rising up in the cracks. Dark humors surely escaped, too," Short Miss Acutt said.

"No one believes in bad humors anymore, Miss Acutt," Miss Thursdale said.

"Dear, that doesn't mean they don't exist," Short Miss Acutt said.

"Regardless . . . At market this morning, there was hardly a thing to buy. The shortages have started already, food, dry goods, and the like. The shopkeeps said people are hoarding," Mrs. Elgin said.

"Did you notice the traveling vendors? The elixirs and charms to ward off what's on the way. A waste of money, if you ask me," Miss Thursdale said.

"Certainly, but we'll all have to protect ourselves in the end," Mrs. Elgin said.

"Sister found our father's old sword in the hope chest," Tall Miss Acutt said.

"Jane and I are keeping knives under the pillows," Miss Thursdale said.

"My husband will put another lock and a bar on the door soon. If you want the same, he'll install them for you," Mrs. Elgin said.

"Still worried about his work, dear?" Short Miss Acutt asked.

"I don't know whether to fear more he'll be crushed by the wall or lose his job because they've been ordered to stop. Either way, what would become of us?" Mrs. Elgin said.

"There, there. Don't borrow trouble," Tall Miss Acutt said.

The conversation stalled.

"How is Julia? I hoped to see her today," I said.

Mrs. Elgin looked toward the door. "She was behind me when I came up the steps. She must be outside."

A moment later, the front door clicked shut and Julia crept to the sisters' doorway. "Misses Acutt, may I play with Sir— Secret! You're back!" She threw her arms around my waist. Mrs. Elgin cleared her throat. Julia released me. "We don't like the man who moved into your apartment. He's grumpy and smokes the smelliest pipe. I still have the books you gave me. I like to make up stories—"

"Julia, enough," Mrs. Elgin said.

Tall Miss Acutt pointed to the table. "Go and have a cookie with Sir and Secret's friend, Harry."

"Harmyn," I said.

Harmyn stood at her mention with Sir in her arms.

"I know you," Julia said. "You're the boy who helped the rabbit and sang and the grown people cried and screamed. Mother, I told you about it. This is the boy, but his spectacles are gone. Look at your eyes. They're so beautiful." Julia reached to touch Harmyn's face, but Harmyn backed away.

"You told us that day you're invisible. Can't you all see him?" Julia asked.

I looked at the women's faces as they turned to Julia.

"Of course we see him," Mrs. Elgin said.

"May we take the cookies outside? You're just going to talk about the plague, and I've heard enough," Julia said.

"Leave the cookies," Mrs. Elgin said.

"Let the children have them. Please," Tall Miss Acutt said.

"We insist," Short Miss Acutt said. "An early treat in honor of your birthday, Julia. Remind us how old you'll be."

"Eleven. Thank you, Misses," Julia said.

I smiled at the children as they left the apartment with Sir Pouncelot at their heels.

"That was kind of you, Miss Acutt," Mrs. Elgin said.

Tall Miss Acutt clasped her sister's hand. "We remember the Brown Famine from our girlhood. We don't yet know what the plague will bring."

DIARY ENTRY 16 MAY /38

After the visit with the neighbors, when Harmyn was yet again confused for a boy, again I offered to buy her some new clothing. But no. She told me, "I am Harmyn, I'm a Voice, and that's what matters," and then was near tears when she said, "It's safer to dress as a boy anyway. Aoife did it all the time, and tried to make Wei do it, too.[28] Don't you want me to be safe?" With that, I couldn't argue. Old Woman insisted I let this be, so I shall.

Tonight Nikolas taught Harmyn how to play chess, which she learned quickly. She's very bright. A shame she's had no schooling. This I'll have to attend, once the plague is over.

At last, Nikolas and I had time alone together, the first in weeks. We've exchanged dozens of notes, but it's not the same. When what was between us was simply companionate, there was no physical craving. Now I want to touch him; sometimes it's only affection, to hold his hand, to feel his arm around me, but when desire sparks— what restraint is at odds with the impulse!

So tonight, we walked as we have a thousand times. Neither said or did anything, but the energy changed, and he had no warning when I turned in midstride and pressed my body to him tongue to thigh. No pause, no protest. He lowered me to the ground, our hands searching what our clothes kept hidden. Stayed hidden. (For now?) He started to laugh when we finally rolled apart. I asked why. "It's embarrassing," he said. "Tell me anyway," I said. "I ache everywhere," he said. "So do I," I admitted, "almost unbearably."

When I returned, Old Woman had a talk with me. She could tell something was different between us. She said she knows I'm well aware of what is and isn't acceptable "beyond the woods" as much as he is. Then she took several jars of dried herbs and one book from her shelves. There is plant lore a woman should know.

22 MAY /38

FATHER AND I HADN'T SEEN ONE ANOTHER IN MORE THAN A month. When he returned from his trip to Osrid, he sent a terse letter inviting me for tea. He made no mention of what I'd said about my mother.

I didn't go alone. For some time, I knew I'd eventually have to tell him about Harmyn, although I dreaded it. I asked her to come along, but with a warning I might lose my nerve. She agreed to wait outside and not wander too far.

Because Father was expecting me, I used the hidden key to open the front door. It didn't budge. I rapped the brass knocker. Father fumbled inside, let me in, and turned to secure three locks.

"A precaution, for the coming plight," he said. "Follow me."

We went to the third floor. The storage room had a new door, also with three locks. He opened it, the space stuffed full. "Flour, beans, dried fruit and meats, pickled vegetables, salt, spices, tea," he said. He offered the ring of keys.

When I looked at him, I hadn't meant to convey judgment, but I had.

He hardened his face. "You have never known want. I have never forgotten it. You are my daughter, and what is mine is yours."

"Promise me if there's a call to share, you will," I said.

"I'll determine that if the circumstances arise. Otherwise, that's for you and me. Also, perhaps, to barter. Money will be useless if the affliction lingers. Take them." He held out the ring. "The keys to the front door are there, too. You'll need them."

"Why?" I asked.

"You are coming home, aren't you?"

"I'm all right where I am," I said.

"Take them anyway," he said, his tone hard, his eyes sad.

After I accepted the ring, he walked downstairs. On the second-floor landing, I noticed several maps and a stack of books outside the spare room. On top was the edition Fewmany had given him of the chronicles from The Mapmaker's War era. The quest for a link to a noble past continues, I thought. A shiver streaked up my spine. I had no tangible proof that Father had been right all along, but I sensed the names he sought were Ciaran, Aoife's brother, and that of the boy Ciaran raised as his own.

That afternoon, however, wasn't the time to reveal what I knew in my blood.

I found Father at the stove when I entered the kitchen. Two plates, two forks, a knife, and a pie lay on the table. Under the ochre bowl was a shortsheet from the ward leaders, calling for volunteers. I moved the bowl across the room, to where my mother had sat near the windows, once curtained, now barred. As I turned, I saw the back door's ancient bobbin and latch had been replaced with a knob. A huge lock and metal bar held it shut.

As a child, I'd often felt trapped within that house. My mother's little fungus, keeping to the shadows. With the bars and locks, I felt imprisoned, although Father meant to create a fortress.

He served tea as I cut the rhubarb pie.

"I saw the shortsheet. What will your service be?" I asked.

"There's an option to contribute to a fund instead. I'll do that," Father said.

"The courtyard is barren. Offer the land to grow food."

"I wouldn't know how to tend it."

"I could. I'm helping to build gardens. One could be here," I said.

He took the plate I pushed toward him. "You were oddly gifted to do that since you were little. The courtyard became such a green, cheerful place once you took interest."

I filled my mouth with a morsel to avoid a response. The ability was inherent to a degree, I thought, and the courtyard was less pleasant once Fig Tree was cut down.

For a minute, we ate and sipped in silence.

"An acquaintance mentioned you spoke before the Council last month," he said.

I stared at the blank space where the bowl had been.

"Is there something you want to tell me?" he asked.

"No."

"Rather, something perhaps you should?"

A deep inhale to think, a slow exhale to decide. "That depends on whether I can trust you."

"How can you say that?"

In that very moment, I knew that what had occurred, because of the symbol, was a matter of both betrayal and fate. Father had used my innocent knowledge for his own selfish desires—to secure Fewmany's good graces and the boons that brought. Yet, still, what happened between Fewmany and me was inevitable. Had Father not presented me to him as an eleven-year-old girl, I would have been surrendered by some other means.

"Where's your allegiance now?" I asked.

"I don't understand," he said.

"Of course you do. What were you thinking when you saw the symbol I'd drawn, cutting my hair, frightening me, but worse, using me for your ends—and his. I had no idea what you wanted from me. I did not lie to you. Mother knew that, didn't she, although I'm sure she said nothing. And then, to encourage me as you did, the apprenticeship, not a single other girl among my group, before or since, neither you nor him believing I dreamed of it but waiting for me to divulge—what? How? I *did* dream of the symbol first, only later finding one, still without a clue what it meant."

The remorse in his eyes didn't reach his mouth. Anger rushed through me, and as it did, I watched his shame force him to look away.

"What did he promise you if the hoard was found?" I asked.

"Land and a title."

"He can't give that to you."

"The King can."

"Not this king. The old one is dead."

"But King Nikolas—you are—"

"His closest friend and confidant."

"You could sway him."

"I could—but I won't."

Father lowered his head. I took pleasure in the wounding, but I chose not to pierce deeper with the fact Fewmany would never get the hoard and never have the chance to fulfill his promises to Father, or me, or whomever else Fewmany involved in his quest.

"I ask again—with whom is your allegiance? Do I matter more now, Father?"

"You're all I have," he said.

I felt a slip within myself. The little girl who once adored him entered the vacant space. "I am, aren't I?"

When he twisted the ring on his finger, my throat closed.

"What do you have to tell me?" Father asked.

"Do you remember the story you told me about the day I was born?"

"One fine autumn twilight, a pigeon, a dove, and a sparrow entered an open window and flew three times widdershins around a room. They lit upon the wooden sill to chirp and coo about the new black-haired babe lying in a cradle—that was you—and nodded to one another when their conference had ended. Shall I continue?" he asked.

"No. I remember it, too, and that you thought their visit uncanny. Years later, did Mother tell you what I told her—that I could speak to creatures and plants?"

"I recall this."

"What did she make of it?"

His expression twisted in thought. "You were imaginative, more so than most children. You had an affinity for animals and flowers. For you to have said such a thing isn't surprising."

"She claimed not to believe me. Did you believe her disbelief?"

"I don't recall having a sense one way or another. Parents tell things about their children which are mere anecdotes, nothing more."

"That wasn't. I don't believe it was trivial to her. If it were, she would have said nothing to you. She warned me not to confuse what was real with what wasn't. I was very careful after that not to reveal myself at all," I said.

"What do you mean?"

"I communicate with creatures and plants. Birds, squirrels, toads, ants, fish. Trees, ferns, flowers. Anything. I know what they think and feel, what they remember, with no more effort than it takes to talk to a person."

"Since when?"

"It happened the first time when I visited my grandmother. I was almost four. Thereafter, I had to learn to manage what came."

"So, the courtyard . . . the birds . . . that fig tree."

"My haven among friends."

"The Council meeting?"

"I gave the warning about the plague. I observed the plants first, then the animals. To the latter, anyone could see they were sick those three weeks, and not one adviser could dispute that. It was my duty to use this knowledge so we could prepare," I said.

"How did the King react when you told him?"

"Nikolas has always known the truth about me," I said. "He insisted I speak to the Council, although I didn't want to because of the suspicion I'd face. Once upon a time, women like Mother and me were burned at the stake. Better that than to suffer for our strangeness, perhaps. And you—has your weird daughter made things difficult for you now?"

Fear glazed his eyes, but I sensed it was for me, not for him.

"My reputation isn't at issue," he said. When he touched his cup, it rattled against the table so hard, some of the tea splashed out.

Unbidden, I remembered that dinner after the fever, when she knocked the salt cellar, telling me, "Mind what is spilled, girl, and watch it doesn't spread."

"You're shaking," I said.

"The shock of the secret you kept. I wish I had known," Father said.

"It would have made no difference if you had," I said. "There is something else."

I told him that several years before, I'd met a young orphan, one who seemed neglected, but there was nothing I could do about it. When I returned from my recent journey, I encountered the child again. By then, I'd read the arcane manuscript. Harmyn, too, was a Voice, lost in the world, like my mother. I had taken responsibility for her, helping as best I could.

On purpose, I left out many other details, ones I'd have to reveal in time.

"Why would you take a child into your charge? You're hardly old enough to bear one. What means do you have?"

"I'll manage. This isn't an ordinary child, Father. She needed someone who would respect her gifts."

"How old is she?"

"Twelve. Would you like to meet her?"

"That seems reasonable, don't you think?"

"Wait here." I went to the front door. Harmyn sat on the front steps petting a stray dog. "Come in."

When we waked in, Father stood in the parlor. Harmyn approached him with an outstretched hand. "I'm pleased to make your acquaintance, Mr. Riven."

He stared, bewildered.

"She minded her manners. Could you do the same?" I asked.

"Your eyes," he said.

"It's a color Voices have. Zavet did, too," Harmyn said.

He approached her, knelt, and clutched her shoulders. I almost intervened, afraid for an instant he'd hurt her. He began to cry.

"I've seen you before, wandering the streets, and singing. Like nothing I've ever heard." Suddenly, he took her in his arms. The child circled his neck as he sobbed. I had seen him broken like this only once, after my mother died. I wondered if I'd made a mistake bringing Harmyn to him. If I had, in fact, been unwittingly cruel, to force him to look into the eyes of what he'd lost. I took a breath, held it, and stepped toward them.

I touched his back. I felt him shiver, but it wasn't from emotion. Harmyn was humming to ease whatever pain had ripped out of him.

He slumped with his palms on the ground, then stood with his back to us. He blew into a handkerchief.

"I apologize. I'm not sure what happened," he said.

"It'll all right. Harmyn tends to have an effect on people," I said.

He squared his coat. "We should get better acquainted. Do you like rhubarb pie?"

"I do," Harmyn said, following him around the corner.

ROTHWYKE DAILY MERCURY.

26 May /38. Page 2, Column 5

ACCIDENT TAKES SIX—Yesterday, at half past two o'clock, a calamity occurred at the northwest section of the wall. Witnesses report a crane used to move the stones began to sway, and a cracking sound was heard before the suspended load dropped. The weight and momentum loosened several stones which had been recently laid, and three fell upon the unwitting, imperiled victims. Among the dead are five journeymen and one apprentice. Mr. Vinter, the foreman, has supervised several projects of this kind and indicated all due measures had been taken to ensure the crew's safety. He stated the crane's defect will be assessed and all other equipment evaluated with doubled rigor; until that is complete, construction is suspended. Fewmany Incorporated has expressed condolences to the families, with a redress officer assigned to their attendance.

WEEKLY POST.

31 May /38. Page 1, Column 2

SIX CRUSHED TO DEATH; CAUSE IN DISPUTE; HALT ORDERED—The recent death of six men, killed by falling stones from the yet-complete wall in the northwest quadrant, prompted further inquiry into the circumstances. Initial accounts described a failure of one crane, from which a stone fell, and subsequently knocked three stones of a similar size and weight from their placements, resulting in the men's demise. The crane did fail, but the cause of its collapse is in question. A source revealed occasional geologic tremors have not ceased since, though this has been refuted elsewhere, and where the crane stood, a deep rut in the soil is visible, which the source asserts was not created by the equipment's movement or placement.

Two days after the fatal incident, King Nikolas issued an order for all construction to stop until further notice, citing a "reasonable concern" that the geological instability affecting multiple wards in Rothwyke extends to the green as well. We are all aware of the state of our streets and sewers, and notably the New Wheel development.

The wall project entered its third year in April. Less than one-tenth of the project is estimated to be complete. Fewmany Incorporated, retained by the kingdom of Ailliath, has previously stated the fortification would be in place within four years.

3 JUNE /38

ON THE DAY OLD WOMAN RETURNED TO HER VILLAGE, SHE packed a change of clothes, her favorite cup, and a tuft of Cyril's fur. She kissed the two goats and remaining hens—she'd sold the sheep and other animals because we knew we couldn't care for them as she did—and stared long at her cottage.

"Protect them, little house," she said.

Harmyn carried our friend's bundle. We held her arms as we stepped into the woods. On Cyril's grave, Old Woman laid flowers. On Reach, who had dead leaves clinging to his branches, she placed a reverent touch. She led us to another tree I remembered well—the half-hollow one with a hole at its base, where a spiral stair of stone led to a tunnel connecting the woods and town. Roots twisted around the hole, leaving only a small place to stand within the tree.

"We've arrived at my shortcut," Old Woman said.

The Guardians, as it turned out, knew the secret of the hollows and used them with respect. Instead of traveling hundreds of miles to her home village, Old Woman would walk a few steps, with an animal leading the way.

A moment later, a fox appeared and sat next to the tree.

"My escort is here," Old Woman said. She turned to Harmyn. They whispered to each other, then embraced.

I struggled to suppress my tears. I told myself, yet again, she wouldn't be that far, not really. She'd be safe with her people; they could care for her if she got sick with the plague; she wouldn't be responsible for caring for me once I did. I could endure what was about to happen without her calm counsel.

When Old Woman tried to release her, Harmyn held tighter. "We'll see each other again, child."

Harmyn pressed her lips shut and rubbed her wet eyes.

Old Woman wrapped me in her arms. I felt small again, the child in the shadows, hiding and listening to her stories of a dragon, a dwarf, a woman-wisp, and an orphan. Mystery, I knew then, as much as myth.

"What a mighty woman you've become, little dreaming mushroom," she said.

At the mention of her long-ago nickname for me, I burst into tears, sputtering words of regret and adoration.

"It has been my honor," she said as she kissed my cheeks. "Have courage. Mind Harmyn with love, and yourself."

The fox yipped. Old Woman took her bundle, kissed us one more time, and followed the fox into the hollow.

A blink and a blur and she vanished.

Through the rest of the day, Harmyn and I tended chores. At twilight, Nikolas arrived with new books, provisions, and dinner. He told us more about the wall's collapse. There were lawyers involved now, the kingdom charged to be in violation of the contract. Then he informed us about the recent preparations in town.

Once that conversation ended, I read as they played chess. Harmyn cheered when she beat him for the first time. Impressed as Nikolas was by her quick learning, he admitted his pride was wounded. After their last match, he said he had an important matter to discuss with us. He wanted us to move to the castle, where Harmyn and I would have a wing to ourselves with each a private room.

"We don't know what will be required of Harmyn once the plague strikes, or of you," he said.

I didn't say so, but I believed my part to be done, save caring for Harmyn, which struck me then as an ironic responsibility. No longer an archivist, I was now the keeper of a child, and I wasn't confident I'd have the skill for it.

"I'd rest far easier knowing you were both in town. Further, if the third phase is as acute for us as it was for the animals, Harmyn can't care for you alone," he said.

"Not to worry. It won't be so terrible. I'll sleep like the girl who pricked her finger on the spindle," I said lightly.

"You'll recall that kingdom slept, too, under the curse, but in *this* version, your prince will slumber helpless as the rest of them," he said.

"How would you explain Harmyn's or my presence, no relation by blood or marriage, only guests? Not to mention, it's known I spoke to the Council. Perhaps it's best I maintain distance," I said.

"It's probably better if you are there. Advisers will see you're sick, too, quelling those suspicions you're so worried about. As to the explanation, I'll say Harmyn is a guest of the kingdom, a talented singer from one of our small towns, and she's in your charge. You're a distant relative who happens to be a longtime friend from our school days," he said.

"That's absurd. There'd be no reason for both of us to stay at the castle, and she hasn't sung a note since we took her in," I said.

"You haven't heard me. I've been practicing alone in town," Harmyn said.

"So, she has been, and if the reason I suggested doesn't suffice, give me another one. The basic fact is, I want to protect you," he said.

"I don't need your protection," I said.

"True, but is it so difficult to admit you want it?" he asked.

"He's right," Harmyn said.

"About what?" I asked.

"That you don't know what's about to happen. I can't tend you by myself. And he's offering us something we've rarely had."

"There are adult considerations involved," I said.

"Excuses," she said, her tone angry. "I want to go. I can't be alone with you. You can't understand why yet, and I can't explain. I simply know this. Please. We can give away the rest of the animals; we can come back to mind the garden; the cottage will be here for us."

"We need to give this more thought," I said.

"No, we don't." Her breath quivered until the cry broke free. "Don't worry about what others might think! What do we want? What do we need? I've never had a father, and he's the closest I will ever get."

Her admission struck me full in the heart. Nikolas looked at me as he went to her. The moment he put his arm around her slight shoulders, Harmyn clung to him. I swallowed the envy which rose up for Nikolas's instinctive affection and Harmyn's warm attachment, knowing I should be grateful for both.

Whatever concerns I had regarding his invitation's impropriety, I couldn't defend them against Harmyn's wishes or my veiled own.

"Two weeks, then. That'll give Nikolas time to prepare for our arrival and for us to do whatever we must here," I said.

She broke from him and hugged me. "He needs us, too," she whispered.

7 JUNE /38

WE WERE ALMOST FINISHED WEEDING THE GARDEN WHEN Harmyn said, "Something's happened. We have to go to town."

No horse stood in wait near the cottage, so we hurried through the woods and across the green. I followed Harmyn to an intersection in a southwest ward. By that time in the morning, most people should have been at their desks and stations. Instead, people stood on the sidewalks with shocked expressions.

Nearby, a news-speaker struggled to maintain his controlled tone and cadence. His well-trained avoidance of reaction faltered as he repeated the announcement.

Due to the coming plague, Fewmany Incorporated and its subsidiaries will suspend operations in Rothwyke, effective the twenty-first of June until further notice. We regret the disruption this will cause and assure all Fewmany Incorporated employees that they will be retained again once the pestilence has run its course. We appreciate those we have served and anticipate your patronage in the future. May Ailliath stand strong through this scourge.

Nearby, a young woman rubbed a slip of paper between her fingers. "Did you receive one, too?"

"What is it?" I asked.

"A furlough notice."

"No," I said. I wondered if my father had known of the plans and, whether he did or not, if he'd received his own slip. It would serve him right, I thought, but he won't suffer much for it. I couldn't fathom why Fewmany had done this.

"I didn't know who owned our shop. None of us did, not even the manager, but we do now." She started to cry.

"There, now, don't—" I stopped myself. She had every reason to be distraught. "I'm so sorry. This is a terrible shock."

"Terrible—yes. As if the coming plague wasn't terrible enough." She wiped her eyes with her apron. "What am I going to do? The slip says I'll be paid my full wages until my last day, but what then? I've nothing but a few coins set aside!"

Harmyn approached the young woman with a pink tulip. Strange, considering there was no flower vendor or pot nearby, and none bloomed so late in the year.

The child held the petals up to the woman's nose. She accepted the gift with a smile, but her tears flowed faster. "These remind me of my grandfather and his garden! It's been so long since I've seen him."

"Maybe you will soon," Harmyn said.

"He would be glad, I know." She looked at us. "You were kind to stand with me. I should go back inside now."

"Let's go this way," Harmyn said to me, pointing east.

Everywhere, people talked of the announcement—on the streets, in taverns and teahouses, in doorways and open windows. Harmyn held my sleeve.

"What's wrong?" I asked. She told me that the people's shock was shifting to anger. "Practice now. Breathe. Pay attention to your steps. Let it out through your feet."

We went toward Old Wheel, now a memory rather than a place. When we reached the plaza, the gold-toned tiles cracked, I saw a line of men holding clubs under the portico at Fewmany Incorporated. They blocked the lobby entrance. I glanced up to the twelfth floor. I wondered if Fewmany stood at a window and watched the growing crowd outside.

People gathered together, shouting:

"Four months king, and look what's become of us in his reign!"

"A war close to our borders—"

"And the plague—"

"We need the wall completed more than ever!"

"Halted that, didn't he? Now thousands won't have work! Coincidence?!"

As Harmyn and I stood by, I felt more than heard a vibration steady as the drone of bees. Harmyn hummed to try to calm the crowd, but the effect reached only the people near us.

"I need to talk to Nikolas, but you don't look well," I said.

"My chest hurts. There's too much poison coming in and I can't release it fast enough. The shadows are feeding on it, getting stronger," she said.

"We should go home, then," I said.

"I have to learn how to endure this. Will you hold my hand? It helps me stay in one place," she said. When I touched her palm, she gripped tight.

A sleek black cat with a torn ear leapt in front of us. Her yowl urged us to follow her along a safer route on the broken streets.

When we reached the castle's outer wall, the guards checked a list, on which our names appeared, and one escorted us toward the gatehouse. At last, Harmyn released my hand, staring up at the towers, then at the columns in the Great Hall. Within minutes, an officer showed us to the corridor which led to Nikolas's office. Hugh stood guard. With Hugh's approval, she left to look around while I talked to Nikolas.

I knocked, Nikolas told me to enter, and I stood opposite his desk.

"I haven't much time. What is it?" he asked. He hadn't looked so distraught in weeks, not since those first days after his parents died.

"I know what's happened," I said.

He thumbed through papers on the desk. "Well, news traveled fast, didn't it? I just had a meeting with the ward leaders. They pleaded with the Council and me to intervene. I—we—made no promises, false or otherwise, and I vowed to do what's in my power, but in this situation, there's a limit. My advisers have pressed me to negotiate with him."

"How?"

"Rescind the order to stop work on the wall. Offer a contract for more fortifications in the kingdom. Offer him something—anything. The thing is, I know the advisers aren't concerned only for the citizens. They have their own interests in mind. They have their own lands and enterprises at risk. They all deal with Fewmany in some way. We have to come to some arrangement. So—I've had a summons sent for him to appear this afternoon."

"What if he refuses?" I asked.

"Even he wouldn't dare ignore a summons," Nikolas said.

I approached his desk. "He'll honor it more for the sport than out of respect."

"He'll counter, and I anticipate I'll have to agree to a compromise I'll question for the rest of my life. You know how the very idea repulses me, but I can't indulge my personal ire at the people's expense."

"No. I am quite literal. What if he refuses? No agreement, no compromise, no poisoned bargain?"

"He can't." Nikolas's expression went blank. "He won't."

"He can, and he almost certainly will."

"It's going to be an arduous negotiation, but if we can work out some plan . . ."

I shook my head.

"But he can't. Surely he must know how many people are affected. How many people are dependent on their positions," Nikolas said.

"Of course he does."

"Doesn't he have concern for them?"

"Only if he gets what he wants," I said. This I knew, without a doubt.

Nikolas clenched his hands behind his neck. "They warned me not to halt construction. What was the worst that could happen? I thought. A protracted contract dispute, which we'd win—terms haven't been met, costs far higher. What he's done now makes no sense at all."

"However, you don't know for a fact that stopping the wall had anything to do with this. He might have been planning it for weeks," I said.

"You have no idea what responsibility I bear."

"Not for Fewmany's actions," I said.

"No, but that makes my burden heavier now, doesn't it?" Nikolas paced between his desk and the window. "What I don't understand is how he benefits. Soon enough, the people with no wages won't be able to buy anything, and the conglomerate owns half the businesses where they buy, not to mention hundreds of buildings where they rent."

The answer came with clarity. "He has a greater prize to claim. The hoard is the means to an end. He's willing to risk everything he's created for it, because when he returns, he can use the treasure to resurrect what was his. Then, he can salvage everything that faltered during the plague. Buy it all."

"You said he won't get through," Nikolas said.

"He won't."

"What if he did? What if you've made a mistake giving him the map and enough hints to lead him that close?"

"The odds are extremely slight. He doesn't know he must follow bees, and he'll be reluctant to do so. He doesn't like them."

Our eyes locked. We realized the error at the same moment.

"How well do you know his mind, Secret? Do you think he'll give up after the first hollow leads nowhere, the tenth, the twentieth? You know the nature of bees, so tell me, what are the chances of finding another hive like the one we saw? I remember what Aoife wrote—what Leit told her—some people cross into the realm by accident. What happens when someone knows what he's looking for?"

"He won't cross," I said, almost shouting to hide the edge of my worry.

"What made you think you could be so duplicitous? Why did you even try?"

"What choice did I have?" I asked.

"'I didn't find the hoard, Fewmany.' 'No, I won't go on a journey to look.' 'No, I won't work in your library.' What was it between you? What power did he have over you, or still does? You told me you're supposed to stop him. Trust me, you said. What are you going to do now? No response? Well, then, we'll have his greed and your complicity to thank for leading us to ruin."

My face stung as if he'd slapped me. "Is that what you think?"

"Oh, yes."

"What of your hubris?" I asked. "Don't you think your people would prefer that wall be built late than not at all? The crowd I saw today—they believe you provoked Fewmany and this is his retaliation. Who will they blame in the end?"

"Late or never, we're doomed. Regardless"—he paused, his eyes savage—"I'm not the one who poured the vials."

"You agreed," I said.

"And you did it. How does it feel to bear that burden?"

"Only in conscience. You'll bear the judgment of history. What will the chroniclers say about you?"

"Stop," a voice said. We turned toward the doorway. Harmyn's head shook with disappointment. "I could hear you shouting from the hall."

"Go back outside," Nikolas said. "This is between us."

"Watch your tone. This *is* between us. Leave her alone!"

"Don't shout at me!" Nikolas said.

"Stop! I feel sick from the feelings in this room. Whatever you said—
I couldn't hear and I won't glimpse—you can't take it back. Beyond
hurtful. Cruel. The damage is done. You turned on each other." Harmyn
spoke the truth with sadness, no attempt to shame.

Nikolas met my eyes. He shoved a bound journal under his arm. "I
have a meeting to attend. See yourselves out."

DIARY ENTRY 12 JUNE /38

Fewmany is missing.

In a note from Nikolas, I learned FM failed to heed the summons
and no one could account for his whereabouts, not his secretary,
not his top men, not even the servant who answered the door at
his manor. Nikolas wondered if he'd already left for his "journey." I
replied I didn't know and I'd talk to my father.

Father said no one had seen FM since the morning of the 7th.
When FM left and didn't return, no one thought much of it because
everyone knew he was leaving for a trip soon. Officially, to Thrigin
and Prev, business and pleasure, but only Father knew the truth.
When I asked, he admitted he knew about the furloughs. He said
most of the top men tried to convince FM otherwise, not only
because the accounting didn't bear it out. For so many to be out
of work at once would be terribly disruptive. All FM had to say to
that was, None should be paid for work they can't do. Fewmany
Incorporated isn't a charity. So, outside of Rothwyke, business
will continue as usual, but if/when the plague spreads, they are to
furlough everyone in those places, too. His top men will stay in
charge and do as he said until he returns. Father asked how long that
might be. Months, I said, not entirely a lie.

But something didn't feel quite right, something I couldn't
explain. After the argument with Nikolas, I wondered if I'd been
wrong all these weeks. Perhaps I've done what I was meant to do,
and the journey is his to take. Nevertheless, I went to the manor
myself. No answer when I rang the bell. I walked around the west
side to find everything gone—horses, carriages, saddles, and bridles.

I remembered then about the key Naughton said was hidden under the boot scraper. It opened a west wing door and led to stairway to the basement—kitchen, pantry, servants' quarters. Everything was in order. Pots hung clean, plates stacked, glasses in neat rows, silver in drawers, beds made, but not a single garment on a hook, comb on a wash stand, pair of boots under a chair.

When I reached the first floor, I noticed a burnt smell. In the hall—no table, no rug, no statues. I checked each door, none locked, not one of them—each chamber, empty. The east wing's hidden door was unlocked, but I didn't open it or enter the corridor.

I went upstairs—the burnt smell stronger—and tried the door opposite the library. Spotless. The other rooms, the chamber of wolves. Empty. I ran across to the library and found nothing inside—no table, no supply cabinet, no books—and proof of a fire. Hearth charred, mantel scorched, bookcases up to the east gallery black, ruined books disposed of. No books or manuscripts or maps anywhere. This stunned me most of all.

Then I went outside, across the green, and that's when I saw the wheel tracks leading toward the trees. The gate was wide open. I walked into the grove and asked what had happened. The trees showed me carts loaded with boxes, headed north, night and day. When the animals came forward, I asked if they'd seen him, Naughton, Mutt, anyone. No one but the drivers taking his possessions away.

Why did he do this? Where is he?

17 JUNE /38

TWO DAYS BEFORE WE LEFT THE COTTAGE, HARMYN AND I washed linens, tidied the space, and started to pack our belongings. At the castle, our rooms were waiting. Earlier in the week, Nikolas introduced us to everyone—servants, staff, officers, advisers. Nikolas showed us to our wing and let us select what we needed from storage. Harmyn had a good time at this, choosing what went into a room of her own. By letter, I told Father of our pending move. In his reply, he didn't question me and invited us to live with him, if circumstances changed. He mentioned there was still no word from Fewmany. Father didn't know I'd been to the manor and found everyone and everything gone. Although I hoped Fewmany was beyond Ailliath's borders by now, I'd been vexed by the persistent feeling that wasn't so.

On that second to last night, I sent Harmyn out to gather blueberries for dinner. As she did, I went to fetch water. All seemed as it should be, the insects' whir, the last of the birds on their way to roost, the burble of the stream. A fox glanced at me as she dipped her head to drink. This tranquility I'll miss when I return to town, I thought.

I walked back to the cottage and set down the bucket on the table.

A sitting shadow shifted on the bed.

Trembling, I lurched back.

"So close she was," the dark shape said.

Fewmany.

Shaking, I lit the three candles. In the light, I saw he was dressed in a shirt and jerkin, the strap of a quiver across his chest. His hair was untamed. Short metallic whiskers bearded his face.

"What animal led you here?" he asked.

"A squirrel," I said.

"Where is the old woman?"

"Away."

"There are bags by the door. Are you leaving as well?"

"How did you find me?" I asked. My thoughts spiraled. Where was Harmyn? Had he done something to her? Why hadn't the animals warned me of his presence?

"'Twas obvious once I pondered pieces in a new light," he said.

"You've been hunting for me."

"Such a strong word, my keeper of tales. Searched, tracked." He stood with effort, clutching his bow in his left hand, touching his belt with his right, the hilt of the bone-handled knife visible above its sheath. Both of his hands were gloved.

I forced my breath to slow and deepen. "I went to the manor to look for you. What happened to the library?"

"Lamp, paper, fire. A mishap. Drowned my sorrows, I did, for what was lost, but do not fret. I shall honor my agreement although the reward is diminished."

Had he meant to put me at ease with those words, despite his armed menace?

"Your collections. Why are they gone?" I asked.

"The plague will unleash an unprecedented level of rabble. My Mutt endured a terrible three weeks, yet he is a simple beast with no need for coin or barter. I couldn't risk vandals and looters with my treasures. There are places great men, too, hide their private hoards." His smile was wry, almost teasing.

"Why are you here?" I asked.

"I want you to come with me."

"You have the map."

"There is one prize to which it will not lead, or so you claim."

"What's that?"

"The dragon."

At last, the fragments revealed their pattern. My meeting with him when I was an apprentice, the menagerie on his office wall, his comment about hanging a top hat on a dragon's head. In his library, the books on dracology. The after-dinner visit to his trophy room, among the dead, the waiting plaque. Our discussion in the map room when he spoke of the elusive hoard. The direct question whether I'd seen the great beast when I found the treasure.

I stepped near the door. "Leave. Now."

"Don't lie to me," he said.

I willed Harmyn to keep away as I silently called upon the animals for protection. Fewmany flinched as if injured as he came forward.

I walked backward through the doorway. A hum hovered at my ear.

He followed me. "What happened to you when you were away? The girl who left was not the woman who returned. I know you spoke to the Council of your preternatural knowledge, but was it that? No. No—because what you knew was not beyond Nature, but of it. Your command of the beasts—'tis but a parlor trick, isn't it, compared to the powers you possess."

"You've gone mad."

"Lead me to the dragon. Hold it in thrall so I can slay it and mount its head. End its reign. Remember how you felt when you took the deer. This—imagine *this*. Come with me."

No matter my will, a fiery helix whirled through my body. Within the plea was his offer, spoken in the summoning voice I had so often heeded, wanted to heed.

A buzzing blur crossed my eyes. "I will not."

"Come. Let us see what you're truly made of. What dominion can you hold? With who else but me? Who rightly sensed your gifts? Who tested you for mettle and found the strength of iron? Who understands you?"

I ran then, away from the truth and the knife he grasped.

Through the dark, across the glade, into the woods, my feet battered the ground. He chased me, his pursuit dogged although he limped and panted. A full moon illuminated our steps.

Among the trees I knew so well, I wove round and round, and hunter that he was, he embodied instinct, anticipating my every turn.

He means to take me, not kill me, I thought, but I couldn't be sure as I felt him gain closer, closer.

Memory returned Egnis's whisper: *His proof.* If I took him to her, what would he do? What would she? She, who first saw All. She, of the myths who said to her orphan child Azul, if she were to die, "All would dry in endless light or all would rot in endless dark."

Running for my own life and yours—do you believe me, descendants and survivors?—I fled with the world at stake. To betray her would lead to darkness; to betray him would reveal so much light, in time.

My side seized with a cramp. My breath failed to sustain me. My strength waned. I was prey, bested by the rapacious pursuit, and I fell. To the animals, I called but none came, not a wolf, boar, fox, or bear—but bees, a line of them merging into a cloud, their orbits spiraling.

"Why did you run?" he asked as he collapsed with his hands against his knees.

"To get away."

"What are you worth to me, dead?" He laughed—maniacal and beautiful—both, yes—as the rage engulfed me and the bees gave voice to it with their drone.

One of you, sting him, I said.

He cried out in surprise. They swarmed him. He flung his hands around his face.

"Oh, they rarely sting unless provoked," I said. "Breathe slowly and don't move."

Another, give your life, I said.

He slapped his temple, which agitated the bees near his head. He barked in pain as more came to defend one another against the threat.

He lunged—I dodged aside—the knife slashed across my left hand—he ran forward in a dance of panic. The blade fell to the ground as he flailed, abandoned to instinct as the bees heeded theirs. The more who died, the more who stung.

I grabbed the knife. Two images flashed in my mind's eye. The scissors on the table near my drawing of the symbol. The dagger in my hand beside the dying doe. My urge, in each moment, to take the blade and kill him. I clenched the bone handle. My body remembered how to slit a clean cut.

He cowered, shielding his head with his arms, then crawled to a leafless hollow tree.

I did not avert my eyes as the bees surrounded him.

"Please!" he screamed. "Have pity!"

"Poor Fewmany," I said with mocking contempt as I walked to him. I leaned into the swarm to look at his face. In my next breath, my fury burned away to sadness and gave way to horror. The wound under his chin left a putrid smear on his shirt. The bruise under his eye I'd noticed weeks before now consumed that side of his face. His flesh swelled with the poison throbbing from the barbed sacs. He flinched when another pierced him.

To their own deaths, the bees heeded my will to do harm, but in their frenzy, I didn't know if they would honor my command to stop.

"Come," I said aloud to the wrathful sisters, calling them with an image of a hive, heavy with brood and honey. They returned to me.

One crawled to the center of my forehead where the queen's venom once anointed me.

We know who he is and what must be done. There is no way without us, the bee said.

As the bees rushed away, I knelt in front of him. His amber eyes sought mine the colors of night and day. Never had I felt so much love and hate at once. I set the knife aside and grabbed his left arm to help him sit against the tree. A viscous ooze covered the sleeve. Under the cloth, the brand wept blood, thick as sap. My own blood dripped into the stain.

"Why did you stop them?" he asked.

"That you must ask reveals the difference between us," I said.

A scuffle made me look up.

Fewmany turned as a brown rabbit crept from the tree's base. He pulled himself toward her, half of his back against the dead bark, the other half to the open space within. She inched near his offered hand.

The tree was hollow, but not hollow through. I understood then why the animals had not come when I called and why we were here, now.

I wasn't meant to kill, but to deliver him.

"Remember what the old woman told you?" I asked. "Follow the symbol, for it will lead to the riches you desire. And watch for rabbits."

The little creature stood on her haunches, out of reach. Fewmany inched closer, balanced on his hip, hand out.

I took up the knife, raised to my feet, and kissed his forehead. He stared at me, the blade.

"Follow her," I said.

The rabbit leapt into the darkness.

I kicked him into the hollow.

His arms reached out.

And he was gone.

BLOOD AND TEARS STREAKED MY FACE WHEN I UNCURLED AND sat back on my heels. Harmyn lowered to the ground across from me.

"Give me your hand," she said, her palms open.

"Did you see what happened?" I asked.

She clutched my injured hand between hers. "Yes."

"Did you know he was coming?"

"No. I'm not as aware of everything as you think I am." She hummed two tones, low, high, low, high. A vibration coursed through my skin. The wound became painfully hot, then as quickly cooled.

When she released me, I touched the thin ridge of a scar. An owl hooted. Another answered.

"That was a summons. Nikolas will be here soon. We should go home," I said.

I stood on weak legs. Harmyn ducked under my arm to help me walk.

"That weight crushing your heart? You can lift it off," she said. "Tell Nikolas everything—what happened at the manor, up to tonight."

When Nikolas arrived, Harmyn excused herself for a long walk. He sat down at the table. I served him tea, and I said, "I must tell you what happened between Fewmany and me." Then I did, from beginning to end. The time for secrets was over.

20 JUNE /38

THE DAWN BEFORE THE SUMMER SOLSTICE, THE DAY BEFORE THE PLAGUE of Silences sickened us, the sky released a relentless gray drizzle. From the room's window, I looked out to a flower garden, roses in full bloom; beyond it, the castle's outer wall. Harmyn didn't rouse for breakfast, so I ate alone, then went to Nikolas's office. He'd left a stack of letters for me to translate, a job I volunteered to assist with because I wanted something to do which required mental effort. During the prior weeks, Nikolas had corresponded with kingdoms near and far. Most appreciated the forthrightness of his warning and offered to aid how they could. Nikolas believed the goodwill visits he and his forefathers had taken had achieved their ends. As dire as our circumstances were to be, he took their kindness as a sign of hope.

By afternoon, the rain worsened, but Harmyn and I left the castle to visit my neighbors in Warrick, then my father. The street drains filled quickly and threatened to flood. The sidewalks were covered with water. People grumbled under their umbrellas, scurrying through their day as if the next one would be exactly the same. They turned to look at the light-haired child behind me who splashed with pleasure. Some of the people softened their faces and some hardened them. Everyone could see Harmyn at last.

When I entered the walk-up, several children were on the stairwell playing. Julia waved for Harmyn to join them. Lucas, who had a fading bruise on his cheek, jostled with two boys over a spinning top. Jane and Dora were on their way out, but we spoke long enough for me to learn Dora still had her job, but Jane was furloughed from Fewmany Incorporated. Jane planned to do her service in the ward garden, which would be built nearby. When we visited the Misses Acutt, I learned Mr. Elgin received confirmation he'd have work repairing the town's streets and buildings. He was one of the hundreds of men the town and kingdom had jointly hired because so many had been furloughed, and the repairs were critical. The Misses didn't seem too afraid about becoming sick, but they worried about feeding Sir Pounce. Even if they gave him their meat rations, it might not be enough and they'd have to get more somehow. Before I left, I emptied my pockets of silver and placed it in a teacup.

Once at Father's, he served tea and butter cookies. We sat together as he asked Harmyn questions about her gifts. What she could do, what she could not. His interest delighted her; her candor charmed him. I sensed him seeking beyond her, however, trying to understand the other Voice he lost. I said nothing of what happened to Fewmany; I wasn't ready to tell him. Before we left, Harmyn hugged my father, which made him smile. He kissed my cheek as I squeezed his hand. I came away with a hint of my mother's perfume, which made me wince.

We were soaked to the skin by the time we crossed through the castle's gatehouse. Harmyn spent a long time in the deep tub in our shared water closet, a luxury she'd never had, until I banged on the door for my turn. A chambermaid informed us Nikolas had been kept in a meeting and a tray would be brought for us. Our dinner was simple—boiled eggs, a loaf of bread, and a bowl of cherries. The rationing, declared three weeks prior, was under effect for everyone.

In her room, Harmyn played a music box with changeable discs. The melodies wafted in the background while I wrote to my friends. From recent letters, I knew Charlotte was happy with her new husband, Barnaby Frigget, and stepdaughter, Liddy, and Muriel was visiting with relatives near the coast. Neither had been in Rothwyke for the initial infection, but I was nearly certain, in time, they, too, would be stricken.

Harmyn was already in bed when I went to wish her good night. The last twinkling notes slowed to silence. My skin prickled into gooseflesh. "Do you remember the old bronze cogwheel you gave me some years ago?" I asked.

"What you want to know is if I *knew*, about it and you." She rubbed the amulet at her neck. "I couldn't say so then. I didn't understand what was happening to me, or why you were the one who had to have it. The cogwheel was a piece of the Wheels, which Aoife saw when she warned the Guardians they might be invaded."

"She watched the children sing along with the music. I had a rupture about that two years ago." I sat on her mattress. In the manuscript, Aoife described the settlement's center, where there was a silver-roofed well and gear-powered musical Wheels. "Well, then. The ward's name. Old Wheel. A name so old, no one remembered the reason it was called that."

"That's one of many things which will be remembered soon," she said.

"What did you notice among the shadows today?" I asked.

"They're ready to come out."

"What does that mean?"

"You'll see. Don't be afraid. I'm here," she said with a reassuring smile.

I smoothed the sheet at her side and almost, almost kissed her forehead, an impulsive maternal gesture which surprised me. My heart lilted, then pounded once, twice, full of blood but empty, lonely.

In my own bed, I drifted off to sleep. When I awoke again, the clock read nearly half past ten. I hadn't seen Nikolas all day. That I wouldn't be able to hear his voice for weeks, possibly months, distressed me. I stepped into slippers and put a robe over my linen gown.

As I walked from the guest wing through the parlors to the stair which led to the second floor, I heard laughter and muffled conversations. Servants, guards, and several advisers, whose duty kept them away from their own homes, gathered in corners and doorways. I assumed they didn't want to squander those last hours with sleep.

The hall which led to Nikolas's new room was lamplit, but there was no guard at its entrance or his door. A pendulum clock ticked nearby. No light shone under the threshold, but I knocked anyway.

Nikolas grinned when he saw me at his door. He wore trousers but no shirt. The last time I'd seen him dressed that way, he was a boy exploring the woods. Since then, on the quest, by accident, I'd glimpsed him change quickly. That was autumn, winter. Cold. This night was warm. "It was dark and quiet in your wing when I checked an hour ago," he said.

"You could have waked me. You're without a guard at the moment," I said.

He peeked into the corridor. "Hugh's on post tonight. He must be in the water closet. That weak bladder of his." Nikolas gestured for me to come in and left the door open.

"Isn't someone supposed to take his place?" I asked.

"I'm too tired to chastise anyone now." He walked across the room. The chamber had once been his father's, now his as the new king. Nikolas's furniture and belongings had been moved.

With furtive volition, I closed the door then joined him at an open window. The rain fell on his outstretched hands.

"How's Harmyn?" he asked.

"Exhausted but in good spirits. How was the meeting with the mayor and ward leaders?"

"Tense but productive. They're as prepared as they can be. At least they're trying to work together, unlike a few on the Council who are skeptical, even hostile, about our plans. Some advisers told me I've been too caught up in the minutiae. I should have my mind on the trouble with Haaud, especially since we learned Emmok's alliance agreement with them. This complicates matters because of our accord with Emmok, Charming's marriage sealing that. Yes, I admit, I might be too involved, but I care how we manage in Rothwyke. What we learn here will affect what's done once the plague spreads. And then, this I heard from an adviser I trust, there are Council members who believe I lack ruthlessness, that what's coming will reveal me as weak and my subjects will resent me even as they laud my goodness."

"What do you think?"

"I'm worried, despite my best efforts, I will fail my people, even though I understand much is beyond my control. I'm afraid what fear will bring out of us."

"So am I." I paused. "I saw my father today. He and Harmyn are forming quite the friendship. I worry how he'll fare, though. Unable to speak, unable to hear, and he's so accustomed to being around people, talking. He wants me home again, even with Harmyn."

"Will you go?"

"No."

I reached my fingers to the raindrops. They were cool and cleansing, so different from tears, which I suddenly felt streaming down my cheeks.

"Why are you crying?" he asked. Nikolas touched the inside of my arm and slipped his wet fingers through mine.

"I don't know," I said. "The only word in my thoughts is *why*, but I don't know to what or whom I'm asking it. I'm afraid, too. Afraid we shouldn't have gone on the quest or accepted the vials or agreed to re-lease them. Afraid what the plague will do to you, and me, and Harmyn, my father, everyone. I don't know how I'll tolerate the silence. I remember what it was like when I was a child, unable to speak, even when I wanted to."

"I'm afraid, too. But I'm glad we'll be afraid together instead of apart. I can't imagine enduring this without you." He kissed the center of the queen's sting. He'd done that once before, the day he visited me at my father's house and I told him about the manuscript. That kiss held me together with the force of unconditional love.

This one possessed the same power, but it made me shatter. All that had been guarded, sealed, walled fell away.

I gripped the back of his neck, drew him close, the kiss voracious.

What I believed was fixed became a new thing—a new love con-joined with desire; volatile, quick, fire and air; heavy, fluid, earth and water. Transmutation, I thought.

When he eased away to catch his breath, he looked toward the bed-room door.

"No one knows I'm here," I said. "Keep it closed."

His quiet laugh was seductive, wicked. The light in his eyes para-lyzed me. His fingers twisted into my silver hair's loose braid. I swept my hands against his skin, muscles, bones. I kicked away my slippers and wriggled out of my robe. My bare feet arched on the marble floor as he loosened the tie of my gown's bodice. I swayed where I stood, afraid I would fall.

I led him toward the bed. We stretched across the mattress. I sighed when his mouth left mine, then breathed in with a start as he opened the top of my gown and set flame to my flesh. I clutched his gold hair and traced the cords of his neck. I wasn't sure when to stop, how to stop, if.

When I pushed him to his back, I planted my knees next to his hips and locked his wrists above his head, kissing him until the need for air drew us apart. My palms drifted across his face, throat, chest.

He knew what I'd done with someone else, and I knew he, too, had sated some curiosity. Neither was as surprised by the other's revelation as we perhaps should have been. I was grateful then as my fearless hands slipped lower and he arched into me.

Nikolas clutched the bare curves of my thighs. "I've thought—imagined—it's not that I don't want to—but—"

"But not yet," I said, willing though I was, thinking of what herbs I'd have to brew.

"Despite your advances, I shall remain a virgin king," he said.

"Just barely," I said.

As I stripped him naked and he did the same to me, I tried to remember what I'd learned from those salacious books, then abandoned myself to the pleasure of giving and receiving. To touch, to be touched, transcended the erotic. I didn't know how starved I was—so hungry to be held, to hold—until his bare skin fed mine.

When we finally exhausted each other, I leaned against his side.

"I don't want you to, but you'll have to go soon," he said.

"Must I? Let's blame it on the plague. I'm sure we're not the only ones entwined tonight."

"I'm serious."

"So am I." I searched myself for remorse, for shame, for modesty—and found none. I felt the purity of my own desire, and regardless of all I had been taught, this was a sacred gift. The aliveness was mine. "You're beyond reproach. I'll bear the judgment as long as you promise this will happen again."

"My valet will come in after first light. I won't compromise your virtue."

"You have, with my full consent," I said.

He laughed. "Regardless, you're not staying." He laid his hand over my left breast. I touched him in the same place. A pulse thread its way into my palm, spiraled around my heart, and joined another cord he'd wound there long ago. I squeezed my eyes shut but couldn't stop the tears.

"What is it?" he asked.

"You truly love me."

"Truly."

"Always."

"Always." Nikolas shifted the pillow under his head. "Will you tell me tonight, before morning comes and I can't hear your voice again until the plague allows it?"

"Tell you what?"

He traced the queen's hidden stings, waiting.

"I love you, Nikolas."

"Love, I love you, too."

I settled into the curve of his body. His arms wrapped around me. Never in my life had I felt so safe.

- Part III -

WEEK 1

Under a table, against a wall across from a fire,
I sat, swaddled in spiderwebs.
    Across the room, a basket wobbled back and forth.
    Infant screams filled my ears. The ogress loped
    toward the cries. A feral stink billowed from her
    skirt's hem. A crow called. Glass cracked.
The ogress listened for another sound.
      She bent at the waist, spilling yellow mushrooms
      from her apron, and searched through the shadows,
      across the floor, to the corner—

I awoke with my throat raw from screaming. My limbs splayed across
the bed as I tore myself from the dream's clutches. When I opened my
eyes, I saw the haze of first light. I remembered where I was, whose bed
I'd left hours before, that it was the twenty-first of June, the summer solstice.

"It's morning," I said but heard no sound. The plague left me speechless.

I tried to sleep again, but a soothing hum in my chest kept me awake.
What is Harmyn doing now? I wondered as I dressed. When I knocked
on her door, she didn't answer. As I crossed through the parlors—resisting
the urge to climb the stairs and find Nikolas—the vibration grew stronger. My feet led me onward, beyond the private residence, through the
main courtyard, under the gatehouse, to the castle's outer wall.

On the green near the entry gate, several guards, servants, officers,
and advisers clustered together, unable to see who sang above. I found a
stairway and reached the top.

The rising sun shone full on Harmyn's face. I noticed her eyes were a
deeper violet, and the indigo rims of her irises were thicker.

She sang in tones, the sound purer than a bell's chime, truer than
a crystal's ring, an element in and of itself. Harmyn smiled as I stood
transfixed, listening as the matter within me churned, shifted, changed.
I wanted to hold the resonance like a stone. A stone, I thought, the

philosopher's stone of alchemy . . . what if it isn't tangible but incorporeal, like light, like sound? *This?*

Through a gap between clouds, a flight of blue swallows appeared, circled over Harmyn's head, then spiraled around me. One hovered near my face and said, *The sickness has not spread. You will receive word when it does.* Relieved, I thanked him.

When Harmyn finished her song, a shudder streaked from my center through my skin. The birds converged above us and parted into four groups flying north, south, east, and west.

Harmyn swung a little bell from side to side in front of her. I noticed then my hearing was slightly muffled and my eyesight somewhat clouded.

"You can't speak, but I can hear you," Harmyn said, then tapped her temple. *And you can hear me.* Her words reached me in the same way I communicated with creatures and plants.

Can everyone speak this way? I asked.

No, but I can, with whomever I choose. It's something I discovered I can do, she said.

How?

In a dream, she said. She pinched the amulet at her neck.

Why are you singing now, here?

I discovered some songs can clear away the poison, like a breeze. Everyone will struggle enough with their own shadows without getting sicker from what other shadows leach out. I'll do this in the morning to help everyone feel better. They should feel a hum in their bodies even if they're not close enough to hear me, Harmyn said.

I did. That's why I came to find you, I said.

Harmyn peered over the wall to the street. She waved at the small crowd gathered below. As we returned to the castle, people looked at her with a curious awe, almost with fear, and a few bowed their heads to her. She returned the glances with a peaceful smile.

I have a job now. I need a uniform. Could I have some new clothes? Harmyn asked.

Not bothering to contain my surprise, I told her I'd take her out after breakfast, as we had an open day. We weren't due to help in the Warrick garden until later in the week.

As we walked to the ward of Dalglen, adjacent to Warrick, the morning's bustle seemed like every other, except for the quiet. The shops and offices, which weren't among Fewmany Incorporated enterprises, were open. There, the workers and customers went about their routines. Tell-a-Bells chimed along our way, but the wearers, now mute, didn't list their tolls aloud. Not a single newsbox had a speaker; word of what was happening within Rothwyke, Ailliath, and abroad was left unspoken.

Those who stopped to greet acquaintances touched their throats or mouths and shook their heads. Some reached into pockets or satchels to grab notebooks or paper slips. Their conversations took place as an exchange of written words.

When we arrived at Margana Bendar's shop, she was outside sweeping. At the sight of us, she set aside the broom, startled me with a light hug, and then stood staring at Harmyn.

Harmyn pointed at the blue crystal in her necklace. "You know who we are," she said in the Guardians' language.

Margana nodded with tears in her eyes. I thought of Old Woman and Naughton for a moment. All Guardians wore their blue in some way, always in plain sight. I'd never made the connection with her.

"I'm not afflicted, so I'll speak," Margana said quietly. "Word traveled among us in the past weeks. We've been told about you three—you, Secret, and you, Harmyn, and the king—and that a change was coming. Our aid is crucial now."

Were you born among or away? I wrote in my notebook, referring to a distinction Aoife made about those who were Guardians by birth, like Wei, or by integration, as Aoife was.

"Among. My mother and I moved here when I was thirteen. If you listen carefully, you can still hear the lilt of my accent," Margana said. "I heard you sing this morning, Harmyn. Such a beautiful voice."

"Thank you. It's my honor to serve," Harmyn said.

"So, then, we could talk more, but you came here for a reason today. What is that?" Margana asked.

"I'm to get new clothes. Secret said you could make something special. I would like a uniform," Harmyn said.

"Let's see what we can do," Margana said, gesturing for us to follow.

Two women and three children sat inside the shop, their hands busy embroidering designs on fabric scraps. From some of their faces, I could tell they were new to the skill or hadn't used it in some time. Draped over the center of the table near them was a length of cloth, Guardian blue.

Margana piled several books on the table. "Sit down with these and see what appeals to you. And on those shelves, you'll find fabric samples. Touch them, look at the colors, and decide what you like. I'll come back to talk with you soon. Secret, a word . . ."

Margana paused to praise one girl's needlework, prompting a gap-toothed smile. I stepped out alone.

Compared to other wards, especially those central and south, Dalglen had moderate damage. The street in front of her shop had no major repairs, and the buildings had the usual cracks of their age. On that block, several shops and offices were closed with massive chains or boarded windows. Nearby, a teahouse, a tavern, and an apothecary remained open. I watched customers step in and out.

"Well, they are busier than usual," Margana said.

Distressing to see others closed as they are, I wrote.

"Men came yesterday evening to shut the buildings. This morning, a few workers forgot they had no jobs and arrived at their usual times. I'll not soon forget the looks on their faces," she said.

How are you? I wrote.

"Aside from a dry throat, I'm well. I likely won't have enough work in the coming weeks. My service, though, is through the practical trades—teaching piecework and tailoring—but some of my pupils wanted to learn embroidery and applique and how to sew. That's who's here today. How are you?"

Sight and hearing not as sharp, but otherwise fine. Not speaking, not difficult yet. I'll serve in the gardens, try to keep busy, look after Harmyn.

"I didn't expect a boy. I'd been told Voices are usually girls," Margana said.

Looks deceive. She's accustomed to wearing boys' clothes. She's allowed some eccentricity, I suppose, I wrote.

"Is she as gifted as I heard they could be?"

You cannot imagine.

"Secret, look! Margana, I want one of these," Harmyn said.

She stepped out with her arms flung wide. The violet silk frock coat had exaggerated saffron-colored lapels and flared to her knees from a fitted back. Silver buttons as small as blueberries dotted the length of the placket. The cuffs reached to her fingertips.

"With some alterations, it's yours. It's one of my play pieces, which has found for whom it was made," Margana said.

"May I accept?" Harmyn asked.

I nodded.

"Thank you! Let me show you the drawings I like, but I have some ideas to change them," Harmyn said.

Inside, Harmyn went to the table where two books lay open on top of the blue cloth. I brushed my hands across it, so smooth, I couldn't resist caressing it.

"Incredible, isn't it? I didn't order the bolt but it arrived with my name on the tag. The courier refused to take it back, saying payment was in order," Margana said.

What are you going to make with it? I wrote.

"I don't know yet. It would make beautiful drapes or a stunning dress. So then, Harmyn, show me what you liked," Margana said.

When I drew close to Harmyn, near enough to hold her, a chill ran through my arms.

At the end of that first day, Harmyn and I had an informal dinner with Nikolas, and we retired to one of the parlors. Harmyn surprised him with a conversation I couldn't hear. Nikolas seemed relieved he could communicate with her. They played a game while I skimmed a book. Afterward, Harmyn excused herself to go to bed.

Nikolas beckoned me with the curl of his fingers. With his guard trailing behind, I followed him to his office. Once the door closed behind us, he pulled me close and kissed me with cheerful ardor, which I returned. Nikolas withdrew a clothbound notebook from his pocket and wrote,

I enjoyed our pleasant evening.

Which one? I wrote underneath.

He smirked. **You seem well enough. Any pain?** he wrote.

No. You?

Arms sore, right much worse than left. At meetings today, men moved stiffly, some kept rubbing hands. Everyone silent, but I've been told that's not the case for all.

Correct. Perhaps Harmyn can explain soon enough, I wrote.

When I passed the notebook to him, he put it away. From the look in his eyes, I could see he was tired. I wished for the comfort of a conversation, especially then at the close of the plague's first day and after what happened the night before. Absent that, I wrapped my arms around his waist and leaned into his heartbeat. His sigh confirmed that was enough.

WEEK 2

IN THE MIDDLE OF THE SECOND WEEK, ON THE THIRTIETH OF June, we went to the first concert on the plaza. As long as everyone was able to hear, musicians retained by Ailliath and Rothwyke would give a free performance one evening a week.

A carriage would take Nikolas to the event. Harmyn and I decided to walk that evening. She and I arrived early, before the time Father said he'd meet us, and took a peek behind Fewmany Incorporated to see the stalled construction. Skeletal beams etched against the sky. The completed buildings had cracks along the sides. I dared to step across the open ground. The faintest groan reached my feet. There had been no recent reports of tremors or widening crevices. What I felt, I was certain only I could feel.

As we stepped back toward the plaza, Harmyn spotted Father and rushed to him. He waved with his left hand—gloved—and took a notebook from his pocket. He struggled to hold the pencil in his right hand, his fingers stiff.

Harmyn gestured for him to put it away. "I'm not sick. I can talk and also . . ."

Father's eyes glowed like a boy's watching magic tricks. She was speaking to him within his thoughts. Father pointed at me.

"He wants to see me three times a week, to teach me to read and write," Harmyn said.

Father gave me a serious look. His request didn't surprise me, but the splinter of jealousy, which needled my stomach, did.

As Harmyn and Father spoke without a sound, I looked out to the growing crowd. Based on their clothing alone, I could tell the people's stations and watched them cluster together. Some children and adults chatted in their notebooks, but most people gestured in greeting and stood in groups. Nearby, a woman kept her voice low as she talked to three others. Since we'd sickened, I'd noticed the few who could speak whispered instead, as if out of respect for the majority's silence.

Aside from their muteness, the children seemed well, at least physically. The adults didn't fare the same. During those first days, the adults showed increasing signs of afflictions. Some had limp, atrophied, or spastic arms; a few were affected this way in the legs. Now and then, a person would venture out hunched or contorted, struggling to walk as if carrying a weight. Others had bulging veins in their necks and temples, so profound it seemed painful. By then, I knew I wasn't the only one whose vision and hearing weren't clear.

A cymbal crash startled me. Lord Sullyard, a Council member who lived outside of Rothwyke and wasn't yet afflicted, read a welcome on behalf of Nikolas and Mayor Pearson. After that, the conductor handed a horn to Nikolas, who made everyone laugh with a first bleat and impressed them to applaud as he held a long low blare.

As the orchestra began to play, Harmyn pointed to children she knew from the Warrick garden, including Julia, and ran off to join them. She stopped to select a colorful pinwheel from a basket of them offered by a young man in a blue vest.

Father struggled to write a message. **Come dinner end week w/ H. Elinor cook. You look well. No pains?**

I wrote below his words, **Will do. Yes, well.**

I was about to write more when I felt a light tap on my arm. Leo Gray shook Father's hand, then mine when I offered it. He held up a notebook. At the bottom of the page, he'd written,

This is my wife, Hyacinth, & my son, Solden.

I nodded at his wife, who was as beautiful in person as she was in the luminotype on his desk. The boy looked at me politely and refrained from blowing his own pinwheel.

She wore her notebook around her neck like a pendant, the pages held between two gold covers with a tiny pencil slipped into a slot on the side.

How wonderful we have this amusement, Mrs. Gray wrote.

Indeed, I wrote in my notebook, then handed it to her.

Leo says you were his favorite apprentice, she wrote.

I learned much from him. He's a brilliant teacher.

She glanced at him with affection. **How are you doing your service?**

New gardens. You?

Reuse League. Clothing, furniture to mend.

Leo slipped between us and opened his hand for my notebook. Mrs. Gray waved herself away.

Still no word from Fewmany. Wesley & Cuthbert furloughed. Only Rowland and me now, he wrote.

Didn't know. Sorry, I wrote.

Time for Cuthbert. Eyesight awful. Worry about Wesley. Married now, wife expecting in September.

With luck, affliction will lift soon. How do you fare?

Sore upper back. Muffled hearing. You? he wrote.

Vision bit clouded. Hearing also muffled, I wrote.

Strange what has befallen us.

Quite.

Ages since I danced with my wife. Good to see you. Leo returned the notebook to me. He caught Mrs. Gray's waist and outstretched hand.

Father had taken a seat among colleagues from the twelfth floor, all of whom held handkerchiefs or wore gloves. When I studied the crowd, I noticed no one else covered his, or her, hand that way. I couldn't imagine what that meant.

I stood alone, listening, content to do so as the lamplighters made their rounds and the sky blurred to a soft pink. I watched Nikolas dance with three women—once with an elderly woman wearing her daymaid's apron, then with another somewhat older than he wearing a fashionable dress, and finally with a girl no more than twelve who was impressively graceful and whose cheeks flamed red.

Harmyn appeared at my side flushed from play. "The air is cheerful. It was good for Nikolas and the mayor to do this for everyone," she said.

I nodded. I knew advisers had pressured Nikolas to be austere—don't drain the coffers for anything but the absolute necessities—but he had agreed with a minority of ward leaders who believed entertainments would give some relief from the daily and mounting worries.

When the orchestra stopped for a break, Nikolas found us at the edge of the crowd. He extended his hand to Harmyn with flair.

"No, thank you. No, please, I don't want to. Ask her now," Harmyn said, her serious tone at odds with his playful invitation.

He turned to me. I shook my head. He withdrew a slip of paper and pointed to one line among several.

You know I'm light on my feet, he'd written.

I laughed as I read retorts he anticipated he'd have to give.

It's time you learned a proper waltz.

Afraid of some good-natured teasing from your father?

This constitutes socially acceptable contact.

I shoved the note into my pocket. He offered his elbow and led me near the dais. When the music began again, he pointed to the couples stepping one, two, three, one, two, three. Study them, his eyes said. I accepted the sweep of his arm, looked down to watch the pattern of my feet, and gazed back at him once I felt in rhythm. Where my hands touched him, I held on for dear life, grateful for each moment I didn't have to let go.

WEEK 3

IN AN EMPTY LOT TWO BUILDINGS FROM THE WALK-UP WHERE I once lived, volunteers from Warrick worked to build a new garden. I helped three days a week, often with Harmyn in tow. Each visit, I'd look in on my former neighbors. Mrs. Elgin kept to home, taking in piecework, while Mr. Elgin worked on the town's drains. Sometimes Julia and Lucas were off playing with friends. Dora had her secretary job, but Jane, having been furloughed, struggled to keep herself busy. The Misses Acutt's days were the same as they'd been before the sickness struck, although they, as had Jane, decided to do their service in the garden.

That week, the garden volunteers were ready to break up the soil which plows had turned. We took up our shovels, picks, and hoes as the morning's mist lifted. Julia offered to help that day and spaced herself between Harmyn and Jane. Across from us, the Misses Acutt stood with their elderly friends.

No one gave Harmyn and me strange looks anymore. Although some people recognized me from when I lived in Warrick, most had no idea what to make of the tawny-skinned, silver-haired young woman with mismatched eyes or the violet-eyed child with her archaic clothing. Instead, now they watched Harmyn with curiosity, as most knew she was the one who sang to Rothwyke every morning.

Usually, Harmyn ignored the glances, keeping silent to thwart any more attention to herself. But that day, she sat next to Julia, the two of them smashing clumps of soil in their hands, and studied everyone. The people with the worst afflictions moved slowly.

All eyes fell on Harmyn as the first notes of a folk song drifted through the air. The Misses Acutt looked at each other, then at their companions. Together, they clapped and mouthed the words of a tune from their youth. Spontaneously, the rest worked in time with the melody, then another and another. When Harmyn stopped, everyone applauded.

Harmyn nodded her thanks, moved to a new spot on the ground, and peered over at Jane. This time, Harmyn sang a ballad, which made the younger adults smile at one another. Jane pressed her lips together, trying to seal off the grin which wanted to crack through. As Harmyn mangled a series of notes, Jane grabbed her knees and shook with noiseless laughter.

Harmyn had glimpsed them, searching their secret pasts for happy moments. She hadn't asked permission—how could she have explained that gift of hers?—but I wouldn't scold her later. Harmyn knew the rules she must follow. Her choice to break them that morning brought only joy.

After we completed our work and put away our tools, the volunteers left with smiles. Several people waved at Harmyn, and one elderly man patted her head. I noticed the adults walked away with ease in their steps.

My own merry feelings endured as we tended Old Woman's garden and visited Father that evening. But when Harmyn came to my room before bed, I sensed a somber shift before she said a word.

"I understand why the adults suffer with physical ailments the children don't have," Harmyn said. "Eventually, I think many will figure it out for themselves, too, unless their shadows are very strong and won't let them. What you see, or can't, are *manifestations* of deeds done. Harm done to others over and over, or even only one cruel moment. Like beating someone, or saying cruel things."

I thought of my blunted sight and hearing and felt a twist of regret as I looked at Harmyn. The first weeks she was with Old Woman and me, I had been dismissive and angry toward her. When I thought of Father's crippled right hand, my stomach knotted. That hand had held the scissors, twelve relentless nights. And what of his left, which he kept gloved?

"Some people remember what they've done, but sometimes they forget. Well, they don't forget, really, more so it's denied. It gets buried but never goes away. Their bodies reveal the truth now. Their bodies remind them of what they've done."

Should this be explained to everyone? I asked within our thoughts.

"No. It's a mistake to make people aware of things before they're ready. I also don't know yet what will happen when everyone enters the next phase. Whatever has to be resolved might take the whole period of the plague, maybe far longer."

Other than those who weren't in Rothwyke for the first spread, why have some been spared? I asked.

"Have you noticed most of them are Guardians?" she asked. "Remember what Aoife wrote about them, how they rear their children and how they treat each other. I don't think the plague could make them sick because they don't have the same kind of shadows we do. Not as many or as dense anyway."

What about the people who aren't Guardians and who were here when the plants and animals got sick? I asked.

Harmyn rubbed her wrists as if they hurt. "I can only guess they've been lucky to have gentle lives."

WEEK 4

DIARY ENTRY 13 JULY /38

How welcome the simplest routines are, giving order to our uncertainty. Harmyn sings every dawn to growing crowds. In the mornings, we work in the ward garden, or tend and harvest Old Woman's. Today, we delivered cucumbers, green beans, and lettuces to a charity market, where those in dire need don't have to pay for vegetable rations. In the afternoons, Harmyn does as she pleases, as long as Nikolas or I know where she is, a rule at his insistence. She's made friends with Julia and others in Warrick, so she's often there with them. I read in my room, or if Nikolas needs help, I'll translate correspondence. I'm grateful for intellectual work. How bored I'm beginning to feel!

Most evenings, we three have a meal together, followed by a restful time reading or playing games. It's less odd because of my time with Nikolas on the quest and the months we lived with Old Woman, but I remember always going to my room after dinner. After Harmyn's in bed, we take walks, but exercise hasn't been the sole purpose. He's led me to dark corners, where we've unbuttoned and unclothed as little as possible, the satisfaction quick. Once, I pulled

him into the secret room (if those walls could talk of who else had
been there, he joked) but we haven't dared a night like the one
before the plague. Surely the staff, definitely Hugh, suspects by now.

Muriel wrote me. She's with her parents on the coast, where they
fled after learning of the plague. Both are afflicted. Her father's face is
red "as if he's overexerted himself." Her mother complains of a sore
throat and thick tongue. Muriel was unusually effusive about how
anxious she is to return to the conservatory. She wanted to visit friends
this summer, but her parents refused to give her the travel money. "I've
begun to resent what I see now as stifling dependence," she wrote.
From Charlotte, I received a letter with an apology for her delay
because she's moving to a new house and expecting a baby soon.

Father's restless. He told me land acquisitions are stalled until
Fewmany returns. (Little does he know . . .) All he does now is
manage the men managing the lands. Not speaking is a torment, but
he can "speak" to Harmyn, which might be one reason he's so glad
to see us—her?—when we visit. Their lessons are going well. She
learns remarkably fast.

WEEKLY POST.

16 July /38. Page 1, Column 1

CONTINGENCY LEADERSHIP FOR AILLIATH AND ROTHWYKE
TO BE SELECTED—Next month, committees will meet to name prox-
ies for King Nikolas, Mayor Pearson, and other important positions.
Concerns over how the sickness will progress impelled both offices to
prepare now, in the event any among them lose their full faculties. A re-
gency council, comprising the king's advisers, will elect a proxy to serve
in His Majesty's stead. Under the kingdom's statues, because the king
has neither a wife nor direct heir, the Council can either select a distant heir by blood or marriage or a member of the Council. Lord Ashby,
speaking on the Council's behalf, stated the king may give a recommendation, but as the kingdom's statues read, his request might not be
honored. The king himself will name interim officers, in the event those
who currently serve cannot fulfill their duties. In Rothwyke, Mayor
Pearson will meet with mayors and selected officials from at least seven
towns. A committee will elect the mayor's proxy and determine how
many officers and clerks will be needed as interim staff.

From the Plague of Silences Recollection Project Archives,
Selected Excerpts

Diary No. 92. Female, 51, occupation unknown

This week, for the four of us, 16 oz ham, 4 eggs, 8 oz butter, 4 oz
cheese—half of what we got last week. Standard ration of veg, at
least until the ward gardens are ready to harvest. The boys gripe of
hunger. They want more meat, which isn't always available on the
sleight market. Last week the newsboxes became bread boxes, by the
king's decree, and anyone can get a loaf with no ration stamps required. Mrs. P— has a beekeeper friend who will barter for honey.

Y— assures me I shouldn't worry about our rent. We're fortunate, if he's being truthful. The Post reported hundreds of eviction
notices were sent this week. Ward leaders want rents reduced or
delayed. Rothwyke has no law about this, for circumstances in
which we find ourselves, and negotiations are landlord to landlord.
I heard from Mrs. E— there's talk about establishing new poor-
houses. She said Mrs. Agister, who usually arranges orphan aid, has
tried to rally one of her groups to help. There's a rumor the king
might order relief, too. I didn't think myself unaware before, but I
had no conception of how marginally so many lived. Three weeks
without work, and here they are.

Diary No. 181. Female, 28, milliner

A— complains of a numb arm but says nothing about the cords in
his neck like he's been shouting at the top of his lungs. Which he
did often before the sickness. Yesterday I went to cuff the youngest, and the pain in my hand doubled me. Stopped me dead cold.
I knew then the things we've done, they're showing. I went to
the shops and wondered about the secrets behind those limps and
twisted backs. Like me, has it made them think about what hurt
they've caused?

Diary No. 307. Male, 54, physician

Preliminary reports from colleagues received. Children presenting
with usual complaints (coryza, dyspepsia, etc.) aside from the loss

of speech. Adults as well, but among them, we've seen a notable increase in those suffering from limb difficulties, swelling of tongue/throat, degrees of hearing and vision loss, various aches and pains. Youngest with these same ailments is 16 (three cases thus known); appears they've been struck by this so-called plague differently from others of the same age. Also, strangely, an observable increase in those complaining of impotence, not only among the mature gentlemen but also several too young to endure this debilitation. Only Dr. V— and Dr. G— report a disturbing phenomenon, spontaneous bleeding on hands, as if wicking through the skin like water through wood. The patients are all prominent men, advisers to the King, top men with FM Inc.

Interview No. 223. Male; age during plague, 10; current occupation, blacksmith

The first weeks. There was no one way people reacted, old or young. You could see it in their faces. Do you remember? Shock. Anger. Humor. Acceptance. Then soon enough, the silence was normal. Frustrating, too. You're talking to me because you want to hear from those who didn't write, or couldn't. I finished my fifth year before the plague, but I wasn't a good student.

My parents, they couldn't read or write. They were working at eight, ten. Their jobs? Mother in a pottery. She worked the kilns until she was old enough to apprentice. She painted. Father, always in coal, a trapper, then a hurrier in the mines until his family moved to Rothwyke, then a heaver. He was very strong.

Yes, right, they came of age before the child work laws, but you know those were broken. Blind eyes turned. Desperate families needed the money. Who cared about the children then, really? Funny thing, I'd forgotten this. When that rogue Fewmany closed the companies, even the kids got furlough notices. You didn't know that? Oh yes. My sister worked in a match factory. She was fourteen. Cried and told Mother she'd turn to the streets if that meant we wouldn't starve.

So—the silence, not speaking. In a way, we became like animals. Pointing. Gesturing. We had to read faces. I had a friend who could grunt. It was surprising how much could be said without words.

During that phase, ah, the sleep was so strange. I've talked to other survivors who remember it. Gray, often dreamless. Calm but empty. It was a heavy comfort, but so difficult to wake up in the morning.

WEEK 5

IN JULY, SEVERAL OF NIKOLAS'S FRIENDS RETURNED FROM THEIR high academy terms and travels abroad. As timing would have it, they suggested an evening out just before Nikolas's twenty-first birthday. I declined when Nikolas asked if I would like to join them. He spent most of his time with men far older than he and not for social pleasure. I wanted him to have a night with his fellows, enjoying their company as he hadn't in a long while.

While he was away that night, Harmyn and I went to the castle's library. She practiced her handwriting, copying the words from a sea adventure Father, whom she now called GrandBren, had been reading with her. Her dexterity didn't quite match her determination—her letters remained childlike—but neither Father nor I could fathom how quickly she'd grasped reading and learned new words. My extra tutoring proved unnecessary. What required an ordinary child years to master, she was achieving within weeks. Father promised to teach her arithmetic and history next. The evenings I watched them together, I remembered the lessons he'd given me, and I thought of my brothers who had never been, absent from Father's spirited lectures. I wondered now, with a needling curiosity, how much Father missed the presence of those sons.

That night, while Harmyn sat nearby, the past slipped into the present as I turned through the old chronicles leading up to The Mapmaker's War. My untrained eye could detect no remarkable variance in the writing, but I knew enough about binding to observe several of the books had been taken apart and stitched together again.

I read slowly, searching for Aoife. How careful they'd been to erase her. How thorough her disappearance. In those pages, she was a nameless apprentice blamed for provoking the war. No mention that she'd been the kingdom's mapmaker, that she was from a prominent noble family, that she had married Wyl and bore twins soon after. They, too, the infant girl and boy, were gone.

What Aoife had written herself wasn't merely an artifact of memory. Her manuscript sealed a gap in history. She un-told lies which had been repeated for generations. A translation of her autobiography belonged in the royal archives as well as libraries beyond it.

If I were to provide this, I perceived danger in revealing too much, specifically about the realm. Aoife had used an incantation, I my intu-ition, but we both gained entry because of the bees. What might others attempt, even achieve, if this were known? I could leave out those men-tions. No one would know. Only I could read the Guardians' language as Aoife had written it, and the manuscript would stay in the realm forever once I gave it back.

Then I considered Aoife would want everything told. Throughout the pages, her refrain was "tell the truth." More than a thousand years later, I held the power to honor that.

A chill rushed into my blood so fast, I shook.

Harmyn glanced up from her work. "What's the matter? I feel the cold from here."

"I'm not only Aoife's descendant. The dreams and ruptures I've suf-fered, those were fragments of her life. I realize now—the 'you' in the manuscript wasn't only an address to herself. The 'you' speaks to the part of me that is . . . *her*."

"And?" Harmyn asked lightly.

"How it that possible? Her experiences weren't mine, yet I know them. The manuscript itself confirms it all to be so."

"You received the shape of your hands and color of your hair from people who came long before you. Why should it be difficult to believe memory is a trait which can't be seen but is also a part of the body? Not only for you, but for everyone."

"Honestly, Harmyn."

"Frankly, Secret, your desire to deny what you have proof of is im-pressive," Harmyn said. She closed her book, stacked her papers, and wished me a good night.

I stayed behind to read more of the chronicles, but I couldn't concentrate. My thoughts splintered, wondering why Aoife had written the manuscript, then of my mother. What had she thought when she read it? What of the logs and diaries she kept for her work? Years before, I'd searched them for hints about what she'd done with the manuscript after she received it, but I'd looked for nothing else. The sudden compulsion to skim them now left me uneasy and nauseated, as if something within me, yet again, forced its will.

Unable to sleep, I paced the residence's first floor, from the wing Harmyn and I shared through the parlors to the main staircase and back. The pendulum clock struck one as I stood at a window between the drapes. Footsteps tapped against the marble floor. I almost hid behind the fabric until the person passed, but I peeked out and saw Nikolas.

He startled when he saw me move, peered to see who it was, and approached me. He took my hand, held it flat, and traced with his finger on my palm,

Waiting up?

No, I traced on his. **Good time?**

Yes drink laughs drink your night?

Read

I was grateful we couldn't speak. I didn't have to hide a tone in my voice, which might provoke more questions.

He dared to hold me close then. I hugged him tight for comfort. I felt he wanted the same but of a different sort. His grip slackened. He kissed me high on the cheek under my left eye. A shocking pain blurred my sight. I pushed him away as if he'd struck me.

I touched my face in surprise. A deep soreness lingered.

I took his hand.

Not angry at you. Face hurts, I traced.

Why?

?

WEEK 6

At the start of the sixth week, Margana delivered Harmyn's new clothes. From the moment Harmyn put them on, her presence changed. She appeared taller and older, stately but welcoming.

Her uniform made her seem like a visitor from a distant land. The violet coat was unlike what anyone in Rothwyke wore. Buttons dotted the placket of her white linen shirt, plain enough with a stand-up collar. The fall front trousers were made of black wool with a gray pinstripe, and the wide legs swished when she walked.

I joined her on the wall the first morning she wore her new garments. In that, she will stand out, I thought, and that was the point. As she began to sing, I felt proud of her, and a touch of envy. She didn't hide from anyone now, not even with her clothes.

After she finished her songs, for an audience which filled the streets as far as I could see, we borrowed a horse from the stables and went to the woods with two satchels. With hers, Harmyn went to change into old clothes and then to fetch water. From mine, I laid out our breakfast—milk, bread, and the season's last blueberries we'd picked on our way.

As I poured the berries into a bowl, I glanced at the scar on my left hand, a reminder of a deed I'd done, but I suffered no affliction for it. I dared to think of Fewmany then. That last night. His gloved hands. How he limped and flinched as if in pain. The wet wound under his chin. He showed signs before the rest of us, I realized. I wondered what he'd done to merit the injuries.

Harmyn set the pail near the hearth and plopped on her seat at the table. With an exhale, I forced him out of mind. I watched Harmyn eat, looking waifish out of her uniform.

You're staring at me, she said as she chewed a piece of brown bread with her mouth open.

I'll mind my manners if you mind yours, I said.

She smirked. *What is it?*

You're not the child you were six months ago. When I watched you today, I thought how brave you are. How strong. You've had no proper person to teach you about your gifts, but here you are, using them beautifully, I said.

Thank you, and I have so proper people. Old Woman and you, Nikolas and GrandBren. Aoife, at least her words. And the . . . people . . . who come to me in my dreams. As for being brave, what choice do I have? I can't do what I'm meant to if I'm afraid, she said.

Of what? I asked.

My own abilities, and how others might act toward me, and what's ahead, she said.

I looked away from her. To some degree, I remained afraid of those things myself. We continued with our breakfast, and when we were almost done, Harmyn said,

We're going to have visitors soon. Don't be angry, please. I've shown some children the opening at the margin. They need to be here. I need to be with them away from town, and you need to be with them, too.

My body stiffened. My woods? I thought. A possessive response for what didn't belong to me. That I'd so often found refuge there gave me no claim. That I had a peculiar affiliation with the creatures and plants gave me no right. As a child, in my loneliness and silence, it was where I could simply be, making it possible to endure countless hours when I wasn't in Nature's company. How could I deny that to anyone else?

Secret? she asked.

In all the years I've come to the woods, I've seen no one except Old Woman, and Old Man, and Nikolas. So, my guess is no one wished to come. The stories everyone was told as children instilled a fear of the dangers they'd find. For an instant, I thought of Fewmany but didn't mention him.

All the more reason to welcome them, she said.

It's not entirely safe, though. The animals guided me. When you came, I could have called them to find you if you got lost, or before you were eaten. I could, I suppose, ask them to help, I said.

Although we had weeding and harvesting to do, that would wait. Harmyn followed me to the woods' edge. The twist of branches, which Nikolas and I found upon our return, had become an impenetrable wall of leaves and flowers. A drape of vines fell across the solitary opening, wide enough now for a horse to ride through.

I called the creatures and waited until groups arrived—sounder, herd, sleuth, pack, skulk, cast, murder, parliament. To the animals and birds, I explained I wanted the children to be free to wander the woods without threat, under their protection. They argued with memories, ancient and recent, of excessive hunts, heartless cruelties, and brutal violence. Although I knew I could command them to heed me—a power I wished not to exploit—I made them a promise.

The children's first instinct will be wonder, and this I'll nurture in them. Some might do harm, I know, but most will not, not if they're taught to respect and cherish all beings here, I said.

For some time, I listened to their conference although they didn't make a sound.

At last, an immense boar said, *We agree, as long as we're allowed our justice based on our instincts.*

The whole of them nodded behind him.

So it is, and thank you, I said.

As the creatures disappeared into the trees, I nodded at Harmyn. Her eyes softened with relief.

Harmyn stood outside the entrance as the first group approached from across the green, pointing at the abandoned wall in the distance. They were girls and boys, seven in total, the youngest nearly five, the oldest about twelve. I stepped back to watch them enter. Their heads turned, eyes wide, mouths slightly open in amazement.

"I have a friend for you to meet," Harmyn said as she gestured to me.

They stared at me with guarded expressions. A girl and a boy with the same brown hair and brown eyes clutched each other's hands.

Tell them my name and that I'm not a witch, I said.

"This is Secret. She's not a witch, but she has a special way with plants and animals. She's sick like you, so she can't speak. She's going to lead us on an adventure today," Harmyn said.

I beckoned to them.

Our progress was slow as they stopped to touch leaves, smell flowers, and look for what scuffled among the branches. Soon enough, they smiled and laughed, chased each other around trunks, and sat on the ground to observe whatever they could see.

Through Harmyn, I could tell them the names of things—not only bird but robin, not only tree but larch—and I took delight in the way they mouthed the words into memory. When we found something they shouldn't touch or eat, I mimed horrible itches and ripping pains. I showed them how to hold insects gently, how to pick a ripe berry, how to explore with respect and gentleness.

When it was time for them to go, the youngest girl refused to budge. Her hands were full of treasures, a twig, a feather, a stone, a wilted flower.

"I promise, you can come back," Harmyn said.

Crying, she plopped on the ground. I knelt across from her. When she peered up at me with tear-streaked cheeks, I looked back with damp lashes. Somehow, she knew I understood her sadness, mingled with joy, heavy with longing. *I want to stay,* her eyes told me. I nodded; *I know, I know.*

I wiped her face, helped her stand, and led her to the waiting group. Harmyn and I walked them to the entrance at the woods' margin. One by one, they stepped out to the green, each looking over a shoulder for a farewell glance.

WEEK 7

ON THE THIRD OF AUGUST, HARMYN AND I WENT TO FATHER'S for a visit. The house smelled of fresh bread and fish stew. Elinor had not yet left for the day and was in the kitchen when we arrived. Aside from the way she held her right arm close to her body, she appeared to have no other visible afflictions. With a damp cloth in her hand, she motioned for Harmyn to turn around.

"You haven't seen me since I got my new clothes," Harmyn said. "What do you think?"

Elinor squared her shoulders and swept her hands across the front of her blouse as if to say, very fine indeed.

I helped Elinor store away what she'd cleaned. Neither reached for her notebook. By this seventh week, hardly anyone bothered with small talk.

When Harmyn heard the front door unlock, she rushed into the parlor. At the sound of footsteps, I turned to greet Father. He waved at us and left the room with Harmyn at his side. When he returned, he was down to his shirt and vest. Elinor handed me a wooden spoon and waved good-bye. Harmyn and Father settled side by side at the dining table for a silent conversation.

As I had several times before, I stood watching them. Again, I wondered if Harmyn had been an ordinary child, would Father have taken to her as he did. I heard her laugh as I stirred a pot. My teeth gritted as I looked at them rollicking with a shared joke. I couldn't recollect a moment when I'd made such a bright noise among those same walls.

They acknowledged me when I served their plates. Father placed his notebook on the table, wrote a message with his atrophied hand, and pushed it past the ochre bowl.

All's well, my pet?

I took the mechanical pencil from him, the body of it damp, and wrote, **Warrick garden growing. Reports encouraging in other wards. Misses Acutt ask of you. Plenty to read in castle library. You?**

Anxious to travel, nowhere to go. Still no word from Fewmany. Unlike him. 12th-floor men worried.

Remote where he is. FM Inc. in good hands, isn't it? I wrote.

The notebook lay open between us. I set down the pencil, glanced at my index finger, and wiped away a reddish smear.

We ate in silence and helped Father tidy up when we were through. Once Father and Harmyn sat together in the parlor, her voice confident even as she struggled over difficult words, I ventured upstairs with two lamps. I'd taken no book with me that night. There was something else I planned to read.

As the evening light faded in my old room, I opened box after box in the storage area across the hall and carried those which held my mother's old logs and diaries. Piles of Father's boxes filled the room. He'd moved many of them from the third-floor storage to lock away food and supplies. I placed a lamp on a low stack and sat under the light. From the corner of my eye, I saw the faded blue chest with the painted animals. I had a sudden impulse to open it, remove the nesting dolls, and throw them out of the window, but I didn't.

Fortunately, the logs and diaries had been stored in chronological groups. Her records reached back to the years after she obtained her degree from Altwort. For someone who kept so little of her past, she had preserved all of this. What I was searching for when I placed that first diary on my lap, I didn't know.

I turned through the pages, her handwriting meticulous, sometimes finding a note or simple sketch in the margins. Most entries were written in Kirsauan, but she shifted among several languages throughout. After studying the initial pages, I discerned the text she'd been translating was an ancient one in a dead language. Astronomy, long before telescopes. I looked at the year. She had graduated from high academy that summer. In the page corners were notes to herself—paid rent; Prof U tea at 3; ordered paper.

In a different box, I found her last diaries. I could hardly breathe as I flipped through the final months of her life. Again, I studied the very last one, which I'd skimmed when I stored away her belongings after she died. This time, I looked more carefully, through the pages kept during the days I was sick with the fever, far fewer ones filled in the weeks which followed, until the end where she'd written: "A map is to space as an alphabet is to sound."[29] A sentence straight from Aoife's manuscript and the hint for the cipher my mother had created. I thumbed through the blank pages and found tiny sketches. My heart knocked when I realized she'd practiced what she drew on the cipher—boat, leaf, jug, wheel, slipper, mushroom.

I reached into another box. That diary was from the year before she'd met my father, so I sought him in the following one. As I searched, I found detailed, whimsical drawings along some page edges, as if she'd paused in her work to daydream.

Then, in obvious contrast to the language in which she'd been writing, there was a name. Bren Riven. As I turned the pages, I could comprehend nothing else. However, in the margins, she'd drawn—and colored—intricate flowers, leafy vines, interlocking shapes, flying birds. The dates corresponded with what I knew were the months they exchanged letters, which soon enough became a courtship. Again and again, my father's name appeared like rare blossoms among the text. In the next diary, one month in, she drew a jeweled ring surrounded by a heart. Their engagement. Not long later, two circles overlapped, again held within a heart. Their marriage. The dates revealed a gap in her work for several weeks. Her move to Foradair, the town where my father was born, in the kingdom of Ailliath.

Of the diaries I'd seen, no other had cheerful illustrations like these did. Without words, she spoke her feelings. She was happy.

My breath fluttered. Oh, she had loved my father. I remembered the way she turned her face to his, how she touched him with tenderness, how devoted she was to him. I knew such love now, and as quickly as I felt its expanse within me, I tensed every muscle to brace against a collapse, a black hole widening, widening to annihilate me from within.

WEEK 8

THAT EIGHTH WEEK, ON THE FOURTEENTH OF AUGUST, THE weekly concert commenced as usual. Since the fourth one, the event had been moved to the green because the plaza's gold-toned tiles were so buckled, they were dangerous to walk, much less dance, across. That night, Harmyn and I decided not to attend. I wished to be alone and didn't want to have to guard myself against the pity, sadness, and anger I felt as I watched so many adults together, their debilities unavoidable.

Harmyn simply needed her rest. She could barely stay awake past nine and slept like the dead until morning.

Nikolas, however, was obligated to make an appearance. By this time, there was a lottery drawn for the girls and women to dance with him. That he didn't mind, even enjoyed. He liked the festivities, even if no one could talk.

When he returned that evening, he knocked on my door and asked if I was too tired for a walk. From the look in his eyes, he meant nothing more than that. Minutes later, I met him in the small courtyard and took his offered arm. He seemed deeply quiet, as if something was on his mind.

He led us to the tower where we'd stood the night before we left for the quest. That evening, what came to mind was my first visit to this place, Charming's wedding day when I first saw the whole of Rothwyke from above. Five years later, our town was crumbling, our people sick.

Like a little boy, he sat on the walkway between the battlements. I lowered next to him and took my notebook from my pocket.

What troubles you? I wrote.

Among many things miss parents. Much on my mind. He handed a letter to me. **Read this while I write. Good news there.**

Harmyn, gifted Voice; Secret, distant daughter of Wei; Nikolas,
king of Ailliath,

A thousand years ago, our people were hidden, but never in hiding.
That changed after what happened on the land now claimed by your
kingdom. For this, we do not hold your king Wyl responsible alone.
Other men counseled him to the decision and still more consented to
do their bidding. Such is the culmination of individual wills leading to
collective action.

As our histories witness, the violence couldn't be contained. That we had
never threatened, harmed, or robbed a neighboring people meant nothing.
Within three years, we mourned the deaths of untold thousands killed in
their homes and in battle, Guardians and neighbors alike. Once that first
great war was done, there came others, and in time, a new form of pillage
executed not by kings alone but by men of enterprise. Again and again, our
people were discovered, the land that sustained us taken by force, those who
survived bewildered by the choices of strangers.

Now our numbers are a fraction of what they once were. By necessity to save ourselves and be true to our ways, we have lived in hiding for generations. The Ancient Elders tell us a shift is at hand, and the time has come for us to emerge again to fulfill an ancient promise or perish at last.

We send this letter in peace and with the offer of aid.

As you have noticed, our people are already among you in Rothwyke. They serve with the intent to bring comfort to those in need. Within and beyond your borders, we will give our protection. We know of the strife among the kingdoms. Our warriors, who have long protected the Ancient Elders, will now be at your call to stand alongside your troops, if and when they are needed. There are those among us willing to give their lives for the era waiting to come.

We ask for no compensation or exchange of trade. Our request is that if at another time, in some way, our people require aid, yours would reciprocate. If a friend can share with a friend, a people can share with a people. Despite the conflict and suffering in our world, we continue to believe this.

You know we're never as far away as it might appear. You need only send a message to the address noted below, and a dispatch will reach us within hours.

> *To the reign of love,*
> *Dru Kai*
> *Milan Visham*

When I finished, I held the letter on my lap as Nikolas continued writing. Even if I'd been able to talk, I would have been speechless. The three of us named, not only Nikolas; The Mapmaker's War mentioned; the Ancient Elders—they meant Egnis, Ingot, and Incant, didn't they? From what I'd witnessed in the past months, I had no doubt what was at hand was significant, but until that letter, I hadn't begun to comprehend the magnitude. Fear and hope snarled in the pit of my gut.

I gave the letter back to Nikolas with a look of astonishment. He smiled but shrugged as if to say, he, too, had no words.

He passed my notebook, open to the start of his message.

Much bad news today. First, war. Eastern Giphia in Haaud's control now. Kirsau holding tenuously. This could turn if

Seronia and Bodelea, or both, join Haaud's side, as they have before. Confirmation Haaud & Emmok occupy Uldiland, H west of river, E what's east. Advisers debating whether to send aid to Giphia & what to do about Emmok. But we're under no direct threat. There's been no specific ask for help from any-one. Yet.

Second, rents. Some building owners are willing to accept our deal to cover rents BUT one who owns arable land wants to require labor of tenants. He claims what the kingdom will cover is a pittance & that would make up for it. This is a most egre-gious suggestion but appears majority of Council & town reps willing.

Third, received word an adviser is dead. Not from Roth-wyke but was here in March. Sickened with plague. Palsied arm. Both hands bled. Died clawing at his chest. He was titled, which means his eldest son takes position. I'm tempted to find an ex-cuse to strip him if only to have one fewer cocky myopic on Council.

Fourth, letter from my sister. Youngest niece sick with chin cough, should recover, but of course Pretty is worried.

Last, missing parents. Grief still comes in waves & this one has leveled me.

He was staring into the full moon's light when I looked at him. I sensed more than saw a flutter ahead and called to what was there. The moth abided, landed on my fingertip, and sat with his wings spread. His golden antennae were delicate as feathers. Carefully, with his permission, I lowered him to Nikolas's knee. When Nikolas reached for him, the moth climbed on his waiting finger. Nikolas lifted him to the sky, circled him with the moon, and watched him fly away.

When Nikolas turned to me, the tenderness in his eyes softened the shape of my heart.

In the notebook, he wrote, **You are my refuge. I love you.**

You are my anchor. I love you, too.

When I returned to my room, I tore out the pages, folded them tight, and buried them in my satchel. I would hide his words at Old Woman's cottage and hold the feeling where no one could steal it.

WEEK 9

DIARY ENTRY 17 AUGUST /38

Yesterday, the plague surprised us. The adults' condition is unchanged. The children can speak again but <u>cannot hear</u>. If only that were all. The young ones have physical afflictions, too. This afternoon, Harmyn and I played with a group in the woods. How they shouted because they could! Of the nine, three seemed to suffer most visibly. Reg walked with a crutch. Daisy hunched at the shoulders whether she stood or sat. Lia had a red blotch which covered her whole cheek.

When I asked Harmyn why the next phase struck only the children and what was happening to them, she couldn't tell me. Or wouldn't. Truly, what could they have done to have these marks and infirmities?

This is a break in the pattern. Think now . . . plants and animals in spring, first phase on the summer solstice. A sound guess—the adults will enter the second phase at the autumnal equinox. FIVE more weeks of this, then a season unable to hear?!

A letter from Charlotte arrived, dated 29 July. Birth imminent, as of that date. She warns me I'll want to take a knife to myself when I end up in her condition one day. No word from Muriel. Perhaps she's traveling back to the conservatory.

Aside from a meal last week with Father, I've not returned to the house. Harmyn is now allowed to take a carriage for her lessons. I feel a desire to burn the diaries—as I did for Aoife's manuscript—but a curiosity about them, too. I doubt I'll find her in those millions of words, but still I wonder. Several times, I've started a letter to Leo to ask about her, even one to Remarque, but I cannot gather my thoughts.

Tender greens to harvest in the ward garden, and come autumn there will be beets, carrots, cauliflower, potatoes. Soon we'll plant the next crop.

WEEKLY POST.

16 August /38. Page 1, Column 3
NEW! Horology & Mechanics Club (all welcome)

Every 1st, 8th, 15th, 21st, and 28th, six o'clock, Carncloch, 18 ½ Upper Peet. Those interested in mechanical devices, join us as we reveal the mysteries of springs, escapements, and gears. Students will dismantle broken clocks, old Tell-a-Bells, and faulty music boxes and learn to repair them. No skills required, only curiosity.

Performance Guild

Town Concert: 21st, six o'clock, on Green
Ward & Area concerts and performances: Refer to posted placards, updated weekly

Craft Guilds & Music Guilds

Ward & Area instruction: Refer to posted placards, updated weekly

Athletics—Men's & Boys' League

18th and 20th, on Green, six o'clock (evening)
Relays, javelins, weights, fencing

Athletics—Women's & Girls' League

19th and 21st, on Green, three o'clock
Badminton, weights, fencing

From the Plague of Silences Recollection Project Archives, Selected Excerpts

Diary No. 832. Female, 40, laundrywoman

I'm blind in one eye now. Why? Because I turn away and allow it. He's the master of the house, his ways, his rules. Like my father. I'll not have a soft boy grow to a weak man, he says. Said. Now the beatings happen in silence, and now I truly SEE. The shame I feel, because what do I do? I've no means. Mother would send us back if I went to her. She suffered this, too, so why should she help free me? This is our lot, isn't it? Oh, what did I not see when we courted, which might have warned me? Too late once married, trapped myself, trapping my children.

Diary No. 31. Male, 29, occupation unknown

Terrible terrible. Mr. H— found Mr. M— hanging from the neck in the cellar. A mystery why, although there are rumors he was in substantial debt. He's to be buried tomorrow. J— and some of the fellows will meet at Bull and Ram tonight. None of us shall be nagged upon his return home pickled and cured.

Diary No. 307. Male, 54, physician

Most perplexing, the abrupt change which came. Group met to identify the visible afflictions of late; will send to colleagues with an initial report. As named,

- The wasting—loss of muscle; shrinking of limbs or spine; concavity of body, esp. chest or abdomen; also includes hunched backs and similar unexplained deformities
- The festers—spontaneous wounds, boils, blisters
- The contusions—spontaneous bruises
- The sanguine blot—continual bleeding, typically spotting, from genitalia, anus, and mouth (female and male patients)

Dr. S— asked if anyone has observed that younger patients (15, 16, 17), suffering as the majority of adults, have either borne/sired children or have erupted wisdom teeth. Although he serves in charity, the group agreed we should make note of our own patients. Remarkable, if this is so.

Interview No. 13. Female; age during plague, 6; current occupation, lawyer

I've never forgotten this. We had a new puppy, and it would soil in the house. Each time, I would get angry and scold it. One day, I was outside, screaming at it. The dog could hear, but I couldn't. Remember that—I couldn't hear. A girl with rather short hair and funny clothes came up and took the puppy out of my arms. She asked why I shouted at him, and I said he messed on the clean floor and he should know better. The girl said, "Look how young the pup is. He's going to make mistakes sometimes." I said, "No, he's a bad dog and deserves to be punished."

It was then I noticed the girl's strange eyes, almost lavender in color, and she asked, "If you were your dog and he were you, what would you expect him to do?" I said, "The same, because that's what you do to teach someone to behave." I remember I started to cry hard then. She touched my hand, it felt very warm, and she asked, "If you were your dog and he were you, how would you want him to react?" Through my tears, I said, "Be nice with hands and words." She said that would be wonderful and asked how that *thought* made me feel. The girl laughed when I said, "Like a smile and a sunny day." She put the puppy on my lap, and we petted it together. She told me next time he made a mistake, maybe I could try treating him the way I'd want him to treat me.

Then I felt a kick on my backside and turned to see my stepmother screaming down at me. I watched her face twist and that auburn hair wave like flames on her head. I realized I couldn't hear the men working on the drains, or the blacksmith one block away either, but I'd heard every word the girl said to me. Mother pulled at my sleeve to make me get up. She kept shouting as I held the puppy, who shivered against me, and then she had some sort of fit on the steps, stomping a beetle.

Later, after the sleep, I knew the girl was Harmyn.

My stepmother's name? Audrey. Born C—, married W—. Why?[30]

WEEK 10

HARMYN INSISTED WE GO TO NIKOLAS'S PRIVATE OFFICE AFTER dinner. She had been in a subdued mood for days but gave no explanation when I asked what the matter was.

Nikolas and I turned the high-backed chairs near the fireplace toward the window. I put my notebook on my lap. Harmyn peered at the weapons on the wall, drawing her hand away quickly when she touched a mace, scowling when she stared at the gold sword. She raised the flame on the lamp at the end of his desk, which was covered in stacks of documents.

"What I want to tell you now, I need you to listen," Harmyn said. "You know why the adults have their afflictions. The children's, though, are different. Theirs aren't from the deeds they've done—but the harm done *to them*. Secret, when you gave me the vial, and you saw the bruises and cuts and how I screamed, it's because I . . . remembered . . . what happened to me. The other children remember, too, but not all at once, as I did."

I pressed my hand against my forehead, dreading what I was about to hear.

Harmyn continued. "Many of them understand their bodies hurt because of what's happened to them. Things adults have done, parents, family, neighbors, even strangers. Some older ones who can write are asking each other questions. Some have been brave and told friends, and the bravest have told adults. I know some figured out that the adults' afflictions reveal their hidden guilt.

"It's no surprise, though, when the children tell, most of the time no one believes them. They're told they're lying or making up stories. Or the adults try to justify things, or turn on them, making what happened their fault. Physicians tell them it's impossible for an old injury to appear again, or for scars to break open, or bad feelings to make their bodies hurt. What the children claim can't be true. Especially not among the wealthier families. No, the beatings and abuse, that only happens among the poor—like me, remember? The marks showing on them now? Well, they got those recently, from an accident or fight with a friend. There's a reasonable explanation. As for the invisible hurts, the pain no one can see—oh, that's their imagination."

That instant, my left cheek began to ache. A memory flashed; I saw myself at my full-length mirror after the fever, touching a greenish bruise under my eye. Fur and feathers on the floor, broken windowpanes behind me.

"I've glimpsed," Harmyn said. "I know what's happened to them. Not only the slaps and beatings. I know what cruel words they've heard, being told they're no good, useless, other terrible things. The times nothing was said but they noticed the sharp looks and heard the angry sighs and felt alone because they're ignored. I know why their bodies are bleeding in places they shouldn't—and no one should suffer that."

Now my heart pounded and my stomach churned with nausea.

"You have to understand—I feel what they feel. Everything. Grief, anger, confusion, shame, rage. It floods into me. What the Guardians are doing does help. The fun activities, especially the physical ones. But all of that energy has to go somewhere. It's part of the shadows. Secret, the children who've come to the woods and sit motionless—they've forced the feelings inside. The ones making trouble, they're letting it out."

Nikolas leaned over with his head in his hands.

"Nikolas asked me what he's supposed to do," Harmyn said. "I don't know. You tell me. Who's going to admit what they've done is wrong? How's that supposed to stop? Adults protect adults anyway."

He looked at her. His entire body tensed.

"I know quite well what measures are in place for the worst cases. I've watched children die all over town, not only in Elwip, thanks to those laws and the charity workers who heed them," she said.

Nikolas remained seated as Harmyn stood, but they faced each other. Whatever he said to her, he didn't bother to take my notebook and tell me.

"I'm giving you warning. Once the adults get sick like the children, I don't know how everyone will endure," she said.

I pointed to the notebook, then to my ear.

Nikolas grasped the pencil. **So, all you can do is sing and try to make it all better?** he wrote.

His sarcasm shocked me. I nudged his arm, but he ignored me. The caustic words brought tears to Harmyn's eyes. She drew several jagged breaths and didn't speak until she calmed them.

"I'm trying to do what's in my power—which I'm still learning—as you should do what's within yours. You could do more for your people. You're the king," she said.

Not so simple. Balance of interests, rules, laws, he wrote.

She shook her head. "Excuses, that's what those are. That's all they've ever been. Right now, there are more people living on the streets than during your father's reign. I know you know this. I know you've seen the numbers. But I saw you in the southeast wards when I was little. I saw what you did, bringing food sometimes, talking to people. I know what kind of person you are under that title," she said.

Nikolas rose up from his chair and took a step toward her.

"No right to speak to you that way? I have every right to tell you the truth," she said.

He rushed at her with his hand raised—I leapt to my feet—and he stopped still.

"Go ahead. Do it. See how it feels," she said. She stood tall, her expression fearless.

He turned to lean against his desk.

"Yes, sir, I'll go to my room," she said. She glanced at me and disappeared into the hall.

What is wrong with you? I wrote.

I don't know what came over me, he wrote.

Something ugly, to be sure, I wrote.

When I found her, she was sitting on her bed in the dark.

You were provocative with him, but his response was undue. He shouldn't have threatened you, I said within her thoughts.

I don't care. I'm not afraid of him, she said.

What you told us, I don't know what to say. This is horrible. And you, for you to feel and know what you do, I can only imagine how hard that is, I said.

That's why I'm so tired. By the end of the day, I only want to sleep. The plague has to run its course and all I can do is try to help everyone from tearing apart. Tearing at each other, too. I could barely manage that with Nikolas, she said.

That seems too much to ask of yourself, I said.

But that's what is required of me, she said. *Stay for a while.*

I climbed next to her.

She leaned against me. *Tell me the Myths of the Four. Start with when Egnis found baby Azul in the river and brought the orphan back to life,* she said.

WEEK 11

AFTER OUR GARDEN WORK, HARMYN AND I FOLLOWED THE Misses Acutt to the walk-up. Four weeks prior, we began to accept their invitations to tea. Sometimes the other neighbors would join us, sometimes we were alone. On that day, Jane went to her weaving class—Dora was still working—and we hadn't seen any of the Elgins since the children sickened with the second phase. Tall Miss Acutt said Mrs. Elgin told them Julia and Lucas had a terrible coryza. I suspected otherwise.

On our way to the building, I noticed few children playing outside. Before the ninth week, groups of them were out on the streets with balls, jump ropes, marbles, and hoops and some with instructors teaching an activity, such as drawing or music. As we walked, I glanced around at the open windows. Now and then, a little face peered out.

The Misses made our tea while Harmyn and I visited with Sir Pouncelot. I drank mine quickly to let Harmyn sit with them to talk, she using her voice, the two of them writing. Despite the sisters' pantomime of protest, I dusted and swept and cleaned. I thought of the dutiful girls in the tales I once loved and of Old Woman who taught me to appreciate a chore well done. It pleased me to help them, because I wanted to.

When I was finished, I asked if they'd seen the Elgins.

Mr., once last week when returned from work. Mrs., keeps to herself more than usual. Hardly at all since little ones lost hearing, Short Miss Acutt wrote on the large slate board on the low table in front of them.

Any little ones. Parents so cautious now with the sickness, Tall Miss Acutt wrote.

No, sister. Think they hide the children, Short Miss Acutt wrote.

Why? Tall Miss Acutt wrote.

You've seen what some look like, Short Miss Acutt wrote.

I hope we don't suffer so when our time comes, Tall Miss Acutt wrote.

I motioned to Harmyn it was time to leave. She slipped a knotted handkerchief full of silver behind one of the settee's pillows. We bid our good-byes. Outside the apartment, I grabbed Harmyn's sleeve to direct her upstairs.

A light rap, a steady knock, then a rhythmic pounding—and at last Mrs. Elgin opened the door. Clearly, she didn't want to invite us in, but did. Baskets of clothes were lined up near a long table and an iron. Julia strained to pull herself up from the floor where she was playing a memory game with her brother. He looked up at us with a hopeful expression. The skin under his right eye was swollen and a purplish blue.

I clenched my teeth as I smiled at Mrs. Elgin. She returned a weak one.

"May we take Julia and Lucas to play? We'll have them home before dinner," Harmyn said.

She shook her head. She mimed a sore throat and sneezing.

"The fresh air might do them good. They'll be no bother," Harmyn said.

A subtle vibration purred at my chest, one I knew Mrs. Elgin was meant to feel.

Mrs. Elgin stood with the children behind her. She looked at us as she nibbled the inside of her lip. The urge to slap her rose so fast, I almost couldn't stop myself from doing it. Let them out, I wanted to scream at her.

"Please," Harmyn said. The vibration grew stronger.

Mrs. Elgin peered at the children's faces. She nodded with a sigh. I gestured for them to come along, and they smiled with relief.

Can they make it all the way to the woods? I asked Harmyn.

I believe so, she said.

In her notebook, Julia asked where we were going. I told her it was a surprise, and some distance from home. She nodded and grabbed Lucas's hand. He tried to pull away. She looked at him sternly and seemed to mouth the words *Be good.* They walked ahead of me with Harmyn. Lucas held his right shoulder much higher than his left, and his upper arms seemed fixed to his sides. He stomped hard as he walked. Julia seemed smaller, frail, the hunch high on her back drawing her down.

As we crossed the green, Lucas pointed to the abandoned wall, pulling Julia's hand to go there. Harmyn stepped in front of them. I watched their eyes open wide as she spoke to them within their thoughts. They followed Harmyn through the woods' entrance and into the trees.

Children sat in three groups, and I was certain there were more exploring elsewhere. I was glad to know they felt adventurous and safe to be there. Some of them I didn't recognize, which meant children were bringing their friends.

Julia and Lucas stood side by side and looked around. Suddenly, Lucas ran straight ahead, arms flung wide, howling like a wolf. Julia clasped her hands at her heart and started to cry. Before Harmyn or I could step toward her, another girl near her age approached. They exchanged messages in the girl's notebook. Julia wiped her eyes, waved at us, and followed the girl to two others who played a clapping game under a tree.

I sat with the youngest children and helped them sort leaves and stones. Harmyn played hide-and-seek with Lucas and several boys.

After the sorting, I invited the group Julia had joined for a walk. Past the huge rounded rock, past Reach, I led them along the narrow path to the glade. The four girls gasped and clutched whoever's skirt they could reach, including mine.

Your house? one girl wrote to me and showed the rest.
A friend's, I wrote.
House in woods BAD, another girl wrote.
Secret will take care of us, Julia wrote.

To the cottage we went. They explored outside—the garden, the shed, the pens where the sheep, goats, and hens once lived, and the shady spot where Old Woman had found me as a child. Inside, they sat on the benches, lay on the bed, and studied the shelves. They laughed until they were breathless when the smallest among them climbed into the large cauldron and mimed being cooked alive.

I led them to the stream as each carried a pail or bowl.

Walk in water? Julia wrote to me.

We removed our boots. I stood with the water slipping past my calves as they leapt on the rocks and braced against the rush on their legs. When one found a frog and dared to pick it up, I was impressed the others looked on without disgust. Their joy in discovery made me almost as happy as I'd been when I explored at their age. In that instant, I wished Nikolas had been with me to witness and remember as well.

The girls called out when they spied a fox. They turned to me and pointed toward the opposite bank. I asked the fox to sit so they might admire her and commit her red fur, black paws, and white-tipped tail to memory. She yipped for good measure, but they couldn't hear her. That absence made me heartsick. Not once in the girls' time that day did they listen to birdsong, wind rush, or stream burble.

I plopped down on the damp ground, dipped my hands in the water, and patted my face to hide my tears. What have I done? Look at them, I thought. The girls were laughing, but all I could see were their contorted bodies and wounds. Again, the conflict spiraled within me. If releasing the vials was a matter of fate, why had I been chosen? If it had been one of free will, why did I consent? Regardless of whether it was both/and or either/or, my actions had caused pain and strife, which would only worsen. I thought of the prophecy which foretold these events. What a poisonous legacy I bore. I remembered what I'd been told in the realm, "Whatever you choose, your world will never be the same again." Yes, with children as the sacrifice.

When I led the girls back into the trees, Julia linked her arm in mine. She held out her notebook with the words **Thank you, Secret. I've never been to the woods before and this was beautiful.**

We found Harmyn and Lucas building a tower of sticks. He looked at me and grinned wide enough to show his missing teeth. His eye was no longer swollen, and the color had dulled to nothing more than a dim shadow. Harmyn had healed the bruise with her miraculous touch.

Julia and Lucas waved good-bye to their new friends.

As we led them home, Harmyn told me she'd noticed a change in the children that day. "In their bodies," she said, "tiny flecks appear and vanish like pinpricks of light. There's something within the darkness. More than shadows are there now."

At their door, Mr. Elgin answered our knock. The children's father touched their heads as he mouthed, Thank you. Hidden, the lock turned. The bar slipped into place.

❦

Dear Secret,

These days, we all must determine how to fill our quiet hours, and you've taken on a project well suited, haven't you? Of course reading through your mother's diaries would provoke questions. I am glad to oblige.

I had been in my position two years when your mother joined us. Cuthbert and Rowland had decided to tolerate me, at last, although they grieved the loss of their prior manager, who according to rumors, desiccated bit by bit until they found his venerable husk slumped over his desk. I intend not to repeat his fate.

Yes, when I told you we envied her, I was sincere. Your mother had a reputation not only because she was a woman doing the work of men, better than most men, but also because she was among the most rarified in our field. If you choose to study ancient languages at any high academy, I expect you'll hear your mother's name mentioned as the one who deciphered Pelensian Form A, or alternatively, as one who claimed to, as most credit Professor Ozol Yakup. There are, too, apocryphal stories of her ability to know where obscure languages are still spoken though she never visited these places.

Tales like this, legends really, are why men like Rowland intimated she was a witch. I confess, rational man of our age that I am, I found it difficult to believe one mind could hold all hers did. Rowland was also convinced she heard voices. When I asked her about her ability, her remark that it was like hearing screams which never cease—well, that gave me pause, but only a pause. I'm sure she meant what she said in a figurative way.

Please don't bear too great a grudge against our old pungent friend. Rowland matched your mother in ambition but never in talent. When Fewmany retained her—and how he crowed that "acquisition"—Rowland never recovered from his diminishment of favor. The pet projects upon which those two conferred happened no more; rather the projects emerged without Rowland's involvement. Fewmany made no secret that he wanted the best man he could find for any job. To Rowland's dismay and horror, the best man was not he, and worse yet, a woman.

During the years she worked for Fewmany Incorporated, I visited with her rarely. We communicated by letter at her insistence. Fewmany accommodated her wish to work from home. I recall she required this, otherwise she wouldn't have worked for him. You asked about her demeanor among us, and I will be truthful and say she was not so much cold as guarded. Beyond good morning and good day, what weather we're having, there was no small talk. I confess, and please know I mean no disrespect or insult, but those who know your amiable father puzzled over the match.

I'm afraid I've not been as helpful as you might have wished. I regret she and I weren't better acquainted. Although her diaries are written in languages you don't know, I hope you won't dispose of them. Matters of confidentiality and privacy aside, she was one of the greatest minds among us wordtinkers. It would be a travesty to not archive her work.

As to the plague, I'm glad to know you haven't suffered terribly, unlike many among us. My wife and I endure throats and tongues sore like a bruise. Solden lost his hearing, which saddens him because he enjoys music. He also has the sanguine blot and complains of a weight on his shoulders. Some days, he seems withdrawn and exhausted, but otherwise, he's an active boy. We're fortunate we've not had the difficulties of some of our neighbors' children, tantrums and destructiveness. He has, however, had those strange fits in which one stares into the distance and doesn't move.

If anyone has heard from Fewmany, he hasn't divulged the contact. This is unprecedented.

Do let me know if there is anything else I can address for you.

Sincerely,
Leo

WEEK 12

THE STOLEN MOMENTS WITH NIKOLAS HAD BECOME MORE DES-
perate than exciting. Although I asked him to take me again to his room,
somewhat joking when I said he was old enough to have a lover, he
refused. His desire for me wasn't in question, but the extent hadn't been
tested because he feared being caught for my sake, and his own. He liked
that he was held in a virtuous light.

Regardless, I wanted a night alone with him.

I thought of the masquerade ball and the yearning which laced my
blood and I could not sate. I had no regrets about what I'd almost done
with the masked hunter. My actions revealed my true nature, beyond what
I'd been taught to believe and believed about myself. I wasn't as innocent
as I assumed. When the hunter kissed me, when Nikolas kissed me under
Reach, when I closed his bedroom door the night before the plague sickened us, my body responded before my mind could deny what I felt.

My body knew the truth.

To have what I wanted required a plan. Father gladly agreed to keep
Harmyn for a night. He didn't ask why, and if Father had any suspicions,
he revealed no hint. Of all the guards in Nikolas's service, Hugh was the
one he trusted most. I chose an evening when Hugh would be protecting his door, whether Nikolas was behind it or not.

At the start of the day, I left a sealed letter on Nikolas's desk. While
Harmyn and the children played in the woods, I tidied the cottage, studied the instructions in Old Woman's plant lore book, and foraged what I
could instead of using what she'd tinctured and dried.

That afternoon, I returned to the castle to help Harmyn pack her
satchel and to add items to my own. I told her the truth—that I was
going to the woods overnight—but made no mention of Nikolas. As we
rode on the same horse to Father's house, she said, *It's no secret what's between you and Nikolas, not to me.*

You understand why it must be, I said.

I do, and one day, you won't have to hide, she said.

Once Harmyn was with Father, I crossed through town toward the
woods. As the insects joined in their summer evensong, I stood at the
cottage's threshold, my bare toes pressed into the earth. Bats darted across
the sky on their hunt. On the table were bottles of vinegar, oil, and

honey, a salad fresh from the garden, and bread from one of the boxes. The bed was made. Thoughts attempted to intrude, admonish—what was I thinking, raised a proper young woman, what if someone found out, this was undue, he was the king. I had sought approval for so long, for so much, and this time, I allowed no judge other than my own heart.

The sun continued its descent. I lit candles on the table and sat down, anxious.

Then I heard the hoofbeats. I walked outside to greet him. Nikolas reined his horse, extended his arm to me, and presented a wildflower bouquet and a pheasant's plume. I smiled, feeling the echo of the boy I'd always loved in the gesture. He released the horse to graze near mine and followed me inside.

He dropped a satchel on the ground, wriggled out of his coat and vest, tossed his cravat aside, and rolled his shirtsleeves. I watched him pull off his boots and set them near the door.

He is at home. With me, I thought.

I placed the flowers in water as he took cheese and honey-almond candy from his satchel. From his coat pocket, he removed a notebook and pencil. He laid my letter flat on the table.

> *Come to me in the place I found my voice,*
> *where I will be through the night.*
>
> *Yours, Secret*

He scratched a few words and pushed them toward me. **Invitation I couldn't refuse, though I evade regal duty to do so.**

What did you tell Hugh? I wrote.

Needed respite.

Does he know where you are?

Drew map. Swore not to disturb me unless there's trouble.

I crossed my arms and tilted my head.

Said he won't betray me, Nikolas wrote.

Always liked Hugh, I wrote.

You have a beguiling influence, Nikolas wrote.

As I turned my response toward him, I sensed Fewmany's specter. I banished it before it lingered too long, reminding me of how I learned certain truths about myself.

Only for the willing, I'd written.

Nikolas laughed without sound, its absence stark. **Sorry I was late. Told you about meeting planned in Ilsace, now confirmed I'm leaving tomorrow with advisers. Will meet reps from I, Giphia, & Thrigin to discuss war.**

There will be no talk of that tonight, my love, I wrote.

As we sat outside for dinner, a flight of swallows took its last dash south before the light slipped away. We peered into the patterns of the stars and stared into the trees where owls hooted.

There were no letters, reports, or longsheets among us, no notebook open for a conversation in broken sentences about the problems in Rothwyke, Ailliath, and kingdoms beyond. As it had been on the quest, I was content with my best friend and the silence.

I lifted my chin to a breeze, then turned when I sensed his stare. A column of fire ignited through the core of my body. My breath was shallow, fast, barely enough.

When I stood, I reached my hand to him. He clutched my palm, rose up, and followed me inside. He swept his hands down my back and gripped my waist. I spun toward him, caressed the stubble on his jaw, and gasped when he kissed me.

I pushed him away. He stroked my arms as I loosened the buttons of his shirt and the first on his trousers. I brushed the suspenders away and pulled the shirt over his head. He shivered as my nails scratched across his back. Nikolas reached for the buttons of my dress, but I caught his wrists and guided him to sit on the bed. The stars and waxing moon shone through the windows and open door. The candles remained lit. I began to undress, my eyes on his while his gaze roamed.

He gripped the sheets at his sides. His anticipation delighted me. Revealing myself openly was an act of spontaneity, trust, even power, my own, meant to please myself, and him.

Naked, I approached him. My fingers slipped through his gold hair as he held my waist and kissed a circle around my navel. Blood rushed into the well of my hips. My eyes closed as I searched for a word, finding euphoric.

He stood and let his trousers fall away. My silver braid unraveled in his hands. He caught me in his arms, lifted me off my feet, and laid me on the bed's center. My limbs vined around him, embracing him so long and so close, I lost sense of our boundaries. When he kissed my throat, neck, mouth, I reached for him, the thrum of his blood contained by such thin flesh. He shifted his hips aside, breaking my hold, and looked me in the eye. His expression was so serious, I laughed and swiped a tickle against his ribs.

He curled inward as if I'd hurt him. I touched the same place again, gently, and he flinched. He kissed my cheek where the soreness lingered without a mark. Our eyes met, then our hands in a guiding gesture. In time, our bodies merged in divine union.

We entwined and drowsed, twice and again, discovering a synchronicity between us, a balance between force and surrender. At last we slept without dreams, drunk on love. I awoke to birdsong, his head on my shoulder, twisted sheets. For a while, I pretended the world was as simple as it had been that night and morning, nothing but the present. Flowers, a modest meal, a strong tender man, the moon giving birth to the sun.

WEEK 13

WITHOUT FAIL, HARMYN SANG EVERY MORNING. THE CROWDS outside the castle's wall had swelled into the hundreds. People of all ages, all stations, stood together. Few wore Tell-a-Bells anymore—the habit proved hard to break—but almost everyone had a bell in his or her hand. The people rang them as Harmyn stepped up to the battlement waving her own bell. When she stopped, they did, too.

Harmyn sang for half an hour, rarely more or less. Those beyond the range of her voice felt soft whirs in their chests, like a cat's purr, but each person who could hear her experienced a spiraling rush which spread through the limbs and head. As they listened, or simply stood, some pressed their hands at their hearts; some stared at their palms; others kept their eyes shut. Almost everyone sang with her, even though most adults couldn't speak and the children couldn't hear.

When Harmyn finished, she chimed her bell three times. The crowd responded with the same.

By the thirteenth week, the crowds thinned after Harmyn left the wall, but several people gathered at the gate, waiting. When she and I left the castle grounds together, it was no longer without notice. The first few instances when I watched people approach her, I feared for her safety, even though I saw Guardians close by, watching, their blue prominently displayed. Margana stood among them several times, giving us a wave. I wouldn't leave Harmyn's side, no matter how the crowd pushed.

How insistent the people were as they reached for the child.

Some wanted to express their appreciation, bowing before her, touching her clothes, giving her notes—thank you for singing; you brighten my day; you have the most beautiful voice I've ever heard.

But most were desperate, and they knew, although they didn't know how, Harmyn could help them. They held out their afflicted arms to her. They presented their children, some with wounds that wouldn't heal, most infirm in some way. They offered bags of coins, jewelry and time-pieces, baskets of food. Each week, more people fell on their knees before her, begging for relief they believed she could give.

And so, she did.

Harmyn sat cross-legged on the street, hands held open, and everyone grouped around her. She began to hum, but it wasn't as simple as that. Instead of singular notes rising and falling, she hummed in chords. Impossible though this seemed, I couldn't deny my own ears. I looked at everyone as the notes within the chords changed. From their bodies, I could tell who Harmyn reached, sometimes watching a bruise fade, an atrophied hand relax, a dark expression lift.

Once she was done, Harmyn pressed her hands against the ground and exhaled with a puff. Then from the satchel she'd started to carry, she handed out fresh flowers, enough for everyone.

Where did you get these? I asked her the first time she did this.

From the ground, she said.

Did you ask permission to take them from the castle gardens?

They didn't grow there, she said. She gave me a red poppy. Later, I would realize why.

WEEK 14

DIARY ENTRY 23 SEPTEMBER /38

My 21st birthday. A pigeon, dove, and sparrow sang at my window, which fell on deaf ears. It's the second day I cannot hear anything.

This isn't like being alone in an empty room or awake while the house sleeps, in a meadow on a summer day or in a forest in the middle of winter. I feel defenseless. My body is constantly tense, waiting for signals of danger.

The sore place on my cheek—that's now a lurid green-edged purple bruise. There's a knot behind my navel, which I haven't felt in a very long time. My arms feel tired and the flesh looks doughy. And my bones ache, not like they did when I had ruptures; this is more subtle and incessant.

Because Father insisted on a cake for my birthday, we went to the house. I sensed he did this more out of obligation than celebration. Father's glove is gone—no more blood. He has no visible marks like I do (my eye shocked him), but he's hunched over and struggles to keep his chin up. Unless Nikolas writes to tell me, I won't know how he fares until he returns from his trip. I hope they left before the equinox, as I insisted.

To walk through town is ghoulish now. Almost everyone has an affliction, many with several, and some worse than any seen among the children. It's awful—twisted limbs, crippled gaits, wounds seeping through clothes, eyes narrow with pain.

I am responsible for this. If anyone knew, I couldn't blame them for what they'd do to me.

If the pattern holds, the children will sicken with the last phase in 3 weeks.

Harmyn says as we worsen, all is not dire. The gold flecks she saw in the children are brighter, but she can't explain what they are. Something magnificent, she thinks. The adults already have the spots. I dared to ask about myself. She said I have a fleck on my right hand at the web of my thumb.

Charlotte and her baby, Tom, are doing well. The longsheet reports have her worried. She's asked for reassurance if— when—the plague spreads, the sickness isn't as awful as it seems. Muriel returned early to the conservatory, to her "well-rested favorite piano," where she can practice without interruption or complaint. Among my letters, I've posted one to Mr. Remarque. What he has to say about my mother will be unrestrained, I'm sure.

WEEKLY POST.

———◆———

20 September /38. Page 1, Column 3

KING'S PROXY NAMED—The Council elected Lord Humphrey Sullyard to serve in His Majesty's stead, in the event the king succumbs to an incapacity and is unable to fulfill his duties. An agreement will be signed to grant Lord Sullyard all due powers, which will revert to the king as soon as his health is restored. From Penridge, Lord Sullyard has served on the Council for 31 years and was one of King Aeldrich's closest advisers.

Rothwyke Services Log, Excerpt

20/9. Subtle ground rumbling in Areas 11, east 10, south 8. First activity since June. Will monitor.

21/9. Again, same intensity of rumbling, lasting only seconds, reported in all Areas. No new damage to buildings or streets reported.

22/9. Multiple reports of a "murmur" and "low groaning" sound as minor tremors swept through, then a "roaring," "booming," or "thunderclap" when they stopped. Tremors strong enough to rattle objects. No structural damages reported as yet.

23/9. Shocks coming at intervals day and night. Earthquakes unknown in this region. What is this?

24/9. Still more shocks, less frequent, less intense.

25/9. Four shocks today.

From the Plague of Silences Recollection Project Archives, Selected Excerpts

Diary No. 579. Female, 14

I pretended to go to my drawing lesson and went to the woods instead. I must go because I feel calm when I do. I must write in my diary because I don't want to forget. Today was special. Secret took us on a walk. We watched bees repair their hive and ants clean mouse bones. I sat for a long while by myself. The sun moved, the wind blew leaves, and a snail crawled by. My heart felt full and I realized everything seemed so clear and bright, unlike being in town, where it feels so dark all the time, even in daylight. I'm glad no grown people come to the woods. It's their fault, I think, the darkness. Let it stay there.

Diary No. 127. Male, 41, accountant

Watched everyone at their desks as they stared off from their ledgers. It seems none of us can concentrate for long. Mr. E— walked up the aisles banging his cane. He struck Mr. R—, which he's done before numerous times. As usual, Mr. R— said nothing; we said nothing. When I came home, K— could see I was out of sorts. There is a heavy feeling in my chest, which worsens each day. After she went to bed, I locked myself in the water closet and screamed until my throat burned. The feeling is somewhat better now.

Diary No. 365. Female, 11

I might have a mind sickness. Am I the only one? I see what's on the outside of people and I wonder if they have sickness on the inside, too. I know I'm not supposed to think the things I do. It is wrong, the things I wish. But I can't stop. The thoughts spin around like the zoetrope I saw once. Oh, how a smile comes to my face and my heart feels blackly glad when I think of smashing _____'s head with an iron. Stabbing over and over and over until what I touched is bloody as meat. That would stop it. It would never happen again.

Diary No. 307. Male, 54, physician

Thus far 37 patients this week, each has the same afflictions which emerged in the children five weeks ago. Again, more female patients with the sanguine blot than male, and some of them telling the same preposterous stories. In addition to the visible afflictions, most complained of phantom pains throughout the body. Purgatives, all around.

Interview No. 214. Female; age during plague, 15;
current occupation, teacher

The second phase, I was lucky. I remember seeing other children, and then the adults, most everyone sick with the wasting and also the festers. My brothers and myself, we had aches in our chests, but none of the ailments so many seemed to suffer. Momma and Poppa, neither they were as bad off as our neighbors, poor souls. My friend O—, what a mess she was, her family no better. The smell in her house—the bucket where they kept the bandages before they burned them. Her father, brings tears to my eyes to think of him, O—'s father had to crawl to get around. He couldn't work at all. My father would visit him every night no matter they couldn't speak. Poppa was a clever man, and he took an old chair and put wheels on it and pushed Mr. I— up and down the sidewalk giving a how-do to everyone.

WEEK 15

NEITHER THE MISSES NOR JANE WAS AT THE GARDEN AT THE start of that week, which worried me. As Harmyn and I neared the walk-up, Mr. Elgin and two men sat on the front steps. One smoked a pipe, one clutched a large cup, and Mr. Elgin rubbed his right arm, held in a sling.

They looked out at the street. Two young men and a young woman stood on the opposite sidewalk. They had touches of blue on their clothing. In the street, a group of children with wooden swords rushed at each other and a horse-sized effigy of a green dragon. Sawdust puffed from its side when one child stabbed it with a direct thrust. He turned to the men, waving his sword in triumph. The boy was Lucas. Mr. Elgin managed a grin and nod to acknowledge he'd seen his son's deed. The children—mouths gaping wide with battle cries only the young people could hear—rushed to join the kill.

I knocked on the Misses Acutt's door. When no one answered, I tried the knob. The door opened, but the apartment appeared to be empty except for Sir, who groomed himself in the parlor.

On the second floor, Jane and Dora's door was open halfway. I waved my arms until Dora gestured for me to enter. I wondered why she was home instead of at work. Julia looked up from the floor where she sat with Flowsy and two other dolls. Together on the settee were Jane and Dora, holding hands with fingers entwined. Tall Miss Acutt perched on the chair's edge with a doll in her hands.

We had seen each other the week before, so the bruise on my face didn't startle them. But when I entered their semicircle, Julia pulled on my skirt. I looked down at her note.

Skirt too long. Ask Mother fix? she'd written.

I shook my head. I would do that myself, but I was waiting for the change in my body to stop. Within days, I had shrunk two inches and my arms had withered like old branches. I looked hideous. **Thanks, but I can later**, I wrote back.

Julia slipped the notebook under her knee and handed a doll to Harmyn, who sat it on her lap.

I took the chair opposite Tall Miss Acutt and gestured to Jane to give me the slate board next to her. As she did, she dabbed her mouth with a handkerchief. Her lips faded to rose. The linen absorbed a red stain.

Mr. Elgin outside, I wrote.

Dora wrote, **Can't work anymore. Saw his arm?** then erased our words with her sleeve as Julia glanced up from her toys.

I nodded. In a few days, she'll be as inanimate as Flowsy, I thought. **Why are you home today?** I wrote to Dora.

She stared at Tall Miss Acutt until our elderly friend nodded, then wrote, **Jane took with the blot. Mrs. E & Short Miss A have it, too.** She poised her hand to write more, then jotted, **Are you well?**

My stomach lurched. I knew what she meant as I nodded. Even if we had been able to talk and hear, we wouldn't have been able to ask of the unspeakable. I watched Dora lace her fingers with Jane's in an act of comfort, blatant before us guests, and then I knew Jane had told Dora what violation had been done to her. I wondered if Short Miss Acutt kept her secret from her sister, Mrs. Elgin from her husband.

We looked at one another then shifted our attention elsewhere. Before the plague, as well as during the first phase, this pause from contact was an ordinary part of conversation. Sometimes awkward, often only a rest. But in the second phase, this break felt like a small abandonment.

I noticed Harmyn looking at Jane, who stared toward the windows. Harmyn held her amulet and closed her eyes. Although none of us could hear her, she began to sing, but her voice didn't soothe. Julia held Flowsy against her chest as if to shield her. Tall Miss Acutt hurried from the apartment. I doubled over as my lower belly cramped and my hips throbbed with pain. Dora clawed her fingers into her hair as she rocked back and forth. Jane pounded her fists against her legs as tears coursed over her scarlet cheeks.

Helpless and weak, we watched as Jane dropped down to her hands and knees, slamming her head against the floor. Harmyn touched Jane's shoulder. Harmyn's gaze fixed into an unknown distance, her eyes fierce. When Jane rose up, Harmyn stroked her forehead and stared at her until she looked back and nodded. With a wave, Harmyn called to Dora, who embraced Jane full in her arms.

Julia crawled close to me and leaned against my leg.

Well? I asked Harmyn. What she'd done reminded me of what happened with Nikolas, when she glimpsed into him after his parents died. But then, she'd had permission. We'd not given our consent.

Harmyn's entire body shook. *I'm sorry. I meant to help her, but when the shadow came out, it called out ones from the rest of you. Old shadows which belong to your mothers and grandmothers and their grandmothers, but they're in you, too. I don't understand what happened. I didn't expect that.* Harmyn put her head in her hands. *The only reason you don't have the blot is because those horrible things didn't happen to you. But Jane, poor Jane. I had to help her see, it wasn't her fault.*

WEEK 16

FOR WEEKS, THE DISTANCE BETWEEN FATHER AND ME HAD WIDened. I avoided the house and him to the degree that I could. Although Father knew I held him responsible for what happened with the scissors and the symbol, my feelings hadn't settled on this. By second phase, I couldn't look at him without resentment, but I had no clear understanding why that was so. I sensed, too, he avoided me, using Harmyn as a shield, which only fueled my jealousy.

One evening, as I made tea, I watched Harmyn rush into the kitchen to find a treat in the cupboard. Father had found a sleight market supply of what seemed like an endless variety of sweets—syrup candies, brittles, nougats, liqueur-filled truffles. In this time of restriction, the excess piqued me; the indulgence more so.

The goodies weren't the issue, however. I'd received plenty of treats and gifts from him in the past. The frivolity, the play, the joy—that infuriated me. When I was a child, my father gave attention with an instructive approach, from the way he read to me to the outings we had together. What fun I might have seemed secondary to what useful thing I might learn. Father was a teacher to Harmyn, as he'd been to me, and though I tried, I could recall few instances of laughter with him, in that house.

That night, I walked toward the parlor with my cup, planning to read alone. Harmyn, with a fistful of candy, opened her mouth and shut her eyes as if she'd heard a hilarious joke, and bumped into me. I grabbed her arm, scowled, and hushed her.

She froze, eyes wary.

What did I do? she asked.

I forced myself to take a breath. I hadn't meant to be so harsh, but I reacted without thinking. I knew I shouldn't feel as I did, but I couldn't help it. Still, I didn't apologize.

The child blinked. *Your poison spilled over, didn't it?*

I nodded.

Then I'll leave you to sit with it, Harmyn said with dispassion.

Sit I did, unable to concentrate on my book, aware of the dark corner where I once hid as a child, memories flitting so quickly through my thoughts, all was a blur. After I placed the cup in the basin, I stood near the dining table and faced where my mother once worked. My right hand tingled as a streaking pain burst between my hips. I remembered the afternoon she gave me the nesting dolls, when she told the story her years in fosterage and of her dead brother, Szevstan, and mentioned my stillborn ones. What she said to me, "Lucky thing I kept you. Lucky thing, I kept you."[31]

Before I could stop myself, I went into my old room. The pain in my body worsened the moment I stepped inside. Unable to endure being there, I carried the boxes I needed into the spare room and sat with her diaries, searching for a vestige of two lost boys. Eight years had passed between my parents' marriage and my birth, so I continued where I'd left off weeks before.

When she resumed her diary after the move to Foradair, the cheerful drawings became less frequent. Marks began to appear at some page corners. I puzzled through that diary and the next until I realized she'd kept record of her bleed days. The words blurred as I searched for a change in the regularity. A year and a half after they wed, the marks vanished. Several weeks on, there was a note written into her diary.

I didn't sleep last night, thinking of the child within you.
At last! I am so happy, Zavet. I love you.

The volume of her translations remained steady as ever, until seven months later when she wrote nothing for a week, and then her work resumed as usual.

That gap in time held my first blue brother.

Sweat dampened my armpits as I tore through diary after diary, counting marks, seeing them disappear again two years later, finding the message from my father, "All will be well. I wait with joy for our baby," and then again, a week of her absence, followed by words, words, words.

My second blue brother, who fell from her body and hardly interrupted her schedule.

After that, I couldn't search for myself.

I went downstairs, stared at the ochre bowl on the table, and thrust it over the edge. The shatter gave me a frisson. Father and Harmyn walked in as I wrapped the shards in an old dustcloth.

GrandBren bought me an archery set. Come try it with us, Harmyn said. She had the bow over her shoulder.

I blanched, reminded of the hunt for the deer and for me, then fumed, annoyed at their amusement. As I opened my satchel to find my notebook, I said to her through the silence, *I need to be alone with my father.*

I'm going to the water closet, she said, which I knew Father heard because he nodded.

With a gesture, I told Father to sit down. I handed him one of the two pencils I kept with me.

Broke the old bowl. Sorry, I wrote.

Father looked at the space where it had been. His expression conveyed surprise tinged with sadness. **Too broken to mend?** he wrote.

Yes. Want to talk to you. I've been reading through Mother's diaries. Found record of your engagement, marriage, note you wrote when she was pregnant first time, I wrote.

He seemed confused until the memory swept in. His smile was reflective.

What do you remember? I wrote.

I was so happy with the first. Hopeful. I was older than your mother. The wait for a child was longer for me, he wrote.

How was she?

Nervous. She had never cared for a baby. Didn't know how she'd manage. Didn't sleep well. Nightmares. Otherwise healthy.

And when he was stillborn? I wrote.

Father rubbed his brow. He wrote, **I felt as if someone had gouged a piece out of my heart. No indication anything might be wrong. So shocked.**

And she was—?

Numb for some time. As if she couldn't believe what happened, he wrote.

The second?

Confess, I was more cautious, more protective of her. Still happy. Your mother—brave, reassured me all would be well. Nightmares again. Acute aversion to many smells, unlike the first. Wouldn't wear her perfumes.

Looked forward to the baby?

Father's pencil hovered above the paper. **She did, in her own quiet way.**

And when he came blue?

Why do you want to know this? he wrote.

I'm curious, I wrote.

I was devastated. Wrong to feel so, but felt she betrayed me.

I forced myself not to look at him. Not once, not a single instance, could I remember him speak an unkind word about her.

Why? I wrote.

I wanted a –s– child. Never believed physicians who said mental effort bad for women, but she worked as much as ever. Did that cause harm? Don't know. She knew how I grieved the first, he wrote.

That *S*. He struck it out, but the truth slipped. He had wanted a son. I pulled the notebook toward me.

Did she? Grieve? I wrote.

She wasn't one to dwell, he wrote.

Did you see their births?

No. But there for yours. INSISTED.
Did you see them after?
Father nodded.
What did they look like? I wrote.
This is morbid, he wrote.
I want to know.
Perfect, but blue.
Why?
The cords. The first, wrapped round his neck. Second, a knot like a fist, he wrote.

An electric pain ripped from my navel through the tip of my tongue. I remembered what she'd called my brothers—Noose and Knot. I thought of Aoife and the twins she bore, whom she did not want and did not name in her manuscript.

You named me. Did you name them? I wrote.
Duncan. Riley.

His head dropped as a tear inched down his cheek. I tried but couldn't touch him. A cold sweat broke through my skin. Noose and Knot. Duncan and Riley. My brothers who never were.

Harmyn returned, narrowed her eyes at me, and slipped next to him. I almost told her to leave us—my father, our loss—but I knew the moment she rested her small hand between his shoulders, she would soothe the wound, ripped wide open.

AS SOON AS WORD CAME THAT NIKOLAS WAS A DAY FROM HIS RE-turn, I sent a message, through a winged courier, which read "Harmyn will be at Father's the night of the ninth."

I received no reply. When I tidied the cottage that afternoon, I anticipated he might not meet me if duty kept him to his office. As I built a fire to hold off the evening's chill, I realized I'd never spent a night alone there. When I was a little girl, I'd imagined what it would be like to live as Old Woman did with the plants and animals as my sole companions. My quest allowed an exploration of that solitude. I found it suited me; I wished for no more than the peace it offered. However, once Nikolas accompanied me, I found comfort in his presence and conversation, and now, there was far more to our friendship. Perhaps I wasn't the lone creature I thought myself to be. Still, a part of me longed for the rigors of study and work that engaged the mind. These thoughts chased one another in circles as I made the bed, a meal, a cup of tea.

This I preferred to what had begun to stalk me. Fragments of memory, dark and unwelcome.

A storm swept into the woods, but I didn't notice until the lightning drew my attention. I turned back to reading Old Woman's plant lore and startled when a hand brushed my shoulder. Nikolas was soaked, but I hugged him anyway. He kissed me through a rumble of thunder I could only feel. He held the left side of my face when he noticed the bruise, then patted my shoulders when he realized I'd shrunk.

Two bottles of wine were on the table. We went to the shelves. He took two cups as I grabbed bowls and walked to the hearth. I ladled the soup I made. Being near the fire was warmer, so I spread a blanket for us to sit there. When I turned to look for him, he was naked from the chest and wrapped in a quilt below. He handed me a cup and settled beside me. Unbidden, I thought of Fewmany's hand, a crystal glass, the red wine.

We ate and had a second cup before he reached for the obligatory notebook.

Good we timed our departure from Ilsace with your prediction. Were back in Ailliath by the equinox. I wasn't prepared for the silence. One adviser said he hears his heartbeat & coachman said he endures a constant ringing, like a Tell-a-Bell which won't wind down. The afflictions, how quickly they came on. I woke up the first morning with a light bruise on my side & a feeling of weight on my shoulders, both worsened to the point they are now. How are you? he wrote.

You'll see later, I wrote.

How is Harmyn? Your father?

H still singing, with friends in woods most days, very tired at night. Father has hunched back & it's hard for him to keep his head up. Everyone at FM Inc. working half days now. Father said they're exhausted, trouble with concentration, I wrote.

What I saw coming through town, I wasn't prepared for. As if survivors of a war walk the streets, he wrote.

Yes, that's what it's like, I thought as I reached for the bottle. I filled our cups to the rim. Nikolas put his aside and stroked my arm. Loneliness welled up through my body. The force made my palms and soles ache.

I held my breath until I suffocated the urge to cry and banished the fragment I glimpsed. My little hands, reaching for my mother.

The notebook lay open at my knee. I wrote, **Since you lost your hearing, have you noticed unpleasant memories coming back to you?**

As he nodded, his eyes were hard.

I realized I hoped he'd say no, even expected him to. Nikolas, I thought, was always so cheerful and well liked, someone I would have called happy. No doubt since his youngest days, everything possible had been done to please him. A desired son, a treasured heir, given a square place in the center of the world. He had always been surrounded by friends and, as I'd seen at the castle, attended by staff and servants who had affection for him.

I would have thought you've had a nearly perfect life, I wrote.

Wrong, he wrote.

How so?

Not now.

He closed the pencil within the notebook. As he unbuttoned my dress, I almost pushed him away. What was to happen didn't require all of me to be unclothed. He stopped to look into my eyes. He'd felt my resistance. I nodded with my consent. When my dress's bodice fell away, he swept his palms along the lengths of my arms. I pressed my lids shut as the hollow feeling claimed me.

He traced his hands along my shriveled arms with curiosity, with affection, but not disgust. When I finally glanced at him, he pressed his palm against my cheek as I tried to look away. I drifted my fingertips to his sides above his waist, carefully, but he bent to his right as if I'd struck him. I almost pulled back, but I knew if he'd braved my hideous limbs, I must return the witness.

I guided him to turn to the firelight as I eased the quilt away.

"Oh, Nikolas," I said into his deaf ear.

A swollen red streak striped his side as if he'd been whipped without restraint. I followed its margin, felt its furious heat, kissed the flawless skin above the wound.

He drew me up by the shoulders. He kissed me, too, above and below my bruise. We held each other until love was stronger than the pain.

WEEK 17

DIARY ENTRY 11 OCTOBER /38

I wonder what the children were thinking when they went to bed last night. Who was frightened? Who was relieved? Harmyn assured me it was gentle, like going to sleep. We went to see about Julia and Lucas. There they lay side by side in my old bed, Flowsy tucked next to Julia and a blanket folded at Lucas's neck. Mrs. Elgin was fretful, her hands fluttering. The neighbors will help look after them, and I said to send word if I could help, too. I mentioned to no one I paid the Elgins' rent through next summer, for the children's sake.

The streets are so deserted now, not a child in sight. This only makes our shared desolation worse. The hearing loss—we are all so insular. Caught within ourselves. The only means to reach someone now is to look, or to touch. We don't want to look too long or too closely, afraid of what we'll see. We aren't supposed to touch, not beyond a handshake or quick pat; affection is not for public spectacle.

I don't know how I'll endure this for two more months. What I miss. Nib scratch. Birdcall. Wheel crush. Twig crack. Footsteps. Music. His voice. My own. The third-phase sleep—I welcome it. Blankness, no thought, empty. Unless we dream, unable to wake up. At least now when the ogress comes for me, I can escape when I open my eyes.

From the Plague of Silences Recollection Project Archives,
Selected Excerpts

Diary No. 101. Male, 23, liveryman

Even here in Gomfrey, owners selling horses for bargains to stables out of Rothwyke. Nags go off to the sleight market. Not all beef is beef these days. Us at the margins, maids and laundry women, laborers, men like me, it's becoming dire. The ones who pay our wages, more and more working half days or not at all, so they can't keep us. I have three horses left. Mr. N— behind on his payment and won't sell the horse so I split the feed from the other two to keep the three alive. Can't let Ruffian starve. At least I have enough to eat and the lot owner lets me keep a proper bed in the stable since the landlord evicted me.

Diary No. 307. Male, 54, physician

I wouldn't have believed this if I hadn't seen it with my own eyes. Throughout Rothwyke, the children sleep. The adults who can hear say they make no sounds. Of the ones I observed, I saw them twitch and shift. I feared if there was no movement at all, the risk of bedsores was imminent. Whether they can hear again, I cannot say. They don't respond to loud noises. Physical sensitivity is compromised. I discerned no response when they were pricked, pinched, touched with a warm poker or cold, or sprinkled with water. Mysterious, eerie. The ones I've seen still have the afflictions from the prior phase. Perhaps this will heal in their rest. Alone, when my imagination takes on a life of its own and my own troubles get the better of me, I wonder if we might fall into an eternal sleep, never to awaken. Ridiculous, of course. The animals recovered. So shall we.

Diary No. 415. Lord Humphrey Sullyard

Haaud's continued occupation of Uldiland bodes a coming invasion into Thrigin. Most of us believe that is likely, if not assured. For now, because of the mountains, Thrigin can hold the shared border with Haaud, but that could quickly change with any movement coming from Uldiland. To the north, Giphia fell. At last. Haaud now pushes farther into Kirsau. Ilsace is sending troops across. They are next if Kirsau falls, and it would only be a matter of time for us. Ailliath remains neutral, signing no pacts, giving no aid, keeping minimal troops at our border. I can't imagine how we'll hold off much longer. The king must see reason here.

We await several towns' revised population tallies, detailed to the household, sex and age and occupation, and plans for ration storage, ward gardens, etc. Places the envoys visited on the way to and back from Ilsace have been most prompt to respond. Lord Milton thinks they were reassured—that is, the mayors, leaders, and subjects—to see the king himself, to hear from him, his written words at least. They took him at his word then, regardless of past frank correspondence, that they must remain vigilant. The plague, should it strike them, requires their preparation. The king was correct to insist on this.

Interview No. 124. Male; age during plague, 17;
current occupation, porter

There were five younger than myself. I didn't sicken with the second phase when they did. That upset them. They didn't think of me as grown. I didn't either, but Mother said I was always beyond my years, and she wasn't surprised I got my wisdom teeth at sixteen.

The next oldest, they avoided me, fifteen and fourteen they were. The youngest were ten, six, and three. My sister, the one who was ten, she was a delicate girl. She didn't like seeing everyone disfigured. She was also terrified of the sleep, but I didn't know this soon enough. We'd been told of the sleep when we could still hear, at a ward meeting. The adults were expected to tell the children, but my parents didn't want to frighten the younger ones. The ten- and six-year-olds heard from friends. I didn't know this at first. Not until the end of the second phase when L— cried every day and I convinced her to tell me what the matter was. I was never so happy we could write some as I was then. She believed she would fall asleep and never wake up. I told her no, that wasn't true. She would sleep the way bears do through winter, then wake up very hungry. She laughed at that, then cried with relief.

I was glad the children slept before the rest of us. As the weeks went on—shops and offices closing, the hobby and athletic clubs not meeting because so few went. Almost everyone had tetchy moods. The smallest thing could cause a turn. Drop a package, brush a passerby, wait in a stalled line. There would be shouting although no one could hear and pushing and brawling. Public drunkenness like never before. Attacks, assaults, vandalism, as if men went mad. People falling to the ground for no reason having tantrums, crying, sometimes staring off at nothing. Do you remember?

I was glad to fall asleep at night. It was such a deep sleep, not like it was in the first phase. As if a force were pulling me down, into a cave, under water.

WEEK 18

AT THE START OF THE EIGHTEENTH WEEK, HARMYN ASKED TO meet in Nikolas's office. She didn't wait for us to sit down before handing me a letter. It read

Dear Secret and Nikolas,

I could tell you this, but I decided to write instead. I had to think about what to say first.

When I told you I saw little flecks of light on people and inside of them? With the children, the spots have started to look like shiny holes.

I'll try to explain what I've seen and how I understand it.

I want you to imagine a hole like the hollow of a tree. The tree is Now. Step through the hollow. On the other side, you're in a time and place you may or may not remember. This is Then. A past.

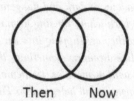

In Then, you might find something that was taken from you, left behind, or given away. Not like a coat or a toy, but that could be there, too. Sometimes it's a belief, or an emotion, or a thought. No matter what it is, the missing piece is a part of you.

A person has many holes. Those all connect Then and Now. None is separate from the rest. See in my drawing how they overlap.

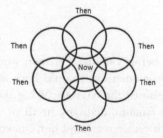

You are probably wondering, what about the shadows?

Shadows cover the holes between Now and Then, moving between them. The shadows are thought and feeling, and they know something has been lost. When the shadows get stirred up, that's when they can spill into what I call the poison.

I should give you an example.

You'll remember when Aoife told how Wei glimpsed what happened to her father and the little girl on the tree. Wei's hand got bloody when she touched Leit. That's because she went into the space between Then and Now and saw her father at the very moment of the wound. Then, he left behind his blood and part of his voice. What was taken from him was his faith and hope. A shadow took the place of what he lost and covered the hole between Now and Then. So, if he thought about the horrible thing that happened or something reminded him of it, that's when the shadow came out into Now. He could hold it back, but Aoife felt it as darkness— as poison. She was right to be afraid he'd fail to contain it and hurt someone. That shadow was very very strong and full of rage and guilt.

Not everyone has shadows so dark and dangerous, but all shadows hold pain. All shadows want back what's missing to make things whole again.

As our children sleep, they are slipping into the holes between Now and Then. To them, it feels like dreaming. Sometimes they are only dreaming. Sometimes dreams mix with memory, or it's memory alone.

I should tell you, though, not all holes lead to Then as they've known it. Some of the Thens are what could have been. And some Thens are for people, ancestors, who came before them, and they can see into these. There are many realms which exist at the same time, too. Inside of everyone, there are different Nows and Thens, even futures. The children are going to these places. Some will stay there and won't come back. The ones who do return won't be the same.

The adults are next, soon enough.

Harmyn

I finished reading before Nikolas. Harmyn stood with her arms behind her back. Whatever questions I could have asked, none of the answers would have explained the Mystery. What she told us was beyond comprehension, more fantastic than any myth or story I'd ever read. In all the moments I'd felt cautious around her, I never feared her, but I did then. My gift with creatures and plants was extraordinary. Her gifts were supernatural, the extent of them unknown.

Nikolas jotted in his notebook, **Too bewildered to ask anything other than are the children in danger?**

Of course they are. Last count from the wards, how many don't have proper roofs over their heads? How many more in the next weeks? she said within our thoughts.

He shut his eyes, obviously resisting the urge to barb back at her. **I meant from the plague. 18 children died last week. The registrar says that's almost the average for a <u>month</u>.**

Oh, yes, the death toll will rise, she said with a tone so matter-of-fact, the hair on my neck stood on end. *That's what I meant by some won't come back. To us, they're gone.*

IN HIS WEEKLY ANNOUNCEMENT, SENT THROUGHOUT AILLIATH and to several kingdoms, Nikolas made a plea for volunteers to help before the third phase struck the rest of us and until the sickness ran its course. To this point, we had managed with neighbors helping neighbors. However, the children who'd recover and the healthy adults among us wouldn't be able to care for the sick adults alone. As well, he wrote letters to specific ward and charity leaders requesting their guidance to prepare for volunteers and a system to assign them. To Dru Kai and Milan Visham, the Guardian leaders who contacted us in August, he sent a message to accept part of their offer.

The Guardians' reply wasn't delivered by post, as expected, but in person, with a request to meet the three of us.

At breakfast, a castle officer told Harmyn and me to report to the meeting chamber once we were finished. I arrived first. As the door opened, I noticed two people wearing black trousers and identical tailored coats, Guardian blue, with white turn-back cuffs, and gold buttons molded with the symbol in the center. The man had skin darker than mine, with light eyes and black hair cut close to his skull. The woman's eyes were slanted with heavy lids, the irises black. Her hair was gray, cut straight over her brow and shoulders.

Another man stood next to the woman, dressed in the same uniform. When he smiled, I stepped forward to embrace him.

Naughton.

Harmyn and Nikolas walked in as I released him. Nikolas's eyebrows arched with inquiry, his expression both amused and suspect. When his attention turned to the guests, they didn't bow. I hoped he remembered from Aoife's manuscript that the Guardians had different ideas about authority and meant no disrespect. They accepted the offer of his hand. When Harmyn extended hers, they couldn't hold back their stares when they touched her.

Nikolas leaned toward Harmyn. Suddenly, a high-pitched ring pierced my ears. We clutched the sides of our heads. I heard a rattle of keys in the hallway and the flap of drapes moved by the wind.

"I'm sorry," Harmyn said. "The king asked if I could make it so you could speak without notebooks. I meant to with only thoughts, but that's what happened."

"Is it permanent?" Nikolas asked.

"I haven't practiced this. I don't know how long it will last," Harmyn said.

"Well, then, welcome to Ailliath," Nikolas said, his voice a little deeper than it had been, the tone even warmer. "May I introduce Miss Secret Riven, and—Harmyn."

"Thank you for the audience. I am Dru Kai," the woman said in our language with a pronounced but musical accent. Pointing to her right, she said, "This is Milan Visham and Connau Kess."

"I knew him as Naughton," I said.

"Ah, she's told me about you, in good regard," Nikolas said. "Shall we sit?"

"Milan and I request a private meeting with you," Dru said. "Connau wishes to speak to Miss Riven."

"We'll go to my office, then," Nikolas said. He opened the door to allow Dru and Milan to walk ahead. Nikolas paused with his fingers on the doorknob as he looked at Harmyn and me. "I get to wish you two a good day as I haven't in months."

"Wait." My cheeks blushed as I walked to him. "Harmyn knows and I don't care if Connau does. I've missed the sound of your voice and I love you and—" I kissed him as quick as if I'd stolen it.

"Miss Riven, such forwardness! I love you, too." Nikolas gave us a nod.

When we sat down, Harmyn rolled her eyes. Connau tried not to smile.

"I know you Guardians are far more lenient about certain displays than we Ailliathans," I said.

"We are. I won't pry, but I'll remark I'm glad you share the mutual affection of a man worthy of you," he said.

I nodded with a grin. "Do you mind if Harmyn stays?" I asked.

"No."

"Why did Dru and Milan come instead of sending a letter?" I asked.

"They wanted to discuss the arrangements for volunteers as well as the war, in person. We were also curious to see for ourselves what we've read in the announcements." Connau studied the bruise on my cheek. "Although the King's descriptions were accurate, I wasn't prepared for what I've seen. This is hideous, Secret."

"You cannot imagine," I said. My right ear popped. "We might not have much time to speak, and I have questions."

Harmyn curled herself on the chair as if she were about to listen to a good story.

"Then ask," Connau said.

"Several days before the plague started, I went to the manor. Everything was gone. The collections, the library, Mutt, the servants. What happened?" I asked.

"After the evening you met him, when you returned from your journey, he wasn't quite the same. He told me he had an important trip to take soon, but nothing more. He ordered the rooms to be packed, and he arranged for everything to be moved, the sort of duty he typically entrusted to me. Around this time, the staff said they heard him scream in his sleep. The maids told of his sheets stained with blood and seepage, as if from wounds. I heard no complaint from him. Strange, because he's prone to whine when he doesn't feel well. After the ball, he went to the office every day, but he took his meals in his room and had no guests. It was painful to see him in that state. So quiet. Mutt his only companion, sitting in the library with his automatons, not even calling the musicians to play for him."

"The fire?" I asked.

"I assume he knocked over a lamp and left the library. By the time someone smelled smoke, the fire had spread. The staff helped with buckets of sand and wool blankets. He worked beside us, but—I'd never seen him as he was—enraged, howling, and when the flames were out, he took the fireplace iron and beat the burned cabinets," Connau said.

"Why did he dismiss the servants?" I asked.

"There was no one at all?" he asked.

I shook my head.

"I have no explanation. In my case, a week after the fire, I received word I must resign without notice and depart immediately. Unusual orders, but I did, leaving a letter for him at his door."

"So, you'd been in communication with your people about him?" I asked.

"Yes, of course. I admit I was reluctant to leave him, not only because he was sickly. Almost ten years I'd been in his service. It's the strangest thing how, in time, kept secrets become shared secrets. The deference to him was difficult, that isn't part of my innate constitution, but he wasn't as harsh to me as he was to some others. And there were many fascinating and jolly moments in that house," he said.

"Do you know where he is?" I asked.

"Officially, I've been told he's no longer the threat he was."

"Do you know what happened?" I asked.

"No."

Except for Harmyn and Nikolas, whom I told the night it happened, no one else knew how Fewmany had hunted me, that he asked for my help to kill the dragon, and that I'd pushed him into a hollow tree. I believed I could trust Connau with the truth, so I did.

Connau stretched out his open hand. I accepted it. "You understand the magnitude of that one choice not to lead him there or, depending on one's perspective, to follow. There will be tales told of you one day, Secret."

Tales of the keeper of tales, I thought. I held my breath but the tears came anyway.

Connau looked at me with those gentle brown eyes and wrapped my hand in both of his. I thought of Aoife, the tender moment she had with a Guardian the first time she visited the settlement, more than a thousand years before, not far from where we now sat.

"What has upset you?" Connau asked.

"I was truly happy in my position. I believed he cared for me, even though deep down, I knew he meant to use me for his ends." The scar on my left hand, where Fewmany's blade had cut me, began to burn. Harmyn placed her palm over it. "He flattered me with his trust. He talked to me as no one ever had before. I admired his ambition and intelligence and wit. I felt like a treasure to him, and I was, but not the kind that matters. He seduced me, and I allowed it. I feared him, and when that waned, that's when I put myself in the most danger. How close I came to doing as he wished. I hate him now, with the visceral certainty

I felt as a child, but I also—because I can't deny the good times—I loved him, too. There is no peace being pulled between those extremes."

"Does it surprise you I loved him, too?" Connau asked.

"Yes," I said.

"When he was filled with wonder and curiosity, he was impossible to resist. You understand what I mean," Connau said.

"I do." The burn in my hand became a throb. I paused as I dared to ask the question. "How did he feel about me?"

"I believe to the extent he could, he cared for you as well. Your affection wasn't unrequited."

"It was wasted," I said.

"Not on him, lonely as he was. Besides, if you hadn't had that bond between you, you couldn't have achieved what you did. It's both that simple and that compli—"

I clutched my ears. Instead of silence, I heard the faintest rush of my heartbeat.

He can still hear you, Harmyn said within my thoughts.

"Thank you for listening. Thank you for everything," I said.

He nodded, the little bow familiar; his body had not forgotten Naughton. When he stood to leave, he reached out his arms. He held me as I cried for what Fewmany and I had done to each other out of love, grief, and greed.

WEEK 19

OUT OF GUILT, I FINALLY RELENTED TO HARMYN'S REQUEST TO invite Father to dinner. I had no good reason to refuse for so long, other than the castle, like the woods, was a secluded place where certain memories, and those who embodied them, didn't intrude. Since I learned my brothers' names, I'd not seen Father except for a weekly obligatory cup of tea and jotted conversation.

The night Father arrived, we greeted him in the front parlor. He walked slowly, bent forward, his head tilted like a turtle's. He dressed more formally than the occasion called for. When he bowed to Nikolas before they shook hands, I was reminded of the flagrant exceptions Nikolas allowed Harmyn and me. Harmyn hugged Father around the waist. When he leaned forward to give me an awkward kiss on the cheek, I detected a whiff of my mother's perfume. My temper riled. I lagged behind as they walked, wondering why Father had expended a precious drop. I froze when I realized that day was the seventh anniversary of her death.

Harmyn asked Nikolas to have our meal without attending footmen so that we could talk together. She would give us respite from our deafness but didn't want to draw undue attention. Dinner was as frugal as any Father might have at another house that night. I watched him for signs of disappointment—at the King's table at last, but with no extravagance—but he seemed content. The conversation included us all, until Father mentioned the war. He and Nikolas leapt into an earnest discussion, which piqued me until I realized this was inevitable given their shared interest. Both were students of history in their own intimate ways.

When talk turned to preparations for the third phase, Harmyn leaned toward Nikolas and said, "GrandBren can stay with us, can't he? We have plenty of room."

I stirred my cooled leek and potato soup. One more person at the castle could be accommodated. The servants, staff, Council members from Rothwyke, and their families were to be kept within the walls, along with the volunteers who would tend us. Vacant rooms on the residence's second floor, once used by the royal family, were reserved for Lord Sullyard and several advisers who would aid him in the coming months.

"We will," Nikolas said. He nudged me with his foot under the table. Through a few written conversations, he knew some of my recent thoughts and feelings about Father.

"I recall Elinor's daughter is coming soon from Clyton to care for her, and he considered hiring her to tend him as well. Perhaps he'd be more comfortable in his own home," I said.

"What do you want, GrandBren?" Harmyn asked.

Father glanced at us, but his eyes rested on Harmyn. "I'd prefer to not be alone. There is room for you and Secret at the house."

"What do you want, Secret?" Harmyn asked.

"I'd prefer to feel safe, and that will be here," I said.

"Then you can both have what you want, if Nikolas gives his permission," she said.

"Mr. Riven, the invitation is open. You needn't answer now," Nikolas said.

"Thank you," Father said.

When Harmyn suppressed a triumphant grin, I wanted to smack her.

After we finished our meal, Harmyn announced she'd planned a tour and presented Father with a hand-drawn map of the main buildings marked with Xs. His face brightened with delight. She was an enthusiastic guide, sharing facts and anecdotes she'd gathered from the staff in written interviews. Even Nikolas learned things he didn't know. Father behaved himself by not asking too many questions.

In the main meeting chamber, Harmyn didn't reveal the secret room but did speak at length about the kings' portraits and the crest of scales.

"Nikolas, yours is the last one, correct?" Harmyn asked, her finger on the scale's transparent edge.

He nodded. Harmyn had meant the last scale on the row, but there was a double meaning. As Father and Harmyn turned back to the wall, Nikolas looked at me. In those eyes the color of myth was a resolute peace. His was the last and final. His son would pursue his own quest, if he chose one.

The penultimate destination was the library. Nikolas allowed Father to see some of the kingdom's oldest records—writs, deeds, treaties. Wax seals attached to ribbons, which served as signatures of venerable dead men, dangled from several of the documents. Nikolas unlocked a cabinet which held a portion of the kingdom's chronicles.

"You're welcome to look at them," Nikolas said.

A fevered boyishness lit Father's eyes. He laid a bound volume on a stand. Harmyn turned up the flames on the nearest lamps. Father traced the parchment edges with reverence as my fingers drifted over the text. I didn't resemble my father, but in that moment, we mirrored each other. From the observant expressions on Nikolas's and Harmyn's faces, I knew they noticed this, too.

Through my cold feelings came the thought, This love we share is truly in our blood.

Father's hands began to tremble. He cleared his throat. "I've read the translations, but to touch the original chronicles—the excitement overwhelms my nerves. This one is seven years before The Mapmaker's War. What of the ones prior, and during?" Father asked.

"All here," Nikolas said.

"And you could sign a pass so he can read them," Harmyn said.

"Yes, Harmyn, I could," Nikolas said.

"There are maps, too. I found an old one of Foradair," she said as she pulled open a narrow drawer. Father hurried over to look.

As they searched for the street where Father lived as a child, I leaned close to Nikolas. I thought of the treasured old map in Father's study and the thin veils which covered it—of mines, ports, trade routes, battle sites. I wondered how he would respond if he saw Aoife's map and I told him what it was.

Quickly Father and Harmyn glanced at several other charts, and then she said, "We have one more place to see, which Nikolas is very kind to allow."

As we walked down the hall, Nikolas and Father lagged at a snail's pace behind in conversation. Outside the corridor to Nikolas's private office, Nikolas acknowledged the guard's bow. The guard pushed the pocket doors aside and allowed us through.

I realized, even before Harmyn told me, why she led Father there. Within my father was the memory of a noble past, of a man who had been raised as Ciaran's son but born first as Wyl's heir.[32] Aoife, his mother, hadn't named him in her manuscript, but I was certain he was named, along with this title and deeds, within Ailliath's chronicles after the war.

"GrandBren will have deep feelings about this place," she whispered. "He's going to have profound dreams during the sleep. He'll question them even as he believes what they show. Eventually, you need to give him a translation of Aoife's manuscript and tell him the whole truth."

"In time," I said.

Dangling from the ancient torch hangers, oil lamps burned. Our shadows drifted across the floor. Along the way, Father touched the corridor's gold walls and the doors, chained and locked. When Father stepped into the king's office, he hesitated. He stared at the hearth, the desk, and the sword among the weapons. A shadow crossed his face not of darkness but of recognition.

"I feel I know this place," Father said.

"Perhaps you met here with my father once," Nikolas said.

"No. I'm certain," Father said.

Father walked to the fireplace, stepped along the mantel's length, and placed his hand on one of the stones. From where I stood, I could see the crack he touched, bold as a scar.

When he turned to us, he looked at me in a way that made my skin ripple into goosebumps. Whomever was in our blood lived again.

Harmyn reeled back with a yawn.

"Hint taken," Father said. "An expert tour you gave us, Harmyn. Very well done. My thanks, Your Majesty, for being a gracious host."

"You're welcome. A carriage should be waiting at the gatehouse to spare you so late a walk," Nikolas said.

In the main courtyard, Father said his good-byes to Harmyn with a hug and to Nikolas with a handshake more relaxed than the evening's first. Father asked me to remain behind. I tensed, wondering what he wanted.

"You have time to talk. Make use of it," Harmyn said.

Father, aware of the coachman's proximity, motioned me to follow him away from passersby. "I've many, many questions, but there are two matters at the fore. First, I saw the map you gave to Fewmany. Was it fake?"

I didn't expect this revelation or his directness. "No."

"From where did it come?"

"I can't tell you."

"What can you tell me, then? What do you know? Where is he?" he asked, his tone worried, not angry.

I realized Father had lost Fewmany, too, not only as an employer. They were both poor native sons of the same town, both men of uncommon obsessive pursuits, and both bound by the twists of history which came down to us. Beyond the respect and trust they shared, there must have been fondness, at least on Father's part.

Let's have this out at last, I thought. So, I told Father the truth. I told him the arcane manuscript my mother received not only revealed her as gifted but also divulged mysteries of Nature, time, and space. I explained the links—hollow trees—and the gaps, which bridged one place to another, and how animals served as guides.

"That's what I did for Fewmany. I gave him a guide beyond the map. The hoard is real. The dragon is real. I saw each myself. They exist in a realm concurrent with ours," I said.

"The brooch with the symbol?" Father said.

"Of course he showed it to you. It was proof," I said. "Remember what you told me as a child, so often I memorized it? Fact is what happens in real life; fiction is what is make-believe. History is fact, and story is fiction. Myth is the make-believe history of the beginning and ending of everything. Legend is the strange child born of history and make-believe. Tale is a phantom with a body of fact and a heart of fiction. Well, the distinctions aren't so clear. They exist all at once. This, Fewmany must learn for himself. I would not lead him. You will never see him again. His quest will require his lifetime."

"You're lying. You must be," he said.

I glared at him, the wound of the scissors and symbol open again.

"Why would I lie to you now? There are things of and beyond this world you can't even imagine. Mother, Harmyn—they're proof. The manuscript—I've thought to give you a translation. You'd get answers to so many of your questions. You'd see what happened among us isn't only about a fantastical search. Far more is at stake," I said.

Father crossed his arms and placed his hand over his mouth, his thumb spinning the ring on his finger. He stared at me for several moments. "But he's alive."

"I assume so," I said.

"Never to return?" he asked.

"Probably not."

He shook his head, bewildered, but didn't tell me what he was thinking. "The other matter," he said. "What is the King to you?"

I paused to consider the formal address and his intent. "He's my best friend."

"What are you to him?"

"The same."

"The plague has dulled a number of my faculties but not my vision. I see the way you look at each other."

"That doesn't matter. Before my mother, you no doubt looked at another in a similar way."

"How quick you are to dismiss the heart's import," he said.

"Merely the implication you suggest," I said.

"And what do you think that is?"

"The possibility I could be his intended—which he hasn't expressed—and although you know very well the traditions to which he's bound."

"You believe that's my only reason for asking?"

"Why else? Any reference you ever made to my future in this regard involved finding a man of good station, although I can't imagine you hoped for better than one with a modest title, at least some wealth." I was being cruel, but I did speak honestly. Father had been practical rather than emotional about these matters, although I knew he had married my mother for love. She'd loved him, too, but I knew that wasn't the reason alone. She'd once said of him, "He was the only one who'd have me as I was." This, I felt, was my sad inheritance, from one strange woman to the next.

He winced at the same time my ears started to ring.

"Secret," Father said, "does he love you?"

"Yes."

"Do you love him?"

"It doesn't matter. We both know his fate here," I said.

Father's head bobbed as he struggled to look at me. "So if I weren't the son of a chimney sweep, you'd have hope?"

"Even if you were landed and titled, that would make no difference."

"Why not?" he asked.

All went quiet. Father handed his notebook to me.

My mute tongue wanted to lash him with a truth that would sting. Instead, I wrote, **I'm meant for a different life, that's all.**

Still want to attend high academy. Still my scholarly pet, he wrote.

With that, he eased the tension between us. He patted my hand and turned to the waiting carriage. Better I hadn't ruined the end of the evening with what I wanted to say: Unlike what my mother did for Father, I would spare Nikolas the embarrassment of a peculiar wife.

Dear Miss Riven,

Please accept my apologies for my tardy reply. I found myself detained in Prev as I negotiated the acquisition of the—oh, I'm bound to secrecy, aren't I? Suffice it, then, of a codex once thought lost to history, only to be discovered in a box of linens purchased by a walleyed churnmaid. And yet, stranger things have happened.

Indeed, I have followed accounts of this Plague of Silences. I'm glad to know you fare well and bravely. Gruesome affliction to rob one of the precious faculties of speech and hearing. This I fear more than buboes, vomiting, and leeches combined. I cannot remember the last time I endured more than a day without a hearty conversation. Weeks, months? Unthinkable!

Now to your inquiry.

What do I remember of Zavet Molnik, as I knew her then?

She was beautiful in the way of exotic creatures, fearsome even, with hair that could not have been more black, skin no more flawless, eyes no more rare in color. That violet, an enchantment. Ah, this—during a switch between classes, early spring it was, the leaves that newborn green, she set down her books to fix the combs in her hair and then it fell, a lustrous (pun intended) drape upon her shoulders. The fellows walking with me froze upon the sight, struck dumb, and though she looked toward our direction, she seemed to take no notice.

I thought her lonely, as I never saw her in social company, unless there was some obligatory function to attend. She might have had a friend outside our academic circles; I do hope so. The majority disdained her, her audacity to step outside of her proper place, and those who took an interest, and there were some, lacked the courage to approach the odd beast in her solitude.

For those men, the judgment of others was intimidating, but so was she. Your mother possessed a formidable genius, which you know, and an iron will, which you might not. The dismissiveness and derision leveled at her when she spoke in seminar discussions would have brought a meek man to tears. She shed none. How she held herself against the ire, I don't know. It was as if—yes—as if that was not the worst she'd endured and her very life depended on bearing it.

Even though she wasn't well liked, I am sorry to tell you that, Miss Riven, she commanded our respect in due time. She couldn't earn what was owed her, frankly. We recognized we were dealing with no ordinary animal, and her genius and tenacity are what secured her place among the best minds. Strange, isn't it, the exceptions men make when it serves their interests or fancies.

Another memory, several years later. I happened upon two former classmates at a tavern in Kirsau, and of course we began to reminisce and ask of our fellows. Ferrill—tragic halitosis he always had, who could blame his wife for cuckolding him?—I digress—well then, he said Brandemere had turned up dead, found buried in his garden, and how chilling was that. How so, other than the obvious? Thorpe and I asked.

Don't you remember, he said, that night in the library? Some of us were late studying. Zavet Molnik was off in the shadows and surprised us when she rose to return a book, then gave us pause as she stood in the moonlight coming through the window. Brandemere shouted, Give us a howl, and we laughed. Her back was to us and she said, As you will when the shovel meant to bury you brains you first? Live full these next seven years.

At that, I did remember, as well that several of the fellows made a game of it, teasing her. I dared not, superstitious as I am. Not once did she turn to look, responding to each voice, each prognostication more specific than the last. To my knowledge, Brandemere met the worst fate, and the rest, well, several foretellings have in fact come true.

Coincidence, yes?

I haven't received word from Fewmany since early June. He sent a letter then informing me he was leaving for an extended trip. He didn't say where, which is unlike him, and strange, too, that he has fallen silent. I confess, I am worried. Also perplexed, because along with the letter, he sent his atrocious dog for me to attend.

I would gladly oblige more questions if you have them and welcome your correspondence if only to ensure me of your welfare. May we share a conversation again once this unpleasantness is past.

Sincerely,
William Remarque

WEEK 20

THE FIRST WEEK OF NOVEMBER, NIKOLAS CONFIDED IN ME about the worsening situation outside of Ailliath. A third of Kirsau was under Haaud's control. Giphia and Ilsace had intensified negotiations to get aid from our kingdom. East of us, Thrigin had blocked Haaud's advances into their kingdom and had obstructed Haaud's supply lines into Uldiland.

Nikolas was determined to keep the kingdom out of the war. For now, he had enough advisers willing to work to that end. However, he feared what would happen if he succumbed to the third phase. With Lord Sullyard named as his proxy, whom Nikolas liked and respected although they agreed only half the time, this marginal hold could collapse, even if circumstances remained the same among the allies and enemies beyond our border. As for the plague, Nikolas worried whether the efforts to prepare throughout Ailliath would continue as he intended. He wondered if there might be some who'd prefer he didn't recover from the sickness. Once he did awaken, in what state would he find the kingdom?

Nikolas was the one who asked Harmyn if there was anything she could do.

From her place on the parlor's floor, surrounded by colored pencils, she scrutinized him. She chewed the edge of her amulet. *I can, but the pain you'll have might make you wish you hadn't asked me to do it.*

What kind of pain? he asked.

How you felt when your parents died. Maybe worse, she said.

His expression went flat, his thoughts whirring deep.

Can you do the same to me? I asked.

You have to sleep through like everyone else, she said.

Why? I asked.

I can't risk you, she said.

I realized then not only the danger involved in Nikolas's request but also that Harmyn knew far more than she revealed. *Tell us what you know,* I said.

I won't. I mean to protect you. You have to trust me, she said.

What would it be like? he asked.

Similar to what Wei did with the Guardian warriors. She went into their memories with them and helped them take back their lost pieces. That's the only way I know to explain it, Harmyn said.

That doesn't seem so awful, he said.

It depends on what the shadows hold, she said.

Can Secret be with me? As a witness, he said.

The shadows will be very dark, very ugly. I worry how that will affect her, she said.

I don't care, I said.

What Harmyn said next, she said to me alone. *You understand you'd do for him what Aoife did for Leit? The worst things that have happened to Nikolas, you will hear him tell it. As much as you love him, you will feel that measure of his pain. Can you endure it?* she asked.

I'll have to, won't I? I said to her.

I've warned you, she said.

To both of us, she said, *Nikolas, think about this. Ask more questions before you decide. If we start, we can stop, but I'm not certain how that would affect you during the sleep later. We can start tomorrow night. You shouldn't eat much for dinner.*

The next evening, at half past eight, Harmyn sat in the parlor with Nikolas and me and sang. No one could hear her, but I felt a thrum behind my eyes, which made me drowsy. Nikolas bobbed his head as if he fought sleep. Harmyn walked across the parlor, pulled a chair away from the wall, and set it under a falling guard.

When we entered Nikolas's former bedroom, Harmyn placed a lit candelabra on the floor next to three cushions. Inside, there was a bed, a wardrobe, and a table covered in glasses. Although it was cold enough for a fire, none warmed the chamber.

She gestured for us to sit. Our ears opened with a ringing and a pop. A horse's whinny and a chilly gust entered the open window.

"Secret," he said, reaching for my hand.

"Are you ready?" I asked him.

"I must be," he said.

Harmyn sat across from him, cross-legged, her bare toes visible. She said she was going to lead him to one of his shadows and then to the hole it covered. She warned him he would likely leap from hole to hole. He shouldn't fight it, or anything he remembered or felt as he did. As his witness, Harmyn reminded me, I was to level no judgment. If I was compelled to ask him questions, they should be open ones. What I agreed to do was sacred and what I heard, I could tell no one else.

"I'm also your witness, Nikolas," Harmyn said. "Everything you see and feel, I will, too. You can be silent, or you can speak. Understood? So then. We need to be able to see our hands or feet. Feel your fingers and toes. Keep breathing, no matter what happens. Especially you, Secret."

Moments later, Harmyn placed a tiny sailboat next to Nikolas's knee.

"Where did you find this?" he asked, a joyful surprise in his voice. Then a darkness entered his eyes; yes, as if a shadow had fallen.

"What do you remember?" Harmyn asked.

"We went to the coast, Mother and my sisters. The manor where we stayed had a lake with a pier. I played there with a boat on a string. I made a friend, a boy my age. We were about five. Roger was a servant's son, but I didn't care. My father arrived at some point. Before we were to leave, I gave Roger the boat as a gift. I didn't know my father saw what I did. That night, Father handed me a sailboat. At first, I thought it was a different one, but it wasn't. He said the boy couldn't have it, and neither could I, and he had his valet take it away. I cried to my mother. I could tell she thought what he did was mean, but she told me to obey him. When he found me with her, he said, 'Leave the charity to your mother.'"

"How did you feel?" Harmyn asked.

Nikolas traced the little boat stern to bow. His breathing hitched. "Sad because I wanted my friend to have it. Angry because I wasn't allowed to. Shame because I disappointed him."

Harmyn watched him, then asked, "Where are you now?"

"One of the wards. I'd awakened early and decided to race my horse on the green before school. On my way home, I took a different route than usual, through a poor ward. I remember the old privies and buildings in need of repair and the tired looks, which seemed deeper than a lack of sleep." He sighed. "None of that has changed. It's worse now, with the plague. That morning, I got lost and found myself in an alley, and in a doorway was a little girl. There was a box next to her, and matches strewn all over, as if she'd been robbed. I went to check on her, and when I touched her, she was stiff. I carried her to the street. A man took her from me. Asked nothing."

"You never told me this," I said.

"I meant to. I was too shocked, and then, well, I couldn't."

"When did it happen?"

He wouldn't look at me. "You probably don't remember. We took a long walk after school in the woods. Not long after you turned fourteen," he said.[33]

"I remember. That's the day my mother died," I said.

"I found the little girl that morning," he said.

"Who did you tell?" Harmyn asked.

"My parents. Mother promised to talk to one of the women's leagues about it. But Father," Nikolas said, as he began to shift from side to side, "Father said he was going to make sure my guards kept me away from those places. He had no idea how often I went off to ride alone. And then he turned back to his longsheet, flipped it up like a shield, and said, 'Sometimes death does favors.'"

Nikolas began to pace. "She was a little girl. Four, maybe five. Pretty long brown lashes. She smelled as if no one had washed her dress. I carried her like a contorted doll, and I never learned her name." A pause, then, "No, not there. I don't want to think about that."

"You do it now, or while you're asleep during the plague with someone else leading the kingdom," Harmyn said.

"You don't have to, Nikolas. You can stop," I said, although as I did, I wasn't sure for whose sake. I could feel the black energy seep out of him, into me.

"You can't escape this. You must go in," Harmyn said.

Away from the candles, Nikolas became a shape stalking the room. "The carriage stops. The windows are open. It's a beautiful day, so breezy, there's hardly a stink from the horses around us. I can hear a newsbox. Father's Tell-a-Bell rings and he starts listing his toll."

"How old are you?" Harmyn asked.

"Seven."

"What happened?" Harmyn asked.

"A face appears next to mine," Nikolas said. "We frighten each other and we laugh. He has the dirtiest cheeks and bright blue eyes. He's on the curb on tiptoe looking in. I have an apple in my hand, and I see him stare at it. I give it to him. I hear Father clear his throat, and I wave the boy off. I hope Father didn't see what I did. He doesn't say anything, so I think he didn't. When we return home, I go to my room to play. Father walks in with a riding crop. He comes at me, swatting my legs and backside. He chases me. He doesn't say a word, but I know why he's there. Then he hits me on the thigh and on my hip and the worst one lashes my side and I fall on the ground and curl in a ball and I see him raise his arm again but he walks away. Doesn't say a word. Walks away."

"How do you feel?" Harmyn asked.

"How do I feel," Nikolas said. He picked up a glass from the table and dropped it on the floor. "Like that."

"Don't go near him," Harmyn whispered, grabbing my wrist as I tried to stand, a cry thick as sludge in my lungs.

"Don't go near me. What, are you afraid? I won't hurt you. I'm a good boy. A bad prince but a good boy." For several minutes, he paced the room with the boat cradled in his arms. When he returned to the table, he picked up a cane. "That was the first time Father hit me, but there were others. Rare, but I remember them all."

An ominous stillness was the only warning before he tossed the boat into the air and hit it with the cane with all his might. In one swipe, he struck the glasses. He beat the table, screaming with every blow. When the cane broke, he upended the table and kicked it until the boards cracked. With a piece of that, he pounded the bed, the wardrobe, the walls.

"Stop him, Harmyn. He's going to hurt himself," I said.

"This is the shadow. He has to release it," she said.

Her calm vigil infuriated me. She did nothing to ease his pain, although I knew she could. Her grip on my arm didn't soften, even as my tears streamed out for what he'd suffered, then and now.

At last, he dropped the cane. His keen gored straight through my heart. He held his side, collapsed on the bed, and wept, inconsolable.

"He's about to come back," she said, loosening the hold on my arm.

I crawled up next to him, tugged his shirt away, and pressed my hands against his ribs. The bruise on my face pounded in time with my furious pulse. His pain flooded me, swirling to my center, toward the black hole yawning within. He started to shake, like an animal that barely escaped being prey. As the movement became more intense at his hips, tremors ripped through the rest of him, ceaseless.

"He's having convulsions. Do something," I said.

She sat across from me with her palm on his forehead. "He's all right. The shadow is breaking apart. Nikolas, I'm watching from the gap. It's within your reach. Get it back."

His entire body relaxed. As Harmyn hummed, I laid my hands across his bare chest to embrace the lilt of his good heart.

WEEK 21

DIARY ENTRY 12 NOVEMBER /38

Charlotte's parents hired caregivers, but she's returning to help.
"Her duty" as the only daughter among four children. Latest from
Muriel—her father tried to have her tuition refunded to force
her to return and care for them, but the conservatory refused. She
wrote, "They have a houseful of servants. They don't need me. This
is a battle of wills. I fear what would happen if I capitulated. Please
don't think badly of me. You above anyone understands my wish to
have a life of my own, narrow as it is."

Every night, Harmyn sings everyone to sleep and takes Nikolas
into that room. Whatever she's doing to him seems sinister, even
if it is necessary. Since the first time, he won't allow me to go. He
doesn't want me to hurt, too. A part of me wants to be with him,
but he's right, I can't bear it. It's awful enough when he comes to
me afterward to lie on my lap. His need, so open, I want to shrink
away. But I sit there stroking his head while he cries, and I cry
from the wordless pain welling up in me, until we physically can't
anymore.

Although he seems on the verge of fury or tears, he tends
his responsibilities as usual. To some minds, he overstepped

his bounds last week. I'm certain what Harmyn forced him through has much to do with this. He declared an act of seizure, usually done only in a time of war, of several dozen buildings throughout Rothwyke. The banks cannot claim them now. No one can be evicted, and the vacant apartments will be used as shelters. Nikolas decreed in writing the owners will regain possession once Ailliath—not only Rothwyke—is free of the plague. All the more reason now he can't sleep in the next phase. He's angered quite a few powerful men who don't possess his compassion.

Julia and Lucas are restful. The Misses seem very frail. Dora's office will close next week. Everyone is so tired, she said, so tired.

WEEKLY POST.

8 November /38. Page 1, Column 2

SHELTER REGISTRY FORMED; ALL RESIDENTS MUST VISIT AREA OFFICES; VOLUNTEERS TO ARRIVE SOON—Per the King's decree, Rothwyke residents who have been evicted or otherwise find themselves without homes will be granted shelter through the plague's duration. Those in need must register with his respective Aid and Relief League area office and will likely receive assignments within the same day. To conserve wood and coal, the apartments will be shared, such as a space meant for four will now hold eight. The discomfort of the over-crowding will be temporary, if the plague's sleep falls upon the rest of us as expected on 21 December.

Residents who shall remain in their own homes must register their households with the area offices by 30 November to indicate whether they will have family or hired help. At this time, the Aid and Relief League, ward leaders, and town officials have not decided whether to require location to group shelters for those without care or to arrange daily visits from volunteers.

Regarding our young ones, they are expected to recover on 6 December. In conference with parents, ward leaders, and Aid and Relief League workers, certain walk-ups and houses will be designated as group shelters to care for them while the adults sleep. Efforts will be made to keep children with their siblings and friends within their own blocks. Families will receive assignments no later than 15 December.

Within the next two weeks, residents should expect to see many new faces as volunteers move to Rothwyke to assist with daily tasks and municipal services. Most will be assigned to group shelters. All others will be housed in buildings under the King's decree or be accommodated as guests by our residents. The majority of volunteers will travel from other towns in Ailliath; some will be visitors from nearby kingdoms.

From the Plague of Silences Recollection Project Archives, Selected Excerpts

Diary No. 293. Male, 36, luminotypist

Delivered portraits. Beautiful, if I say so myself, even of the homely ones, uglier still with the withered arms and legs and sunken chests. This plague. Not sure who was more grateful for the barter. Relieved now, but won't be if I'm pissing pins and needles next week. Had a glass at The Toothless Manticore, got a gash stopping an indecent assault, carried a fellow home too weak to stand on his own two feet. Taverns and teahouses open, almost every shop except for dry goods closed. Walked until nightfall, nothing else to do. Noticed on several street corners, sculptures of fanciful beasts. Made of wood, paper, fabric, and metal, very colorful and expertly crafted. Some have cranks, which when turned, animate the beasts' heads, jaws, tails, and limbs. Waved to a man in a dashing blue coat who was repairing one.

Diary No. 468. Female, 9

Awake must write fast. In dream I was in Rothwick but it wasn't Rothwick in that funny way you know a place but don't in a dream. I was with many cildren standing on a gold road and these very big weels were turning and making music chimey and tingely. We had just begun to sing toghether the song from the big weels and I heard screeming. I turned to see people running toward us and smoke rising from the huts in the distens. And then I saw men with swords chopping and grabbing as our people ran away but some toward them with axs and shovles. A little girl with light purpl eyes who was Harmin but not Harmin stepped out from our group and turned to us and said We will come back another time and right then as a sword came at her head I woke up.

Diary No. 307. Male, 54, physician

Periods of wakefulness now, lasting seconds in some cases, others half an hour or more. Children will respond to names. Said they've been dreaming, pleasant ones and nightmares. Odd how many have mentioned dreaming of dragons and gold, objects such as chalices, rings, coins, and crowns. Not all rest so easily now. Incidents of quaking fits and violent outbursts (kicking, punching), which require some children to be bound. Sadly, last week, the death toll doubled. Thus far this week, although not confirmed, it appears the toll will double again. After speaking with parents and examining bodies, no cause seems clear. The children simply stopped breathing. Why? The registrar promised to give us tallies with sex, age, ward of residence, but he said there appears to be no concentrations. Total dead from 11 Oct, start of second phase, to 4 Nov: 341.

Interview No. 7. Female; age during plague, 11; current occupation, children's health advocate

Probably not many admit they thought about not waking here. I did. Weren't only because I saw what might be, working my fingers to the bone until I was long in the tooth. There's worse things than being poor, and that's feeling like you can't live with what happens in this world. How old was I? Eleven. Old enough. By then, I paid attention to the newsboxes. The horrible things happening in other kingdoms, that dragon menace burning villages, all sorts of trouble in Rothwyke. Among the people I knew. My dearest friend's mother was blind in one eye because her father beat the woman senseless. Everyone knew. No one did a thing. He stayed. She never left. But she had no choice then, right? I had another friend. She was older by two, three years. We saw her belly grow. She said she was getting fat, and then the fat was gone, but her parents took in a baby nephew, they said.

And then. My grandfather, he was good as gold. I never heard him say an unkind word about anyone. He liked his drink some, but he was never mean. He worked every day of his life. He loved me, called me his Little Bird. If ever I was sad or afraid, I could go to him and he'd make me feel better. Then one day, he was dead. Walked to his job one morning and fell like a heap. How could he leave me as he did?

So when I slept, I saw where I could go. You saw them, too, didn't you, the other places you could be, still you, but different. I thought to do it, never to wake up again where my grandfather wasn't, never to know again the terrible things that happened and happened, over and over, everywhere.

Why did I wake? I remember, I was in and out of dreams, searching like, to find where I might want to be. In one, there was Grandfather. He took my hand—oh I remember how happy I was to touch him—and said to me, "Little Bird, there are people you don't know yet who need your tender heart. What I gave you, give to them."

More than thirty years on, I still cry when I think of this. I still cry when I think how the children who woke up were never the same again. Those who didn't wake, well, how great their suffering must have been here, and how good they went to their peace.

WEEK 22

THE TWENTY-SECOND WEEK, I WENT TO THE WOODS ALONE. THE garden required tending, the cottage some dusting, wood some chopping, but I couldn't muster the vitality. For several nights, I'd dreaded sleep. Once I slipped in, I fell into the lair of the ogress, with her filth and feral stink, where she boiled children alive and ate them, bones and all. I awoke each time unable to breathe, clawing the air.

I left Harmyn and Nikolas with the promise I'd return in three days. Alone, I walked among the skeletal trees. When I was hungry, I foraged mushrooms and the last apples. When I was tired, I slept where I found myself, with a creature to keep me warm. For hours, I wept as Aoife had early in her exile—for every reason why. For all that happened, all I suffered, all the pain I'd caused.

The second morning, a crow alerted me to the approach of two men on one horse. I stood near the garden as they arrived. Hugh helped Nikolas from the saddle and nearly dragged him into the cottage. Their intrusion angered me, and Hugh could tell.

The moment Hugh placed him on the bed, Nikolas wrapped in a quilt, turned to the wall, and curled into himself.

Miss, Hugh wrote in the notebook I handed him, **phosishen said plage simtons bad. Harmin told me to bring him said you will know what to do.**

Tell her I <u>don't</u> know. She must come, I wrote.

Please something is very wrong, he wrote.

Hugh patted Nikolas on the shoulder before he left. When I brushed the hair from his face, Nikolas cringed away from my touch. I fed the fire. I made tea he wouldn't drink. I looked around the cottage. On the high shelf where I'd put it months before was Aoife's manuscript. As he slept, I sat with paper, pen, and ink and began to translate her words, compelled to do so at last. The ink's smell, the paper's texture, and the whir of clear thoughts made me cry. When I found the white flower Egnis gave me pressed within, I cried more.

Near twilight, I went to the stream. I set the full pail aside to watch the sunset through the trees. A fox drank, then raised her head, looking to my right. Nikolas shuffled toward me and dropped at my side. When I took his hand, he felt ghostly, more form than substance. His pupils were dilated, the irises eclipsed. I wrapped my arm around his back, almost expecting it to slip through his flesh. I couldn't tell if he breathed.

A stag crept along the water's edge, his majestic antlers held high, the setting sun behind him. He moved as a silhouette, without dimension, still beautiful. I pointed to him, Nikolas's favorite among beasts, but Nikolas observed him with indifference.

I pulled my notebook from my pocket. Nikolas took it from me. He studied the bruise on my cheek. As he scrawled on a blank page, I expected him to ask, why is it there? who did this to you? Instead, I read,

Veins are strands in the rope of fate & we cannot untie the knots which bind us.

I leaned away from him. His body was near me, but his voice, as I knew it, was not inside.

Oh the burden of knowing the good & evil your blood has done, fathers kings mothers queens

I tried to take the notebook, but he wrenched aside to scrawl,

Oh the horror you will repeat their deeds, war without, war within, war on innocents strangers & kin

With a swipe, I snatched the pages and threw them as far as I could. I knelt in front of him and clutched his icy hands in mine. "Where are you, Nikolas?" I asked aloud. He cocked his head as if he'd detected a noise. "Are you lost?" I asked. His eyes met mine. "Please, come back to me," I said.

He blinked, then stared as if he couldn't figure out who I was. My fingers thrust through his hair and I kissed him, breathing him in. He drew back to look at me. His pupils contracted with a glimmer. When I moved to sit on his lap, a stagnant energy broke free, spiraled into an ascendant flow, and released into another kiss, this one returned. As his hands swept under my skirt and found the warmth of my skin, I knew I had been lost to him, too. We tore at each other, searching for the heat of our bodies, that moment, now.

ON THE TRAY ALONG WITH OUR BREAKFAST WAS A NOTE FROM Dora Thursdale, addressed to Harmyn and me. "Please come to the Elgins as soon as you can," she'd written.

We skipped our meal and took a horse from the stables. Along the route, few people were outside enduring the cold. At one corner, a young man sat on a stack of longsheets and puffed clouds into the air. Two blocks from the walk-up, a bearded man with a blue scarf hurried to a bread box carrying a cozy-covered teapot and several cups. The bread box attendant served loaves with gloved hands, and the man poured steaming tea for the attendant and three customers.

When we reached my old building, a group of people were gathered near the front steps, their faces mournful. We hitched the mare and went inside.

The Misses Acutt stood in their doorway, clutching handkerchiefs. Short Miss pointed to the stairs. Harmyn rushed ahead of me.

Not Julia, please, I thought, appalled that I did.

The Elgins' door was open. Neighbors and garden volunteers stood in groups of two and three. Dora handed me a card which read "They lost their Lucas."

On a board near the window was the boy's body. His mother, vacant with shock, slumped in a chair nearby. Her hands dangled into the clutches of women who knelt on both sides, one of them Jane.

In the children's room, Harmyn sat cross-legged on the bed. Julia was awake. Her eyes held mine as I approached. I shifted Flowsy to lie on her shoulder. On the pillow next to hers was Lucas's wooden sword.

My mother's voice came to me: "Your brothers Noose and Knot, dead before they were alive, spared you the grief of their loss, if you had loved them." Hearing this again infuriated me. That I thought of Duncan and Riley deepened my sorrow.

"I'm so sorry," I said aloud.

She wants to talk to you, Harmyn said.

She knows what you can do? I asked.

By now, all the children know, she said.

I heard an avian whoosh and a snap and then Julia said, "I begged him not to go."

"I don't understand," I said.

"When you sleep, you're going to dream of things that happened, things that didn't, and things that could," Julia said. "You'll see people you know. Sometimes they'll be the same as you know them, but not always. They might be younger or older, or nicer or meaner."

I remembered Harmyn's letter with the overlapping circles. "You and Lucas saw each other in these dreams?"

"We played and had good times, and we visited each other when we were grown."

"Then what do you mean, you begged him not to go?"

"When you sleep, you find out you don't have to wake up here. You can go into another dream and stay there. He said he didn't want to come back."

"Why not?" I asked.

Julia stared ahead toward her room's entrance. There stood Mr. Elgin, his arm useless in the sling, his face blank with grief.

She leapt from the bed, charged him, and clawed at him as he backed into the parlor. He doubled over when one of her blows struck his groin. The visitors stared, deaf to her screams and shocked that she moved, as I ran to stop her. She pushed through the adults toward her mother, who reached her arms out in a gesture of entreat, not consolation.

The girl slapped her mother across the face. "You did nothing. You never have, and Lucas believed you never would."

Harmyn darted past me and circled Julia in her arms.

"I'd rather die if I had to be like you. But I don't. I won't be," Julia said.

I touched Julia's shoulder. She turned from Harmyn and clutched my waist. I couldn't look either of her parents in the eye.

Seated on her bed, I held her. She wept for her brother, but she also wept for herself. She didn't have to tell me why. As she hugged me, my arms ached to the marrow for the times I reached out for nothing and finally learned it hurt less to hold back. Like me, she should have been able to turn to her mother for comfort, but how could she when her mother was a source of the pain?

Harmyn sang lullabies until Julia slept again, peaceful.

"Why did Lucas leave?" I asked.

"There wasn't enough love to keep him here."

WEEK 23

I HADN'T SEEN CHARLOTTE SINCE NIKOLAS'S DEPARTURE BAN-quet a year and a half earlier. When she sent a note she wanted to visit, I almost refused. I'd written to her about my bruise and various pains, but I didn't want her to see me so damaged. My mood rarely lifted beyond apathy but invigorated to a seething anger when the knot at my navel tightened and the ache below intensified to a churning throb. In the end, I relented with some hope seeing her would cheer me.

She arrived for afternoon tea. As she stepped into the parlor, I saw a nurse holding an infant and a little girl in tow. The children, Tom and Liddy. I stood with effort, forcing a smile. Tears slipped down Charlotte's face as she kissed my right cheek. Her mouth moved as if she were speaking, then she stopped, reached into a tapestry bag, and took out a notebook.

Sorry, she wrote. **I'm not accustomed to the silence.**

I gestured for them to sit. Charlotte lowered next to me on the settee as the nurse took a chair, with Liddy at her knee. My hands tingled as I poured our tea. The weakness in my arms had become worse within the past days. I pushed cups and saucers to the nurse and Liddy, who eyed me with horror and fascination. With my silver hair, tawny skin, mismatched eyes, purple bruise, and wizened shape, I surely looked like a monster. From Charlotte's expression, she appeared to instruct her stepdaughter not to be rude.

I took out my notebook. **We haven't any cookies for her. Rations remain strict.**

Please no, I understand, she wrote.

She studied my face and hands and burst into tears again.

Secret, I've so missed you & I am so happy to see you but forgive me you look as if you're in terrible pain. Have you not told me the truth in your letters? she wrote.

No lies, only not whole truths. Didn't want to worry you, I wrote.

My parents did the same, she wrote. **Father is so thin. He'll hardly eat. He says he can't stomach it. Mother has the blot & her body shrunk—like yours. He's lethargic but Mother walks through the house looking behind drapes & under beds & in wardrobes. I asked her why & she said she wants to make sure he didn't come back but wouldn't say who he is. She's imagining things.** Charlotte paused, then added, **Let me introduce Liddy.**

Charlotte called the girl to us. Liddy had large brown eyes, a broad forehead, and perfect auburn ringlets. I gave a welcoming smile, but her bottom lip puffed out and her eyes grew wet. Charlotte hugged her and, although I couldn't hear what was said, I could tell Charlotte spoke to her kindly. A moment later, Liddy took the nurse's free hand and walked across the room toward a pastoral painting which filled a fourth of the wall.

She's a good-natured girl yet often shy. Perhaps I should have left them back, but I wanted you to meet them before— Charlotte held her pencil—**before you sleep. Are you afraid?**

Yes, I wrote.

Weekly Post reported 729 children died thus far. No warning. They stop breathing & they're gone. I couldn't bear it if that happened to mine.

I could give no reassurance her children, once sick, would survive.

To the extent we were able, Charlotte and I had a conversation. She asked about my father and Nikolas; I asked her of her husband and home. Charlotte hoped she might meet Harmyn—I'd written of the young singer in my charge, but nothing of her uncommon abilities—and I said she was helping a friend pack for a move, but didn't say that was my father. She inquired what I planned to do after the plague; I inquired what she would do while we slept for three months. While she amused me with anecdotes about her new life, I was glad my affectionate feelings for her hadn't changed, despite distance and circumstance.

During a rest while we drank another cup, the nurse walked over to give the baby to Charlotte before she and Liddy bustled away to explore another room. His wispy hair was the same color as his sister's. Charlotte held him on her lap, clapped his tiny hands, and kissed his fingers. Tom smiled with his whole face, dancing his arms and legs. Gracefully she lifted him and offered him to me. I raised my hands. My strength was unpredictable, and I'd never touched an infant, much less held one. Charlotte persisted. I kept my groan silent as I extended my withered arms.

When his warmth touched my chest, my heart flooded with tenderness. I had no discomfort as I cradled him tighter. He was awake, his brown eyes on mine. He gave me careful study. I brought him to my shoulder. I pressed my cheek to his heavy little head and breathed. What Nikolas told me about his nephew Iwen, I thought, Babies do have a scent. I closed my eyes when I felt him sigh.

I glanced at Charlotte. She held up a message.

Looks like you're ready for your own, she'd written.

That instant, the pain oozed back into my body. I returned Tom before my arms slackened and the loneliness turned my blood icy. My muscles contracted against my bones; my organs seemed to shrivel.

I'll not have any children, I wrote.

Of course you will. After this horrid sickness you'll find a smart, kind man & have darling little Secrets. You shall. You must! Charlotte peered around, then wrote in small letters, **I recommend the bother before.** She arched her eyebrows.

I shook my head as a flush rose to my cheeks, not for her suggestive remark but for the blunt realization which came to me: I have the power to end this.

Charlotte didn't stay much longer. I promised to arrange our next visit so she could meet Harmyn and see Nikolas. We clutched hands, she kissed me, and I went to my room.

Yes, I thought as I sprawled on my bed, whatever inheritance I carry from Aoife can finally be spent. Indeed, if she'd never become pregnant or had purged herself of the twins, she wouldn't have married Wyl. She might have continued to map Ailliath or journeyed away to another kingdom. There would have been no exile. No travel to a distant Guardian settlement. No marriage to Leit, no birth of Wei. Skip across generations—no fraught mothers and troubled daughters, no Katya, no Zavet, no Secret.

Yet, there I was, the last daughter of this line. I knew, because my mother had been one, there were Voices in my blood. As Aoife had explained, a Voice could be conceived only if the father had Guardian blood himself. So, if more of these strange children had to be born, let them come through someone else, as Harmyn had. Let those dormant seeds split into growth. And if I were not to bear a Voice, only a daughter, odd as I was or not, she need never exist at all. Our miserable legacy could die with me.

By dinner, the revelation's comfort had worn off and my dark mood returned. I was in bed by the time Harmyn sang her lullaby to the castle and asleep as she dragged Nikolas through another maelstrom of shadows.

During my slumber, I plunged into a dream.

A crow called. Glass cracked. There were screams—animal, human, either, both. The feral stink—the ogress was near. I saw a black feather, falling. I reached for it . . . and I dropped to a forest floor. A familiar voice called my name. I ran to embrace Fig Tree, covered in fruit, but the ground tremored, rent apart, and pulled me away from her. The ogress leapt over the abyss, and when her feet touched the earth, she revealed her full face. Mother. She grabbed my arm and eyed my hand, which had turned into a mushroom. "My little fungus," she said. Her maw gaped wide and—

When my eyes flew open, they met Harmyn's, lit by candles. The black hole in my chest expanded until its edge threatened to turn me inside out. I rose up and knocked away Harmyn's extended hand. *Leave me alone*, I said.

I ran to the second floor. A whoosh filled my ears. The pendulum clock ticked. The guard outside Nikolas's room snored in a chair. I leapt on Nikolas's bed, burrowed under the covers, and clung to his side. He roused with a start, then he held me as I trembled.

"Don't let me go," I said.

"What's happened?" he asked.

The lurch in my gut brought up bile and certainty I didn't dare swallow but couldn't spit out. "A terrible dream," I said as a hideous feeling came over me, worse than dread, a pure mortal terror. My bruised cheek pounded.

"Breathe, Love." He shook me. "Why aren't you breathing? Secret, what's the matter?"

That, I couldn't tell him because I didn't know. What crushed me wouldn't be named. I crawled on top of him. "Don't send me away. Please. Let me lie here for a while."

He cradled my head against his bare chest. A moment later, I heard no heartbeat. Dead silence.

WEEK 24

THE RING OF KEYS PRESSED AGAINST MY LEG AS I SAT AT JULIA'S bedside, tidied the Misses' apartment, and walked to my father's house.

At the door, I turned the three locks and set them once inside. Father wasn't there. He'd moved to the castle the day before. Father donated the food he'd hoarded to the Aid and Relief League and left everything else in the house except for some clothing, some bedding, and his three-hundred-year-old map.

With the drapes drawn, near dusk, I could hardly see in the parlor. I found a lamp on the mantel. The simple act of lighting it flared my memory of certain dark rooms in another quiet house.

The truth is, I didn't know what I'd come to find. When I stood in the place where Father had discovered her dead, I wondered where she'd found the mushrooms. Child of a forest that she was, surely she learned from her own mother what was safe and what was poisonous. On one of her afternoon walks, had she crossed the green, entered the woods, and searched the shade for her last meal? Had she bought a pint from a market vendor and noticed someone had made a lethal mistake, as had happened before?[34] How great her misery must have been to welcome the deliberate agony of that death. The fortitude she had to not take to her bed but to sit at her table, waiting for the final throes.

With the lamp turned high, I went to the third floor into Father's bedroom. Everything seemed in order, although his pillow was missing.

I peeked into his wardrobe. There hung his fine suits. Then I looked into hers, full of blouses and skirts, a coat, evening gowns, walking shoes, slippers; the drawers packed with undergarments, stained cloths, handkerchiefs. On the dressing table, the items appeared to be in the places they'd always been.

I went downstairs to my old room. The boxes of diaries hadn't been disturbed since my last visit. One deep breath, then another, and I pulled out the diaries from the year before I was born through the first years of my childhood. There were the bleed days and the absence of them. No marks for three months and a page torn from the binding—a note from my father, expunged?—words, words, words, then nothing from the twenty-second of September to the seventh of October. From that date onward, while some entries seemed shorter, there was no break for anything other than a typical off day.

I huddled with my head to my knees. How many hours I'd spent in that same position, barely breathing to enter the quiet blackness where I felt nothing, not even the urge to cry.

Within myself, the thump of my heartbeat whispered in my ears. Louder then, I heard the flutter of a page, a little girl's giggle, and a hiss. Again and again, the sounds repeated until they came to me as if sung in a round. There came random hitches of silence as the flutter, giggle, and hiss looped.

I felt myself contract, drawing me into the shortened sleeves and hem of my dress. Three quick throbs surged under my ribs and with them, three separate images of my father, his turned back, his eyes on a letter, his tight mouth pressed shut.

Crouched there, I was once again a little girl, alone with my books, so quiet, so quiet, because there would be a hiss for the slightest noise, an observational "oh" or tiny titter, and sometimes Father, present but absent, stood by and did not defend my simplest expression.

Look at me! I screamed inside, the words I couldn't say as the mute little girl with the knot at her navel tied to her tongue.

He must have seen what she did to me, yet did nothing, I thought, or did not see, because he couldn't face the truth.

She didn't want me.

Oh yes, she did her duty. She kept me fed, clean, and warm. She kept me out of harm's way, behind that pen in a corner when I was very small, sealed off in the house and courtyard when I was older.

Duty is not love, I thought. This wasn't a revelation, but Aoife's own words about her twins, whom she didn't despise but admitted she tended with the diligence of an animal mother without the love of a human one. A cruelty, to bring innocent lives into such absence. My palms and soles stung as I tried to recall a single hug or kiss for comfort or affection from my mother—and could not. Not once.

I returned to the diaries. That my mother worked as much as ever after I was born seemed impossible, not without help.

Suddenly, a light blinded me. Elinor and I didn't hear each other scream. She dropped a stack of folded sheets on the floor, knelt down, and looked at me with concern. I knew she'd worked for my parents since I was too young to remember. Although she'd expressed sympathy after my mother died, we had never spoken of her.

I fumbled in my pocket for my notebook. **Why are you here?**

Forgot to cover ferniture for dust, Elinor wrote.

May I ask you questions? I wrote.

She nodded.

Who took care of me when I was a baby?

Not sure what you mean, she wrote.

Mother worked much, I wrote, then gestured toward the diaries.

My daughtur Bess she had her second boy then. Wet nerse. Mrs. R milk didn't drop. My face must have betrayed my feelings because she added, **Common. No shame.**

Did Bess live in my parents' house or with her family? I wrote.

She kept you. Bess very fond of you. Quiet gentel little babe. Mr. R came to see you every day but Mrs. R nervuse mother. Cried when she held you. I told her she was new to it that was all.

Dear Elinor, I thought, assuming my mother was merely frightened rather than resentful. **My father?** I wrote.

So proud. Big smile when you were in his arms. Elinor glanced at me, lingering on the bruise. **You grew to a fine young woman. She was a good mother.**

No, she wasn't. You felt the silence in this house. I slammed the notebook closed and picked up the pile of sheets. Lamp in hand, I waited for her in the hall. I followed her from room to room, pulling furniture into groups and draping them with the fabric, as if we were about to leave for a long holiday.

When I saw her to the door, she touched the left side of my face. I pressed my hand against hers, rough and kind. She kissed me, walked down the steps, and waved to the lamplighter attending his work.

Door locked, vesta in hand, I returned to my room. I burned the diary page by page. Although I wanted to destroy the others, I knew what would satisfy me most. From the faded blue chest, I took the nesting dolls. I wrenched them apart, matched their hollow bodies, and lined them up. To the fire I fed them, one by one, screaming into the flames' fury as the thirteenth blazed and its solid core turned to ash.

THIS, I THOUGHT, WAS A DREAM.

My body swayed with the sweet notes of a lullaby. When I opened my eyes, I found myself in my gown, covered with my cloak, my boots laced, standing in the glade outside of Old Woman's cottage.

"You must call on the animals. They must be witnesses for the children," Harmyn said.

"Haven't I done enough? Don't I have a say in this?" I asked.

"You do. But you know better than anyone the gentle alchemy which happens when something, or someone, listens."

I remained silent.

"The plague is almost over for them, but shadows still hide what they must see," she said. "Please, Secret. We need you."

The bare trees reached toward first light. My breath hovered as a mist as I said, "Hear me. Heed me. Come to our aid." A gust whipped my silver hair as a chorus answered. *Whir chirp hum yip grunt bell screech howl.*

Children streamed out from among the trees. Babies slept in the arms of the older ones, and the younger ones trailed hand in hand. As they gathered to sit on the ground, the animals came to join them, creatures of every kind for whom the woods was home.

"I need something to stand on. Call a stone for me," Harmyn said.

"I can't do that," I said.

"Only because you've never tried before."

I tried, and failed, to roll a stone from the abandoned wall and the huge rounded rock in the woods. Then I touched my hands to the earth, asked for a piece of its deep heart, and felt the ground rumble. A hidden power welled up within me. Under Harmyn's feet, a jagged gray rock cracked through. As I stood, she rose above me, higher than my shoulders.

Harmyn called for the children's attention. "There are things left unsaid. You're here to speak them. Unless you do, you will remain trapped in the shadows."

"What are we supposed to say?" an older boy asked.

"The darkest secrets of your heart," she said.

"Why must we tell them?" a girl asked.

"Because the time for silence is done and the truth must be revealed," Harmyn said.

"What is *she* doing here? She's an adult—and she's not wearing blue," a child hidden in the crowd said.

"That's Secret. She played with us in the woods," a little voice shouted.

"And she called these animals to listen to you," Harmyn said.

"Won't the adults look for us?" one asked.

"I sang them to sleep. No one is coming. You're safe here," she said.

A little girl with a wren perched on her finger approached. "We can tell anything?" she asked.

"Anything," Harmyn said. She scaled down the rock's side and knelt next to her.

"No matter how terrible?"

"Yes."

"Will you listen, too?"

"I will listen—and believe you."

The little girl looked down. "My uncle made me go into the room and touched me in bad ways and he said if I ever told—"

So began the litany of heartbreaking truths. One at a time, each child sat with Harmyn and the animal who offered its witness. Child after child after child, telling what they had suffered themselves or from the witness of what happened to others. Cruel words, cold glances, benign neglect, bitter hunger, harsh beatings, tragic deaths, quick slaps, heinous violations, and lingering silences. For some, the hurts and horrors had repeated for months and years. For others, terrible shocks occurred only once, but the pain never went away.

As I listened, time ceased its natural cycle. The sun lagged in its arc. I noticed a cloud swirling around the sun, impossibly red, with a long neck, wings, and tail.

She who first saw All saw this, too.

Throughout the day into the cold night, the children and animals huddled together. Wolves and foxes suckled infants, although they had none of their own. Hunting beasts brought their prey, which the children cooked and ate with the reverence of sacrifice.

They were silent when dawn came again, until Harmyn said from the top of the rock, "Do you feel lighter now?"

The children looked at one another as if the collective truth was more than they could bear. A long low hum of discontent began to rise.

"Secret, stand up here with me," Harmyn said.

I climbed next to her. As far as I could see, children and animals pressed together as one breathing, feeling, beautiful being.

Julia, who had spoken hours before, tore from the crowd and stared up at Harmyn.

"What is it?" Harmyn asked.

Her body shook as she parted her lips. The word escaped; the question, Why? Her mouth softened again as if to speak but instead she screamed screamed screamed with rage.

As Julia paused to gather more breath, a wolf and a baby joined the cry. Then the throats of the children and beasts opened and gave way to a raging which threatened to shatter the earth, sky, and all that was between.

"Scream until the shadows break their hold!" Harmyn shouted. "See what they hide!"

Harmyn took my hand and leaned into me for support. I anchored my feet against the rock, my legs suddenly strong. I felt the circle of the earth spiral through me and into Harmyn's palm. I remained still, allowing what had begun, but I trembled with fearful awe.

"Enter the rage! What does it hide?! Scream!" Harmyn called.

As the sun continued its ascent, a burst of rays filled the sky. The screams transformed. The children keened with grief, clutching their chests, each other, until the sobs gave way to peals of laughter, clear and bright as bells. They embraced one another and held their middles and rolled in ecstatic fits.

When Harmyn started to sing, the spiral reversed through me, returning to the earth. As the animals took their leave, the children hummed the melody along with her. They clapped at the song's end.

"What happened?" I asked.

"The first turn of a new world," she said.

WEEK 25

ON THE SIXTH OF DECEMBER, ALMOST TWO WEEKS BEFORE THE winter solstice, the children awoke. They staggered into the rooms of those who had watched them and out to the desolate streets. At once, there was much to feel—sorrow for the dead, fear of what was to come for the rest of us, relief for those who recovered.

Among the children who survived, there was a restless energy about them. This I saw for myself as those who visited the woods before returned to play. They talked among themselves with fervor, ran with exuberance, and seemed to vibrate when sitting still. Even when they comforted each other—all of them had siblings or friends who didn't awaken—their faces shone with vitality.

As a respite from our worries, the Guardians—not yet identified as such, but they were responsible—arranged for celebrations across town. The afternoon of the eleventh of December, thousands joined for food, drink, and revelry.

Because of his meeting schedule, Nikolas couldn't be with us. Father and I escorted Harmyn and Julia to the Area 4 festivities, of which Margana's shop was part. Children who knew us from the woods ran up in greeting, then dashed off to watch jugglers and acrobats. On a dais, musicians played as the children danced. Along with the adults, they stuffed their faces with savory pies and sweet cakes.

Margana stood near her shop's door. Against the wall were baskets of clothing, fabric swatches, ribbons, and belts to create makeshift costumes. Harmyn and Julia rushed over with their friends. I noticed Solden Gray, hesitant to join in. A moment later, a girl his age led him to the group, which he approached with a shy grin on his face. I turned to look for Leo. When our eyes met, we waved, relieved to see each other, but didn't move from our places. I sensed we were both too worn to scrawl a conversation.

A hand brushed my arm. I flinched in pain, not surprise.

Margana held out her notebook. **My scraps are in good use**, she'd written.

How kind to treat everyone, especially the children, I wrote.

It is our way, she wrote.

How do you feel? she wrote.

I'm ready to sleep. Too much pain these last weeks, I wrote.

She held my hand as she looked into my eyes. Be strong, she seemed to say. When she released me, she wrote, **I'll be so glad to speak to you again.**

I nodded. When I glanced up, I saw my father with Harmyn and Julia. He wore a hat with four dangling points with bells on each end. He had never looked so silly, and I burst into a belly laugh along with the children.

Once the full moon was high and the cold almost unbearable, the crowds began to return home. Harmyn asked if Father could take her back to the castle while I escorted Julia to the walk-up. I asked what was wrong.

I don't know, Harmyn said. *For a few days, I thought I was feeling a change in the children, but that's not it.* She held Father's sleeve as they stepped away.

At the Elgins' door, I dreaded to leave Julia, which she intuited, because she kissed me on the cheek and squeezed my hand.

By the time I returned to the castle, it was almost nine o'clock. In the parlor, Nikolas was stretched out on a settee near the fire. He held a glass of gin, the first time I'd seen that, and he looked more relaxed than he had in months. The week prior, Harmyn ceased their nightly ordeal and said Nikolas would be well through the plague's end. His body bore no sign of the plague's ravages, and he could hear again. When I eased next to him, he offered a sip of his drink, which I tried, wincing at the taste. He held out his notebook with a message that Father and Harmyn had retired and Harmyn seemed quite anxious.

I glanced toward the parlor's entrance. Hugh was gone. Skipped to the water closet, I thought. Exhausted, I leaned into Nikolas. He draped his arm around my shoulder. I closed my eyes.

Suddenly, he slipped away. The fire glowed as embers, there was a bright light, and a note at Nikolas's fingertips. Harmyn stood by with a lamp and her hand on Hugh, who cried as he knelt in front of Nikolas.

On his official stationery, Nikolas scrawled a letter with his full signature. He gave it to Hugh and gripped his arm. Hugh bolted from the parlor.

I looked to Nikolas, then Harmyn. My ears popped open.

"His wife is due to give birth in two months. Nikolas gave him a letter to fetch the physician, but there's no use," Harmyn said.

"If the labor is delayed, that might not be so," I said.

"She's not the only one. Every woman who is pregnant is sick, too," Harmyn said.

"Why?" Nikolas asked.

"Because Nature has a cruel wisdom," I said, without a doubt of its truth.

Seconds later, I rushed to the nearest water closet. I vomited until my gut was empty but continued to heave. Nikolas burst in and crouched at my side. I knew what he was thinking. My cycles had come as usual; I'd drunk my teas without fail. I shook my head. He sighed with relief.

The knot at my navel wrenched violently. I showed no hint of pain as my belly began to cramp. "A dreadful shock. I'm going to my room. Find Harmyn and check on your servants and staff," I said.

I walked away upright, although I wanted to crumple. In my room in a cold sweat, I alternated between sitting and pacing. The agony intensi-fied. I didn't ask for help. Whatever rupture was about to occur, no one could stop it. I wanted no witness, especially not Nikolas, who had en-dured enough on his own and didn't need to see more of mine.

The clock on my night table ticked to midnight. On my bed, I crouched on my hands and knees. My mind slipped loose, and I was aware of

> —young and wide-eyed, Bren. Next to him,
> a physician. Between them, a table covered with metal
> tools. I refused those men who urged me to my back, to
> submit to their prying eyes and fingers. I crouched on the
> floor, knees, palms speckled with dirt—

Then I was held under pressure, in blackness.
I pushed my abdomen against a terrible throb—
a clot that failed to knot—

> On all fours I screamed with rage and strained with wrath—

On my back, my limbs fell wide as the throb tried
one last time to bind, but I breathed—I breathed—

> I was both before the cut, then—

I was separate and afraid. I cried. Whispers reached
my ear. *Hush, baby.* I wailed. *Calme-toi, bébé.* I screamed.
Usu mchanga. I howled. I heard a noise and turned to

suckle the shhh until it rose to a chilling hiss, the sound of
the throb. A hard node where the blood could no longer
enter seized to hold my tongue silent.

For seven years after, I could not, would not, speak.

A small hand pressed over the queen bee's stings. I opened my eyes.

"Inside, I always knew," I said to Harmyn, "she never wanted me. My
blue brothers. Noose and Knot. Duncan and Riley. Better I'd been born
dead like them. Better I'd not been at all."

The child wiped the tears from my face.

"Why did I survive? Why must I know this truth without a doubt?"
I asked.

She climbed on the bed, lay on my stomach, and curled in like a snail.
I rested my palm on Harmyn's head as I felt a hum from my navel to my
throat, which cleansed the wound that wept there but did not heal the
damage done.

WEEK 27

THE DAY BEFORE THE WINTER SOLSTICE, NIKOLAS, FATHER, AND I
rose at dawn to be with Harmyn. She opened Father's and my ears, led us
to the castle's outer wall, and instructed the guards to let us through the
gate. At the first chime of Harmyn's bell, the legion of children crowded
near the entrance sat on the ground, ringing their own. Few adults were
among them. When Harmyn began to sing, the young ones joined her,
their projection clear, the union of their voices transcendent. They had
been deaf, then asleep, for months, but they knew every note and word.

As I listened, I welcomed a respite from pain. The second phase had
debilitated me. After the night the unborn bled away and the truth of my
birth became conscious, I could barely hold against the force drawing me
into darkness. Like so many others, I tried to keep a brave face although I
felt as if I were dying inside.

I refused the tears which came as she led the children in a song I
knew, translated into our language, but not from our time.

Innocent, remind us what is pure.
Innocent, remind us what is true.

Innocent, awake from the great sleep.
Behold what waits for you.[35]

This was a Guardians' song of welcome for their newborns. Centuries before, Aoife heard this joyful sound when she visited the settlement to warn them of a possible war, when she labored with Wei, and as Wei sang it with her dying father.

When they finished, Harmyn shook the bell over her head. The children rose to their feet and took candles from their pockets. Harmyn gave Nikolas a candle and vesta.

"Light it, and touch the wicks in reach," she said. "These candles will burn in their windows through the long night. Tomorrow morning, a very new day will begin."

With ease, Nikolas bent on one knee and offered the flame to the nearest children. He watched them turn to each other, sharing the fire. A little girl in a patched coat whispered to him, then kissed him on the cheek. He extended his palm, which she accepted, and he kissed her mittened hand.

When the crowd began to thin, Harmyn gestured for us to return to the castle. The distant noises on both sides of the wall fell silent to my ears.

After lunch, Harmyn and I went to Warrick for one last visit. Mr. Elgin let me in without meeting my eye, and Mrs. Elgin sat at the window wrapped in a blanket. Julia wrote in her notebook that a family had been assigned to my old apartment and three volunteers, who would take care of everyone in the building, were in Woodmans'. I asked if she wanted to go to the castle to be with Harmyn, but she insisted she stay. She and several children from the block were going to live in Jane and Dora's apartment and help how they could while the adults slept. She said she missed her brother, and she was worried about the adults, but she was glad she could play again and take care of Sir Pounce. Harmyn promised she would visit often.

Downstairs, in the Misses Acutt's parlor, two beds were near the fireplace. In one, Jane and Dora sat reading longsheets with Sir near their feet. The two sisters were on the settee, the tall one holding a skein of yarn, the other knitting. I went to the bed, and the three of us gathered our hands in a firm knot. I stroked the cat, who answered with a tremendous purr. When I walked to the Misses, I leaned over to kiss their downy cheeks. They patted my hands as if to assure me all would be well.

That afternoon, in the castle's library, Father surprised Harmyn with a butter cake and three small gifts. At some point, he'd asked Harmyn the month of her birth—December—and how old she'd be—thirteen. **Because we'll soon be asleep,** he wrote, **we must celebrate now.** She hugged him so long, he started to laugh.

I had a surprise for Father, too. In a cabinet, to which I gave him a key, was Aoife's original manuscript and one copy of its translation, which I'd completed through several nights I avoided sleep. I gave him a letter.

Dear Father,

In this text, you will learn about the mapmaker who was blamed for starting the war. Aoife had a different view of events, and you'll understand why the chronicles were rewritten as you read her autobiography. If you've noticed people among us wearing a certain shade of blue, they are the Guardians. Despite what occurred in this land a thousand years ago, they've agreed to help us in our time of need.

When you read about the Voices, especially Wei, Aoife's daughter, you will better understand what my mother was and what Harmyn is.

Most significantly, there is an answer you've long sought. Pay attention to Ciaran. I'll say no more than that.

The dragon mentioned; she is real. She is no menace. When we awaken, I'll tell you myths unlike the ones you told me.

Your daughter,
Secret

Father drew me to his hunched shoulders and wouldn't let me pull away. He feared, I knew, he might never get to hold me again.

That evening, dinner was in the Great Hall. Everyone from Nikolas and his advisers to the servants and their families and all volunteers joined for the meal. Although most of us wouldn't eat again for months, few had an appetite. There was wine, however, a small glass for each. Nikolas climbed up on the head table, invited everyone to stand, and raised a toast to our health and the future of Ailliath.

That night, Nikolas had a late meeting with Lord Sullyard, who, Nikolas sensed, looked forward to taking the throne and was clueless he would not. I didn't want to go to my room yet, which I shared with Father, Harmyn, and several volunteers. Instead, I walked the castle grounds. In the stables, I pet the horses and cuddled my favorite mouser, the elderly gray fellow with the white chin. When I returned to the residence, I went to get a gown, robe, and slippers from my trunk and changed in the water closet. I entered the quiet room again to put my clothes away and to wait to see Nikolas one last time. Father was already asleep. The volunteers dozed on their pallets. Propped up in bed, Harmyn chewed the edge of her amulet and read a book on her lap.

You seem calm, I said as I sat next to her.

I am. The children are well again. I know what to expect the next three months. And I won't be so lonely now that Julia and my friends are awake, she said.

How did the children know those songs today?

From their sleep. She glanced at a nearby clock. *If you're going to visit him, be back before the stroke of midnight.*

A fairy-tale warning? I said.

She smirked. *Then you know to heed it.*

As I stood to leave, the composure I'd held finally cracked. I swallowed a cry. *The shadows I've felt these last months. They will be worse now, won't they?*

Some will. Some won't. No matter what, you won't be alone. I promise.

I nodded and left the room to go to Nikolas's. My ears popped. The guard stepped aside as I knocked. Nikolas let me in and shut the door. When he approached me, I wrapped my arms around him. He held me tight. I thought of the good-bye which wrenched us apart that summer three and a half years before—before Fewmany, the manuscript, the quest—and then of the night before the plague sickened us. Nikolas kissed the center of the queen's stings. He reached into his trouser pocket then, between his fingers, held the ancient coin minted with the stag.

"You still have it," I said.

"It's always with me." He searched his coat. "For you. She said to say she apologizes."

On his palm stood the carved stag he'd given me, which Harmyn had destroyed during one of her malicious fits the previous winter.

"That's not possible. She burned it," I said.

The stag, his sailboat, the tulip she gave the young woman, the red poppy she'd given me. Yes, Harmyn possessed Wei's most profound gift. She could enter the nexus between Now and Then and retrieve a remnant from a past not her own. Beyond the threshold of Nature, she touched the very matter of realms beyond. She had plucked that red poppy from Aoife's Then, during a moment of peace, in a time of hope.[36]

Suddenly, I wanted the burden of everything that had been revealed, unresolved, to fall away. I wanted to feel nothing but the weight of my body, light in my heart. I slipped the stag into my robe's pocket, then dropped my clothing at my feet.

"This isn't what I intended when I invited you here tonight," he said, glancing at the door but making no move to stop me.

"I don't have my herbs, so the pleasure, I'm afraid, will not be consummate."

"There will be no complaints."

I went to him with the desire of a maiden and the gaunt body of a crone. My fingers released every button on his vest, shirt, and trousers. He stripped on the way to his bed, returned naked with blankets, and tugged me to the floor near the fire. Soon would be a cold season we wouldn't be able to touch each other. My hands committed his flesh to memory. He twisted my hair at my neck, eased my head back, waited to kiss me. I told him I loved him again and again, the whisper of my words full on his lips. We hurried, then dressed. Near the hearth, he held me as I trembled.

"I'm so frightened, Nikolas."

"I know," he said.

In the hall, the pendulum clock struck the first chime of twelve.

"I must go to my room," I said. My next breath drew longer than the last. "You'll see about me, won't you?"

"Every day, without fail."

My lids strained to stay open. "If I don't wake up, take care of Harmyn. Look after Father."

"I promise," he said.

I stood and swayed. He lifted me in his arms. I circled his neck. "I love you."

"I love you, too."

A hinge groaned. A step creaked. I dropped like a feather. He kissed me. "Sleep, my beauty," he said.

WEEK 28

From the Plague of Silences Recollection Project Archives, Selected Excerpts

Diary No. 536. Female, 16

One of my charges woke up this afternoon. His eyes moved around as if he searched for something. We were told this happened to us, but in the later weeks. Our instructions were to be gentle when they get like this. I said, Hello, Mr. C— and reminded him he was in a shelter, and I'm P—. He didn't act as if he heard me, but I spoke softly that he'd been resting well and oh, what a lovely snowfall we had last night. Then his arms were grasping in the air and he had the look of someone falling. His eyes closed and his arms dropped. I hope he didn't have to stay in that dream for long.

Diary No. 143. Male, 12

I spend half my days in a laundry keeping the fires fed. Once, I cut nothing other than meat on my plate; now I cut wood. The group leader, one of those people wearing blue, not only lets the girls try their hand at chopping but encourages them. All the girls are encouraged to do new things, but then we boys are, too, as if there's no difference between us. I hate the laundry and would quit but F— and W— work with me as well. W— said we should consider that doing our service will put us in a good light once all returns to normal. We don't say so, but we know things will not.

Diary No. 415. Lord Humphrey Sullyard

The king shows nary a sign of weakness. His vigor is as mysterious as the plague itself, possibly more so in that by all accounts he suffered as the rest these past months. Tyson-Banks asked at today's meeting what curative spared him of the sleep, and might we, as his loyal men, receive the boon. The king insists there is no medicine and explained not everyone endures in the same way from phase to phase. Quite on the aside, some wonder if that child in his charge works sorcery. That singing seems a form. How light I feel when I hear her.

I confess a disappointment I'm not in his seat. King for a season—how could I not pine for it? I remain at his right hand each day and, despite our differences, find I cannot help but respect the sincerity with which our young king conducts himself. His father would have involved us in the war by now. King Aeldrich never would have thought to consult anyone lower than a mayor, or done so, in preparation for this plague. As for the halts on Rothwyke's wall and similar projects, I fear the king has made difficult work for us once Fewmany returns and his top men have recovered.

Interview No. 190. Female, age withheld, occupation withheld

You know my name, so this conversation isn't anonymous. I signed your agreement, so it is confidential. I believe I can trust you. Besides, what proof is there other than my word?

Not everyone who died during the sleep *died* in their sleep. Oh, no. The truth was out, even if the facts weren't known. It wasn't spoken in the first phase and couldn't be heard in the second. In the third, all was silent, a dreaded one, because what might happen after the sleep was over?

Let me see those numbers again. Rothwyke's children, 1,159 plague dead. One of those, I know, she didn't slip away. Our neighbor killed her. Several children on our block had the blot. He caused it for at least six. Her mother had to get rations, and he offered to watch her, and when the mother came home, _____ was gone. Stopped breathing, he said. How do I know this? After I woke up, there was talk, but it wasn't rumor.

More adult deaths than children, I see, statistically quite a few more. Two of those for certain, not from the plague. Oh, no. That neighbor I mentioned, someone made certain he slept for good.

And the other, well, from what I saw in my dreams, I knew what I had to do when I awoke. What I did might not have been just, but it was righteous. Sticks and stones can break your bones, but words can kill your spirit. He would never make Mother and me feel so small again. She was asleep next to him, half the person she'd been, she'd shrunk so much, and I did it there. He didn't struggle. I didn't leave a mark.

☙

The first weeks of the sleep,
oh, my beautiful impossible dreams,
full of magic and wonder—
        Journeys by sea upon a boat made of feathers,
        by air in a bed lifted by balloons,
        on land carried by animals, grand and fierce.
                I met fascinating people and
                collected many beautiful things,
                which fit in a purse as small as my hand.

From these splendid travels,
I returned to a time before,
to moments of contentment and joy—
        I leaned against Father as he read a new tale,
        harvested the garden with Old Woman,
        walked among the trees with Nikolas,
        listened to the stories of creatures and plants.

And when my visit to that Then was done, I entered other Thens,
made of the warp of memory and the weft of imagination,
where I was myself, with what could have been—
        I ran from the hollow tree when Mother called, to her
        wide smile and open arms. She carried me to join our
        dark-haired family dancing in the woods. I heard no
        story from a bee who told of the dead girl, the wound,
        and the wolf, neither Mother nor I stung.

The night of the summer ball at the castle, my parents left me at home with Auntie, and when I started at my new school in autumn, the prince was a boy I knew by name and sight, but I would never be sure he knew the same of me.

> I played with my older brothers, Duncan by six years, Riley by four. Duncan, black hair and eyes, serious, brooding, who liked to take things apart; Riley, brown hair, blue eyes, funny, brilliant, who played the violin as if he were born to do so. Strong Duncan carried me on his shoulders; protective Riley kept me near his side.

I dreamed of a symbol—circle, triangle, square—but felt no urge to draw it, and later, at a performance hall, my father introduced me to Mr. Lesmore Bellwether, an acquaintance, who regarded me with amber eyes and disinterest.

❦

THE FIRST TIME I STIRRED AWAKE, I SURFACED FROM AN OILY darkness. For several moments, I couldn't remember where I was. When I did, I glanced toward Father's shape, wondering where his dreams led him.

Thirst parched my tongue. I strained to whisper *Water* several times before someone hurried to my side. A young man held a cup to my lips. He said his name was Tucker, that I'd been restful, and it was now the fifteenth of January. As I waved him away, I counted I'd been asleep twenty-five days.

"Would you like a change of gown? I'll call the women to tend you," he said.

"No, thank you. Has my father been well?"

"Aside from quaking fits now and again, yes. He's more wakeful than the rest of you, but with no distress."

Tucker washed my hands with a warm cloth. The cuffs of his blue shirt were damp. As he wiped my face, my left cheek stung as if he'd hit me. I leaned away.

"I'm sorry. I tried to be careful," he said.

"I still have the bruise," I said.

"Remember, the children had their afflictions well into the sleep, too. No cause for alarm."

"I want to see Nikolas. And Harmyn."

"I'll have someone fetch them, but you might fall asleep again before they arrive." He walked off. A bell chimed soon after. I heard him speaking in the hall. When he returned, I looked around the room. There were twelve beds, three empty.

"We have more people in the room," I said.

"We had to do this. The adults need more attention than the children did in the early weeks. They're more prone to fits, and they have more frequent periods of wakefulness. The ones without hired help or family have been moved to the shelters, for their safety. Do you want to hear of recent news?" Tucker asked.

"No, thank you."

"Very well," he said as he settled on a chair near the fire with a longsheet. "You might like to know, the King visits at least twice a day, and Harmyn sits with you and your father every night. There have been friends, too, Julia, and Mrs. Frigget, and Miss Bendar."

"That is comforting. Thank you," I said.

I thought to write Julia, Charlotte, and Margana brief letters, but I felt too tired. As I waited, I listened to a clock's tick, stared out of the window, and moved what parts of me I could, both arms, my eyes, and the toes of my right foot.

The door clicked open.

"Good morning, Tucker."

"Good morning, Your Majesty."

I cut my eyes to watch Nikolas cross the room.

"May I have a private word with Miss Riven?"

"Of course."

Nikolas sat next to my hip. "Hello, Love," he said.

I grabbed the V of his green damask vest and hugged him tight.

"The caregivers tell me you haven't been fretful," he said. He set me back on the pillows and clasped my hand. "Good dreams or bad?"

"Good enough. How are you? You're not sick," I said.

"Much to everyone's surprise, even my own. I cannot convey the relief I feel to be clearheaded again. And how strange it is to be fully aware of what's happening now, to feel a different sort of quiet, like an anticipation, but also—" His eyes filled with tears.

"What's happened?" I asked.

"It's so peaceful, Secret. Remember when Aoife told how she felt when she first visited the Guardians—that peace she couldn't explain? Then when she found her new home, how they lived and ordered their days, everyone taking part in work and play, how the children were cherished among them?"37

I stroked the scar under his thumb. "I remember."

"Right now, we have a sense of what that's like. This isn't simply the absence of strife, or the ordinary balance of how we all get along, or pretend to. You can see it in the children. The plague changed them."

"You're the first adult to survive. How are you changed?"

"I accept my true nature, as I couldn't before. Harmyn led me to see it, but it was my choice to claim it, as a person, and as a king," he said.

"So it must be for the children, too," I said.

I wanted to know more, but my head lolled against the pillow. "I'm being pulled in. Tell Harmyn I'll speak to her—"

The sleep's nightmares, unlike any we had before or since.
Remember them, survivors? Uncanny as imagination, if it was that;
plain as memory, if it was so.
Revealed there, in those shadows,
were the truths of broken hearts and greatest fears.

> Bound by rope, I struggled on the dining table as Father carved my raw thigh with the scissors and served my meat in the ochre bowl to Fewmany, who ravenously ate, asking for more.

In corners, I sat alone time and again; swarmed by beetles and ants, emaciated until I turned to dust; kept occupied by building the same tower with the same ten blocks; buried under a pile of musty books.

> I crouched in a cage made of Fig Tree's dead limbs. My mother dragged a dying doe to its door. Around Mother's neck were strung a fledgling swallow and a fluffy kit. She forced me to watch as she flayed, gutted, and stewed them, then watched me starve as I refused to eat.

Again and again and again, the stinking ogress
stalked, menaced, and penned me—and each time I
got away, she chased me into the dark woods,
where I ran and ran and ran.

> I wore a red silk gown, fitted to my flesh as a second skin,
> with a cowl and cuffs trimmed in fox fur and a train so long
> I saw no end. I wed a man who stood in shadow and
> accepted his ring, gold with a jewel the size and hue of a
> drop of blood. There was dancing and wine and a feast,
> then a carriage ride into a deep valley through a night of
> stars and new moon. By the light of a single candle, I went
> to a room at the top of a spiral stair, to a bed clothed in
> white. I found delight in the thought, I'll leave no stain.
> As I hummed, I shed the gown, slipped across the sheets,
> and coiled under my silver hair. He entered in the dark with
> hands made of fire. Come to me, I told him, and I felt his
> heat. Touch me, I bade him, and I didn't burn. Love me,
> I begged him, and then I did. The pillows burst into flame.
> I stared into my husband's amber eyes and kissed his
> mouth and bit his lolling tongue. I forced him to his furry
> back as the headboard blazed. The light shone on the
> dragon's head, red as poppies and pomegranates, mounted
> above us. Smoke curled from its dead snout, and in the
> plumes, I saw the world we'd made beyond our bed
> —scorched, barren, laid bare; earth, sky, and sea.

OUT OF STILLNESS, I AWOKE TO FIND HARMYN SITTING NEXT TO
me. Nearby, Father snored in whiffles. The lamp nearby burned bright.

"Nikolas didn't ask me to do this, but tonight marks a year since his
parents died. There's no one else he'd prefer to keep him company," she
said.

"I haven't the strength for this. The sleep is a slow black drowning,"
I said.

"Do you want to see him, if I can help you feel better?"

A puff of a laugh escaped me. "Yes. Do what you can."

She held my wrist. A current streamed into my limbs. I stretched, welcoming the movement. I sat up and looked at her. The lines of her face were stronger, comely more than pretty. Between the gap in her robe, her chest seemed fuller. Her light hair had been cut level with her chin.

"How are you, Harmyn?" I could see dark circles under her eyes.

She smiled. "Well enough."

"Are you still singing? What do you do while we sleep?"

"I must sing, as much for myself now as for everyone else," Harmyn said. "I'm not on the wall anymore, though. I walk through the streets and visit the shelters. I go to the woods, too, where so many children go to play now, even more than before. You'd be proud of them, being mindful of the plants and animals, teaching the new ones what you taught the first. And sometimes I visit Margana's shop and take Julia with me. Speaking of, she's well and happy with her housemates. The neighbors, nothing unusual among them, although Mr. Elgin has had some violent fits."

"Father?"

"No need to worry."

"Nikolas? Are you two on good terms?"

"Yes. We're positively combative at chess, and he's taught me to ride, which I'm good at now. Sometimes, we race on the green and take rides in the woods. We visit town together, without advisers, to see about things. And the talks we've had. He's a profound thinker, isn't he?"

"A pragmatic philosopher, as long as I've known him," I said.

I asked for the luxury of a bath, which Harmyn drew for me. I felt strong enough to tend myself, but she sat outside in case I needed someone. As I soaked, I stared at my still-withered body and noticed the nails on my fingers and toes had not grown. Despite the cold, I washed my hair, feeling the same length as before. Through the door's crack, Harmyn dropped a clean gown and thick robe.

Harmyn escorted me through the parlors, where people sat reading, in conversation, or playing games. She greeted the guard at Nikolas's door. I noticed a blue sash tied at his waist.

She knocked with a pattern, which seemed meant to identify her. I buried the memory of a certain *rap-rap, rap-rap*. Nikolas called her in. Still dressed in his coat and trousers, he sat in his chair near the fireplace, with documents piled on the floor. He smiled when he stood to greet us.

"I guessed you wouldn't mind a visitor," she said.

Nikolas tousled her hair with affection. "How long do we have?"

"As long as you want. Secret, when you're ready, you'll sleep again without my help. Good night." Harmyn closed the door behind her.

Nikolas gave me a quick kiss. "You'll catch cold with that wet hair." He stood me against the fire. I sunk into his protective embrace.

At last, I said, "Harmyn told me what day it is. I imagine you're missing them terribly."

"I am, even though with all that's happened, it seems so long ago. Harmyn came this morning to see how I was. What I can hide from everyone else, I can't from her." Nikolas dropped his arms and pushed another chair close to his. He reached for my hand once I sat down. "I've missed you."

"Had I not been unconscious, I believe I'd have missed you, too," I said.

He grinned. "Almost six weeks until the spring equinox and this is over. I've talked to several children about what the sleep is like. The blur of dreams and memories, sorting themselves out, with time to rest between them. It seems far less brutal than what Harmyn put me through."

"Do you wish you hadn't?"

"No, the choice was evident. I didn't want to wake to any surprises. Matters are difficult enough as it is. The war—never mind, it's no better or much worse. The plague—we've had representatives from eight towns come to see how we're managing. Everyone is worried what will happen if, when, there's a greater spread. I couldn't reassure them. We don't know where the plague will strike next."

"If any bird messengers have come to tell me, I wouldn't know. Did you ask Harmyn?"

"She said she doesn't know. Seeing the future isn't one of her abilities, she claims."

A stricken look must have crossed my face.

"Has she told you differently?" he asked.

"No, that's not it. I believe that was my mother's gift. Had she been here instead of Harmyn, she might have known," I said.

He stared at my bruise, then looked into my eyes. "Secret, what's happened while you've been asleep?"

"Precisely what the children told you—a blur of dreams and memories, wonderful and horrifying."

"That's not what I meant."

"Whatever you think I've suffered, it's worse than you imagine. My mother—I can't talk about this now." I withdrew my hand from his and paused through a deep breath. There was much I hadn't told him yet, not of my loneliness and isolation, what I learned about my blue brothers, or the memory which returned to me the night the unborn bled away. Soon enough, the whole truth would tear its way out. "The first night Harmyn took you into the shadows, I couldn't comprehend what your father did to you. That you lived with those memories, that pain. But in spite of it, you're able to take his chamber as your own and miss him on the anniversary of his death."

"My love for him weighs heavier in the balance," he said.

"Good that it can," I said.

"And for yours?" he asked.

"I'd say the same. Failings with me aside, and whatever he's done to others through his work—I didn't ask what he'd done to get that blood on his hands—still, I never thought him to be a cruel man."

"He's never seemed so, not as I knew him in an official way, skillful at angling for a diplomatic compromise between Ailliath and business interests, and not as I see him now."

"How so?"

"When he wakes, he doesn't like to be alone. The caregivers talk with him or bring children to him. This I've seen for myself when I've stopped in to see about you. There he was, tucked into a chair with a group of little ones at his feet, telling stories. They all seemed under a spell," he said.

A wistful grin softened my face. "He's quite the bard."

"Sometimes when he's awake, he joins me and Harmyn for a conversation. He has a far better grasp of history than most of my advisers," he said.

I smirked then, wondering if my father was positioning himself in Nikolas's favor. Father had to realize by now whatever Fewmany Incorporated had been, it wouldn't be again.

"He and Harmyn are very fond of each other. It's good to see her laugh as she does with him," Nikolas said.

"Harmyn is the closest my father will ever get to having a grandchild, so he might as well enjoy the semblance of it," I said.

"What do you mean?"

"I'll never marry or have children."

There was no mistaking the alarm in his eyes. "Those are your shadows coming out, tricking you. You don't mean that."

"You've known me for so long, you don't see me clearly, and you don't know me as I know myself. I'm not fit for either. Not meant for either."

"Why would you say such a thing? What, then, of us?"

I closed my eyes, bracing for the inevitable conversation. "What happened between us, I don't regret at all. Months ago, you said you were willing to see where your feelings led, but I had no hopes attached."

"I wasn't entirely sure what I meant when I said that," he said.

"I entered these feelings unprepared myself, more so than you. I don't think either of us anticipated the depth of how we came to feel about each other. I assure you, I had no illusions. We both know what's expected of you."

His expression betrayed no emotion. He paused for so long, I was tempted to say something else, but had nothing to add.

"I wasn't going to speak of this now, but as it's come up, I want you to sleep with this in mind," Nikolas said.

I felt every movement within me become still, breath, pulse, thought.

"I love you—" he said.

"I love you, too."

"That is why I ask you to consider marrying me."

My heart surged, then twisted and sent a leaden ache straight to my feet.

"You're right. We both know what's expected of me," he said. "The goodwill visits, that was a matter of politics, of course, but the diplomacy wasn't limited to war, peace, and trade. There were introductions and renewed acquaintances. The women I met flaunted the refinement bred into them. Some were even charming, or intelligent, or good-hearted. When the time came, there would have been a culling to select those I found suitable, who thought the same of me. But there was no question our happiness mattered far less than how strategic the union would be. Then my parents died, and the plague struck, and in between, as well as before, there was you."

He clutched my arm with both hands. "You are more to me than my best friend. My mother told me I'd one day find a wife and grow to love her because we'd be from the same world and desire the same things. My father counseled me to look for a good disposition, beauty that would age with grace, and the fortitude to manage a proper house. Affection was a matter of familiarity, he said, and in time, especially after she bore me a son, I would be fond of her."

"Well, I wasn't raised in a noble family," I said. "I have no understanding of a courtly life and what rules and duties that entails. I am unsuitable." Unsuitable for far greater reasons than that, I thought. My fists clenched to hold the ache pouring from my heart.

"Didn't you hear what was behind my words? I speak of love, Secret, not lineage. But to address your protest, you are resourceful beyond measure. I hate to invoke his name, but Fewmany saw that quiet but fierce resolve in you. This resolve is how you found the strength to translate the manuscript and go alone on a quest with nothing tangible to guide you, and speak before the Council, and—frankly—to take in a child most people would fear or misunderstand too much to love. Now tell me you couldn't learn a few rules and customs."

"I'm not meant for what you ask of me," I said.

"I know you'd die of misery if you were denied what you cherish. Time alone, the woods, your intellectual curiosity, your books. I would never ask you to sacrifice any of it."

To none of that had I alluded. I didn't have the energy to discuss the true reasons, so instead I smiled and said, "You do have your moments of rhetorical flourish."

He laughed, a release of the golden boy of light I loved in him, always. How could he love me as he did, the dark girl full of shadows? I couldn't tell him no right then, not when he looked at me with such adoration. "I will think about what you asked," I said.

"At least you didn't refuse me outright. I would feel used and tawdry if you did." Nikolas moved from his chair, knelt next to me, and lay his head in my lap. As I slipped my fingers into his hair, sighing from the pleasure of it, a trough of grief returned to take me into the swirling dark hole inside.

WEEK 34

Rothwyke Services Log, Excerpt

7/2.   Reports of minor tremors with "murmur" and "low groaning" in Area 11 most notably around Fewmany Incorporated

building. Last activity reported in September. No new dis-
cernible damage to structures or streets. Will monitor.

8/2. Water leak behind ~~Old~~ New Wheel in former Alley J.
Tremors throughout day, no greater severity, sounds still
reported.

9/2. Leak source undetermined at present. Tremors, same.

10/2. King issued order to evacuate persons within 10-block area
of plaza. Aid volunteers working through night. Attempted
to convince king's representatives action unnecessary but
king's order stands.

11/2. Four minor tremors today.

12/2. Major tremor throughout Rothwyke. Roaring sound reported as far as The Manses.

13/2. Profound structural damage to Fewmany Incorporated
and buildings within two blocks. Interim mayor ordered
structures and area as condemned.

From the Plague of Silences Recollection Project Archives, Selected Excerpts

Diary No. 6. Male, 32, municipal clerk

Time to get another bottle from the sleight market because this
one won't last the duration. Adult deaths, thus far, 1,523. Today, 111
messages arrived to request a registrar to record the latest deaths.
Yesterday, 67. Days before, 59, 55, 61. As there's only myself, Diggby,
and Potts, I need to ask for more volunteers to help. At least it's
cold and we have the textile warehouse near the steamwheeler station to store the bodies until the new mass graves are ready. More
diggers arriving tomorrow. I estimate 4,500 to 5,000 dead come
mid-March for ones we can account in Rothwyke. Some who fled
town are dying, too, but we haven't confirmed numbers.

Diary No. 415. Lord Humphrey Sullyard

Such a harsh winter, bringing not so much peace as immobility. Yet
another week with reports of no significant advances or retreats in

Giphia, Kirsau, or Ilsace because of the snow. Prev's troops, with Thrigin's, are in Uldiland now to help drive out Haaud. Speculation that Prev will press east and fight Emmok, if Emmok doesn't relent. Given our relations with Emmok, we are in a quandary. To aid Emmok would be a boon to Haaud, the benefit to us in some ways negligible; better we back Giphia, since our borders loom with threat. But still the king sends our envoys abroad for talks, more talks! and continues to stall. He says he understands the risks here, but I cannot determine if he's indecisive or naïve. If we're invaded, he will have no choice any longer.

Regarding the king, in anticipation the phases will keep to the predictable regularity, a date at last has been set for the coronation. This coming 1 May.

Diary No. 224. Female, 12

We crept out after our gaurdians were asleep. It was a long walk in a light snow. They called me a spooky goose when I said maybe we should turn back. What if it wasn't true he went away for the plague and was still in the house? R— said that was stupid because he'd be asleep like everyone else. I said maybe he had people taking care of him and they'd catch us. A— said we weren't going to steal anything, only look, and if I was that afraid, I could wait outside.

We were all afraid once we got there. The manor was much larger than we thought it would be. All of those dark windows in the front, sixty-four long shut eyes. We decided to try to get in from the back. G— was about to smash the glass of one big door but R— saw a key in the lock of another. It was very strange to see it that way. Someone else had been there, or was still there. We found some lamps in the kitchen, and matches, so we took those.

I'd never been inside a house so grand, never will again I'm sure. We went into several rooms and a big library, the door and some things inside of that were burned, but the rooms were empty. I expected to see beautiful furniture, and vases and candelobras, and wardrobes full of elegant clothes. Everything was gone.

From the outside we saw the manor had a very long first floor, which we wanted to see. A— was the one who found a door hidden behind heavy drapes that went to a hall. We dared him to go in the pitch black, and he did. He was gone so long, we were afraid something happened, so we went to find him. The hall turned on itself and we walked calling his name. Then we heard footsteps and saw a light and we screamed. I thought Mr. Fewmany was coming after us, but it was only A—. He said we had to see something. The look on his face, I knew it would be awful but I had no idea how awful.

There in one room, piled on the floor—skeletons with old flesh on them, and clothing, and hair and teeth fallen around! We couldn't talk we were so shocked. We agreed we can't tell anyone. We weren't supposed to be there, but oh I wonder what happened and who did that terrible thing.

Interview No. 98. Male; age during plague, 8;
current occupation, carpenter

The third phase, like everyone, I dreamed, but I had none of the terrors I know others had. My dreams were fanciful, lovely, and when I dreamed of myself grown, I liked the man I saw and what would become of him. I liked, too, what I saw of Ailliath, like a promise kept.

When Momma and Poppa took to the sleep, my sister and brother and I missed them, but we knew they would be well in the end. We remember our time as plague orphans—you have heard that before, what we children called ourselves—yes, that time with happiness. No gruel, bedbugs, and rags for us wardrats! No, our guardians took good care of us, twenty or so in that one walk-up. We had the warmest clothes we'd ever had and plenty of food—the whole of the plague, never to know that hollow hunger again—and comfortable beds, each with a stuffed toy to hold. I had a little dog, gray with a brown eye patch. We had small chores, what we could do at our ages. The older ones helped the younger ones with washing up and dressing. When we quarreled, as children do, our guardians were so patient and kind, but many of our friends seemed confused, standing in a crouch as if they expected to get a cuff or shout.

In the mornings, after breakfast and chores, Raisa and Ben would have us in school, but not as we'd known it. They made games of it. We'd eat together—there was no kitchen, our meals were always brought in, always hot—but we'd wash our own bowls and spoons and cups.

After that, we'd put on our coats and our guardians would take us to see our families. They were asleep, but we got to sit with them and see they were all right. M— didn't like going, or his brother, so Henley—he was a guardian—always sat with them as a friend.

Then in the afternoons into the evenings, we'd play with orphans from other houses. We laughed and had such fun. None of us had ever been so carefree, I believe, not we children from Elwip. The plague had given us this gift.

At night, we'd have our dinner, then we'd go to the top floor for entertainment. Gert had a sweet voice. She'd lead us in singalongs as Ben played the mandolin. There were times we children put on a play that the older ones wrote, and we all made costumes and acted. Our guardians enjoyed our antics. I know they were fond of us and we were of them.

Oh, there was the one night Harmyn came. We knew who he—no, she—well, the clothing did confuse us. Yes, everyone knew of her, although some of us had never seen her. There was a guard with her who wore a blue coat with gold braid. I remember this because he let one of the boys try it on. She said she'd lived in our ward and wanted to see for herself we were being cared for as treasures. Treasures, she said. Some of my housemates started to cry, but not out of sadness but because they were moved. We did feel like treasures.

I'm sorry. I didn't expect to be overcome. We had each other and our guardians. We wanted for nothing, not food, warmth, safety or, I say this sincerely, or love. Every plague orphan I've ever met recalls this sense of being precious.

Here is the beauty. Why so much is different now. As we felt this for ourselves, we felt it, too, of our friends. Those of us who awakened from the sleep, after the dreams we had and the way we lived with our guardians, we couldn't go back to how things were before.

❦

Under Fig Tree, I leaned against her sturdy trunk,
eating her fruit, telling her of my first year in high academy,
of the things I'd learned, of the interesting people I'd met,
      but there came a strange smell,
          intrusive, hot, spicy, a hint of jasmine . . .

I FELT MYSELF FLOAT AWAY, THE SCENT BECOMING STRONGER, until I discovered I was awake. I cursed the breach into my alternate Then. Between my bed and Father's stood a woman with a lamp.

"There, there, Mr. Riven," she said.

I almost gagged on the trace of my dead mother's perfume. "What is that doing here?" I asked.

The woman turned. In one hand, she held a bottle. "Remarkable. Did the scent wake you, Miss Riven?"

"Yes, it did," I said.

"Secret," Father said.

"I'll leave you to talk while you can," the woman said as she placed the lamp on the table near our heads. The door clicked open, then shut.

Father had a full gray beard, neatly clipped, and a tasseled cap. A handkerchief draped from his neck. When he rolled to his side, the perfume drifted toward me again.

"I was in a good dream," I said.

"So was I, until it twisted, and I came out desperate to be reminded she had lived," Father said.

"The caregivers indulge such things? How did she ever find that scent?" I asked.

"I brought it with me, among my things," he said. "How strange this is, this sleep. Even now, I almost wonder if our conversation is a dream, as so many seem quite real."

I put my hand over my nose and mouth as a memory of my mother surfaced—a new string of jewels at her neck, the violet gown with the jet buttons, how beautiful in that moment she was.[38]

"This is real, Father," I said.

"Then we'll talk now. I wake more than the rest of you. Harmyn often sits with me. She's losing that childlike softness to her face. Have you noticed? Her jaw in particular—"

"Yes, I have. Is there something you want to tell me?" I asked.

He pushed the handkerchief into his nightshirt. "She reads your translation of Aoife's manuscript to me. Last we stopped, Wei saw how her father received his grisly wound, and a Voice came to train her. Sisay, the ancient Voice, who gave a prophecy."

"Of the children to come, and a great hush," I said.

"Yes. There is something I want to tell you and something I want to know."

"What is that?" I asked, dread thick in my veins.

"I've told you your mother had a sort of foresight," Father said. "Sometimes, what she dreamed came to pass, small things, the look of a room or a street corner before we would see it, or a bit of news. And sometimes, the dreams were significant. She foresaw my mother's death though we lived in two different places, and my title—Geo-Archeo Historian—before Fewmany ever offered a position to me. She had recurring ones, too, and one in particular was so outlandish, it had to be her imagination."

I held my palm against my face to block the wafting perfume. "Why are you telling me this?"

"Before you were born, each time she was with child, she had a certain dream. In this dream, she was pregnant and she couldn't hear a single sound, as if the land and every living thing had become mute. She saw the vision of a hand, three times, the same hand, as it poured a liquid from a vial. She watched it spill and she knew the poison— she called it a poison—had caused the silence. She believed the child she carried would commit this deed and destroy the world as it was known."

Hidden, my mouth gaped open.

"I gave this little thought, of course," Father said. "Most dreams are nothing but a performance of the mind. When you were born, and the three birds came, I knew you were a special child. A good, gentle girl. I told your mother, our babe received a visit of welcome. All is well. She never spoke of the dream again, and it was all forgotten, until."

He leaned at the bed's edge. "There are things you've told me since you returned from your journey. Things which made me pause, contemplate, question. How could it be, though? The very idea. Yet we sickened, didn't we, left mute, deaf, motionless."

Father reached his hand from under his quilts, holding out for me. Someone in another bed stirred. "I cannot help but think of her dream and wonder if she had, in fact, foreseen but was mistaken about what she saw."

"GrandBren," Harmyn said, climbing on his bed.

"You've refused to tell me, Harmyn, and I must know," Father said.

"Please. No. Not yet," she said, shaking him.

"What have you done, Secret? Tell me, at last," Father asked.

"I poured three vials. I released the plague."

I watched the light bleed from his face as my mother's voice ruptured through my memory. "This spill is but an accident, yes, little scourge." I had tipped over a cup of water. "Mind what is spilled, girl, and watch it doesn't spread." Then, it was a cellar of salt, and Mother's fault, as if she'd done so on purpose. "You will be the ruin of me, won't you, girl? You will not make a mess here." In a perfume shop, the bottle fell but didn't break, and nothing I could do could set things right.

from darkness I exhume into dimness
> a crow calls glass cracks
>> a soft weight crushes my fevered face
flutter scuffle howl screech hum
>> my clawing nails strike skin, hair, feathers
>> my nose and left cheek throb
>> against the smothering force I rise
a crow with a bloody chest dives toward a black head
the feral stink of animals and fear burns in each breath
> she swings the pillow screams with pain
> she runs from the beasts at her back
>> flesh lungs throat aflame I fall
>>> into darkness
>>>> into unknowing
>>>>> Mother meant to kill me

❦

OUTSIDE OF FORM, OUTSIDE OF TIME, I THINNED TO ETHER. Feeling and thought faded the farther I drifted into a spiraling vortex, alone, alone.

Until I wasn't.

"Secret, can you hear me?"

I thickened, unable to flow forward.

"Secret, there are things the shadows hid from you. Things I hope you're willing to see," Harmyn said.

The vortex twisted in the distance as another force pulled me into a dense black tangle of memory. A strand broke free. A reflection in a shop window, Mother and me, her little shadow and dark mirror at once. I heard myself say, "She saw herself in me, and this she couldn't bear."

"Do you believe that's why she tried to kill you?"

"Not for hatred alone. She wanted to stop me. She believed her dream about a child spilling poison, but what future did she see? Was it a way it could have been, the world destroyed, or was it what has happened now and she didn't understand the vision?" I asked.

"What if it was both, or either, and still something else?" Harmyn asked.

Behind and between shadows, I slipped, among the instances she shunned our strangeness, struggled to mask how horribly she suffered. Within her many lies was a desperate, twisted truth. "She meant to protect me, didn't she? To spare me of my fate," I said, "as she wanted to be spared of hers."

The darkness faded to a gray haze.

"If not for the animals who came to help that day, I would have died," I said.

"If not for your strength. They came to your aid. You rose with the force of will," Harmyn said.

"Why didn't she try again? Why leave the cipher and manuscript if she believed I would bring ruin?"

"Think. What was different after the fever broke?"

"My hair turned silver. I could speak the Guardians' language. The fever changed me, and she knew it."

"How was she different?" Harmyn asked.

From a distance, shimmering through, an ethereal voice broke the silence, singing in tones. "She had never sung before, but she did then, alone, at night, so beautiful, so pure. As if something lost had been returned to her. Then as suddenly as she started, she stopped. That is when she made the cipher. That is when she abandoned her role in what was to come, leaving it to me. And then she was gone. And then she left me. And then my mother was dead."

With a jolt, I found myself once again flesh, bone, and blood, on my knees in a forest near a tiny sapling. One pale leaf unfurled. At the surprise, I held a gasped breath. I didn't want the terror of the release, but my body violated my will. I inhaled until my ribs strained and screamed through the hole in my chest.

Rage, bile black, bloodthick, flooded into the gap.

Harmyn touched my shoulder. I crawled away, spewing howls.

"This happened after I drank the vial," Harmyn said. "I wanted to die, too. Scream, Secret. Rage for what you lost and you want back."

As I shrieked, the pressure in my skull threatened to burst every vessel, the promise of a lasting final peace.

The web of my right thumb began to tingle. A streak of light flashed from the aperture in my hand. All at once, I was three, seven, fourteen again. I reached up to hold my mother's bee-stung face. I took her hand after she spoke of her lost brother, and mine. I stood in awe as I heard her sing for the first time, wishing I could touch the sound.

As the moments held in a constellation of time, I felt what I couldn't name before. I had felt compassion for her, and deeper still, at the core, love unconditional.

More fragments joined the shifting pattern. I glanced up at my mother as she played a memory game with me, handed me a tattered book, watched me tend flowers in the courtyard, laughed as I jauntily flipped a hood over my head. So fleeting, what I felt from her, a curious affection, as if . . . as if the whole of her didn't despise me.

The love I wanted to give, she could not receive. If she had ever wanted to return it, she could not. Her damage was too deep, her scars too thick, to ever love me. She was too broken to make that choice.

Bright dots appeared across my body, expanding until they over-lapped, glowing brighter at the points of connection. Within me, mem-ories ruptured in new dimension. I was not only myself but many, filled with pieces of other lives, those people my blood had been, those my essence once were. I slipped past shadows, beyond limits, beyond judg-ment, to realize nothing was as simple as it might appear or I wished it to be.

As the openings sealed shut, I looked around at the forest where all was living and all was dying. Beautiful and poisonous, a pale yellow mushroom cracked through the dark soil. With a pinch, I plucked it, watched it turn to gold, and ate it. Light streamed from my fingers and toes as I became again the little girl with black hair, tawny skin, and eyes the colors of night and day; part of the wildness, beauty, and wonder; the duality and paradox; nothing other than myself as Nature meant me to be. A child among the Mystery and too young to find the word to de-scribe what I felt in my own stillness.

Whole.

Harmyn wiped the joyful tears from my cheeks. "This is what the pestilence has hidden in everyone, from themselves and each other. When the plague ends, everyone will struggle to remember how to see this, but no one will forget what was revealed. I told you, Secret, we are all born made of gold."

20 MARCH /39

ON THE MORNING OF THE FIRST DAY OF SPRING, I HEARD THE COO AND chirp of a pigeon, a dove, and a sparrow. The three birds stood on a windowsill, their chests broad and wings tucked back as if standing in ceremony.

I moved to sit up. Most of the beds were occupied. Harmyn wasn't in hers, and Father was asleep in his. Quietly I called to him. He yawned, blinked, and smiled when he looked at me.

I walked to the window. The sleeves and hem of my gown were too short.

We've come with a message, the pigeon said.

The plants are sick in the nearest towns north, the dove said.

Our kind will report how far it's spread when it's known, the sparrow said.

I thanked them and stroked their heads. The caregivers and plague survivors watched them fly in a circle, widdershins.

Moments later, the castle filled with chimes and laughter. Two girls burst into our room with a box of little bells, giving one to each person.

"Everyone up! Harmyn is going to sing in an hour!" one said.

At the open door, Nikolas dodged aside as the girls rushed out. He met my eyes, hurried into the room, and swaddled me in his arms. I held him so tight, he strained to breathe. "My Secret," he whispered. "My love," I said. When Father approached, Nikolas reached out one hand to shake his but didn't release me.

"I have an address to make. You'll join me, won't you?" Nikolas said.

"Once we're properly attired," Father said, pulling at his nightshirt's cuff. He pointed to my cheek. "The bruise is gone."

I touched my face. The full knowledge of what had caused it surfaced under my skin.

"Nikolas, I've had a visit from messengers. The plague has spread to the plants north of Rothwyke. I'll tell you as soon as I know the extent," I said.

He pressed his chin against my temple. "Right now, we can celebrate. We must."

Within the half hour, Father and I walked to the castle's outer wall and climbed up to stand with Harmyn. As she approached us with her arms out, I detected a weary look in her eyes. She hugged Father briefly, then clung to me.

"Why did you come and search for me?" I whispered.

"You stopped dreaming through the shadows. The worst wound took you, and you got so lost. I was almost too late," she said.

I patted her shoulders, noticing they were broader and she was taller. When I looked up beyond the castle's wall, my hands froze. Fewmany Incorporated was gone. A stretch of blue sky filled where it once stood.

Harmyn slipped aside. "In February, the ground tremored and groaned. You roused from the sleep and warned us of what was coming. It collapsed two weeks later."

"No one was hurt," Father said, "but the surrounding five blocks, the building, and everything inside—furniture, documents—gone. A crater swallowed it all, and the hole filled with water. You'd be amazed at the archeological treasures which were forced up."

I shut my eyes when I realized the land itself had taken its claim from the town's shadow of The Mapmaker's War. "Now what?" I asked.

"I don't know. It seems not much is as it was before the plague," Father said, drawing Harmyn close to his side.

A moment later, Nikolas, along with several advisers and town officials, stepped up. Harmyn greeted them, then walked to the wall's edge ringing her bell. When the chime faded, she sang a song of mourning for those who had not survived, one of gratitude for those who had given their care, and one of joy for us all.

When she finished and the crowd quieted their cheers, Nikolas took a sheet of paper from his pocket and gave a concise address.

"Many of you are filled with happiness today, as well as grief, with hope and fear. We wish the uncertain times ahead were not so, but we will persevere. In this, I have full faith because of what I witnessed these long months. I am immensely proud of each one of you. Each one who braved this plague, who gave aid to the sick and companionship to the rest, who kept our children safe and warm, in body and spirit. To those who served as our guardians, thank you. To Lord Sullyard, my advisers, Mayor Pearson, interim mayor Mr. Moore, and those who served Rothwyke and Ailliath, thank you. Last but not least, please join me to thank Harmyn, who in our silence was our Voice and whose gift of song soothed and guided us to this day."

As applause and bells rang out, Harmyn looked out at the crowd.

Nikolas reached into a pocket and opened a small hinged box. He motioned for her to come near. He placed a gold medal on a purple ribbon around her neck. She reached to hold the medal in one hand, her amulet in the other. Nikolas stared at her until she met his eyes. "Thank you, Harmyn," he whispered as he bowed.

She stepped forward to hug him. He held her head against him until she moved away.

"Thank you. Everyone," Harmyn said with tears in her eyes. "To the reign of love," she shouted.

The children were the ones to answer her call, "To the reign of love."

Nikolas waved to the crowd, shook hands with Lord Sullyard and the other men, and turned to Harmyn, Father, and me.

"Breakfast, anyone?" he said. I accepted the offer of his arm as we descended the stairs.

That first day at the castle, as it was throughout Rothwyke, no one was expected to return immediately to their homes, assuming they could. We napped, we took short walks, and we visited with our caregivers and those who shared our rooms. We read letters sent to us as we slept, and we waited to hear word of what happened to people we knew.

I spent the morning in the kitchen garden with a cat on my lap, content in the sun among the growing vegetables, budding roses, and blooming tulips and daffodils. That afternoon, Father and I sat together with the past and future between us but the practical present at hand.

"For what I've done which hurt you, if it has ever made you question my love, I am sorry. Please, return home with me, and Harmyn. There's plenty of room, and we'll not want for the necessities. We need time to see what's ahead," he said.

I had no idea where I would go next. To stay at the castle now seemed undue. I didn't have the means to have my own apartment again, but I could return to Old Woman's cottage. As I pondered Father's offer, I waited for a feeling of contraction, but it didn't come, even though I knew I would go back to a place where dark memories remained.

"Your apology is accepted. I know you love me, as I love you. I will go home," I said. Father cradled me like a child, to which I gave no struggle.

That evening after dinner, one served to everyone in the Great Hall, Nikolas asked me to join him for a ride in the woods. Once Father and Harmyn went off to amuse each other, I waited for him at the stables. In the fading light, a host of sparrows descended to the roof's edge. One lit on my finger.

The plants are sick north of the river, moving east to the mountains, she said without saying.

Not south? I asked.

For now, the river marks the border, she said.

Nikolas approached as the birds took flight again.

"How far now?" he asked, and I told him. "Do you think it will spread beyond Ailliath?"

"I do. We'll know more soon enough."

We mounted our horses, crossed through town slowly as he waved and stopped to talk to people in the streets, then raced across the green. We rode far into the woods, into the night. When we stopped to stretch and let the horses rest, Nikolas caught me from behind and turned me around for a kiss. I let my cloak drop and yanked the coat off his shoulders. We tore away at buttons and hooks until we fell on the cool ground.

Once we curled together under my cloak, I held his hand against my navel. A black stir roiled up to his touch. I wondered how long I'd have to feel the fester of the old wounds before they healed.

He buried his face against my neck. "Marry me, Love."

All I had to say was yes, but I couldn't. He didn't yet know what the plague revealed to me; I didn't know how to live with the truth. "Not tonight," I said.

"Coy answer."

"Better than none."

21 MARCH – 30 APRIL /39

THAT FIRST WEEK, BEFORE THE DEATH LISTS WERE PRINTED, Nikolas told me Charlotte's father had died. I rode out that afternoon to give my condolences. Her parents lived in one of the fine houses in The Manses, near the main entrance, where there was no longer a gatekeeper. Charlotte told me her father slipped away in February. While she'd had a month to grieve, her mother awakened to his loss. "I wish it weren't so, but you understand how I feel," she told me. "I can't believe he's gone. So peaceful, though. I was with him. One sigh, then . . ."

Midweek, I went to Warrick. No one answered when I knocked on the Misses Acutt's door. As I went up the second floor, Julia thundered down. She squeezed me around the waist. When she released me, she took my hand. We saw Jane and Dora first, who were busy moving furniture around the parlor. The Misses' furniture.

"Oh no," I said, my eyes welling up.

"Both of them, late January," Jane said, hugging me lightly.

"A blessing in a way. One wasn't left without the other," Dora said.

After a brief chat, I followed Julia to the stairs. She told me "her guardians" were living on the third floor in the Woodmans' former place, three young women who'd cared for her and twelve other children. The moment we stepped into her apartment, Sir Pouncelot strutted from a bed near the door.

"He's mine now. We miss the Misses, but I think he's happy with us," she said, taking his gray fluff into her arms.

Mrs. Elgin approached with an outstretched hand. I held it between my own. "I'm glad you're well, Secret. Julia said you were very ill for a time, feared almost lost. You've been a dear to her, and I'm grateful."

"So good to see you well, too. I am so sorry about Lucas," I said.

"A piece of my heart is gone," she said.

The door shut. Mr. Elgin was behind us. He extended a white paper rose to Julia. "There's a man in a blue hat outside with a basket of more, if you want to see," he said.

She dropped Sir to take it, her reach both hesitant and excited. "Thank you. Don't leave without saying good-bye, Secret," she said as she rushed outside.

"Mr. Elgin," I said.

"Miss Riven."

"Secret, please, after all this time."

"Then for us, Edmund and Amelia."

Without an invitation, I went to see about Leo. He and his wife invited me in for tea while Solden played with friends in their courtyard. They told me of the loss of several friends and acquaintances, among them our old Rowland and, sadly, Wesley's wife, leaving Wesley with a six-month-old son. They were among the 5,375 adults who died, nearly 17 percent of those who remained in Rothwyke through the plague. The children's total count, 1,159, 11 percent of them.

In the final days of March, I returned to Father's house. That first morning, I carried my bag upstairs and stopped short at the closed door of my old room. My body's memory led me there, although I knew I was to share the spare room with Harmyn. When I stepped across the hall, I found Elinor making one of two beds. Glad to see her, I dropped my belongings and walked to her with open arms. Harmyn and Father found us talking.

"Your bed is on the left, Miss," Elinor said to Harmyn.

"You forgot again. No 'Miss.' Call me Harmyn," Harmyn said. She placed a satchel on the bed to the left.

"Old habit," Elinor said. "Fresh linens in yours now, Mr. Riven."

"Thank you," Father said, carrying a trunk. "Finish up while I make us something to eat. We'll have a proper visit."

The three of us moved through the room, shifting furniture, putting things away. On Harmyn's side, she had a small wardrobe, a little desk, and a case of books. On my side, I had a chest for clothing, my old desk and chair, and a night table with a lamp and the carved stag. Next to the table was the faded blue chest, which Elinor said, when she saw me staring at it, my father had placed there for me.

After Elinor went downstairs, I was about to carry the chest away when Harmyn asked to look. She studied the painted animals on the side and opened the lid. Although I remembered I'd burned the nesting dolls, I almost expected to see them inside. All Harmyn found within was the one-sentence note Mother had left as a clue to the cipher. Harmyn's hands traced along the bottom as if she missed something, but there was nothing else to find.

She closed the chest. "The plague is over. What had to be seen, has been. For you and many others, that was an end and a beginning. You know the truth about what your mother did and also about yourself, your gold. There is more to discover as you find your way to peace, possibly forgiveness." She smiled at me. "But right now, we'll be glad to be together with cookies and tea."

I sighed, wishing for more respite than the next hour would give.

At the beginning of April, Nikolas received word that the war had escalated on every front. With allied troops from Seronia and Bodelea, Haaud was now marching through the rest of Kirsau, with Kirsau and Ilsace viciously on the defense. Prev and Thrigin continued to help Uldiland against Haaud, while Prev did as expected, marching into Emmok to drive out their men and Haaud's.

At last, Nikolas agreed to substantively increase troops at our borders with Giphia and Ilsace, with the order to make no move unless our boundaries were breached. This satisfied the Council to a degree. They were ready for a war they wouldn't fight with their own hands. As well, Nikolas contacted Dru Kai and Milan Visham to ask for aid. Their Guardian warriors would stand along with our army, waiting. Waiting, Nikolas said, because he believed the plague's spread would end the conflict by summer. His refusal to take action for so long hadn't been through cowardice or indecision but faith that a stronger force would prevail to finish it.

Also in April, there was an initial meeting among ward leaders, mayor's representatives, twelfth-floor men including Father, and local merchants independent of Fewmany Incorporated. They were determined to work quickly, and cooperatively, to figure out what to do with so many vacant shops and offices and how to return jobs for the thousands who were still without them.

What would become of Fewmany Incorporated was uncertain, as his surviving top men pondered who might take the helm, or if anyone should. The longer Fewmany was away, the more they felt his grip of influence release, his energy fade from what he had built, the power lost. Having had no word from him in almost a year, some believed he was dead.

In the meantime, the people carried on. Streets, buildings, and sewers needed repairs. What hadn't collapsed into the crater but had been destroyed had to be hauled away. The ward gardens required tending, since volunteers and children had worked to prepare and plant for spring and summer harvests. Long lines remained to get rations. With everyone awake, there was much to cook and clean, that daily rhythm of life familiar. Performers and audiences filled the halls again. The leisure activities which had occupied many during the first months of the plague began again—the athletic leagues, music, crafts, to name a few. The volunteers from other towns and three hundred of Rothwyke's oldest children prepared to leave, some remaining in Ailliath, the rest traveling to Thrigin, Giphia, and Ilsace to help before the plague spread.

The Guardians were no longer hidden in plain sight. The children identified them openly. Everyone knew then, if they'd never discerned so before, that there was something different about the people who wore a certain shade of blue. A quiet, a kindness, a sense of peace.

In those early weeks, the grief consumed us, too—for the dead, for what had been revealed, for what had changed. Everyone had suffered, together and in their own secret ways. No one could deny what they'd seen of the people they loved, the strangers among them, or within themselves. All was not idyllic. Fear, grief, resentment, and guilt took hold. There were still arguments and fights, some of them brutal, but none which could last as they once did.

The children wouldn't allow it.

With words and with their bodies, they wedged themselves between parents and siblings, friends and strangers, stepping in to make peace. We don't have to do this anymore, they said. We dreamed it another way, remember? We know we have a choice.

In mid-April, Nikolas's sisters arrived with their families to attend his coronation. He invited me to a dinner in their honor, which I couldn't avoid. He'd written to them about me and they wished to make my acquaintance. Pretty was remote and inquiring; I sensed her scrutiny. Charming remembered meeting me almost eight years before and said she was happy to know her little brother had someone so close when their parents died and through the kingdom's trouble. How close they believed we were, they didn't say, and if they disapproved, I detected no clear hint.

I received word from Charlotte that she was settled with her husband again. Muriel wrote to say her mother died during the plague. Whether Muriel would return to the conservatory next term remained unknown, her mother's supportive influence absent now.

By the end of the month, Nikolas was no stranger to my father's house any more than I was to his own. With Harmyn among us, we shared dinners and conversations, as amiable as I could have ever imagined. How Nikolas and I felt about each other was no secret, but Father did not pry about what that might mean.

Nikolas and I hid nothing between us. In our time alone, we spoke of what we'd found in our shadows. Eventually, I would talk to Father about my mother's neglect but never tell him what she'd done to my brothers or tried to do to me. To Nikolas, I told everything, even though I feared how that would alter me in his eyes. My grief, rage, bewilderment, shame—he was strong enough to stand to it. He loved me still, as I loved him more than ever. He insisted nothing I said changed his desire to marry me, but I knew I wasn't free of the darkest shadows, only aware of them. I feared what I might do to myself or someone I loved when they returned and leached their poison. Even if I did agree, one distant day, I refused to promise him an heir and didn't quite believe him when he said that didn't matter to him because he didn't need one.

Aside from whether we had a future together, I puzzled over mine. What of the hopes I'd once had for myself? Did I still hold them—high academy, a life of my own, away from Ailliath? What would be possible in these next years as the plague spread?

Through April's final week, Harmyn didn't leave the house. She had no complaints other than she was exhausted. Julia and other friends came to visit, bringing mirth into the house at last. Harmyn studied the lessons Father gave her, history and geometry, and sat in the courtyard with her hands out to the sun.

On one of those days, I heard her and Father walk up to his bedroom. When I went to see what they were doing, Harmyn sat on his bed with an empty box. Father stood in front of Mother's open wardrobe. I detected a hint of her perfume, but I walked next to him and touched the violet gown he had draped over his elbow.

"Before I awoke for good, I dreamed of her in the tower where I first saw her," Father said. "She was beautiful as ever. She said she waited for me, but I had time left, time to make myself and someone else happy, as I did for her. Then she kissed me good-bye and flew out of the window with the wings of a black swan."

As he started to cry, I wrapped my arms around him. "Make room. You've grieved enough."

1 – 8 MAY /39

ON NIKOLAS'S CORONATION DAY, FATHER ARRANGED FOR A LU-minotypist to come to our house early that morning. "Well that we should have a record of our happy faces," Father said. The man set up his machine and a chair in the courtyard, inviting us to sit one by one.

We did look dashing. Margana had sewn most of our garments as gifts, along with something for Nikolas, which I hadn't yet seen. Father looked elegant in his finest suit and a new cravat, which one of Margana's students had embroidered to resemble an ancient map. Harmyn's gift included straight-leg trousers in a thin black wool; the shirt, white silk with dozens of tiny tucks along the front; and her jacket, Guardian blue, embroidered with vines and berries. Margana had made my gown, too, and as I brushed lint from a blue bird appliquéd on the skirt, I thought what an honor it was to wear the color. I thought, too, of the costumes she'd made for me and realized, had circumstances been different, there would have been a masquerade ball that night.

After a late breakfast, a carriage arrived to take Father, Harmyn, and me to the green. Unlike the ceremonies to crown our former kings, this one was to be held outdoors, among the people, where there would be a feast, though modest as the kingdom faced the plague's spread. By now, I knew the plants and creatures had sickened through the northeast of Ailliath, the east half of Ilsace, all of Giphia, Haaud, and Kirsau, the southern edge of Thrigin's mountain range, the northwest of Uldiland, and up to the foothills of Seronia. As Nikolas hoped, the war would not endure once the plague struck so many.

The carriage stopped behind the dais. A footman escorted us to our seats. Father shook hands with several men, acquaintances from before the plague, and introduced me and Harmyn. From the height, I could see an aisle marked with gold ropes, which reached through the crowd to the dais. On a decorated platform was a throne.

Soon, a fanfare announced the ceremony's start. We sat down. Harmyn craned her neck to see what was happening.

The procession was long, attended by heralds, officers of the royal house, members of the Council, bearers of regalia, the royal family, personal attendants to the king, and among the latter, Nikolas himself.

The robe he wore wasn't the one from the night of his departure banquet. This, too, was purple velvet, but trimmed in white ermine, with a jeweled clasp at his neck. He looked confident, strong, earnest.

After several speeches, at last came the moment of coronation.

"Look closely. This was especially made for him," Harmyn said.

"By whom?"

"An Ancient Elder. Ingot," she said.

On a tufted pillow, held by Nikolas's sisters, was the crown. The top was scalloped, each segment alternating gold and silver, with a band of jewels along the bottom edge. Mounted to the two crosspieces within, striped with the same metals, were two interlocking circles of gold and silver, the union between them in amethyst.

After cheers, Nikolas's speech, and more cheers, he stood before the crowd and announced the pomp would now give way to merriment. Musicians began to tune their instruments. He walked to the back of the dais, talking with guests, and placed the robe and crown in his valet's hands. A woodwind piped up the first notes of a spirited waltz.

"We should have King Nikolas honor us with the first steps," Lord Sullyard said. "So, who shall dance with the King?"

Nikolas had turned when he heard his name. He walked over, looked past everyone, and gestured to me formally. "My beloved—friend, Miss Riven."

My instinct to refuse made me freeze until Father nudged me. I tried to ignore the murmurs as I went ahead.

I had never seen Nikolas more handsome than he was that day, his eyes and hair brilliant in the sunlight, jaw firm, square across the chest, steady on his feet. He wore the gift Margana had made—an emerald-green tailcoat piped in a certain shade of blue.

His gaze traced me head to toe as I approached. Tailored perfectly, the lavender gown had fitted sleeves with cuffs which flared like petals. The neckline was modest, but the back plunged almost scandalously low. Silver birds, mingled with blue ones, twirled down from the bodice and around the narrow skirt.

My hand fell into his. His fingers glanced the small of my back as my palm rested on his shoulder.

"Now, aren't you glad I taught you to do this all those months ago?" he asked.

"I'm in your debt," I said.

He led me into the dance, our steps almost perfect. There was applause in the end, and the sight of Harmyn and Father giving us an approving look.

Nikolas held my wrist as the next song began. People clapped when they recognized the lively tune. Couples joined on the green and the rest moved toward the banquet tables.

"No one's looking. Kiss me," he said.

"I will not," I said.

"Shy in public, brazen otherwise."

"You'll provoke rumors."

"Oh, the wicked scandal."

"Be quick, if you must."

Nikolas swept his fingers under my chin and kissed my cheek. "Now I have to be kingly." He smoothed his coat's lapels and bowed. I curtsied.

Above me, three blue birds whisked past in a line. Swallows, a hopeful sign, I thought with a smile, remembering what Old Woman once told me years before.

Into midday, the celebration continued. Volunteers alternated with the castle's servants so that everyone could spend some time at play. I was stunned but pleased to see Father speaking alone with Mrs. Knolworth's sister. Harmyn spent hours with her friends as I visited with mine. Nikolas circled by every so often, drawing me into conversations with his family and advisers, and I acquiesced to another dance.

Near two o'clock, I was ready to go home and went to find Harmyn. I saw her in the middle of the green. As I went closer, I heard her singing to herself.

Descendants and survivors, we know this story, told in the tone of myth.

She turned her face to the open sky, arms out wide. The melody which flowed so sweetly transformed to a chant, primordial yet newborn. Soft though it was, the child's voice soared beyond Rothwyke, past rivers, mountains, and seas. Where it was day, people lifted their heads to listen; where it was night, they turned to the sound in their dreams. The beauty of that voice poured light into every space of every being, every body, giving resonance to all it reached.

As her final note faded, a stillness within and without fell upon the whole of the world. Then, through the release of this impossible pause, the trees in Rothwyke's woods began to rustle and above their reach, swallows flocked in numbers unknown to our land in generations. The swallows descended in a torrent of blue stars and flew into the town. The birds twirled among the buildings and through the streets. The whisper of their wings was a gust in every ear, a breath from a realm not quite their own.

Harmyn's fingertips reached for the last of the flock who flew above and around her. She cringed and looked down.

I heard footsteps and turned to see Nikolas.

We went to Harmyn. The child lifted a bird from the ground. When Harmyn faced us, the swallow lay dead in her hands. A red stain appeared on her white shirt.

"Your chest," I said. "The bird."

"The swallow struck me. Look, her neck is broken," Harmyn said.

"What do you want to do?" Nikolas asked.

"Bury her, but I want to alone," she said, her eyes shiny with tears.

"Very well," I said, close to tears myself seeing the bird. "Remember, we're having dinner at the castle tonight at seven. Come home in time enough to wash."

Harmyn glanced past me, searching. "I remembered." She blinked at us. "You're so beautiful together. I love you both, you know."

Nikolas hugged her at his side. "We love you, too," he said.

She stepped away and, with a little wave, turned to walk to the woods. The flight of swallows gathered again to spiral above me and Nikolas, then soared toward Harmyn.

Nikolas linked his arm with mine. "I never tire of the magic that happens around you." I patted his hand. "There's a carriage waiting." I hesitated. "She'll be fine," he said.

The carriage took Father and me home. An hour passed, then two. Harmyn found some friends and stayed to visit in the woods; no reason to worry, Father and I said to each other. At five thirty, I peered up and down the street from the bedroom window. Below, a young red squirrel was circling our front steps and scratching at our door.

I ran downstairs. As soon as I stepped outside, I saw a horse charging in my direction. Nikolas reined in the horse. He noticed the squirrel.

"An owl nearly brained itself at a window. Something's wrong," he said.

In a swoop, I lifted the squirrel, placed her on Nikolas's lap, and climbed up behind him. The squirrel scurried to my shoulder.

Go to the ancient one, she said.

"Reach," I shouted to Nikolas over hoofbeats.

We went through the northwest wards to the green, cutting between the abandoned wall and what was left to store away after the day's events, and into the darkening woods.

He slowed the horse not far from Reach. I jumped off, set the squirrel on the ground, and called the child's name. No answer came.

Nikolas ran ahead of me and disappeared around the tree's enormous trunk.

I found him with Harmyn on his lap. The blue swallow lay against a root. I knelt at Nikolas's side and touched the bloody rose on Harmyn's chest. There was no heartbeat above the rounded swell. I pressed again, confused. This couldn't be. I stroked Harmyn's small hands. The palms were a pale blue. I brushed her cheeks, slightly warm.

Shocked beyond tears, Nikolas reached out his hand. "This was next to her," he said.

Dear Secret, Nikolas, and GrandBren,

I want you to know I didn't want to leave you, but I had to, to answer my ultimate call. For some time, I knew what my fate held. My dreams told me, and that is where I learned about myself and practiced my gifts in other realms. I didn't worry any of you with this because there was nothing you could do. Nothing to do. As the great Voice Sisay told Aoife, and me, this is beyond our understanding.

Because the plague has spread to so many kingdoms, I've seen to it that those who sleep next will sleep like bears. Few volunteers will be needed to tend the adults, but the children will need care until the adults awaken again. Tell the Guardians now.

As the plague runs its course, you must understand the purpose was never to eliminate all shadows and their pestilence of lies, but to release what could be and expose the rest. As the balance of your world shifts to good, it means nothing without its opposite. Now, as it's always been, this is matter of free will.

I am grateful you were my family. Look for me in dreams.

I love you, so much,
Harmyn

I fell next to him, taking the child in my arms as he coiled us in his. I kissed Harmyn's closed eyes, blind again, blind for good. I wept with grief for a love I never believed I could feel.

A crack broke through my heart, through my spine, and into Reach's trunk. I turned to watch a thin fissure open in the dead wood. The beginning of a sacred hollow.

When we could finally stand, I called the horse. I climbed on first, pulled Harmyn up from Nikolas's arms, and held her between us as he led us to the castle.

Everyone stood aside as he carried her through the courtyards, into

the residence, and placed her on the bed which had been hers. Behind
me, I heard Hugh ask what he could do.

Within the hour, as I sat alone with her in the dark, Father and Margana
arrived. He collapsed the moment he saw Harmyn, kneeling at the bedside.
When Margana entered the room, she dropped a large bundle on another
bed and stood in tears. She rubbed my father's back, then came to hold me.

"We have to prepare her," she said.

"I don't know what to do," I said.

"I'm here to help. I'll be back in a few minutes," she said.

Nikolas lit every lamp in the room while Father and I sat in silence.
When Margana entered again, she placed cloths and a bowl of water on a
night table. She sent Nikolas and Father out.

"Help me undress her," Margana said.

We began to remove the coat, the bloodstained shirt—underneath,
the amulet and medal—her little boots, then the trousers and thin drawers. We paused to glance at each other. I reached to turn up the lamp's
flame and held the light near her thighs. Our Voice lay before us.

Harmyn's body, naked—both male and female.

"Margana, were you told the Myths of the Four?" I asked.

"Yes," she said.

"Were you told Azul the Orphan, as a child, was 'he and she, both
and they'?"

"I heard the same. You didn't know," she said.

"No. Harmyn hid this all along." I cradled Harmyn's face, pressed my
forehead against her, his, theirs, and kissed the divine child's brow.

After we dressed our Voice, Margana held out a length of blue cloth
on the other bed. "In the months since I received this, I could never decide what to do with it. Not until the king's man came to fetch me did I
realize it was meant to be a burial shroud."

We were in tears again as we cocooned Harmyn within the cloth,
their face exposed like an infant's.

Once Margana departed for home, I refused to leave Harmyn's side.
I surrendered to Father's arms as we sat next to the child's body half the
night and then to Nikolas, who held me through morning.

In the Great Hall, Harmyn lay in state. The people of Rothwyke
came to mourn through the next day and night. The children surrounded Harmyn with flowers and covered our Voice in tears. There

would be no burial, because Connau arrived on the second morning with an invitation.

"The Ancient Elders offer the release bestowed to our warriors. We're here to help, if that's what you choose," Connau said to Nikolas and me.

"Of course," I said. "We couldn't deny Harmyn this honor."

A horse-drawn cart brought the child's corpse to the woods, to the glade near Old Woman's cottage. Connau and Nikolas placed Harmyn's body on the waiting pyre. Five men dressed in blue coats, holding bronze shields with a dragon herald, kept vigil over the fire.

That evening, the oldest among them came into the cottage with an urn filled with Harmyn's ashes.

"Connau will show you the way when you're ready," the man said, his mouth twisted in one corner from a ragged scar.

"We'll go alone," I said.

Nikolas held the urn as we thanked them. We entered the woods, Connau and his men going to one tree, Nikolas and I to another. I watched as a doe led them home. When the bees came for us, I held Nikolas's hand as we crossed into the realm.

We walked toward the mountain. I leaned against him as I thought of Aoife, a thousand years before, standing in that same place with Wei at her side, waiting to release Leit. As it happened for her, the clouds shifted into shades of red. The billows took form and down she came. Egnis, she who knew the future present past.

With one wing, she beckoned us into the valley. She stared into our eyes, into the pain, and from the dark, drew out the light and joy of our time with Harmyn. Together, Nikolas and I spilled the vessel, scattered the dust. The dragon huffed, the ashes disappeared, and Harmyn became one with All. As swallows darted past, Egnis spiraled into the air with a plume of violet flames. She flew higher and higher until she vanished behind the rising moon.

Nikolas and I stood in each other's arms until the night became cold and returned to our world as the sun rose again.

ON THE NIGHT OF THE FULL MOON, SEVEN DAYS AFTER HARMYN died, I dreamed of a black-haired man with scarred hands who carried a singing swallow on his shoulder. I followed him into a shed which smelled of sawed wood. He lifted a sheet to reveal a blue chest painted with animals. "Mine?" I asked. "Yours," he said. I opened the lid and peered inside. "Look, there's a secret," he said, pointing to the bottom. With a gouge, he removed a knot in the wood. He caught the hollow with his fingertip and raised the panel to reveal a hidden space.

Wide awake, I fumbled for a light, found a pen with a broken nib, and went to my old room, where I'd placed the chest weeks before. I flipped the top, rubbed my hand along the bottom, and dug at the knot. The dark core rolled away. I clawed the hole and lifted the panel.

I descended into what for so long had been sealed off.

Mother's high academy diploma. Rose-colored silk shawl. Four letters in a language I couldn't read. Map, hastily sketched, not by her. Desiccated human finger, wrapped in a handkerchief. Talisman tied with sinew—sticks, a stone, an iron nail, a feather turned into dust. Clay pendant in the shape of a crescent moon. Small leather bag holding nineteen rings. Carved beast with a coiled tail and bird's wings. Sapphire bracelet with one crystal, Guardian blue. Drawings, almost three dozen, in a young but skilled hand. What they represented, I didn't know, except for three.

A girl tied to a tree, where three shadows loomed close, and a man and a wolf watched nearby.

The symbol.

An infant with eyes the colors of night and day.

My tears rushed not for grief or rage, hatred or resentment. I wept with sorrow for the enigmatic woman who could not bear the risk of being known, not even by her inevitable daughter.

23 SEPTEMBER /39

IN THE WEEKS AFTER WE LOST HARMYN, I WENT TO THE WOODS for hours each day until I retreated there. Old Woman's cottage became my home. I trusted Nature to comfort me, as only it could. Among the trees, I felt our Voice with me, but I missed the child no less because of it.

I guarded against my instinct to withdraw. I lived in the woods, but I didn't leave anyone to grieve alone, which included myself. When the children came to the cottage or found me among the trees, I didn't send them away. We shared stories about Harmyn, took walks with the animals, and rested in the shade, content with the silence we chose. Several times a week, I visited with Father and my friends. Rather than meet at the castle, Nikolas would come to me. We found refuge in the quiet and each other.

Then, on the morning of my twenty-second birthday, I awoke to find a pigeon, a dove, and a sparrow on the windowsill.

Return to the castle.

Messengers await.

You will soon have a choice to make.

When I arrived, I found Nikolas and kissed him in front of a guard who no longer took notice.

"I'm told we have visitors, but I wasn't informed who they are," Nikolas said.

We held hands as we walked to the meeting chamber. His guard opened the door.

There, next to the crest of scales, were two elderly Guardians. I hugged Old Woman as Nikolas accepted Old Man's embrace. When Old Woman kissed Nikolas's cheek, I accepted the clasp of Old Man's strong, thin-skinned hands. We sat at the table and spoke few pleasantries.

"We know what happened to Harmyn. None of us expected the loss I've mourned for our dear child. A gift beyond measure," Old Woman said.

"The child and the two of you made us proud. We're relieved peace remains in Rothwyke, despite the adversities," Old Man said.

"Our people deserve the credit for that," Nikolas said.

"As well as the one who guides by his own actions," Old Woman said. "But we're not here to talk of that and the compassionate king you're proving yourself to be. We're here for Secret."

Old Man placed a package on the table and pushed it toward me. I removed the paper wrapping. My fingers filled with sparks. I brushed my hand across Aoife's minuscule handwriting. Another manuscript. Before I could study it, Old Man pulled it back to him.

"You know there are more works yet to be translated," Old Woman said. "You are the only one who knows this written form of our language. It could be taught, of course, and I hope it will be. Until then, the Ancient Elders believe it's time for the knowledge to be shared. You're invited to join me to live and work and learn among the Guardians. With us, you'll find a place of peace unlike any you've ever known. You'll be allowed to translate the texts into several languages and arrange production of multiple copies. We know Aoife recorded our history, but it's a mystery what she preserved. You can solve this for us."

I felt Nikolas draw me toward him without a touch. I gripped his forearm. He knew what I was thinking. The possibility thrilled me. To be the first to read the manuscripts, to ring it all to the world, to myself.

"Why can't you send them to her here?" Nikolas asked.

"We could. But to live among us is to understand what words alone cannot convey. She might welcome it, after what she suffered through the plague," Old Woman said. With that, I knew she'd received word of what the sickness forced us to see and feel. She knew of some of the shadows which came for me.

"In all paths, there are forks and crossroads," Old Man said. "The future, as you know, is mutable. Fate is not so neatly fixed. You could choose to remain here now to serve with the gifts you possess. You are a woman of tremendous power. No one lesser could have turned an adversary to face his fork, as you did. You entered the mystery of duality—light, dark; good, evil; love, hate—and you are wiser now in its mastery, even if you lack faith that it is so.

"You need not consort with the dark again as you did. You can choose the light and nurture its expanse. The man who sits next to you has always known this possibility. It's what he saw in you when you were children, and you saw in him. His Guardian blood is very old, long before this kingdom's time, but it is strong. A wondrous marriage could come of these forces."

When Nikolas's hand swept into mine, the love between us charged through our palms.

"Do I have to give my answer now?" I asked.

"No, but you will have to decide soon enough. You've sensed this. Your return to the woods wasn't only to grieve Harmyn and what you've suffered. You sought a deeper truth," Old Woman said.

"We've delivered the message. It's time to return home," Old Man said.

We stood together. They kissed us good-bye and left the room, slow but steady.

The door shut. Nikolas held my face in his hands. He knew what I would choose, but the plea in his eyes told me what he wanted. A hum rose in my ears, sourceless it seemed, and I realized this was the sound of the threshold, the liminal space between what was and what could be. He stood firm as I reeled on my feet. I swept my arms inside his coat, wrapped tight, and laid my head on his pounding chest. He drew me close, rocking us together.

"Hold me, Nikolas," I said. "Don't let me go."

Afterword

YET HE DID, WILLINGLY.

My father understood her leaving was as much a part of her fate as the manuscript, the quest, the plague, and he were. Wise as he was, he knew she went to prepare Aoife's manuscripts for untold thousands to read, but more so to mourn and heal. The wounds of betrayal and unwantedness festered deep. The woman my father loved required time to close them, enough at least. Old Woman welcomed her among her family and gave her an experience of acceptance she had never known.

During the seven years she lived among the Guardians, she translated sixteen manuscripts. She found Aoife had written their history, folktales, and myths as well as anthropological studies of their culture. In four languages at first, the words traveled to lands Aoife never knew existed, during a time of transformation which she couldn't have dreamed. The peace and compassion which Aoife, Wei, Leit, and their Guardian family wanted the world to know was taking root and blooming, most vibrantly in the children who awoke from the sleep.

These same seven years, the Plague of Silences spread across the world. The illness afflicted the plants, creatures, and people on our continent in the first three cycles, then crossed the twelve seas to lands far beyond. The war, which my father didn't want to enter, collapsed as the second and third cycles swept through the fighting kingdoms.

What suffering preceded the plague rapidly waned in the years which followed. Many reading this now find our world's history as perplexing as I do. The neglect, cruelty, and violence committed within families, towns, and kingdoms, against our companion beings in all forms and the earth itself—we marvel at what we've been told. How unreal it seems.

Throughout the plague, my father honored his promise to care for his people. With ward leaders, Guardians, and advisers at his side, he traveled to share their counsel with other kingdoms. I was told by many, during my own goodwill visits, what a gentle, centered man he was.

"Strong in the way a tree is strong, not as a storm," someone remarked to me once.

Given the proximity of hollow trees, my father and the woman he loved lived only minutes apart and saw one another periodically those seven years. They exchanged letters, in which they chronicled their respective work and often struggled with what would become of the two of them as a couple.

The plague ended in the spring of 3245. Even though her work was done, she didn't return to Ailliath. She traveled to lecture on Aoife's writings and to witness for herself how quickly the world was changing.

In 3247, my father chose a surname to mark a transition for himself. In September of that year, Nikolas Hart voluntarily relinquished absolute rule to a prime minister and a representative assembly, gender equitable, elected by the people regardless of their occupations. This shift of government had been a matter of conversation for years, with guidance from his Guardian advisers, notably Dru Kai, and a group of citizens and open-minded Council members. He was the first king on our continent to abdicate power, although he retained his title and role of counsel.

Ailliath's people adored and trusted him, but he refused to stand as a candidate. He understood the Old Ways were meant to die while "certain old men and their intractable sons," he told me, tried in vain to keep what no longer belonged to them, and never had. There had been resistance. Not all plague survivors found the initial years of The Turn to their liking, especially not men accustomed to unquestioned power. On the very day the upcoming election was announced, my father lost his friend and most loyal guard, Hugh, who took an assassin's blade through the chest.

On 1 May 3248, my parents, both thirty-one years old, married. Two chronoprints of their wedding day remain in my library because my heart lilts when I look at them. In the first, they're in each other's arms, resplendent in the suit and gown Margana designed, looking into the other's eyes with an intimacy unmeasurable, which bound them until the end of their lives. The second is posed but playful. My mother stands behind my seated father and grandfather, her arms around them, their hands clutching hers. Twined in my grandfather's fingers, dangling from his knee, is an amulet. Harmyn's. The member of my family I never met, I feel.

Two years later, my twin, Duncan, and I were born; four years after that, our brother, Riley. We spent our infancies in the settlement where Ahma had lived and visited often when we were children. When they joined us, my affectionate Ahpa and my beloved Grandahpa, who died when I was eight, found it to be as much of a second home as Ahma did.

Once we were old enough to hear of certain matters, Ahma spoke of them. She hid nothing from us, not the fact she released the plague, the legend which was Fewmany, the mystery which was Harmyn, the lovers she and Ahpa had during their tenuous years apart, or the complicated truth about her own mother. Because of the last, although this wasn't the only reason, she had long refused to marry Ahpa. She feared her shadows, the legacy they bore, and how she might fail a child, if they agreed to have one.

After what you've read from her, I want to assure you I loved my mother, truly and deeply. She was not without flaws, but we never doubted her love. When dark moods overcame her, she sent us to our father or friends until she could quiet them again. Ahma found joy in our presence and delight in our learning. I knew the comfort of her arms and voice, often both at once when she told us stories. I was also in awe of her; only those closest to her knew the extent of her powers, no longer latent. My mythic mother could summon rain, flower valleys, move mountains, and turn tides—that, and more. In the instances when she revealed her gift, she did so to share power with, not over, this world.

From her, my brothers and I inherited a love of Nature and great tales. I received her passion for knowledge and two eyes the color of night; Duncan, her ability to speak to creatures and plants and two eyes the color of day; Riley, the gifts of a Voice and indigo eyes instead of violet.

Unlike our grandmother, Zavet, and Harmyn, Riley wasn't alone. He was among the first Voices born after the plague. While Ahpa served on councils and boards, Ahma traveled with us to help other families with Voices and hosted gatherings twice a year for them. She had so loved Harmyn and my brother that she was determined no Voice would suffer from other people's misunderstanding or fear.

She accomplished still more.

Queen Evensong, spouse of Nikolas, mother of us three, was also

Secret Riven, Keeper of Tales. In her lifetime, Ahma not only translated and distributed Aoife's work but also collected an archive of the plague. With a staff of scholars, she gathered notebooks, diaries, and ephemera, amassing thousands of records. Beginning in 3269, using the first sound cylinders, she started to record interviews for the Plague of Silences Recollection Project. She was fifty-two years old.

My brothers and I didn't know she'd written her own recollections until after she died in 3295, eight months after we lost Ahpa. As I sorted through her belongings, I found boxes of Zavet's diaries, all of the letters Ahma and Ahpa had exchanged, as well as hundreds of letters, dozens of her diaries, and her plague notebooks.

In the old faded blue chest she kept in their bedroom, I discovered two typed manuscripts. She left them with a note: "To reveal at your discretion. I love you always, Ahma." I'm uncertain when she wrote *The Chronicle of Secret Riven* or this text. I might have been able to discern the time periods if she'd left handwritten copies. When I discovered the manuscripts, they contained the same woodcut images which appear in various editions of *The Mapmaker's War* as well as other illustrations done in her hand. She included the diary entries, letters, interviews, and additional relevant documentation seen here. The endnote references, however, are my own.

My brothers and I believe our parents would want descendants and survivors to know the truth, just as they learned the cause and consequences of The Mapmaker's War. Their role in releasing the plague and Harmyn's miraculous contribution perhaps couldn't be told until now.

Mine is the first generation since The Turn. My children's, the second. As I write this, the third is taking its first breaths as the remaining survivors begin their last. Each of us is witness to and a participant in an era many of our ancestors never believed could exist. Caught as they were in the shadows of the past, they could see no other way.

My parents sometimes wept together as they marveled over what emerged in their lifetime—peace and plenty enough, for all. However elated they were, they were pragmatic, too, telling my brothers and me that we weren't free of the darkness. The old shadows linger within us, within everyone, as reminders, as a challenge. Ahma wrote in her diary on the tenth anniversary of the plague's first day, "Our intricate nature continues to tilt its balance toward light. It could, again, turn the other way. I know too well the choice between good and evil, light and dark, is a precarious one. But now that we understand we're guardians of one another, may we choose wisely. May we never forget we are all born made of gold."

To the reign of love,
Aoife-Ianthe Riven Hart
Professor of Sociology, Erritas Academy
23 September 3298

Notes

1. *The Chronicle of Secret Riven*, Chapter XXI, pp. 143–149
2. *The Chronicle of Secret Riven*, Chapter XI, pp. 80–82
3. *The Chronicle of Secret Riven*, Chapter V, pp. 38–39
4. *The Chronicle of Secret Riven*, Chapter XXXVI, pp. 264–265
5. *The Chronicle of Secret Riven*, Chapter XLIV, pp. 328–341
6. *The Chronicle of Secret Riven*, Chapter XIV, pp. 101–103
7. *The Chronicle of Secret Riven*, Chapter XXII, pp. 155–158
8. Regarding Secret Riven's first seven years, refer to *The Chronicle of Secret Riven*, Chapter I, p. 1; Chapter II, pp. 5–14; Chapter V, pp. 38–39; Chapter VI, pp. 44–47; Chapter XV, pp. 105–108; Chapter XVI, pp. 110–111; and Chapter XVIII, pp. 116–119.
9. *The Chronicle of Secret Riven*, Chapter XXVIII pp. 207–210 and Chapter XXIX, pp. 211–216
10. *The Chronicle of Secret Riven*, Chapter XXII, pp. 155-57 and Chapter XXXIII, pp. 247-250
11. *The Chronicle of Secret Riven*, Chapter XXXVIII, pp. 279–280
12. *The Chronicle of Secret Riven*, Chapter I, p. 2
13. *The Chronicle of Secret Riven*, Chapter XLI, p. 305
14. *The Chronicle of Secret Riven*, Chapter XXXIX, pp. 296–298
15. Regarding the first three encounters with Harmyn, refer to *The Chronicle of Secret Riven*, Chapter XXXV, pp. 254–255; Chapter XXXIX, p. 289, and Chapter XLV, pp. 346–347.
16. *The Mapmaker's War* [translation by (E.) S. Riven], pp. 10–11
17. *The Chronicle of Secret Riven*, Chapter XLI, p. 309
18. *The Chronicle of Secret Riven*, Chapter XXXIX, p. 290
19. *The Mapmaker's War* [translation by (E.) S. Riven], p. 8
20. References to another man with similar attributes, which Secret Riven did not specifically acknowledge, *The Mapmaker's War* [translation by (E.) S. Riven], pp. 3, 8, 13, 23, 26, 30, 45, and 53.
21. *The Chronicle of Secret Riven*, Chapter XXX, pp. 221–222
22. *The Chronicle of Secret Riven*, Chapter XXVI, p. 195
23. The Myths of the Four appear in *The Chronicle of Secret Riven*, Appendix II, pp. 363–385.

24. *The Mapmaker's War* [translation by (E.) S. Riven], pp. 49–50
25. *The Mapmaker's War* [translation by (E.) S. Riven], p. 85
26. *The Mapmaker's War* [translation by (E.) S. Riven], p. 213
27. *The Mapmaker's War* [translation by (E.) S. Riven], p. 77
28. *The Mapmaker's War* [translation by (E.) S. Riven], p. 193
29. *The Mapmaker's War* [translation by (E.) S. Riven], p. 111
30. *The Chronicle of Secret Riven*, Chapter IX, p. 64
31. *The Chronicle of Secret Riven*, Chapter XIV, p. 104
32. *The Mapmaker's War* [translation by (E.) S. Riven], p. 211
33. *The Chronicle of Secret Riven*, Chapter XXXI, p. 229
34. *The Chronicle of Secret Riven*, Chapter XVIII, p. 132
35. *The Mapmaker's War* [translation by (E.) S. Riven], p. 216
36. *The Mapmaker's War* [translation by (E.) S. Riven], p. 103
37. *The Mapmaker's War* [translation by (E.) S. Riven] pp. 106–108, pp. 111–113
38. *The Chronicle of Secret Riven*, Chapter XI, p. 77

Acknowledgments

To my family, thank you for your unwavering support and encouragement.

My heartfelt gratitude to those who know the whole story—Alison Aucoin, Madeleine Conger, Tameka Cage Conley, Penelope Dane, Mary McMyne, and Nancy Peacock.

Thank you to kind friends, some of whom were early readers—Nolde Alexius, Martin Arceneaux, Rick Blackwood, Tracey Bourgoyne, James Claffey, Jamey Hatley, Susan Henderson, Tai Anderson Istre, Judy Kahn, Karla King, Ben Lanier-Nabors, McHenry "Dub" Lee, Signe Pike, Ariana Wall Postlethwait, Kathleen Sarsfield, Emilie Staat, Kirsten Steintrager, Kate Suchanek, and Gary "Doc T" Taylor.

For typing the rewrites, thank you, Marianne Konikoff. For help with specific details, thank you, Mark Ensley, Sean Flory, Robert Forbes, Nat Missildine, Chris Odinet, Caroline and Lann Wolf, and Mary Erica Zimmer. For spelling assistance, thank you, Charlotte Alexander, Madison Layne Brown, Karleigh M. Cannon, Finnegan Collins, Harrison M. Conley, Sophia Delahoussaye, Madeleine A. Guidry, Parrish Johnson, Aidan Johnson, Vincent J. Pelletier, Ella Mae Pettyjohn, Kate Pettyjohn, and Kamryn Lacey Reed.

To readers who've embraced the people of these books and their world, thank you.

Thank you to Kathryn Hunter for the illustrations, Jillian Manus for seeing me through, and Atria Books and Sarah Branham for their commitment to this uncanny little project.

Dr. Robin Roberts, thank you for the creative assignment option in your Spring 1990 Women & Literature course. The feminist fairy tale I wrote was the genesis for the trilogy. Dr. Randall Rogers, thank you for sparking my appreciation of history and inspiring my earliest research for this work.

At last, but not least, thank you to a man of integrity, loyalty, and devotion, my partner and my beloved, Todd.